A PLUME BOOK

THE LINE OF DEPARTURE

SPARKPIX

G. MICHAEL HOPF is the bestselling author of *The End*, *The Long Road*, and *Sanctuary*. He spent two decades living a life of adventure before settling down to pursue his passion for writing. He is a former combat veteran of the U.S. Marine Corps and former bodyguard. He lives with his family in San Diego, California.

G. MICHAEL HOPF

THE LINE OF DEPARTURE

A Postapocalyptic Novel

• • •

BOOK 4 OF THE NEW WORLD SERIES

P

A PLUME BOOK

PLUME
Published by the Penguin Group
Penguin Group (USA) LLC
375 Hudson Street
New York, New York 10014

USA | Canada | UK | Ireland | Australia | New Zealand |
India | South Africa | China
penguin.com
A Penguin Random House Company

First published by Plume, a member of Penguin Group (USA) LLC, 2015

Copyright © 2015 by G. Michael Hopf

LIBRARY OF CONGRESS CATALOGING-IN-PUBLICATION DATA
Hopf, G. Michael.
The Line of Departure : a postapocalyptic novel / G. Michael Hopf.
pages   cm.—(The New World Series ; Book 4)
ISBN 978-0-14-218152-2
1. End of the world—Fiction.   2. Regression (Civilization)—Fiction.   I. Title.
PS3608.O635L56   2015
813'.6—dc23   2014048533

Printed in the United States of America
10   9   8   7   6   5   4   3   2   1

Set in Minion Pro
Designed by Eve Kirch

To all those warriors who,
when their nation called,
crossed the line of departure,
some never to return

ACKNOWLEDGMENTS

As I have mentioned in earlier acknowledgments, writing a novel is something an author doesn't do completely alone. Yes, the author sits behind the glow of the screen tapping away for what seems like endless hours creating the characters, plot, and story that will eventually become the book. But once that first draft is complete, an author, if he's doing it correctly, will send it off to a trusted confidante and, in many ways, collaborator: the editor. I have had the honor and great fortune to be surrounded by an incredible editorial team at Plume. I don't know all of their individual names, but the one person who has worked with me to ensure that my novels have been readable, richer, and top-notch has been Kate Napolitano, editor at Plume. Her careful eye and attention to detail has aided me in making *The Line of Departure* the great book it is. She worked closely with me, pushing and encouraging me as I went through the most extensive rewrite I've ever done in my life. It was her insistence and vision that the book could be better that led to the book you're about to read. When I turned it in originally, it was a totally different book. I want to thank her from the bottom of my heart for being open, honest, and professional, as an editor should be.

I am often asked for advice by aspiring writers. Besides my typical response of "Just write," I now follow up by saying, "Get an editor—they're a priceless asset to your team."

Thank you, Kate, and thank you, editorial staff at Plume.

THE LINE OF DEPARTURE

PROLOGUE
OCTOBER 19, 2066
. . .

McCall, Idaho, Republic of Cascadia

Hunter Rutledge exited the warmth of the aircraft only to be greeted by a brisk wind. He lifted the collar on his thick wool peacoat and headed toward the lobby of the small airport. He took a deep breath and tried to prepare himself for the unknown. McCall had played a large part in his family's history, but this was the first time he had stepped foot here. There was nothing like the promise that something "life changing" had happened to encourage him to seek out his roots, and that's exactly what had been promised to him by his brother, Sebastian. Even after badgering him for more information about what possibly could be in McCall that needed his immediate attention, Sebastian stood firm and said it would be better for Hunter to come see himself. How could anyone turn down an invite promising something so profound? Curiosity got the best of him, and so he soon found himself on a small plane, unsure of what to expect.

As he strode toward the terminal building, the first thing that struck him was how small a place it was. It surprised him, especially considering what he had seen on his flight. As his plane made its approach, he had peered out the window like a small child, eager for the view. He marveled at the size of Long Valley, how it stretched north for miles on end. An early dusting of snow capped the exposed granite tops of the two mountain ranges on either side; the white transitioning to the deep green of the pines, then segueing into the patchwork of browns, tans, and greens of the valley floor. He took in every mountain, road, and building he could until they landed just south of town.

Hunter was the deputy chief of mission for the embassy, a busy man whose schedule was dictated by political turmoil—and in this day and age, there seemed to be a nonstop supply. If he didn't have such a great relationship with the ambassador, he wouldn't have been able to make the trip to McCall. His original itinerary took him back to Austin, Texas, today, but when he asked for some leave due to personal family issues, the ambassador granted it without discussion. Hunter was a consummate professional, never one to take a day off, so for him to ask for leave meant that it was something serious. It was just too bad that he didn't know what this serious thing could be.

Just a few feet shy of the entrance he stopped and took in his surroundings. "So this is the fabled McCall," he said to himself.

A large man wearing an orange vest opened the door and said cheerfully, "Welcome to McCall! What brings you here?"

Hunter looked around the sparse lobby of the terminal. Small red leather-bound chairs lined the walls, interrupted every few feet by tiny tables covered with magazines and newspapers. In the corner of the room was a counter with old computer monitors and behind it a board listed arrivals and departures. He took notice that the board only listed one other arrival coming in later in the day, and the only departing flight was for tomorrow morning.

Realizing that he hadn't promptly answered the man's question, he said, "Sorry, I was expecting to meet someone here."

"No one here but us," the man said, shrugging his shoulders.

Hunter shook his head, exasperated. Sebastian told him he'd be there upon his arrival, but being typical Sebastian, he was late.

• • •

Hunter looked at his watch and grimaced. Sebastian was now two hours late. He couldn't wait any longer, not when he was this anxious. After asking for directions, he departed the terminal and headed toward town. He chuckled to himself when he saw the street sign for Van Zandt Boulevard. His own family namesake, emblazoned for all to see.

As he walked, the occasional truck or car drove past, but as a whole, the town seemed sleepy and quiet. Large ponderosa pine trees towered over the houses and small commercial spaces that fronted the street. He had heard so many stories about McCall over the years—it had given his mother a place to call home as a child and was the birthplace of their republic. It was hard for him now to see how this tiny mountain town could have been so instrumental in the beginnings of a new country. The town had a population of less than seven thousand people, but those people had the vision and drive to be independent from the tyrannical forces that collided during the Great Civil War. McCall may not have started as a unique place, but it became pivotal because of one person: his grandfather, Gordon Van Zandt.

Hunter inhaled deeply through his nose. The fresh smell of the alpine air invigorated him. He strode closer to the lake, taking mental notes on restaurants and bars he saw along the way. He wasn't sure how long he'd be in town, and knowing where to eat and, more specifically, where to grab a drink was a priority.

The blare of a truck's horn startled him and brought him to the present. He turned in the direction of the sound and saw an old Ford coming his way. Its side panels were decayed from rust, its blue paint faded to the point that primer now showed. The years of being subjected to the harsh conditions of the mountains had taken its toll on the truck, clearly.

"Bro, I'm so sorry. I'm such an ass. I was tied up!" Sebastian hollered out from the cab.

Hunter peered at his baby brother's beard-covered face. "You *are* an ass. And a late one at that."

Sebastian leaned over and unlocked the passenger-side door. Hunter tossed his duffel into the bed and got in. "So. I'm here. What the hell is up?"

"Nice to see you too," Sebastian joked, making a U-turn in the road and heading south out of town.

"I'm starving. If you're not going to tell me what's up, can we at least stop and get something to eat?" Hunter said.

"No time! Where we're going there's plenty of food," Sebastian said happily.

Hunter rolled his eyes. As much as he loved his brother, they were very different people. Sebastian took after his grandfather in his demeanor and thirst for adventure. He loved life and wanted nothing more than to see the world. As soon as he was of age he had left home and never looked back. Now in his mid-twenties, he had finally taken interest in his roots, and this desire for knowledge had taken him to McCall. Hunter was the polar opposite—steadfast, reliable, and grounded. He knew every detail about the Van Zandt and Rutledge families. It was a priority for him to maintain the reputation the name gave him. He was proud of his family's history, regardless of current revisionism taking place in the media.

"So, where the hell have you been?" Hunter asked.

"Everywhere!"

"I just saw Mom and she's worried about you. You need to call her," Hunter chided.

Sebastian cut him a look and answered, "I love Mom, but"—he paused, clearly trying to figure out how to present the information— "it's just . . . she hasn't been honest with us. That's part of the reason why I asked you to come here."

"What are you talking about?"

"What she told us about Grandma and Granddad were not true. To be blunt, I now question everything she ever told us."

Hunter pursed his lips. "Mom's been through a lot. I don't know what you're talking about, but right now she's being interviewed by the paper about the family, about everything."

"Really? I wonder if she'll tell the truth."

Sebastian took a left off the highway and headed east. The one-lane county road was paved but the lack of maintenance made for a bumpy ride. The towering ponderosa pines were now gone, replaced by the tall grasses and small shrubbery of the open valley.

"If you're not telling me what we're doing, can you at least tell me where we're going?"

"Almost there, calm down! You're going to love it here. McCall is a great place—I can't believe it's taken me so long to get here. I've learned so much about the family since I've been here."

"Since when have you given two hoots about the family?" Hunter asked, an edge in his tone.

"I know I've not been the best brother or son, but when I was in New Zealand a few months back, I had a chance encounter with this woman—"

"How surprising," Hunter interjected. Sebastian had a reputation for being a playboy.

"It's not like that. She was an older woman, and she knew the family. She had known Granddad, Hunter."

"Really?"

"I knew that would pique your interest."

"I hope it's not another person claiming how bad he was. I'm sick of hearing that side of the story."

"I've heard the stories. But what if I was to tell you there's a different perspective?" Sebastian said as the truck slowed and pulled into a gravel driveway.

Sebastian stopped the truck in front of a metal gate and got out to unlock it, hollering at Hunter to drive the truck in. Once the gate was secure again, Sebastian jumped into the passenger side and instructed him to drive.

Hunter paused. He trusted his brother but the entire situation made him uneasy. He peered down the long drive; mature groves of aspen trees to either side gave it an ominous look.

"C'mon, let's go. You're hungry and I got to use the bathroom," Sebastian urged.

Hunter put the truck in gear and drove down the driveway. After a quarter mile, the green metal roof of a house came in view. His curiosity was at a high. He leaned in and stared as more and more of the house came into view. It looked very familiar.

"Is this Mom's old house?"

"Yep."

"I thought . . . I thought Mom said this was gone, that they had sold it."

"That's the first lie," Sebastian blurted out.

Sebastian's excitement for what Hunter was about to see couldn't be contained. "C'mon!" he yelled, and jogged to a side door next to the garage. He pulled out a key and unlocked the door. When the final click of the last tumbler fell on the lock, a bark from a large dog sounded out.

Sebastian grabbed the handle and opened the door slowly so as not to let the dog, a pit bull, out. "Oh, who's a good boy?" Sebastian said to the dog. The dog wiggled with excitement and licked Sebastian's hand intensely. The dog's friendly behavior was the antithesis of its appearance.

"This is Irish," Sebastian told Hunter.

"Hi, Irish," Hunter said, just standing behind his brother. He wasn't much of a dog lover and didn't have too much experience with them, as their mother, Haley, never allowed them when they grew up.

"It's Sebastian!" Sebastian called out.

They entered a small mudroom. The only furniture in the small space was a bench, coatrack, and baskets with boots and shoes. Irish bolted ahead of them into the main part of the house. Both men took off their shoes and followed him. The next room they walked into was a large kitchen. The appliances in it were at least fifty years old, but what stuck out was how clean everything was. Whoever lived there took great care to keep it that way. The kitchen opened up to a large great room with twenty-five-foot ceilings. A large rock fireplace and chimney spanned the distance from the ground to the wood-beamed ceiling. From this room, one could sit on the large sectional sofa and overlook the valley and a creek that was a hundred yards off the back of the house. Jug Handle Mountain stood prominently in the distance.

Hunter was captivated by the view and approached the windows to get a better look. It was stunningly beautiful. He was starting to understand what his grandparents saw in this part of Idaho. His awe was shattered when the realities of the years before came crashing down. Off in the distance, under a large pine tree, sat a gated graveyard. The site of graveyards in this age was common. After the lights went out, the luxury of having funeral homes and municipal graveyards disappeared. If someone died in your family they'd have to prepare the body and bury it themselves. But knowing what those graves meant—the history behind them—took Hunter's breath away.

"Mom said this was a cabin, not a compound," Hunter remarked.

"I know."

"This house is huge. What do you think, three-thousand-plus square feet?" Hunter asked out loud.

"More like four thousand," a voice echoed from the hall beyond.

Hunter turned around quickly. The hallway was dark, but in the shadows a person moved slowly toward them.

Hunter's heart pounded with anticipation as an elderly man with a cane appeared. The man walked up to Hunter and outstretched his hand.

Hunter was confused; there was something about his weathered face that seemed so familiar. When his eyes fell on a scar on the man's right cheek, his stomach dropped. *It can't be,* he thought to himself. He was dead. His mother had told him he had died years before. History books had talked about his demise. There had been a state funeral. His mother told him about how sad the republic had been when one of its founding fathers had passed. So many questions came rushing at him; he was overwhelmed with confusion.

"Granddad?"

"Hi, Hunter."

"Granddad, it can't be you. You're supposed to be dead!" Hunter exclaimed in disbelief.

"You can't always believe what you read," Gordon said.

Hunter was in shock, but he extended his hand to his grandfather's and shook it. Gordon gripped it tightly.

"Let's go sit in my office," Gordon recommended. He led them down the hallway to a set of large double doors that opened to a dimly lit space. The smell of cigar smoke wafted over Hunter. In the room were two large leather chairs with matching leather ottomans. Both were positioned in front of another fireplace, this one made of river rock. Against the wall across from the chairs was a leather love seat. It looked like a museum. As Hunter's eyes scanned the space, he saw pictures of his family and relics of days gone by; men in uniform, flags and medals now encased in shadow boxes. Above the fireplace hung an M4 rifle. Hunter remembered seeing the many pictures of his grandfather during the Great Civil War, always with a rifle in his grip.

"Take a seat," Gordon said, motioning to a chair. "Sebastian, come in here and turn these around to face the love seat."

Sebastian jumped at his command and turned the chairs around.

Gordon plopped himself in one of the chairs and Hunter took the other. Sebastian sat across from them. At first an unnerving silence separated them all.

Sebastian finally broke it by saying, "Granddad, I told you he'd come."

Gordon nodded at Sebastian and turned his attention to Hunter. "Hunter, I'm sorry this is how you had to meet me. And I'm even more sorry that you had to go through your life so far thinking I was dead."

"I don't understand. What's going on?"

"I will answer everything in time. I will tell you everything, like I told your mother many years ago."

Hunter was dizzy from this revelation. His mind couldn't grasp the enormity of it all.

"Why would everyone think you're dead? Even Mom thinks you're dead."

"Everyone thinks I'm dead, except for a few chosen individuals who know the truth. Your mother is one of them," Gordon said.

"Why would she lie to us?"

"Because I asked her to. We had to . . ."

"*Had* to?" Hunter replied, anger rising in his voice.

"I learned a long time ago that life is full of choices. I made the choice to do it this way, and for good reason. You shouldn't be angry with your mother," Gordon said.

"Why, what happened that made you do such a thing?" Hunter asked.

"It's not a short or easy story, but let me first share with you that I've been watching and looking out for you all of your life. I never intended for us to ever meet because . . . well, it could be dangerous for you to know the truth, but two weeks ago a knock at my door led to this meeting. Your brother found me. He's a good detective, I must say," Gordon said with a smile.

Sebastian returned the smile; a sense of pride filled him to have his famous grandfather give him praise. "I'll say it wasn't easy but it kind of fell into my lap, the knowledge that you were even alive."

"There's an old saying: 'Three can keep a secret if two of them are dead.'" Gordon grinned.

Hunter looked at Sebastian intently and asked, "Who was it? The woman in New Zealand?"

"Yes, a woman named Brittany. I was working this shitty landscaping job at a nursery home to make a few dollars and she asked me if I was Sebastian Rutledge. Just like that, she came up to me out of the blue. I don't know how she knew who I was. It really doesn't matter to me. But the conversation went from there; she eventually told me that Granddad was still alive."

"Who's Brittany?" Hunter asked, his focus now back on Gordon.

Gordon, lost in thought, didn't answer.

"Granddad?" Hunter pressed. "Who was she?"

"Someone I knew many years ago. But she's not important to the fact that you're here. I'm so happy that Sebastian found me and that you're now here. We have much to catch up on."

"To say that we have some catching up to do is an understatement."

"Come with me," Gordon said, slowly standing up.

The brothers followed him out into the cold chill of the early afternoon. Hunter watched his grandfather take labored steps toward the small graveyard behind the house. Nine gravestones stood like monuments behind the wrought iron fence.

"This is why I had to fake my death those many years ago." Gordon pointed toward the largest gravestone.

Hunter leaned in and read name on the gravestone. Samantha Van Zandt.

."I don't understand this at all. Grandma died years after your supposed death. Unless—is she alive too?" Hunter exclaimed.

Gordon's eyes grew hazy for a moment. "Unfortunately, she is not. Not a minute goes by that she doesn't cross my mind. I loved her deeply. She was a fine woman. I hope you boys find a good woman like your grandmother."

"But I don't understand—how does our grandmother's death relate to why you faked your own?"

"I made her a promise right there almost fifty-one years ago," Gordon said, now pointing to an old paver stone patio just off the main deck of the house. "I'm happy that you boys are here for many reasons but one is to impart some knowledge and wisdom that I have had to learn the hard way. So often history tends to repeat itself because people forget the lessons of what happened before."

"Then please tell us, please explain to us. Many out there praise you, but others curse you," Hunter said.

"I've never worried about those who criticize. I learned a long time ago that some people just need to do that. But I do owe it to you to explain why I had to make that choice to exit the world. However, I need to start with the promise I made to your grandmother those many years ago so that it will give my decision context."

"I'm all ears," Hunter said.

Gordon shivered from the cold. His gray, thin hair was waving in the cool breeze. He looked at Hunter. Gordon saw his blood and his legacy in those green eyes. Ready to explain his side of his life, he said, "Let's go back inside, grab a drink, and I'll tell you both how it all went down."

JUNE 24, 2015

. . .

"The promises of this world are, for the most part, vain phantoms . . ."

—Michelangelo

McCall, Idaho, United States

Both Gordon and Samantha smiled as they looked upon a hard day's work. Just off the back of their house now stood freshly tilled earth—the beginnings of their garden. Close by, their daughter, Haley, was playing in a sandpit that Gordon had made her after they had settled into their new life in McCall. The deep and rich smell of the upturned dirt filled the air as they shared this moment of contentment and pride.

The roads had cleared enough by early May that the group set out from Eagle to complete their journey from San Diego. Almost five months to the date they had set out to make the trip, they had arrived. When they left San Diego, their group was comprised of six families, but the harshness of the trip and rash decisions of some members reduced that number to three by the time they reached McCall. They had lost many along the way, including those near and dear, but also gained some, including Gordon's brother, Sebastian, Annaliese, and Luke. When they arrived at the first checkpoint in McCall, the celebration was bittersweet. The loss of their son,

Hunter, Frank, Mack, and Holloway hung heavily on the group, but they were determined to make something out of their new home.

So much horror and loss had occurred on the long road, but now the hope was that McCall would be their sanctuary from the new world. There they could rebuild and reconnect with each other, and for Gordon and Samantha, that was of greatest interest to them. The traumas they both experienced had taken a severe toll on them personally, and their relationship had taken some hits. They both recognized the importance of mending those differences, not just for their own sake, but for Haley's. Deep down their relationship had a solid foundation built on love, but it was cracked.

Samantha wanted to immediately forgive Gordon for leaving them after Hunter's death, but she couldn't. Gordon had painstakingly explained his position and she could understand why he would want to avenge Hunter, but she still felt deeply that his departure jeopardized her and Haley. Finally he broke down one night, his tough veneer melting away to show her a man ashamed of putting his son in the position to get captured and killed. He acknowledged that some of his reasoning for not being able to come back right away was due to his utter inability to face her. He felt he had let her down, that his decisions had cost them their only son. He explained what little peace of mind they could ever have would come knowing that Rahab was dead and could never harm anyone else again.

Even with his impassioned explanation, Samantha still felt hurt. She didn't look at the world the way Gordon did, but then again she knew that was why their relationship worked. They shared similar values, but their approach to things was different. After his breakdown and tear-ridden confession, she decided that she had to forgive him completely if they were going to move on with their lives. Someone had once told her that no one can heal if the wound is left to bleed, and with that in mind, she decided that they couldn't dwell on the past any longer.

"I forgot to tell you, Michael Rutledge has enough wood for us to build that smokehouse you wanted. He should be stopping by tomorrow sometime," Gordon said.

"That's great news. I like the Rutledges," Samantha replied with a smile.

"Yeah, they're good people. I've noticed that you and Tiffany are BFFs," Gordon joked.

Samantha shot him a look, "BFF? I haven't heard that phrase in a long time. Gosh, seems like yesterday that was so important."

"Friends are important."

"I know friends are important, it's just that I was so focused on having quote-unquote friends and doing the mommy stuff with the ladies back in San Diego that I kinda lost sight of what a real friend is. You know, play dates, dinner dates, and mommy nights out, blah, blah, blah. Keeping up with everyone else distracts you from the important things."

"I wonder what happened to all of them."

"Well, I'm sure Marilyn and Irene didn't make it out alive."

"Irene, maybe—she'd eat her own young to stay alive! Actually the best thing she could have done was knock off her drunk loser of a husband first; that probably would have given her and her pack of wild children a fighting chance." Samantha laughed.

"Oh, and Marilyn, that snob and her 'look at me and how nice all my stuff is.' I just loved her 'brand name this or that' attitude. I hope that Versace bag kept the Villistas away because her husband, 'the man who hated guns,' wasn't about to do anything," Gordon said.

"Anyway, enough about them. I am just grateful for the good friends we've had and the new ones we've met."

"I like Michael a lot, but he drones on about politics all the time," Gordon said.

"Don't kid yourself, I know you *love* to talk politics."

"What? I hate politics!"

"Yeah, right. You hate politicians but you've never walked away from a good old political debate."

Gordon cracked a large smiled and said, "You're right, but can he talk about anything other than Casadonia?"

"Cascadia, not Casadonia."

"Whatever. I'm not the biggest fan of how the U.S. was run before, but at least I know some of the people who run it now. Trying to secede and break away will only bring bad things."

"Wait a minute, didn't you tell me other states had seceded without issue?" Samantha asked.

"Yes, but I can't believe President Conner's going to let it keep happening. Also, what do Michael or the other Cascadians know about governing?"

"Michael must have some sway—he's convinced Sebastian to join his cause."

"Don't remind me," Gordon lamented. He had been to a couple Cascadian Independence meetings. He listened to what they had to say and liked most of it, but he just couldn't get his mind around pushing for secession, especially since he had allies in Cheyenne. For him it didn't make practical sense, but Sebastian was a convert, and a proud one at that.

"Whatever you do, don't be an ass to Michael. I like him and Tiffany."

"What you're asking me is to not piss him off by saying something like, 'Michael, please shut the fuck up about the Republic of Casadonia'?"

Samantha leaned over and kissed him and then said, "You're a pretty smart guy—that's exactly what I'm asking you to do."

"Hey, look how happy she is," Gordon commented to Samantha while nodding over to Haley. A grin stretched across his face.

"Yeah, she's adjusted well. It helps being here. I know things aren't perfect, but I wouldn't have guessed it would have gone so well."

"Right, with everything that has happened, I would have bet that even McCall would have been a soup sandwich," Gordon said, still grinning. He continued, "They've done such a great job, holding it together up here. These are good people."

"It's also a matter of timing; you heard the stories about weeks after. They had their issues too."

"I know, but they dealt with them swiftly. Mayor Waits and Chief Rainey have been a godsend to this area."

"When is your next shift?" Samantha asked.

"Not till tomorrow. I appreciate you letting me get out there and help. It means a lot to me."

McCall police chief Rainey had asked Gordon if he'd volunteer to be a part-time police officer. At first Gordon jumped at the chance to help, but Samantha resisted. But after spending a few weeks settling in, she saw the importance of Gordon having an active role in their community. She knew he had much to offer, and this was something he was good at; but she now had her eyes on something different.

"I know I was resistant at first but this town has been good to us, and we need to give back, just as long as it doesn't take you away from me too much."

Gordon grabbed Samantha's hand firmly. "Hey, I love you. I won't do anything without first running it by you and getting your input."

"I've wanted to suggest something to you but I think I keep talking myself out of it." She paused. "There's an opening coming up on the McCall City Council. I thought that . . ."

"You want me to run for city council?" Gordon asked, a bit of shock in his voice.

"Yes, I think the best way to keep us safe is to have you in place to make decisions."

Gordon sat back and thought about it. He hated politics, and nothing in life came without the politics of the position attached to it.

"It will also keep you home more often. When you do your night shifts, it's lonely in bed."

"Sam, I don't know what to say. Let me think about it."

"Well, hurry up, there's a special election in August."

"You are definitely full of surprises, I will say that," he said, grinning.

She looked at his rugged and scarred face. "I know there isn't a guarantee what tomorrow will bring, I just want you here when the unknown comes."

"I will be."

• • •

When they had arrived in McCall, they were interviewed by Chief Brent Rainey. New people were welcome, but under certain criteria. Fortunately for them, they passed the first test; they owned property within the city limits. After much back and forth with Rainey, Nelson, Gretchen, Melissa, Eric, Seneca, and Beth were allowed to stay too. Sebastian, Annaliese, and Luke were considered Gordon's family and allowed in without question. The agreement to let the others come in required that they actively participate in the police patrols and other community-based endeavors created by the McCall leadership, including teaching responsibilities at the school, harvesting of community farms, and road maintenance. Gordon and his group were happy to pitch in in exchange for a safe place to call home.

For the first few weeks, the entire group had to stay with Gordon and his family, but eventually they found housing elsewhere. Gordon loved his group, but when the last of them left for their own home, he was happy for them. The abundance of homes came from the fact that McCall had been a town built around recreation. Payette Lake and Brundage Mountain had provided a recreational industry that helped the town economically after the logging mill closed down in the 1980s. With an emphasis on world-class recreation, the town blossomed and many people from out of town built and purchased homes. After the lights went out, many of these homes were vacant. Some of those owners made their way to McCall, but many would never again lay eyes on their second homes. The surplus of homes was a blessing for Gordon's group. Of course if the owners ever arrived, they'd be asked to leave, but so far this had never happened. Rainey's department was in charge of this placement program and so far it had worked out successfully and without incident.

While Rainey had allowed Gordon's group to stay, he was not open to every person or group that came along. Brent Rainey was a no-nonsense man, a former cop and transplant from New York. Upon his early retirement from the New York Police department, he moved to McCall and settled down. He had never stepped foot in Idaho, much less out west, but he was a man in search of a new life. His wife had died from cancer years earlier, and McCall provided him a respite from those painful memories and a place to start fresh. Every time he looked into the face of a newcomer he approached with an open mind, hoping that they might be sincere—he had his own life to use as an example. However, he also knew the realities of the current world, and the town couldn't allow anyone who would disrupt the peace, or those who had to be taken care of constantly. It wasn't that McCall was without generosity, it just couldn't be everything to all people.

From his first meeting with Rainey, Gordon found him to be a man he could deal with and trust. Knowing that the town was being managed effectively gave Gordon peace, but he still had an urge to contribute to something that would ensure his family's safety, hence his volunteering for the police department patrols.

Gordon, Samantha, and Haley had just sat down to eat dinner

when a loud knock at the door interrupted them. Gordon looked at Samantha with concern. Their experiences over the past five months gave them pause whenever an unexpected person was knocking.

"I'll be right back," Gordon said, standing from the table and quickly walking to a table next to the front door. He opened the drawer and pulled out a pistol.

He approached the door cautiously and peered through the peephole to discover Rainey and another officer standing there. He unlocked and opened the door. "Hi, Chief."

"Gordon, sorry to interrupt, but I wouldn't be here unless it was something important," Rainey explained, his Brooklyn accent still thick, even after years of living in McCall.

"Not a problem. C'mon in," Gordon replied and fully opened the door.

Both men stepped inside the foyer, hats in hand. "Nice place ya got here," Rainey commented.

"Thanks. So, what's up?"

"Just over an hour ago, we stopped a convoy of vehicles at our southern checkpoint. We need you to come with us to verify who they might be."

"Verify?"

"Yeah, you see, these were military vehicles and one man is asking for you specifically."

"Seriously?"

"You know me, I wouldn't be bullshitting you. Do you mind grabbing your gear and coming with me? I'll bring ya back right after. I need to clear this up."

Gordon hesitated for a moment, his mind trying to scan who could possibly be asking for him. "Uh, sure. Let me grab my coat and stuff. Did he mention his name?"

"He said his name is Smitty."

Elko, Nevada

"Please, please don't hurt us!" a woman cried. Blood ran down her face from a deep cut on her head.

"Mommy, Mommy!" screamed her daughter.

"Take her inside the house with the other women," a young corporal in Pablo Juarez's army ordered.

Two soldiers hovering over her immediately grabbed her by the arms and yanked the woman to her feet.

"My daughter, please don't hurt my daughter!" the woman begged.

"Stop!" General Alejandro barked as he exited a vehicle that had pulled up to the scene outside the house.

After General Pasqual's demise, Alejandro, then a major, had been promoted to general and commander of Pablo's forces. Alejandro was a man of few words, so when he did speak, his soldiers paused. It was this demeanor that kept him out of Pablo's crosshairs. Alejandro was short and thin, but what he lacked in stature he made up for in reputation. Never one to shy away from a fight, his friends nicknamed him El Luchador, or The Wrestler, as he was well known for his ability to beat anyone on the wrestling mat. It was a name he was proud of.

Both soldiers carrying the woman stopped in their tracks.

"What is going on here?" he asked.

The corporal approached and saluted.

Alejandro didn't return the salute. His face grimaced with anger at the man's ignorance. "Don't ever salute me on the battlefield, ever!" Alejandro was referring to an order he had handed down as soon as he had taken over for Pasqual. The guerrilla war they were fighting against the Americans had forced them to embrace different tactics and to do away with typical military decorum. American insurgents had been able to target officers after they had been identified from something as simple as a salute. In this age, it was necessary to take all precautions possible.

"Sorry, sir," the corporal responded, his face now ashen.

"What are you doing here?" Alejandro asked again.

"Sir, we are taking the woman into the house with other women we have gathered."

Alejandro walked up to the woman and looked at her. Her eyes were swollen red, tears mixing with blood. He brought his hand to her face and she flinched from the anticipation of being hurt. "Shh, I won't hit you." He brushed her hair out of her face.

The woman couldn't control her sobbing, loud wails piercing the air. She looked at Alejandro but frequently her eyes darted off in the direction of her daughter.

"What happened here?" he asked her.

"We . . . me and my daughter were hiding and—"

"Her husband was an insurgent, and we killed him," the corporal interrupted.

"Is this true?" Alejandro asked softly.

Her eyes widened with the mention of her husband's role.

Alejandro now gripped her jaw tightly and asked again, "Is what the corporal said true?"

"We were only defending ourselves!" the woman blurted out.

Another door on Alejandro's vehicle opened up and out stepped Pablo. Simultaneously men poured out of a vehicle parked behind it and surrounded him. All eyes turned toward him as he strode up and stopped just a few feet from the woman.

"Your husband was an insurgent?" Pablo asked.

"Please, we didn't have a choice," the woman pleaded.

Pablo examined the woman, her dark hair, olive skin, and brown eyes. "You're Hispanic, aren't you?"

"Ah, yes, yes," the woman answered, hoping that the admission of her heritage would benefit her.

"So why oppose us?" Pablo asked.

"My husband . . ."

"Was he not Hispanic?"

"No, I mean, yes, he was. He just thought . . ."

"Thought what?" Pablo asked.

"Please don't hurt us."

"My dear, I'm not going to hurt you," Pablo said, looking the woman over. "So what did he think, your husband?"

"He, ah . . . " the woman said, then paused. She wanted to answer correctly but didn't know how to answer.

"Never mind," Pablo blurted out.

"No, please don't hurt us."

"Your husband fought against us, you probably fought against us, so . . ."

"No, please, no!"

"Did your husband love his country, did he love America?" Pablo asked, curious.

The woman's eyes were wide with fear; her mouth dropped open but nothing came out.

"Well? Answer me!"

"Yes, yes, he loved America, but me . . . I, I love Mexico. *Viva la Mexico!*" the woman cried out.

Pablo looked at her with black eyes then looked at General Alejandro. The serious look then changed to humor as he burst out laughing. The laughter drew even more fear from the woman.

Her daughter's whimpering grabbed Pablo's attention. Another soldier held her by the shoulders. The dirt on her face had now turned to a thin veil of mud as it mixed with her tears.

As Pablo looked at the little girl, he felt nothing. Absent was any remorse or sympathy. His emotional state kept him at the distance he needed in order to accomplish what he had to.

"Please shut up," he said to her. She complied with his command.

He took a few steps away and looked at the carnage that was left over from the short skirmish with the insurgents. The once tidy middle-class neighborhood was destroyed. The homes that lined the street were riddled with bullet holes, their windows shattered and blown out. Bodies of insurgents and soldiers lay scattered on the lawns, driveways, and street. The short battle was hard fought, but Pablo's force was overwhelming and had superior firepower. His men were now coming and going from the homes, taking what spoils they could; in one home he heard the screams of women as they were suffering the wrath of his men in the most violent and personal of ways. As he had told Isabel the night he killed her, he would not offer mercy beyond an offer to join him. Once engaged, his men were given carte blanche to do what was necessary to defeat the enemy.

His trek from Sacramento to Elko had taken him over two months. He had departed Sacramento in mid-April once his Villistas were firmly in place across the city. With each town he took, he spent the time to ensure he placed a force of his Villistas with a sound leadership structure. Elko wouldn't be any different. Once every pocket of resistance had been eliminated, the process of transformation would begin.

While taking each town along the way had slowed his conquest toward Cheyenne, what most frustrated Pablo was the constant sorties run by the remnants of the United States Air Force. Without air support, his troops were sitting ducks, but luckily they were able to maximize their countermeasures, diminishing the effects from the U.S. bombardment. Pablo had also split his main force into two forces of equal size. He led the main force as they marched along Interstate 80 toward Salt Lake City, Utah, while the other force followed along a parallel route south of his on U.S. Highway 50. He had hoped this would make his forces a more difficult target against U.S. airstrikes, while also expanding his reach. His forces to the south had not been bombarded and were making their way unopposed, as if the U.S. military was unaware of them. The two forces would link up again when they began their assault of Salt Lake City sometime in July.

Pablo's goal was to march on Cheyenne by late August. The fight would be tough, but he knew the only way to defeat the United States was to level the capitol and kill the president. He wanted to do it the old-fashioned way, with fighting in the street and hand to hand if necessary, but if he couldn't win that way, he had one surprise that would guarantee him victory. The last he had heard was that his surprise was already in Cheyenne; all that needed to be done was to give the word.

He turned back and faced the woman, his thoughts back in the present moment. He could see the fear in her eyes, pleading to let her and her daughter go free. While others might have seen this woman's daughter as an innocent, he only saw someone who would grow up one day to oppose him. She would grow up angry that her father had been killed and her country conquered, and use her anger and strength to find a way to try to reestablish her father's country. He couldn't risk that.

"I was told months ago that being merciful was the apex of strength. I can tell you now, it's not. That lie almost killed me. I warned this quaint little town two days ago to surrender or die." He paused and took a step closer to the woman, making her cringe. "Your husband made a choice. He believed in something. I have to say, I respect a man who is willing to die for a cause he believes in. I need men like that, but unfortunately, he fought for the losing side. You, on the other hand, are willing to beg and change your allegiance just to live. You cherish your own life above anything at all. You would be willing to sell out anyone just to see the sun rise one more day. Your husband was a brave but stupid man and he died. You're a coward and stupid. That's worse, and you'll die too, but with the knowledge that your daughter died before you," Pablo barked. He pulled out his pistol from his side holster and pointed it at the little girl and shot her.

The woman screamed, tears bursting forth as she struggled to go to her dying daughter.

"Look at me!" Pablo yelled.

The woman's own screams of anguish drowned out his command.

He slapped her face, the force of which caused her to look at him. She saw the pistol in her hand and began to beg for her life.

He placed the pistol against her forehead.

She cried out, "No, you said you wouldn't hurt me."

Pablo was squeezing the trigger but her comment stopped him. "You're right." He turned to General Alejandro and looked at him.

General Alejandro knew the look and answered it by pulling out his pistol and placing it against her head.

"No, no, no!" she cried.

The single shot from General Alejandro's pistol silenced her cries. Her body slumped into the soldier's arms.

"General Alejandro!"

"Yes, Emperor!"

"It's time to go."

"Yes, Emperor!"

Pablo walked back to the truck but stopped just outside of it. He turned around and said, "Good job, General. Today marks another victory for the Pan-American Empire."

Cheyenne, Wyoming

Once a week, President Conner would go outside the gates of the "green zone" that encompassed the downtown area of Cheyenne. He traveled with an armed escort to visit the newly erected tent cities that were quickly popping up along the perimeters of the city. The news that the United States government had established a new capital and that it was functioning had spread fast. People were migrating from all over the mountain and central states with the hopes of a brighter and safer future.

General Baxter didn't agree with his weekly sojourns, but Conner rebuffed him. The days of the president having to abide by every security protocol were gone. Conner knew he couldn't sit up in the proverbial ivory tower and lead. Once he made the decision to leave the bunker, he made it a point to mingle with the people he was sworn to protect. He knew he needed to be one of those leaders of times gone past who led from out front.

The first outcropping of tent cities stressed the government resources, but soon Australia, along with Brazil and Argentina, followed through on a commitment that they had struck with the United States. Within a month of a signed deal, aid began to pour in via Houston. Conner's treaty with the Republic of Texas had worked out for everyone's benefit—having a port to access like Houston's was critical to rebuilding, and its location was important. The ROT was working feverishly to establish diplomatic relations but the process was moving slowly. Only with Conner's help did the ROT get recognized by Australia and other nations, but that was in exchange for unfettered access to the port in Houston.

As Conner walked past the campfires and small gatherings, he was pleased to find people were adjusting. He noticed laughter as he passed many of the fires and tents. He knew the laughter didn't originate from a deep-down happiness but from a place of hope. These people had experienced horrors on the road. Many had experienced loss, not only the loss of their personal belongings, but the deep and painful loss that was so common now—the loss of a loved one. Death had become a familiar part of daily life. The initial shock of so much death had quickly vanished as people realized they needed to adapt or they would be one of the unfortunate ones. Those who had managed to survive to this point were lucky but not guaranteed to live another six months.

Conner found these visits enlightening, and he knew the citizens appreciated it as well. While mostly cordial visits, the encounters had occasionally gotten tense. He never once held a grudge against the people, though; he too might act out now and then if he were living under the same circumstances. For the most part, his interactions had given him a love and respect among the people that few politicians ever receive.

At Conner's request, Pat, the owner of Pat's Coffee Shop, would join him occasionally. They had forged a unique friendship. With Pat, Conner could be himself and remove himself from what seemed like the nonstop decision making. He and Vice President Cruz were still best of friends, but per Conner's request they remained separated. He couldn't risk something happening to both of them if they came under attack, so within a week of returning, Conner dispatched him and his family to Cheyenne Mountain, the bunker installation that he himself had called home for a bit.

Conner never shared the operational details of what was happening with Pat, and he never asked. He respected his place and knew it was not his to interject. But tonight things were different.

"President Conner, we hear rumors of a foreign army coming toward Cheyenne. Is that true?" a middle-aged man asked from across the small campfire. The man was joined by his wife and two teenaged sons.

"I won't lie to you: There is an enemy force southwest of us and they intend to kill off what is left of the United States. I will add that we are fighting them every inch. They will not make it here. I can assure you we are doing everything in our power to stop them," Conner answered.

"Why not just nuke 'em?" the man countered.

"We reserve the right to use all options to protect us," Conner replied, a response from his old politician's playbook of answers.

Conner looked at the family that sat across the orange flames of the fire. Their faces were gaunt and showed the stress of the past six months. Their eyes echoed the same plea for salvation of others he had met. They were desperate, and knowing that an enemy force was bearing down on them made them feel even more vulnerable—and they looked at the president to make a decision. Conner still hadn't come to a resolution within himself about whether to use nuclear weapons. He wasn't opposed to striking a foreign enemy across the ocean again, but to use one on U.S. soil was difficult for him to reconcile. The debate was raging within the situation room and halls of government, and it was a constant source of stress for the president. The man's remark gave him the internal cue to call it a night.

"Thank you all for allowing me the comfort of your fire. God bless you all," Conner said, standing up.

The family thanked him and offered him their hospitality again if he chose to accept it.

As he walked away from the warmth and light of the fire, Pat commented, "You're doing a good thing here."

Conner didn't reply. He picked up his pace as they headed toward his vehicle.

"Everything all right?" Pat asked.

Conner stopped and looked at him. "No, it's not all right."

Pat had never seen Conner this way. Gone was his mild-mannered demeanor; in its place was a man who was stressed and agitated.

"What's the matter?"

"These people are looking to me to keep them safe, and to be honest, I don't know if I'll be successful against the PAE. We keep bombing them, but it doesn't seem to slow them down. This emperor keeps taking town after town. My own reluctance to use nuclear weapons against them is now causing untold death."

"Then nuke them, get it over with," Pat answered simply.

"It's not that easy when you're the one pressing the button. Listen, I killed millions of people months ago after I launched a nuclear barrage against every enemy old and new. Without thinking of the consequences, I ended so many lives. That decision changed how our allies viewed us until I was able to convince them it wouldn't happen again. How many people died here because we didn't get the aid we needed sooner? I promised myself that I wouldn't just do that again. Believe me, it would end this whole thing, I know that. And I know it sounds odd, now when I have all the justification in the world, but I can't do it."

"Stop beating yourself up."

"Easy for you to say, you're not the one everyone is looking to," Conner quipped.

"I get it; I'm not making light of your responsibilities."

"What would you do? If you were in my shoes, what would Pat do?"

Pat remained quiet.

Conner finally broke the silence. "See, not that easy when you have to start considering all the ramifications."

"I mean, are you really asking me for my advice here?"

"No, I'm asking you what you would do. Don't advise me; God, I get that daily. I'm asking you to step into my shoes and make the decision."

With this knowledge, Pat again paused to think. "I, um, I don't want to tell you what to do." He took a deep breath. "If I were you, I would have to know everything; I couldn't make a decision that large without looking at all sides of the issue."

"What information would you need?"

"Um, I don't know, would one weapon work or would I need more? What happens after? Is there fallout?"

"See what I mean? Not easy. When all of sudden all the weight of a decision is on your shoulders, you think twice."

"Sorry, I didn't think about that."

"No shit, you didn't."

"I'm sorry I can't give you the answer you're looking for. But you have to determine which is worse, the contamination of your country from this enemy force or from the fallout."

"I'm sorry. I guess I needed to vent a bit," Conner said, a tinge of defeat in his voice.

"Hey, let's fall back to the shop and grab a drink," Pat offered.

Just as Conner was about to accept, a guard leaned in. "Excuse me, sir, General Baxter is looking for you. He has some important information."

Conner acknowledged the guard then turned to Pat and said, "Another time; duty calls. Do me a favor, jump in the chase vehicle. They'll take you back. I need to go back to the office."

Once inside his vehicle alone, Conner sat in quiet reflection. He wanted nothing more than to hammer the PAE, but he couldn't do what he wanted without the consequences of losing allies again. He found himself pulled in so many directions, attempting to satisfy many different thoughts and groups. There was pressure from one side to reconstitute the other two branches of government, there was pressure to sue for peace, there was pressure to fight it all out, there was pressure to openly negotiate with radical groups, so forth and so on. He could barely even keep peace with his own staff, who argued loudly and passionately for their causes.

Recently, Conner had been looking back on history for examples to follow, and one came to mind: Lincoln. Before the lights went out, there were some academic circles that referred to Lincoln as a tyrant because he implemented policies that were construed as unconstitutional. Some asked, "How can a president save the constitution by destroying it at the same time?" It was a fair question, but history proved Lincoln's actions were sound. In order to win a war, you must not only defeat your enemies, you must crush them. As each day passed without a clear plan to victory over the PAE, Conner began to reassess his own policy of what he termed moderated combat. Maybe, just maybe, he needed to take the gloves off and say to hell with what anyone thought.

• • •

Baxter was patiently waiting for Conner outside his office. The fact that Baxter wanted to meet now portended a lengthy evening.

Seeing Conner, Baxter jumped up and got right to it. "Mr. President, do you want the good news or the bad news?"

"I'm always one that likes to get my bad news first, but before you start, let's step into my office," Conner answered.

Baxter followed Conner into the executive office and took his usual seat.

"This is obviously important and couldn't wait, so what do we have?" Conner asked.

"The Aussies won't supply combat troops."

Taking in the bad news, he asked, "What's the good news?"

"They will supply us more arms, jets, and tanks."

"That is good news, but do we have the people who can fly or drive the equipment?"

"The good news was two parts; they will provide us with advisers to train our people. Bringing in all assets from military installations to come support us here was smart. Their troops levels were depleted but having them here will help."

"That *is* good news. How soon can we have it here? We don't have much time; the PAE will be breathing down our necks soon."

"I kind of left out the second part of the bad news." Baxter grinned sheepishly.

"Shit, do I want to hear this?"

"The ships should be pulling into Houston by late July."

"Late July! Damn!"

"I know, I hate to beat this drum, but this really highlights our need for a new strategy. The meeting ended with you wanting to wait for word about additional troops coming from our allies. Well, it's not going to happen. You saw the PAE's location—they've picked up momentum. If we're going to strike we have two windows where the effects of a nuclear strike will be diminished . . ."

Conner held up his hand. "I hear you, General, but I'm not confident about the decision to deploy nuclear weapons."

"I don't mean to step out of line, sir, but this is an easy decision. I understand the dance we have to do for political purposes, but this is now truly a self-defense situation, unlike the earlier strikes."

"I know the concern and the timetable; I'm just praying another way will present itself."

Baxter stopped talking, knowing that right now wasn't the best time to try to convince the president about this issue. The topic of striking the PAE was being discussed ad nauseam, heatedly debated earlier that day. Conner's staff was divided into three positions: ones who supported a nuclear strike, ones who supported a nuclear strike only if given consent from allies, and those who were absolutely opposed. His top three staff members all fell into a different camp—Baxter in the first, Cruz the second, and Wilbur the third.

"Colonel Barone really screwed us. We needed his men on the move weeks ago. I knew, I just knew we couldn't trust him," Conner lamented. He rubbed his eyes, clearly exhausted. "General, I don't need another comment about nukes; I know what's at stake. Let's meet in the morning with all staff. I want to go over the two areas we have found that are preferable for striking."

"Very well, sir. I'll contact everyone and set up a time," Baxter said.

"Ah, one minute. As it pertains to Barone out in Oregon, I want to know exactly what's going on there. The spotty reports of an uprising is an interesting development. I know we don't have assets available to deal with him, but I want to know precisely what he's up to," Conner stated. His mind was swimming with ideas.

"I don't know how we do that. We've sent several teams out there but they can't make it past his checkpoints. His perimeter is incredibly secure. The colonel has that town locked up tight and we don't want to cause an issue by forcing our way in. It's not the most ideal situation but we know he's contained."

"Contained for how long? Listen, we weren't sending in someone he knew and trusted. Who was the man who escorted the vice president?"

"That guy? I can't remember, but I'm sure the vice president or Secretary Wilbur will remember."

"Let's ask her tomorrow. That man is our ticket for getting the intel we need on Barone."

"So, what makes you think this guy will have better luck? Again, sir, don't we have enough to worry about?"

"We can chew gum and walk at the same time. Plus, if something happens to the guy, who cares?"

"True. And knowing what we're dealing with there will help our long-term strategic plans," Baxter replied.

"Exactly. So find the man and get the operation in play."

McCall, Idaho

On his way into town, Gordon had stopped by and picked up Sebastian. There were two reasons for this. One, he knew Sebastian would want to see Gunny again, and second, Gordon loved awkward reunions and this could prove to be one.

"Thanks for coming with me," Gordon said to Sebastian. Both men were standing just outside the interrogation room.

"Not a problem, brother."

"Hey, how's Annaliese, is she feeling any better?" Gordon asked.

"She just feels out of sorts, she's complaining of abdominal pain and has bad diarrhea," Sebastian said, the stress of her illness weighing heavy on him.

"Is she pregnant?"

"No, we tried one of the pee-on-the-stick tests and it came back negative."

Gordon could see how worried he was, and wished he could do something. "Take her into town tomorrow to see Doc, get her checked out." One of the main institutions that was kept intact and operating was the McCall Hospital. Even without power and equipment, they were open for business.

"That's what we were planning on doing. So, let's get to this, shall we?" Sebastian said, clearly wanting to move past the conversation about Annaliese.

"Sure," Gordon answered. He opened the door and they both entered the small interrogation room.

"Jesus Christ, Smitty, I thought I saw the last of you months ago!" Gordon exclaimed.

The men embraced and Gunny joked, "You can't get rid of an old dog like me that easy."

"Obviously," Gordon replied with a smile then continued, "I brought a friend."

Sebastian walked in right on cue with a smile stretched across his face.

"Holy shit, Corporal Van Zandt!" Gunny exclaimed upon seeing

Sebastian. He looked at Gordon and then replied, "I'm so glad you both found each other. There's nothing I love more than a happy ending."

The men shared small talk then sat down to discuss Gunny's unexpected arrival in McCall. Trusting Gordon, Rainey allowed him and Sebastian to talk privately before he interjected his own line of questioning.

"Well, I know you know what I'm going to ask, so go ahead," Gordon put forth.

"Gordon, all hell has broken loose in Coos. The colonel has totally fucked everything up."

The jovial mood created by the reunion melted away after Gunny's statement.

"What do you mean?" Gordon asked.

"Not a week after you left, the Colonel massacred hundreds of unarmed civilians in the streets. We're talking men, women, and children. The lunatic bastard even had the children shot."

"Oh my God," Gordon gasped.

"I told you, Gordo, the old man had gone a bit loopy," Sebastian chimed in.

"Unfortunately, your brother's right. I didn't always agree with him on everything. The mutiny, I could live with, but this move? Nope, I can't understand it, nor will I go along with it."

"So, you left and came here?" Gordon asked.

"Not right away. Many Marines and sailors joined those civilians who rose up to oppose Colonel Barone. We fought back, but what the colonel lacks in couth he makes up for in resilience. For every step we gained, he'd hit us back so hard, we took two steps back."

Gordon was flabbergasted by this. He leaned back in his chair as if to rest from the heavy news. His thoughts soon raced to Brittany and Tyler.

"The woman and her son?" Gordon asked with concern.

"I don't know. The last I saw of them was well over a month ago. She had joined in the resistance, but I lost track of her, sorry."

"Brittany was fighting against Barone?"

"Who's Brittany?" Sebastian asked curiously.

A bit annoyed by Sebastian's lack of memory, Gordon reminded his brother, "The woman who I saved, remember?"

"She's quite a looker too," Gunny joked.

Ignoring Gunny's comment, Gordon pressed on, "What else?"

"The colonel has taken a firm grip on Coos Bay. No one is allowed in and it's tough as hell to get out . . ."

"Not about that. Brittany," Gordon interrupted.

"Afraid I don't know anything else. I saw her at a meeting. She left and that's the last I saw of her. I'm sorry, Van Zandt; I wish I had more info for ya."

Gordon's mind was racing. In some ways he couldn't help but feel responsible for Brittany's fate. Had he known Barone would've been capable of such brutality, he wouldn't have convinced her to come with him. She stayed in Coos Bay because it promised to be a safe haven. Now, in an instant, Barone had turned it upside down. He couldn't imagine why she'd get involved with resistance efforts, though. He knew she was a capable person; she had proven those skills time and time again in their travels. But now she was facing a force of well-trained and heavily armed men. Anger began to rise in him.

"Hey, Van Zandt!" Gunny barked.

"Um, what?" Gordon answered.

"Sorry to interrupt your daydreaming, but can you tell the police chief we're good to go?"

"Ah, yeah, of course. How many men do you have?"

"It was a fucking miracle, but we managed to get out of Coos with four Hummers, a shitload of weapons, and a dozen people."

"Should be easy to house a group of jarheads somewhere around

here. I can attest to how having the Marines can be helpful for our
security."

"Well, we have seven Marines, two sailors, and three civilians."

"We'll make it work. I promise," Gordon pledged, his thoughts
still swimming with images of Brittany and Tyler. He needed to see
if he could contact them but he didn't know how. Then, an idea came
to mind. "Gunny, do you happen to have a sat phone?"

"Of course. If I'm anything, it's prepared," Gunny answered with
a broad smile.

"Perfect, I need it."

"Who the hell are you thinking about calling? I don't think Colonel Barone has the time to take calls," Sebastian joked.

"Not him, someone who won't hesitate to help me," Gordon replied.

"Who's that?" Sebastian asked, his arms crossed.

"The Vice President of the United States."

Coos Bay, Oregon, Pacific States of America

The infighting and armed resistance Barone had been experiencing
since the day he ordered the civilian massacre had taken its toll on
his forces and on him personally. The last count he had that morning
was that one-third of his men had taken up arms against him. The
fighting had been brutal: Marines fighting Marines, sailors fighting
sailors. Not a day had gone by since the massacre that shooting
wasn't heard in the streets. Directly after the massacre, he locked the
city down and implemented martial law. No one was allowed to
leave or come in. He was determined to flesh out those who opposed
him and finish them off. He had lost control of the town of North
Bend, but Coos Bay was firmly under his will. After a few weeks of
bitter fighting, he had proposed a cease-fire, but the resistance group
refused to meet with him. Without the ability to quell the uprising

diplomatically, the only course of action for him was to crush them militarily.

The rebellion in Coos Bay had also forced him to break his treaty with Conner and the United States. He feared that if he told Conner, the United States would take advantage of his bad situation, so he had ceased all communication. He couldn't worry about it now—he had to win this fight or die.

Against his better judgment, he had taken to drinking heavily. What had been an occasional indulgence now happened almost every night. Tonight was one of those nights. As he paced his office in city hall, he mumbled loudly, railing against "the traitors." The almost incoherent comments were directed at those Marines and sailors who he claimed had enjoyed the fruits of his decision to mutiny, but now had turned against him in open and armed rebellion. Clearly overlooking his own indiscretions, he held a deep-seated resentment toward them. His resentment manifested in the treatment these men received after they were captured. The rules of warfare he had lived under a lifetime were gone. Simpson couldn't have been more right that day months ago when he told him that there was no turning back. Barone may have regretted his actions, but now he was committed to his cause, rightful or not.

Exhausted and drunk, he plopped himself on the couch that sat against the far wall. The sofa now served as his bed most nights. Relations with his wife and daughter paralleled everything else in his life—they had soured and he wasn't ready to face them. He sat staring at the wall covered in maps. His eyes followed the red lines that designated the secure boundaries of Coos Bay. As he traced the map lines, his eyes grew heavy and he slouched further into the comfort of the sofa. He turned his weary head and saw a framed picture of his son, Billy. Barone still hadn't recovered from the death of Billy those many months ago. He directed his blame at his foes

but on nights like this, he would lay it all at his feet. Only to himself
did he regret the decision he made in Afghanistan. If he hadn't mu-
tinied, Billy would still be here.

He drifted off into a fitful sleep, but what seemed like moments
later, he was jolted awake by a loud explosion. He sprang up, glass
still in his hand. Within seconds, the roar of machine gun fire
erupted outside on the street in front of city hall. He bolted to the
windows in his office that overlooked the fiery scene below. Large
flood lights illuminated the entire front of the building and the surrounding fenced perimeter. He watched Marines as they raced toward a plume of smoke and fired near a checkpoint not a hundred
yards away.

"Goddamn bastards!" Barone barked as he tossed the half-empty
glass of whiskey against the wall. He marched away from the windows just as several bullets penetrated the glass. He dropped to his
knees to take cover. "Damn it!"

Barone crawled away from the windows toward the side table
where his holstered pistol sat. He grabbed it and made for the door.
The two Marines who typically guarded him were gone, another one
of his poor commands influenced by alcohol. He scanned both ways
down the hall but saw no one. He was in a vulnerable position and
knew it. If city hall was under assault and they managed to breach
the perimeter defenses, he wouldn't have a chance to stop them. He
rushed down to the first floor, where he saw his Marines moving in
earnest to address the assault. In the darkness beyond the fence he
saw muzzle flashes, but still no sight of anyone from the resistance.

Barone opened the doors and walked out. He could hear the gunfire from the resistance fighters rattle off the building and felt a rush
of adrenaline. Unafraid, he unholstered and began to march toward
the smoldering checkpoint.

Another large explosion shook the ground; a fiery plume of black smoke and flames licked the sky. The intense light from the initial blast blinded him for a moment. When he turned back, he saw an armored Humvee on fire, the gunner now dead, lying atop the machine gun. The anger was building up in him; all he wanted to do was end the resistance and deal a final blow. Tonight would not be that night, but he'd kill as many as he could. When he resumed his march, someone grabbed him from behind. Barone swiftly turned and pointed his pistol at Simpson.

"Colonel Barone, we have to get you out of here, now!" Simpson pleaded.

"No!"

"Sir, they've got superior numbers here. We have reinforcements coming but we need to take you to a secure location!"

"I'm not leaving these men behind!" Barone barked, shrugging off Simpson's grasp.

"Sir, please, let's go! Fight another day!"

Barone jerked away from Simpson and continued toward the center of the fighting.

As he watched him go, all Simpson could think was that Barone was now a man who didn't care whether he lived or died. Knowing that his fortunes were forever tied to Barone, Simpson, armed with an M16 rifle, followed him toward the hellfire.

JUNE 25, 2015

• • •

"People are like dirt. They can either nourish you and help you grow as a person or they can stunt your growth and make you wilt and die."

—Plato

McCall, Idaho

Gordon had split up Gunny's group, half staying at his house and the rest at Sebastian's. With Rainey's approval for them to stay, the next step would be to find them permanent homes. All night Gordon tossed and turned, thinking about the unstable situation in Coos Bay. He worried about Brittany and Tyler; he couldn't understand why she would risk everything and work with the resistance. None of it made sense to him, but then again the world didn't make sense anymore.

As soon as the sun made its appearance, he was up and ready to make the call via Gunny's satellite phone. With Cruz's promise to help him in the future, he hoped this was a way to check on Brittany without inserting himself into the situation too much.

"You do know I could have used this on my trip with the vice president," Gordon chided Gunny.

Both men were outside enjoying the crisp Idaho summer morning, the sun's warm rays providing a contrast to the dry, cool air.

"I don't know what you're talking about. I gave specific instructions to put one in your vehicle before you left Coos Bay back then," Gunny said defensively.

"Well, my friend, there wasn't one in the vehicle or trailer. Believe me, I've turned this thing inside out making sure I got everything out that was useful," Gordon commented as he pointed at the Humvee he had taken on that trip.

"Sorry, Van Zandt, I swear I ordered it to be in there."

"It's all right; I know you can't control everything."

"Here," Gunny said, handing him the phone. "The coverage can be spotty; we lost some of the communication satellites in the EMP attacks."

Gordon took the phone, reached in his pocket, and pulled out a small green notepad. He flipped through the pages till he reached the one where Cruz had written down his number. Gordon didn't know where the number went, but Cruz told him that if he ever needed anything to call him. He carefully entered the nine-digit number and placed the phone to his ear. The first few seconds was dead air, then a series of clicks followed by a ring tone that sounded distant. He raised his eyebrows and winked at Gunny when the connection was made. Knowing that was a cue to leave, Gunny patted Gordon on the shoulder and walked back into the house.

By the eighth ring, Gordon was growing skeptical that anyone would even answer. The initial excitement when he heard the connection and ring was vanishing quickly. By the twelfth ring, he became weary. He was pacing the gravel driveway, kicking rocks. He imagined a phone in some far-off corner office ringing with not a soul around to answer. In frustration, he hung up the phone and put it in his pocket. His mind contemplated what move, if he had any, he should make. How on earth could he find out if Brittany and Tyler were safe? The only solution that came to mind was driving the three-plus hours to Mountain Home Air Force base; there he knew he'd be able to reach Cruz. But he couldn't think of any rational explanation to tell Samantha. He could send someone in his stead but even then, what would be the justification for risking someone's life on a trip that long? With no answers apparent except to try again later, he headed back toward the house.

As he did, a car horn blared in the distance. Gordon walked down the long drive to see an old Dodge truck with Michael Rutledge behind the wheel, a load of wood in the truck bed. He unlocked the metal gate and swung it open.

As Michael drove inside, Gordon saw that he was accompanied by his young son, Austin, who was just seven months older than Haley. He and Haley had grown fond of each other, and their time together was enjoyable to watch. Austin paid close attention to Haley and made sure she never was hurt, while Haley would dote on him. The two were inseparable, and for Gordon it was nice to see Haley so happy after all she had been through.

Michael Rutledge was a few years younger than Gordon. He was tall and lean, standing at six feet, with a full head of dark black hair. Michael wasn't a native Idahoan, but had relocated to the area six years prior, just after Austin was born. He had run a successful dental practice in Lowell, Massachusetts, but fortunes aligned for him and Tiffany when a practice became available in McCall. They both wanted out of Massachusetts for many reasons, one being the quality of life. They had always dreamed of raising their children in a small mountain town, and Idaho had been a part of their lives in the past as they were both avid skiers. With the purchase of the practice in McCall and the quick sale of his practice in Lowell, their dreams became reality when they finalized the move to McCall in 2009.

Michael wasn't shy about sharing his libertarian political views with anyone, especially his controversial belief that the United States was ripe for separation. Many years before the attacks, he had predicted that the country wouldn't hold together if a major event occurred. To date, his predication had come true. He often would comment that it seemed impossible for a large central government thousands of miles away to tell someone living in the mountains of Idaho how to live. He looked at how the country was already divided along red and blue states and how varied the lifestyles and culture were in different areas. Besides language, there wasn't much that someone in the Bronx had in common with someone in McCall. After the attacks, he began to meet with others locally to push the idea of separating from the United States and forming a country called Cascadia. At first many scoffed at him, but as the days turned to weeks then to months without a government response, the idea began to take hold. The founding principles of Cascadia would be a respect for liberty, human rights, and sustainable existence with regard to the biodiverse region. The basic tenets resonated with many locals, and with the absence of any federal government, a majority of people in McCall became receptive to the idea of Cascadia. Whenever he was with Gordon, Michael would attempt to recruit him as he had already recruited Sebastian; he wanted both brothers on his side. Not one for playing politics, Gordon would laugh and wave him off. This was not to say that Gordon wasn't curious. He had even attended a couple of meetings with Sebastian before, but in the end he thought the reality of creating a nation out of the states of Idaho, Oregon, and Washington would be an extremely difficult task, if not impossible. The governments of Idaho and Washington were operating to a certain degree and Oregon was not under any central control. When Gordon would raise these inconvenient truths, Michael would smile and tell him that he was too pessimistic.

Michael parked the truck next to the garage. Before he could turn the engine off, Austin was out and running toward the front door to see Haley.

"Those kids sure do like each other," Gordon said with a smile.

"Yeah, they do, it's nice. So, here's your wood. Where do you want it?"

"Right there, thanks," Gordon said, pointing to the side of the garage.

As the men were off-loading the wood, Michael took notice that Gordon was deep in thought.

"Everything okay?" Michael asked.

"Ah, yeah, a lot has been going on, that's all."

"I heard about the Marines arriving. They're friends of yours?" Michael asked.

"Ha. I imagine there's a lot of rumors flying around in town," Gordon said with a smirk, dodging the question.

"Yeah, you could say that. It's not every day a small convoy of Humvees comes rolling into town. The sight of the Marines got everyone excited. The talk was that the army was coming to help us. I, of course, knew that wasn't the case," Michael said.

"When did you get the word of our new neighbors?" Gordon asked.

"I'd guess around nine thirty. You won't believe it, or maybe you will. Joyce, our neighbor, came banging on our door, screaming that the army had come. I don't know what was worse, watching her make a fool out of herself or that she dragged her kids along, soiled pajamas and all."

"I've heard she's quite the drinker."

"More like a lush. And her poor boys. She still has the four-year-old in diapers. Tiffany doesn't know if she should feel sorry for her or slap her silly. The woman is the most negative person I've ever met."

"I'm not going to sit in judgment. She's been through a lot, I heard, with her husband leaving," Gordon said, attempting to stay above the gossipy talk.

Sweat was now streaming down Gordon's face. He wiped it away with his sleeve and leaned against the truck. "I guess we should have some sympathy for her. I'm sure she's not an evil person, just one who has made some poor choices."

"Are you sure you don't have any interest in politics?" Michael quipped.

"Trust me, never. I hate politics and I especially don't have a fondness for politicians."

"So you won't like me when I'm the president of Cascadia?"

"Oh, no, here we go."

"You mean to tell me you can just keep yourself neutral? I see you active with helping the mayor and Chief Rainey."

"Michael, all joking aside, I am intrigued by the idea. I used to be big into following politics, but I was naïve then. I just don't know if starting a new government is as easy as you think it is. You do realize there's this thing called a bureaucracy you'll have to create, right? I think the concept is easy but then there's the reality of the logistics. Listen, locally, I can effect change, but on a national level, it's another can of worms."

"Just come with me to this next meeting. A couple of Cascadians from Olympia just arrived. We are working together to make sure we can have both of our groups operate as one and have a common focus."

"I have to laugh. Your country hasn't even birthed and you have differences."

"Like anything, people have a common idea but different ways of approaching it."

"This sounds a little like the beginning of political parties, and *that*, my friend, can be a death knell from the very start."

"I'm forever the optimist; we can work through these differences to have our common dream of a free nation realized. I just need people like you to be on our team. So you'll come to the next one? I want you to meet Charles, the leader of the Olympia group."

"Sure, I can do that," Gordon said. He was agreeing because he wanted to be a supportive friend and because he did have a nagging curiosity. If Cascadia ever were to become a reality, he might need to be close to it. Like Samantha reminded him yesterday, he could help his family by having a part in how things worked, and being a part of Cascadia might be the ticket. The Cascadian influence had grown a lot locally and he did agree with the basic premise of liberty and human rights.

"So, these Marines, you must know them—unless you picked up two extra Humvees at the car lot in Cascade."

"Yeah, well, not all of them. I know three of them. The other nine, I don't know at all."

"So what's their story?"

"They came in from Coos Bay, Oregon. There's a couple Marine units there now."

Michael completely stopped working. Gordon's mention of the Marines in Oregon piqued his curiosity.

"Why are there Marines in Oregon?"

"That is a very long story and one best told over a few drinks," Gordon said. He had kept most of his recent past secret. He felt that no one needed to know details, and he also feared people's judgments. McCall was supposed to be a new start. Having people judge him for his past decisions could do more harm than good.

"I'll second that."

"Thanks again for the wood; I can't say enough about how much this helps me out."

"Not a problem, just share some of your venison jerky with me when you have it."

"That is a guarantee, and it reminds me—I'm going hunting tomorrow. . . ."

The phone in Gordon's pocket began to ring. The men looked at each other. The once familiar sound of a mobile phone now sounded out of place.

"Your cell phone is working?" Michael asked with a shocked look on his face.

Gordon quickly reached into his pocket and pulled out the ringing phone. One the screen he saw the number calling was the same he had called earlier. His heart jumped into his throat as he clicked the receive button and said, "Hello?"

"Hello, who is this?" the voice asked.

"This is Gordon Van Zandt. I called earlier; I'm trying to reach Vice President Cruz."

"Gordon Van Zandt, who are you? How do you have this number?"

"I escorted Vice President Cruz from Coos Bay to Idaho last March. He gave me this number and said I could call it if I needed anything. Well, I need something."

The mention of the vice president quickly superseded Michael's interest in the fact that Gordon had a working cell phone. Gordon looked at Michael and held up his index finger, indicating he needed a moment alone. He then stepped away from the truck.

"Mr. Van Zandt, let me put you on hold."

"Please don't hang up."

"One second, sir."

Gordon could hear the man talking to someone. He tried to understand what they were saying but it was unintelligible.

"Mr. Van Zandt, do you have something to write with?" the man asked.

Gordon ran back up to Michael. "Do you have a pen and paper?

Michael quickly rummaged through the glove box and pulled out an old pencil and registration papers and handed them to Gordon.

"Yes, I do," Gordon said to the man on the phone.

"Call this number back in five minutes," the man said, then proceeded to give Gordon a different nine-digit number.

Gordon hung up and looked at his watch.

"Who was that?" Michael asked, stunned by what he had heard.

"Um, I'll explain later, over those drinks," Gordon responded as he paced back and forth with excitement.

"I can't wait to hear."

Gordon stopped his pacing and looked at Michael. "Let's just say a lot happened on the way to McCall."

Cheyenne, Wyoming

Dylan, the chief of staff, came into the conference room with the same exuberant look on his face as the day he had confirmed Cruz's location.

"Take a seat, we're about to begin," Conner instructed him.

"Sir, before we begin, I have some interesting news," Dylan said with a grin.

"Go ahead," Conner remarked, waving him to proceed.

"Mr. Vice President, are you on the conference call?" Dylan asked first.

"Yes, I'm here," Cruz replied over the speaker.

Dylan then turned and looked at Conner. "Sir, remember you were asking about the man who had taken the vice president and madam secretary?"

"Yes, I remember," Conner said. "We were going to ask you about him later. I have a job for him."

"I remember him too, a Gordon—"

"Van Zandt," Dylan interrupted and then continued. "Gentlemen, he called us, looking for you, Mr. Vice President, and . . ."

The phone in the center of the conference table rang.

"That should be him right there," Dylan blurted out as he leaned over and hit the button for the phone line.

Silence fell over the room as they waited to hear the man on the other end.

"Hello?" Gordon asked.

"Mr. Van Zandt, hello, this is President Conner."

"President Conner?" Gordon asked, clearly surprised to be hearing the voice of the President of the United States.

"Yes, this is President Conner, and be advised you're on speaker phone."

"Mr. Van Zandt, hi, this is Vice President Cruz."

"Mr. Vice President, hi, how are you?" Gordon asked.

"I'm good, very good, thank you. I understand you were trying to reach me?"

Gordon felt foolish now. He had imagined a simple call to Cruz, not a conference call with the president and his entire staff.

"Yes, sir, I, um . . . Sorry for calling, but you said that if I ever needed anything to call you and, well, you see, I need something."

"Mr. Van Zandt, sorry to jump in, but your call is, to say the least, very ironic. You see, you need something from us, and your country needs something from you."

Gordon paused, not knowing what to say. He knew that the only way for him to verify if Brittany was okay was with the help of Cruz, but apparently this request could now cost him a return favor.

Conner waited patiently for a response to his last comment, but when one wasn't given he proceeded. "Mr. Van Zandt, what is it that you need from us? We're in gratitude to you for what you did, so please tell us how we can be of service."

Gordon looked around to see if Michael was listening. He wasn't; he was back to unloading the truck. Just to be safe, he took a few more steps away and answered, "Mr. President, I hope my request doesn't come off as silly, but I understand there's been some upheaval in Coos Bay. I have a friend there I'm concerned about. I was hoping you could find out if she was okay."

Conner raised his eyebrows and looked at Baxter, sitting next to him. "You want us to contact someone in Coos Bay for you? Why don't you do that yourself? You could have called your friend the colonel instead of calling here."

"You see, that might be difficult. I know you, meaning the United States, have a treaty with the colonel and, well, let's say that my friend is working against him. I was hoping you could use some of your influence to make sure she and her son aren't harmed."

"I don't think we can help you," Conner said flatly.

Gordon was shocked by his abrupt answer to this simple request. "Why not?"

"We lost contact with Colonel Barone months ago. After he massacred countless number of citizens, he locked down the city and any attempts we've made to make contact have gone unanswered. We've even gone as far as sending men out there, but all have been turned away. He has Coos Bay locked down like East Berlin. No one is going in or coming out."

Gordon's pacing had taken him farther up the long drive. The thick grove of aspen trees that stood on either side of him shadowed him from the rising sun. He stopped and stared through the trees, his mind lost in a fog of questions.

Conner looked around the room when a minute had passed without a response from Gordon. "Mr. Van Zandt, are you there?"

"Ah, yes, I'm still here. I'm trying to think about what I can do, that's all."

"Can I propose an idea that would be beneficial to both of us?"

"Go ahead."

"Again, I can't say how ironic your call is. We were actually trying to track you down."

"Really?"

"Yes, we share your concern for what is happening in Coos Bay. Colonel Barone is allegedly an ally of ours, but we need to be more aggressive in our response to what has happened there. But with our inability to enter the region, we were at a loss as to what to do until your name came up just yesterday. We know you and he have a close relationship, yet you have managed to stay neutral in all of this. We thought that you could lead a mission into Coos Bay to determine what is happening there . . ."

"Let me stop you right there. I don't have any plans on driving to Coos Bay. I'm very concerned for my friends, but I can't leave my family again."

Conner looked at Baxter, who then took the look as his cue to speak. "Mr. Van Zandt, this is General Baxter, the secretary of defense. We know the difficulties of living out where you are, but I can say that we can provide you supplies—whatever you need in exchange for you service. You name it; we'll provide it to you."

Gordon began to pace again. The offer of equipment and supplies was enticing, but he had made a promise that he couldn't break. He could not leave Samantha and Haley again, no matter what he was offered.

"I just don't know if I can risk making another drive like that. It's too dangerous on the roads," Gordon said.

"Mr. Van Zandt, our nation needs you; we are in a perilous position right now. We have an army marching toward us and Barone has gone offline. We need to know what's going on there so we can assess our position against the PAE."

Gordon clenched his teeth out of frustration. When he'd called, he never imagined that the conversation would turn out like this.

"Mr. President, I need a day to think about this. I can't make another drive like that again. I just can't risk it."

"Take another day, think about it," Conner replied.

"Van Zandt, General Baxter again here. You don't have to drive—we'll send a chopper to pick you up and take you to a predetermined landing zone outside of Coos Bay. We'll supply you with a motorcycle to go the rest of the distance. Let us know what gear you'll need and we'll have it on the bird."

"Do I call this number back tomorrow?" Gordon asked.

"Correct, call this number tomorrow morning at eleven hundred hours," Baxter confirmed. He then looked at Conner.

"Mr. Van Zandt, please think about it. You get to accomplish a lot with a single trip," Conner concluded.

"Thank you. I'll call back tomorrow with my decision," Gordon said, and hung up.

When the phone line went dead all eyes shifted to Conner, who was now standing.

"Looks like we're having a meeting this time tomorrow?" Baxter asked rhetorically.

"Same time tomorrow, but I want Major Schmidt present too." Major Schmidt was new to the command structure, but in his short time there he had proven to be trustworthy and offered a unique perspective that Conner liked.

"I'll let the major know his presence is needed tomorrow," Baxter stated.

"Mr. President, you do realize that Van Zandt is a *friend* of Colonel Barone's. How do we know he won't compromise the mission or lie about what's happening there?" Secretary Wilbur said.

"Brad, I agree with Secretary Wilbur on this. He's not a man with a strong allegiance to the United States," Cruz added.

"Why's that?" Conner asked.

"The man shared with me his open animosity toward the government," Wilbur said evenly.

"Animosity?" Baxter asked.

"Yes, he was adamant about how the government has screwed him over," Wilbur added.

"How do you know this?" Baxter asked, now facing Wilbur as he swiveled in his chair.

"He told me, flat out. He has no love for us. The man is an op-portunist and I don't think we can trust him," Wilbur said, answering Baxter.

"How did we screw him over?" Conner asked.

"This guy was a Marine and served in Iraq. Something happened; he wouldn't share with us specifically, but it sounded like his exit out of the military was not a good one," Wilbur said.

"General, do we have access to military records?" Conner asked Baxter.

"That's a good question—not sure. It's not as if we've been concerned with that type of info these days," Baxter said.

"Find out. I want to see who we're dealing with in light of this new info. Make it a priority. I want it before our conversation with him tomorrow," Conner commanded. Baxter nodded in acknowledgement of his latest task.

"All right, let's change gears. We have a war to win," Conner said.

"Sir, may I present my findings on the separatist movements to the group?" Wilbur interjected.

"Yes, please, Madam Secretary, go ahead. I appreciate you doing this so quickly. Ever since our run-in with the Montana Independence Party, it has become increasingly important to keep tabs on these groups," Conner said.

The Montana Independence Party was a loose affiliation of civilian militias that had one common goal: to have Montana break away from the United States. Conner was feeling the pressure from these small separatist groups that had popped up. It was already difficult enough to keep the country together without them trying to pull it apart.

"My pleasure, sir. After several conversations with governors and other state homeland security personnel, I came away with extensive knowledge on what's happening out there with separatist and independence movements. Because of more critical issues, like getting the infrastructure back up and just feeding people, focus on these groups and their activities was not being closely monitored," Wilbur said, handing out sheets of paper around the table.

Laying a map across the table, Wilbur turned to her peers with a serious look on her face. "What we're looking at is a widespread fracturing of our nation." The map she had laid out displayed a different country than what they were used to seeing. The map was color-coded to depict the areas that had separated or had threatened to. The eastern United States was crossed out with red lines from the Mississippi river east. This was the area that Cruz and Baxter had determined to be forfeit. Texas was marked out but now parts of Oklahoma and Arkansas were included with it. Nevada and California were shaded green, with the letters PAE written across them. Arizona had the letters AR marked over it, which stood for Arizona Republic. Other states that were now crossed out or missing from the map of the current United States were parts of North Dakota, South Dakota, Wyoming, Montana, Idaho, Oregon, and Washington. These states now marked off gave a glimpse of a new, much smaller country if some of the groups wanting to break away succeeded.

Conner's eyes ran over the map quickly, his heartbeat increasing when his mind started to process what he was seeing.

"If you look at the paper I handed out, you'll see about five major groups. There are a lot of mobs and gangs, but the groups I'll cover are organized and could pose a problem. We all remember the MIP, and though they are down, we can't consider them out. We will need to monitor them. Major Schmidt was smart to keep a small contingency of troops up there to support the governor. In Arizona we're dealing with a group called the Arizona Republic. They're attempting to break away legitimately by convincing the governor and state legislature to vote on secession. You won't believe it, but their leader is former Congressman Faye—"

Conner interrupted her by blurting out, "Faye? He served with me and was a part of my caucus back in the nineties. The son of a bitch term-limited himself out of office, so now he wants his own country?"

"Apparently he has a lot of support in the legislature but not enough for a two-thirds victory. He has a series of militias sworn to him, but so far they've kept it civil."

"Let's hope it stays that way," Conner stated.

"Up in the northwest, in Washington and Idaho we have a group called the Cascadian Independence Movement, which is split into two factions. The one in western Washington wants to split and are more militant; however, they don't seem to have the means to do much. The other faction is located in eastern Washington and Idaho. They want a split too, but they have expressed they'll settle on a political solution, such as a loose affiliation. The governors from both states said they're seeing many of these symbols across the state." Wilbur walked back to the table and showed a picture of the flag that symbolized the Cascadian Movement. It was beautiful, with three horizontal stripes of blue, white, and green. In the middle of the flag was a silhouette of a Douglas fir tree. It was where the flag got its nickname, the Doug flag.

Conner snatched the picture and shook his head in frustration. "Goddamn idiots. Don't they know we're doing our best to help them?"

Wilbur ignored the comment and continued. "And just twenty miles away from right where we stand is the western boundary of the Republic of Lakotah. They too have a strong organizing body but haven't yet garnered widespread support. There have been reports of some of them here in town. Apparently they're attempting to organize a march here to petition us for a peaceful separation. Their desire is to split off parts of Wyoming, North and South Dakota, and Nebraska."

"They're in our backyard and I'm just now hearing about this?" Conner angrily interjected.

"Sir, we've had our noses to the grindstone with the PAE," Baxter said lightly. Conner grimaced.

"Last but not least is a group of states that have come together from a result of our eastern states plan. The states of Georgia, Florida, Alabama, Mississippi, and South Carolina have formed the Dixie Federation. I mention them only because things are happening back east. Our abandonment has left a huge vacuum and they moved in. They don't pose a problem to us, just thought you should know."

Conner sat and examined the map closely. He noticed that she hadn't explained the changes to Oklahoma and Arkansas. "What happened to Oklahoma and Arkansas?"

"Sorry, yes, the southern part of Oklahoma and most of Arkansas is seeking to join the Republic of Texas."

"You all are looking to me to make a decision, but I need to allow this to marinate before I say we do anything about these groups. Does anyone have anything to add?" Conner asked.

"I was wondering if Secretary Wilbur has any thoughts, since she drafted the report," Baxter said.

"I do. I think we need to aggressively engage these groups in diplomatic ways. We need to see what they're seeking. Sometimes in life, I've found that all people want is to be heard . . ."

"Or to kidnap!" Baxter quipped, referencing the botched kidnapping attempt against her weeks before by the separatist group known as the Montana Independence Party. The MIP had solicited Conner and the United States for peaceful separation. Under Wilbur's leadership, she journeyed there under the protection of Major Schmidt. Things immediately went wrong, as it was an ambush. They kidnapped her with the hope of trading her for a treaty with

Conner. However, Major Schmidt didn't negotiate—he attacked them, and viciously.

"In all seriousness, we should talk to these people to see if there is a peaceful way to handle it," Wilbur countered. "Despite my experiences, I say that," she added.

Conner nodded and concluded the briefing. "Wilbur, thank you. Let me think about this. We are already pulled in many directions. In some regards, I want to just put my foot against their throat and end this bullshit once and for all."

"I wouldn't recommend that, sir. We can't just use deadly force with every group we encounter. What happened in Montana shouldn't have happened," Wilbur stressed.

"I don't know what you think should have happened, but those people were not about diplomacy. What happened, happened, and I sleep fine at night knowing that their threat is disabled and you are back here safely," Conner shot back. "Let's take a short break, reconvene in ten," Conner said.

All in the room got up. Some left while others began to chat with one another. As they did, Conner hovered over Wilbur's map. He didn't like what he saw. If something wasn't done, he wouldn't have a country to preside over.

McCall, Idaho

The laughter of children tore Gordon away from his troubled thoughts. He turned to see Haley chasing Austin. Seeing her smiling face, he knew he couldn't risk leaving; he couldn't break his promise to Samantha. He cared for Brittany, but not so much as to hurt Samantha and Haley again.

Gordon always found himself fighting the urge to say yes when supplies and equipment were on the line. He had developed what

Samantha described as apocalyptic obsessive-compulsive disorder. He couldn't help but try to have everything needed to keep his family alive. He knew his side trip to Oregon wasn't the best idea, but he was grateful for all the equipment, food, medicines, and the Humvee he got out of his adventure. But this trip, even with the president's promise of supplies, just seemed too risky.

"You hungry?" Gordon asked Michael.

"Yeah, I could go for a bite."

They made their way to the house. "Sam? Michael's here!" Gordon hollered as they walked inside.

As he passed through the great room, he saw Gunny and his men out on the back deck, but no Samantha. He pressed forward and suspected she was in the master bedroom. His assumption was correct. He walked in and there she was sitting in the rustic rocking chair in the corner.

"Hey, sweetie, Michael's here. He brought the wood over and I'm going to make him something to eat. You hungry?"

Samantha's attention was on a book she was reading. She lowered it in frustration. "These medical books are like WebMD used to be. If I had to guess based on Annaliese's symptoms, I'd have to say she's going to die."

"What?"

"I'm trying to be funny, but it didn't come out right. Her symptoms match so many things, many of them very bad," she said, then paused to think. "I'm worried about her. She's now been sick for almost a week. Something's not right. I thought I could look in this book but her symptoms match everything from cancer to gout. It's crazy."

"I forgot to tell you, Sebastian is taking her in to see the doc today."

"Finally. What's wrong with him? He should have taken her earlier," Samantha said. Samantha and her sister-in-law had grown close over the past few months; it didn't take long for them to click. For Samantha it meant a lot to have a woman that she could call a sister.

"I don't think waiting five days is life or death. She probably has some type of virus or something. She'll be fine," Gordon said. He walked over and dropped to a knee next to her. Taking her hand he continued, "You're such a sweet sister-in-law to be so worried, but I really don't think we should get too upset just yet."

Samantha gripped his hand and smiled. "Argh, you're right. I'm sure she'll be fine. I just worry. What used to be little things can be big now, that's all."

"I know. So, can I make you something to eat?"

"I'm not hungry, you go ahead."

"Okay," Gordon said, then stood and left her. He closed the door behind him so she could get some privacy.

Outside the door, Gordon's calm demeanor was shaken. His mind again was swimming with worry. He laughed to himself when he thought about all the "worries and concerns" he had before the lights went out. Those distant worries now seemed so petty. When someone was sick, you went to the doctor, got checked out, they did some tests, prescribed some medicine, and you were usually fine within days. Getting sick then was more of an inconvenience, but now it truly was a matter of life and death. He shuddered at the thought and continued his way to the kitchen.

Coos Bay, Oregon, Pacific States of America

The intense fighting the previous night had invigorated Barone. It had been a very long time since he had "hooked and jabbed." At moments it felt as if his men were losing but the tide was turned when reinforcements from the *Makin Island* showed up. Together with his security forces they destroyed the assault and captured dozens of resistance fighters.

He stood in front of the mirror and looked at his bloodied and bruised face. In all his years as a Marine, he hadn't fought so hard. So often, commanders never actually fought, they sat back and led their forces; but last night, he was done with sitting back. He wanted to fight man-to-man even if it meant his life.

He picked up the washcloth from the sink and began the slow and painful process of washing off the blood and grime. With each swipe, his face reappeared, but it wasn't the same face that he saw yesterday. Something was different about him; his men saw it too. Those that remained loyal knew he was capable of action, but they had never seen a commander get into the middle of the action before. He stood toe-to-toe with the enemy last night and fought alongside his junior enlisted men. After their victory, he had gathered his men and gave a roaring speech. He had now become a true leader like those leaders of old.

Not one to miss an opportunity to prove a point, he planned on a public trial for those captured, but not until he could get what intelligence he could from them.

A tap on the closed bathroom door was followed by Simpson stating, "Sir, Mr. Timms is here. He's in the waiting room outside your office."

Barone dried his hands and opened the door to see Simpson standing there, still filthy from the battle. "What's he doing here? We haven't seen him in weeks," Barone commented. "How're you holding up?"

"Good, sir, a bit sore. It's been a long time since I've been in a fight like that," Simpson responded with a grin.

"Good man. You were fierce last night, a true warrior," Barone said, a smile across his face.

"Thank you, sir. We're working hard to get defenses back up. We're also moving quickly on what intel we've gathered so far from the prisoners. We're moving in on some rebel strongholds now."

"Good, very good. When you have the time, go get cleaned up."

"Will do, sir. By the way, I thought you'd like to know that one of the rebel prisoners was Major Ashley," Simpson informed.

Barone's eyebrows rose when he heard the news. "You don't say? So we finally got that traitor. Good. Anything from him?"

Major Ashley was the highest ranking officer to turn his back on Barone following the massacre. He had become the leader of the resistance. Having him in captivity was a blow to their efforts.

"No, sir, his lips are sealed."

"You know what to do," Barone said.

"That I do. I'll get back to work," Simpson answered, then turned and left.

• • •

Barone walked into the waiting room to find Timms sitting nervously, tapping his fingers on his leg.

"Mr. Timms, you look like someone whose doctor just told them they have ass cancer. You all right?"

"Yes, I'm fine. Thank you for meeting with me," Timms said, standing up and stretching his arm out to shake Barone's hand.

Barone ignored Timms's greeting and walked right past him into his office.

"Come in here!" Barone commanded.

Timms followed and quickly sat in a chair positioned in front of the desk. His eyes widened when he saw the broken glass on the desk and some of the furniture in disarray.

"Close the door, please!" Barone ordered.

Timms shot up from the chair and went back to the door and closed it. "That was something last night."

"Yes, it was, but we were victorious and that's all that matters," Barone said as he swept glass from his chair and sat down.

"I heard that—"

"Mr. Timms, I'm busy. I don't have time for idle chitchat. What can I help you with?" Barone interrupted.

Sweat began to bead on Timms's forehead. "Sorry, Colonel. Things have gotten really crazy around here. I know you want this to end, and I think I have a plan."

Barone relaxed in his chair. It felt good to take a seat after being up all night. "I'm all ears, unless it has anything to do with me leaving Coos Bay."

"It's sort of a grand compromise. You don't have to leave but you do need to step down. You can live here, but you'll have to relinquish control of your forces."

"Not going to happen, so if that's all you have, then let yourself out."

"Please, Colonel, listen. The rebellion is not going to stop. You might have won the battle last night but this is far from over," Timms pleaded.

"Don't be so confident in your predictions. Our victory last night was an important one, and we captured their leader," Barone replied.

"You have Major Ashley?" Timms asked, shocked.

"Yes, we're interrogating him now. We captured dozens and they're all being processed now, so don't think that I don't have an advantage here."

"Colonel, I don't think the resistance will end just because you've taken Major Ashley prisoner. You must understand that there are now thousands that are against you and your military rule. You must understand that the only way for this to end is for you to step down, cede control to a newly elected civilian authority—"

"Enough. I'm not listening to this. Please show yourself out," Barone scolded as he pointed to the door.

"Please, Colonel. I'm not against you, but I know my plan will work," Timms again pleaded.

"Why are you so confident?" Barone asked, irritation in his voice. The long night and large quantities of alcohol were being felt. He head was beginning to ache and his body was sore.

Timms sat pensively, not knowing how to respond without angering Barone.

Barone stood up from his chair and made his way toward the office door. "Mr. Timms, if you can't answer that question then I need you to leave. I'm tired and have a lot going on today." Barone opened the door and gave instructions to a Marine guard to get him some coffee. When he turned Timms was still sitting in the same spot.

"Colonel, I have been meeting with the resistance and they expressed a call for a cease-fire . . ."

"You've been secretly meeting with the rebels?" Barone thundered.

"Colonel, someone has to find a diplomatic end to this situation. It's gotten out of hand. There's been too much bloodshed. I know deep in your heart all you want is to have a place to call home. That's all that any of us want, a safe place where we don't have to live in fear."

"That peace ended with the mayor!"

"No, Colonel, that ended with you! I have been on your side from day one. I had my reservations but I overlooked your past issues because we needed you and you needed us. Look around you, Colonel. This can't go on forever!" Timms shouted.

Barone cocked his head in amazement. He had never seen Timms so passionate. He let it sink in for a minute and strolled back to his chair and sat down. "At the moment we have the head of the resistance imprisoned. We killed over a hundred rebels, and took dozens more prisoners last night. And you think this is over? We are winning this and I'm not about to surrender."

Timms exhaled deeply, his frustration front and center. "I'm sorry to hear that you're not willing to talk."

"The talking ended when the mayor told me she wouldn't relent until I was gone. She proclaimed they would fight to the death. I gave her what she asked for and will give her followers the same outcome."

"Colonel, we can end this without your leaving. All you need to do is step down, have your second in command take over, call for elections, and let it go back to what we had before," Timms said.

A knock on the door drew Barone's attention away from Timms. "Come in!"

One of the Marine lance corporals who was standing guard came in with two cups of coffee. He strode over and sat them on the desk.

Timms reached for the cup just as Barone said, "No need for the second cup. Mr. Timms was just leaving."

Timms stood up. "Please consider this plan, Colonel."

The Marine guard followed him out and closed the door.

Barone grabbed his coffee and took a large gulp. He leaned back in his chair and began to process the offer presented by Timms. Deep down, he was tired of the fighting, and he did want a safe place to live out the rest of his life. When he first arrived in Coos Bay, he thought this was the place, but it had turned into a fierce battle for control. His thoughts then went to where he could settle down if he took their offer. He began to visualize a place, a cabin somewhere remote, where he could spend the rest of his days. This vision was then trampled by his need to win. Two competing desires resided inside of him. To accept this plan would leave him with the feeling that he had failed, that he had surrendered. He sat up quickly, pushing the thoughts of retreating out of his mind. He wasn't done fighting and if last night's battle told him anything, it was that he could be close to winning this outright.

Elko, Nevada

Pablo sipped his steaming hot espresso and studied the most recent diagram of Cheyenne. His conquest of the United States ended there. Everything after that would be simply a cleanup of ragtag elements and civilian resistance groups. When he took Cheyenne and wiped out the remaining elements of the United States government, he could officially tell the world that he alone had conquered the once great superpower. With this declaration he'd be able to etch in history the beginnings of a new world power—the Pan-American Empire.

He marveled at his own ingenuity. If someone else had put forth this plan, he might have scoffed at them. Along the way, he had lined up the players and the logistics, all the while keeping the United States distracted with an endless parade of small attacks. He remembered the days that followed September 11, 2001, and questioned why those who had orchestrated that attack hadn't gone further. They had missed out on an opportunity to bring the United States to its knees economically with small attack after attack. Terrorism was an effective way to create chaos, and he knew it could be used as foreplay to an attack that would utterly destroy the country and pave the way for his conquest.

He laughed at how the Russians were so stupid to think they could sell him nuclear weapons without thinking that they wouldn't be tracked back to them or the North Koreans whom he had worked with to design the super-EMPs. Those very EMPs that they had designed would eventually bring down their regime. The price of domination was one worth paying.

He was close to accomplishing what had taken him almost three years to plan. Just 669 miles until it was over. He knew this was just the first of many phases in building the Pan-American Empire, but it would be the most critical. Once the United States fell, he would then turn his attention toward taking down the Mexican government. The EMP's effects, while devastating for the United States, hadn't impacted the southern half of Mexico to include Mexico City. The detonation of the EMP over Kansas meant its effective radius was limited to mostly the United States, Canada, and northern Mexico.

Thoughts of the Mexican government reminded him of his parents, uncomfortably so. He hadn't spoken to them in months and he knew that if he even tried to call, they wouldn't speak to him. That disappointed him, as well as motivated him to be bigger and greater. If anything, he knew his father would eventually respect him for what he had been able to accomplish. Hearing his father chastise him for what he was planning that day outside of Tijuana was laughable to him, considering his father had murdered his way to the top of his cartel. It was his mother who he feared would never speak to him again, and that knowledge did pull at him. Before he executed his plan, he had tried to talk to her, but she was the ever-loyal wife to his father. His parents were now living, protected by his forces, in Mexico. Pablo left them in luxurious accommodations minus the ability to contact the outside world—he couldn't risk it. If he could usurp his father, what would prevent his father from returning the favor?

Pablo glanced at his watch and saw that he was late to a meeting with his commanders. He put down his cup of espresso, wiped his mouth with a linen napkin, and left the house that was serving as his quarters during the occupation of Elko.

During the short drive to his temporary military headquarters, he took the time to look at his handiwork. Every street was littered with garbage, abandoned cars, and an occasional body. Periodically a series of gunshots could be heard echoing in the sky. His men were now going to every home they suspected of having resistance fighters. His command element kept the records they had found in Sacramento of active and former military as well as gun registrants and gun permit applications from the sheriff's records. In order for his Villistas to operate unopposed, one of the first laws passed was a total gun ban. No one, for any reason, was allowed to own or possess firearms. If you were found to possess a firearm, you were killed on sight, no questions asked.

After passing through two checkpoints, he arrived at the old city hall. Walking into the briefing room, he was surprised to see one of his junior officers in a heated argument with General Alejandro. Both men were red-faced and yelling at each other, the other dozen men in the room looking on in amazement at the intense exchange.

"What is going on here?" Pablo boomed.

Hearing his voice, both men stopped and snapped to attention. The remaining men followed by standing quickly.

"At ease! General Alejandro, what is going on here?" Pablo asked.

None of the men in the room sat down; they stood erect and silent.

"At ease!" Pablo yelled again. "Sit down!"

The officers obediently listened and sat down in their chairs, except General Alejandro.

"Sir, forgive me for what you just walked into. Colonel Ramos and I were—"

"Not acting like officers, that's what. Now, what could be so disagreeable between you two?"

Colonel Ramos stood and said, "Emperor, I apologize . . ."

"Shut up, I wasn't talking to you!" Pablo snapped.

Colonel Ramos sat down quickly.

"Emperor, the Colonel and I disagree on how we, the army,

should proceed. He thinks we should use our ace in the hole, to excuse the American vernacular."

Pablo smiled and answered, "I like that turn of phrase, I have to admit. So, Colonel Ramos, you think we should just eliminate the remnants of the American government with our *ace in the hole*, then what?"

Ramos looked at Pablo nervously. He and everyone else were well aware of Pablo's ruthless behavior. "Emperor, with each city or town we take, we lose men and valuable equipment. The replacements aren't compatible. What I'm saying is that if we continue all the way to Cheyenne, we won't have the army we have now. We have to know that the American government won't roll over, so we must prepare for a fierce fight."

"Exactly, a fierce fight is what we need!" Pablo exclaimed.

"Emperor, all due respect, by using—"

"No, we will crush the Americans. I want to look President Conner in the eyes as I take his life. I want him to know he has been defeated. Any other way is cowardly," Pablo declared.

"But, sir, was dropping the atomic bombs on Hiroshima cowardly? That won the war. Was using the EMPs to bring them to their knees cowardly?" Ramos challenged.

The room grew eerily quiet at Ramos's bold statements.

Pablo didn't answer Ramos; he smiled for a moment then stood up. He walked around the desk and stopped behind Ramos's chair. "Colonel Ramos, I appreciate your candid thoughts. I realize my overall strategy may not be what you would do, but I'm in charge here. I do want my officers to openly discuss tactics and strategy, but the use of what you call our 'ace in the hole' has been decided. The device is there, a team is there, and if we have to, I will use it. If it looks like we cannot defeat the Americans on the ground, only then will I deploy the weapon."

The blood had drained from Ramos's face as he looked over his shoulder at Pablo. His anxiety was running high. He knew at any moment Pablo could deal a deadly blow to him.

"There will be no more talk about this. Do I make myself clear, Colonel Ramos?" Pablo asked Ramos directly.

Ramos gulped and answered, "Yes, Emperor."

"Good. And this goes for the rest of you. Once we have closed debate, it's closed. Today, we need to discuss the deployment of our Villistas and timeframes," Pablo said sternly.

"Emperor, I'd also like to propose we discuss our next major objective," Alejandro said.

"Yes, let's talk about Salt Lake City," Pablo said, grinning.

Cheyenne, Wyoming

It had been a long day for Conner; he had always thought it amazing that you could get so physically tired from sitting and talking. One thing he took for granted when he worked in Washington, D.C., was how many resources each congressman or senator had—pages, aides, and staff by the dozens. Not until now did he appreciate the political leaders of the early days, the men who actually wrote the legislation themselves. In the last decades before the lights went out, you couldn't get a politician to even read the legislation they were voting on. So much of politics had become gamesmanship. Leadership and statesmanship had died many years before.

The work he did now was the toughest he had ever done. With his eyes burning and his body aching, he called it a night. He reached up and turned off the light, reflecting on how odd it was that he had already gone back to taking the convenience of electricity for granted. Before the EMP attack, there had been red flags about the lack of security surrounding the power grid, but many ignored it. He himself had attempted to pass the Shield Law, a piece of legislation that would have improved and protected the power grid, but too many special interests got in the way and scuttled the bill. If only they could have known then the horror of what would happen, they might have done something.

He grabbed his jacket and was heading out when his phone rang. If someone was calling him at this hour, it must be important. He rushed to the phone and picked it up. "Conner here."

"Mr. President, General Baxter. I hate to disturb you but I know how you want information as soon as it happens."

Conner felt like someone had placed a three-hundred-pound weight on his shoulders as he sat down in his chair and braced himself for the important information.

"Go ahead."

"It's not critical, but Major Schmidt and a few of his officers just had a melee in Pat's place."

"What?"

"Yes, the place is a mess."

"Why would they do that?"

"A fight broke out, and let's just say that the coffee shop took the brunt of it."

"Goddamn it! How's Pat, is he okay?"

"He's fine, a few abrasions and a bloody nose . . ."

"Bloody nose?"

"He kinda got in the middle of it on the side of Major Schmidt."

"Are they still there?"

"Yes, sir."

"No one leaves, no one. I'll be right there."

• • •

Conner rushed to Pat's Coffee Shop as quickly as his protective team could take him there. The sun had set and the streets within the green zone were lit under the yellowish glow of the large floodlights.

As they pulled up to the store front, a large group of onlookers hovered on the other side of yellow police tape.

His protective team was typically comprised of two to three armored Humvees, but because of the altercation, he had additional support vehicles. The mass of people deterred them from parking up front; his vehicle was escorted to the alleyway behind the shop. The support vehicles fanned out and armed men came bursting out. They took up positions about twenty feet away in an arc of protection. Conner's vehicle pulled into the center; he exited and walked into the rear entrance of Pat's shop.

The damage from the brawl was evident the second he walked into the main part of the café. All the tables were overturned, chairs were scattered around, and the floors were wet with coffee, alcohol, and blood. The fight had been fierce, from the amount of destruction he saw. He looked for Pat, but only saw a sea of uniforms. Men and women from the Cheyenne police, department, Air Force, army, and EMS all stood around doing whatever their duties required of them.

"Mr. President," a voice shouted from across the room.

Conner looked and saw General Baxter.

Baxter approached him and said, "I'm sorry, sir, I didn't intend for you to come down here. We have this handled."

"Stop apologizing. Pat is a friend of mine and if men of mine were in a fight I want to know why."

"It started out as an argument," Baxter stated.

"As these things normally do."

"It appears there were some supporters from the Republic of Lakotah here tonight handing out flyers," Baxter said as he handed Conner a few pieces of paper.

Conner flipped through the sheets of paper. The first thing he noticed was the burgundy flag with the words *Republic of Lakotah* drawn below it. Under that, a short paragraph discussed how now was the time for "the Lakotah people and whoever valued liberty" to have a nation of their own. Following that were dates, places, and names of people who were giving speeches in support of this separatist movement.

"Where's Pat?"

"He's giving a statement out front," Baxter said, pointing toward the front door.

Conner folded the papers and put them in his pocket, making his way for the door. Just out front, he saw Pat standing and talking to a police officer, a bloody rag to his nose.

Pat glanced over and saw Conner; he shrugged his shoulders. His typical grin graced his bruised and swollen face. He finished giving the officer his statement and went to join Conner.

"What the hell happened here?" Conner asked.

"A slight disagreement," Pat said with a laugh.

"You all right?"

"Yeah, I'll live. Although I can't say I believed that when the fight was raging."

"I'll get a team of people over here immediately to clean it up and bring your place back up to speed."

"Thanks, I'll actually take you up on that."

"So, what happened?"

"Well, all was going great tonight. A few of your men, a Major Schmidt and others, were in here enjoying some drinks. They were being loud, just fun-loving stuff, then a small group, I counted five men that I'd never seen, came in. They sat down next to the major and were talking about their hatred for the United States and something called the Republic of Lakotah. I swear they were deliberately trying to egg on Major Schmidt and the others. Next thing I know, the major is yelling at one of the men and a second later, he hits him. All hell broke loose after that."

"Major Schmidt hit the man first?"

"Oh, yeah, but that guy was being a complete asshole."

"How did you get popped in the nose?"

"At first I was attempting to separate them, but those guys were not nice guys. I took sides and of course was on the good side."

"You sure you're all right?"

"God yes, I feel fine. I'm almost embarrassed to admit it, but it was kind of fun. Reminded me of a fight you saw from the Wild West. You know, the ones where tables are being turned over, chairs flying around, men getting hit back and forth. It was a damn good fight."

"Glad to hear you're fine and that you had a good time," Conner joked. He patted him on the shoulder and walked over to Schmidt, who was leaning against a Humvee.

"Major Schmidt?"

Schmidt looked up, saw Conner, and instantly snapped to attention.

"At ease."

Schmidt fell into a parade rest and stood looking straight ahead.

"Major, at ease means take it easy. I have a few questions for you."

"Yes, sir."

"What happened?"

"Sorry for the altercation, sir. These men were separatists and they were disrespecting you and our country. I should not have gotten so angry, but my temper got the best of me."

"It's all right. I have to admit, I like your approach. Sometimes that's what people need, a little ass kicking."

Schmidt was average height, but if you were to ask anyone, they'd say he was inches taller than he really was. His muscular build combined with his bearing gave him an ominous stature. He had arrived in Cheyenne a little over five weeks before, after leading what had grown to be a small army across the country from Fort Drum, New York. His story was one of survival and adversity.

Conner was impressed with him from the start; he was tough, strong, loyal, and fiercely obedient. Schmidt's men and equipment, specifically his tanks, had proven to be critical during the standoff with the Montana Independence Party. What was supposed to be a show of force to help Wilbur negotiate with the MIP turned into the instrument of their destruction when the separatists attempted to kidnap her. Schmidt reacted swiftly and harshly to the MIP and when it was over, not one representative of the MIP was left standing. Back in Cheyenne it elicited comments of an overzealous field commander and a grotesque display of firepower, but Schmidt ignored it all. He was an army man who saw the need to crush what he saw as an enemy of the people who had initiated aggression. When asked about the incident, he simply said, "They started it and I finished it."

Conner too had reacted with shock at the complete wipeout, but understood that Schmidt did what he felt was necessary to ensure Secretary Wilbur's safety and to prevent further attacks against the United States. Schmidt saw the big picture; he knew that if the MIP had been successful, it could have led to Conner possibly trading the state of Montana for Wilbur. Schmidt saw this as another step closer to what appeared to him as the total collapse and demise of the United States.

Conner looked at him appraisingly. Here he saw a man who would literally die for his country, no questions asked. Schmidt was unlike other officers in his staff—he was a true-blue warrior.

"Major, did General Baxter relay the message to you about tomorrow morning?"

"Yes, sir, I'll be there at oh-nine-hundred."

"Good. Now go get some sleep. I need you thinking clearly in the morning."

"I'm free to go, sir?"

Conner looked around; about ten feet away were the Lakotah men, all of whom looked badly beaten. "Yes, of course. I'm the president, and guess what? You're pardoned."

"What about my men, sir?"

"Them as well. Gather your men and go back to your camp."

When Schmidt's fifteen-thousand-strong army rolled into Cheyenne weeks before, there was no place to house them. Like other refugees, they set up a large tent city and called it home. Schmidt had been offered housing within the green zone, but he refused to leave what he called "his people."

"Yes, sir, and thank you," Schmidt said, and disappeared back inside the shop.

Conner looked at the Lakotah men again. They looked harmless for the most part. They were all older men, in their mid-fifties. But that was where the harmless consideration ended for Conner. What these men and their followers represented to Conner was a cancer on the country. He knew he faced a tough choice: he could try to see if the country could heal with them, or if he'd have to cut them out.

JUNE 26, 2015

· · ·

**"A sudden bold and unexpected question doth
many times surprise a man and lay him open."**

—Francis Bacon

McCall, Idaho

Sebastian held Annaliese's hand tenderly, but anxiety was coursing through his veins. Sitting in the waiting room of the Payette Lake Medical Center was torturous for him. Being surrounded by crying babies and coughing and hacking people made him wish he had been more forceful in telling Annaliese to stay home. Her condition had only gotten worse since they had stopped by the clinic yesterday. The doctor had taken blood samples to be tested to see if that could give them any better idea of what her diagnosis was. What the doctor didn't share just yet with Sebastian was that the laboratory was very limited in what it could do after losing most of its diagnostic equipment during the EMP.

When her name was called, Sebastian sprang up. He looked down at Annaliese's face. Her skin was pulled tight and ashen. Since she started showing symptoms days ago, she had lost weight quickly from a combination of a loss of appetite and the pain in her abdomen.

"Come on, sweetie," he nudged.

She didn't say a word; she just leaned forward, grimacing in pain.

He knelt in front of her and placed his hand on her knee. "It's hurting again?"

Unable to speak, she simply nodded.

"Let me go see if the doc will come out here," he whispered.

"No, I can do it," she whispered, wincing again in pain. Her right hand clenched the arm of the chair tightly while her left hand held her stomach.

Sebastian looked at the nurse, who was waiting patiently for them. He held up his index finger to signal he wanted a little extra time. The nurse smiled then approached them, seeing that Annaliese was having a hard time.

"Ma'am, are you okay?" the nurse asked.

Annaliese didn't answer, but began to breathe deeply.

"She's been having severe abdominal pain and she appears to be having a surge of pain right now."

Annaliese lifted her head to look at Sebastian. Tears of pain and fear now began to stream from her sunken eyes.

"Oh, baby, you're going to be fine, I promise."

"It hurts so badly," she whimpered.

"Let me go get her doctor," the nurse said urgently and left them.

"Anna, just sit there, no need to get up. The doc is coming out to see you," Sebastian said as he rubbed her arm.

"Something's wrong. I'm scared," she responded, her voice trembling as more tears rushed down her face.

Sebastian looked around; all eyes were on him and Annaliese. Her pain and the response to it was the worst it had been. She probably needed to go to the emergency room, but deep down, Sebastian didn't know if it would make any difference, because the capabilities at all facilities were limited. But inaction wasn't a trait he was known for and he didn't want to wait for the doc. He saw a wheelchair and hurried over to it. He pushed it back, carefully placed her in it, and wheeled her out of the clinic. The hospital was just across the parking lot, not more than a hundred yards. As he reached the halfway mark, he heard the doctor calling him.

Sebastian called back without stopping, "Doc, just meet us over at the ER!"

The once automatic electric doors of the ER were now left wide open. He wheeled her inside and called out, "I need some help here!"

Annaliese cried out in pain again.

A nurse came running from the dim hallway. "Get her in here!" she said, pointing to an examination area to his right.

He wheeled her into the space and both he and the nurse lifted her out of the wheelchair and onto a bed.

Annaliese curled up in the fetal position in cringing pain.

"What's wrong with her?" the nurse asked Sebastian.

"Look at her, she's in pain."

"I need more details than that, sir."

"She's been complaining about pain here," he said, pointing to her lower abdomen. "She's had bad diarrhea, fever, and now she's having incredible pain unlike anything I've seen before."

"Ma'am, my name is Amy. I need to ask you some questions, okay?" the nurse asked Annaliese.

Annaliese only answered with a nod. Perspiration now covered her face and she was still crying.

"Where is the pain?"

Annaliese pointed to her stomach.

The curtains that separated them from main ER hallway flew open and her doctor from the clinic stepped in. "Sebastian, how's she doing?"

"Not good, Doc," Sebastian said, his voice revealing his concern.

"Amy, she came in yesterday and I took blood; the tests came back—"

"Argh!" Annaliese cried out loudly.

"Her white blood cell count was very high, but everything else looks fine," the doctor said.

"Is she allergic to any medications?" Amy asked Sebastian.

"Um, I don't know," Sebastian answered. "Sweetheart, are you allergic to anything?"

She shook her head no.

"I want to give her something to ease the pain and then we can continue to monitor her," Amy stated.

"Monitor her? I need you to give her more tests, do something!" Sebastian exclaimed.

"I'd recommend giving her an angiogram or CT but that equipment doesn't work anymore," the doctor said.

"There has to be something you can do! Do something!" Sebastian yelled.

"Sebastian, please calm down, we're doing all we can with the limited resources and equipment. Many medical issues have similar symptoms. She could have appendicitis or a severe gastrointestinal problem. Short of doing exploratory surgery, we can't do much," the doctor said.

Annaliese cried out, "Sebastian!"

He took her shaking hand and leaned over to kiss her face. "Baby, you're going to be fine." He turned to the doctor and others gathered in the room and said, "I need to go find my brother. Please watch over her."

Cheyenne, Wyoming

Conner assembled his staff an hour before the anticipated response from Gordon. Just outside the room was Major Schmidt, Conner's guest at the meeting. His presence would be a shock to the others as he was nothing more than a field commander, but Conner wanted his unique perspective on what they should do about the militant groups, given his interaction with the MIP.

Once his staff was seated, he ordered a guard to go get Schmidt. A brief moment passed, then the main door to the conference room opened and Schmidt stepped in, dressed head to toe in a weathered and faded green camouflage uniform. He stepped forward, saluted, and stood at attention near the head of the table.

"Ladies and gentlemen, you all know Major Thomas Schmidt," Conner said. "Major Schmidt, please relax and take a seat."

Schmidt promptly took a seat at the far end of the table.

"Major, you look well considering the incident last night."

"Yes, sir, all good."

"You are probably wondering why I have the major here. Well, it's because of his extraordinary experiences. He has a perspective that is missing from our discussions. I know some of you here have heard the stories about him, but I don't believe you've heard them from the man himself. Major, would you do us the honor and share how you and whom you affectionately call 'your people' arrived here?"

"Yes, sir."

All eyes in the room were sharply focused on Schmidt in curiosity.

Schmidt looked at each and nodded slightly. A slight nervousness was apparent in his tense stature, even seated.

"I was with the First Battalion of the Thirty-second Regiment, Tenth Mountain Division out of Fort Drum, New York. Um, the story is too long, but I'll give you a short history of how I happen to be sitting here."

Schmidt then detailed how the 32nd Regiment along with other functional assets at Fort Drum were called up to mobilize. Like all other military installations across the county, most of their equipment wasn't working and a large number of soldiers didn't show up when mustered. He described utter chaos on the base and even greater turmoil across the state of New York. From small towns to major metropolitan areas, the pursuit of resources quickly turned violent and bloody. He described how the command elements at Fort Drum attempted to work along with the civilian leadership in Albany, but that ended abruptly when the governor and his staff were killed in a mob attack. He became somber when he described how demoralized many soldiers were after the news of New York City being destroyed with a nuclear weapon. Each day saw fewer and fewer soldiers left on base as they escaped with what they could make off with; this prompted the command to take harsh measures that spiraled into bitter fighting on the base. He and what remained of his company left with their families once the base disintegrated into bedlam. With only two vehicles and what they could carry, they made out for their journey west.

"We didn't really have a plan for where we were going. We just kept walking. Along the way we picked up more and more people along with equipment, building upon what we started with. What you describe as 'my army' is nothing more than a ragtag group of active and retired military with a large dash of hardy civilians. We heard about the new capital when we hit St. Louis. By then we had grown to around five thousand. We picked up even more after skirting around St. Louis. I estimate our numbers to be around fifteen thousand."

"Major, tell them about the tanks," General Baxter prodded.

"We came upon an old military depot outside of St. Charles, Missouri, and lo and behold they had dozens of old M60 tanks. Along the way we picked up some old-timers who knew tankers and we were able to get them back up and running."

"I heard about the tanks. How many are there, exactly?" Baxter asked.

"Nineteen, sir. The only thing is we don't have any tank rounds.

We came upon fifty-caliber ammunition but nothing for the tank's main gun."

"I'm proud of you, Major. You have done a damn good job. I know it's not easy. You've been resourceful and you're an example of a damn good American. As for the tank rounds, we've taken care of that," Conner stated.

"Do you have a family?" Wilbur asked.

"No, ma'am, not anymore."

"Sorry to hear that," she replied.

"Sir, can I ask a question? And forgive me beforehand for my directness, but you said you wanted my perspective, so I wanted to ask something that might help clear things up on my end," Schmidt said.

"Sure, go ahead," Conner answered, a grin gracing his face.

"Are the rumors you abandoned the east true?"

Conner's grin faded quickly and a tension gripped his face. He leaned forward from his comfortable position. He cleared his throat, and then said, "Major, we never abandoned the east."

"Sir, to be frank, that's what everyone heard. The word trickled down quickly. Whether it was true or not, we never saw an active response or any communication from NORAD or any federal command element. The rumor and the lack of any type of response emboldened those who took advantage of the situation. The east is a mess, total disarray, massive death . . . so much death, I've never seen so much in my life. People had given up hope and resorted to things I would've only seen in horror movies. Such barbarism and butchery. People killing for a can of beans, people resorting to cannibalism. Society is lost back there."

"We never gave up on the east," Conner repeated again, the wrinkles on his face now more pronounced as he strained to convey sincerity.

"General Baxter, anyone, please tell the major that we never gave up on the east. We just, well, to be frank, we had limited resources and abilities. The east is awash in radioactivity due to so many nuclear plant failures. The first thing a president or any leader must do is prioritize and you do this by being honest with what you can and can't do. We have plans for elevating our recovery efforts to the east but right now we are dealing with issues that could destroy our entire nation. Does my answer satisfy you, Major?"

"Sir, yes, it does. Let me be clear. I wasn't making an accusation. I have a duty to my people in addition to my duty to you and the United States. I promised them I'd get the word straight from you. Many believed the rumors were true and were holding an animosity toward the government. I told them it wasn't fair, that all of you were doing your best. Now that I've gotten the answer I was looking for, I'll present it to them. We are here now to help in any way, Mr. President, that I can assure you."

"I'm glad to hear that, because you have proven to be valuable to our cause. After the incident last night, I wanted to announce we are moving in a new direction as it pertains to the various separatist groups," Conner said, then turned his attention to the other staff. "I am starting a new division to tackle this problem, and Major Schmidt will head it."

Schmidt was clearly shocked to hear this surprise announcement; his thick eyebrows shot up, though the rest of his face stayed stony and reserved.

Conner glanced at Wilbur; he could see the disappointment in her eyes. She had been working on this project from the beginning and had her own ideas on how to approach it.

"Secretary Wilbur, if you could find time later today to meet with the major and brief him on what information you've gathered, that would be great," Conner commanded.

"Mr. President, can I ask what the new direction is, exactly?" Wilbur asked.

Conner thought for a bit, looked at the clock on the wall, and said, "Good question. As you know we haven't given too much attention to these groups until lately, when they've been thrust upon us. That will change because these groups represent a clear and present danger, not unlike the PAE. These are Americans but their selfish desires threaten the sovereignty of the country, and I have no desire to talk with them. We will inform them to disband and if they don't we will eliminate them. It will be that clear cut."

Wilbur looked shocked to hear this new directive. "Mr. President, that is a blanket approach. This is not a one-size-fits-all situation."

"Yes, it is. If we allow, say, Arizona to vote and they choose to secede, what do we do? We're not exactly operating under the Constitution right now. There isn't a Congress to vote them down, and we gave them precedents with Hawaii, Texas, and Alaska. No more. If we keep doing this we'll be out of a job. We won't even have a country. So, there won't be any more negotiations. We won't allow them to leave even if they vote on it."

"What if they won't disband and resist?" Wilbur asked.

Conner turned to Schmidt and said, "Major, we haven't talked about my expectations with this new responsibility of yours, but why don't you answer Secretary Wilbur's question."

A bit uneasy to be put on the spot, Schmidt rose to the occasion. "Ma'am, if they won't comply, we will force them." He then looked at Conner to see if his answer met with his approval. Conner smiled.

"But what exactly does that mean?" she asked, brow furrowed.

"We can't allow these groups to flourish; we need to tamp down on them, we—"

"We need to crush them, just like I did in Montana," Schmidt interjected forcefully.

"What happened there was a travesty and can't be repeated. The force used against them was disproportionate to . . ."

"They tried to kidnap you!" Baxter chimed in.

"But the major and his men killed them all!"

Schmidt sat taller in his seat when she made the last comment, clearly proud of his actions in Montana.

"And that solution didn't work. I told you there are still rumblings of the MIP. They haven't gone away because of Major Schmidt's actions," Wilbur contended.

"They'll rumble and talk but we won't hear from them for a long time, if at all. Their strength is diminished," Conner challenged her.

"Mr. President, I just think this approach is wrongheaded. Some of these groups are peaceful and seek peaceful separation. Doing what you're proposing could cause open rebellion."

"I'm sure Major Schmidt will be more prudent than to go in guns blazing. The groups will be warned and if they don't comply, we'll then arrest them. We will hold them until we can get a handle on things, then we can discuss their needs at a later time."

Wilbur was clearly disturbed by the comments; she also noticed that Cruz was noticeably quiet. "Mr. Vice President, any thoughts on this?"

Cruz spoke via conference call. "I agree with the president, we have to get the country under control and the only way to do that is by eliminating the distraction caused by these groups."

Wilbur, defeated, sat, shaking her head.

Conner asked, "Anyone else have something to add?"

The room was quiet.

He looked at the clock again. "Good. Major, we will meet soon to discuss this further. Let's dive into the plan we're attempting to make with Mr. Van Zandt." He pivoted to Baxter. "General, thank you for finding Mr. Van Zandt's service record. We've all had a chance to look it over. Let me get your thoughts on it before we have our talk with him."

"What do you make of it, General?" Conner asked.

"It's hard to fault the man for what happened in the mosque in Fallujah."

"Other than the shooting in the mosque, his record was exemplary," Cruz added.

"I have to agree with the vice president. He obtained the rank of sergeant in less than four years. Very impressive," Baxter commented.

"Have you read the transcript from the court martial? He was belligerent and demeaning to the Marine Corps and the United States," Wilbur said.

"I can forgive the man for how he conducted himself. He felt like he was being charged for doing the right thing. I remember when this incident happened. It was all over the news," Baxter said.

"His behavior during the court martial was appalling and disgraceful," Wilbur fired back.

"Try putting yourself in that mosque, put yourself in his shoes," Baxter countered.

"General, I spent days with the man, and he is callous and ruthless. I'll add this one positive note: I respect him for his abilities. But I wouldn't trust him completely." Wilbur turned to Conner. "Sir, his disdain for the country is well documented. He openly displayed this to me, and after reading this transcript from the court martial, I can see the man hasn't changed. I just don't know if this is the best man for the job."

"Andrew, you want to add anything?" Conner asked.

"Yes, I agree with Wilbur to a point. Mr. Van Zandt did come across as hard and callous, but he risked his life for us. He didn't falter—"

"He did go off course though," Conner interjected as he interrupted Cruz.

"Yes, he did, but I understand why he did and thank God he did. His actions saved his wife and others in his group from bandits," Cruz said.

"I think I know where you all stand. I believe that Mr. Van Zandt was a man loyal to his country. Why else join the Marine Corps? He volunteered to serve during war, he suffered wounds, and then he ended up a political casualty of the war. I can see where that would jade a man. It soured him and I can understand that. Do I completely trust the man? No. But men can be bought and we have a lot of offer. I trust him to complete the task because he'll want to receive his payment. I don't care if he loves me or not, I just need him to do a simple job. Now, let's see if he is prompt."

As if by magic, the phone rang.

Baxter touched the receiver button and said, "Hello, this is General Baxter."

"Hi, General, this is Gordon Van Zandt."

"Mr. Van Zandt, thank you for calling back. Now, before you tell me—" Conner began to say, but Gordon interrupted him.

"Sir, I don't want to waste your time, but I can't do what you're asking. I can't leave my family again. I've promised them and I just can't. I'm sorry."

Conner grinned uneasily, then said, "Gordon—can I call you Gordon?"

"That's fine," Gordon replied.

"Gordon, I know how hard it is to leave your family under the current circumstances, but let me first present you my offer."

"No need, sir. I can't do it."

"Please, just hear me out," Conner beseeched.

Gordon exhaled deeply, then said, "Go ahead, but nothing, I mean nothing, will convince me."

"Gordon, we will not only offer you every resource you need but I can also promise that the trip will be quick. We'll come grab you in McCall, fly you to Mountain Home, then onto Coos Bay. You will simply go in, look around, and try to meet with the colonel. You know, get a feel for what's going on there. It's really very simple. You're in and out."

"Sir, this is wasting your time and mine. I can't do it."

Wilbur's eyes squinted in disgust as she shook her head at what she perceived was Gordon's disrespect toward the president.

"Gordon, I'd really appreciate it if you'd let me finish my thought," Conner snapped.

"I told you, I can't. If you'll excuse me . . ."

Conner's temper flared. "Mr. Van Zandt, I have your service record here and apparently your old company commander was correct in his assessment of you. He says here in your last fitness report that you 'routinely questioned authority' and 'showed a lack of tact toward superiors.' I can see that displayed here."

"Does my service record also say that I was injured and scarred from your misadventure overseas? Does it mention that I had been nominated for a Silver Star until the kangaroo court?"

Conner didn't answer Gordon's questions and instead changed his tack. "Mr. Van Zandt, why were you even in Oregon? Apparently you didn't have a problem leaving your family before."

"And now you're trying to guilt me into the task? I'm done with this phone call."

"You're making a huge mistake."

"Maybe so. Good-bye, Mr. President," Gordon said, then hung up.

Baxter, Wilbur, and Conner all exchanged looks.

"What's the term the Brits say? Cheeky? Well, Mr. Van Zandt is definitely that!" Conner said.

"I told you, sir," Wilbur said, vindicated.

Cruz, speaking from Cheyenne Mountain, followed up by saying, "The man has gone rogue, that's for sure, but, Brad, I don't think it was a smart move to try and use his past service as a way to leverage him."

"Andrew, once I saw he was committed to not helping us, it was appropriate to call him out for his past indiscretions," Conner said defensively. He leaned on the table and placed his head in his hands.

"Any other ideas on getting human intel on Barone?" Cruz asked.

"Not sure," Baxter answered.

"No idea," Wilbur chimed in.

Conner raised his head and exhaled loudly. "Let's go back to the drawing board."

McCall, Idaho

Gordon placed the phone back in his pocket and looked out toward the rolling foothills of Jug Handle Mountain. The tall grasses melted into an alpine setting of thick pine trees. His eyes followed the trees upward toward the exposed granite peak still covered in snow. The sheer beauty of the area always left him in awe. He swore that the sky here was a deeper blue than what the sky was in San Diego. He wasn't sure why, but the colors seemed softer, more muted in San Diego. Maybe it had to do with the air quality, but whatever it was, when he came to Idaho he would always comment on just how blue the sky was and how green the trees were. Before the lights went out, he often referred to McCall as "God's country," and it was living up to that name, especially now.

The beauty of the vista gave way to ugly thoughts about his recent conversation. He didn't like saying no to supplies, but his family was the most important thing to him. All he could do now was call Barone directly. He knew it was a long shot, but he might be able to convince him to forgive Brittany and not harm her. Then the thought that she could be dead crossed his mind. It wasn't inconceivable that she had perished in the fighting. He vanquished those dark thoughts and told himself that he'd only think of her in terms of being alive.

The large sliding door that led from the great room to the deck opened up behind him. He turned to see Gunny walking out.

"Whatcha doin', Van Zandt?" Gunny asked.

"Just thinking."

"How did that call go?" Gunny asked after walking up to Gordon.

"Not good. I think I pissed off the president."

"Good!"

"Good?"

"Yeah, nice to see you that you still have the talent for pissing people off," Gunny joked.

Gordon laughed.

"So, I'm thinking about calling Barone myself. What do you think?"

"I think that's a dumb fucking idea. The colonel likes you but he doesn't love you. I'm telling ya, the whole place is a shitstorm, a total clusterfuck."

"I need to know . . ."

"Sorry to cut you off, but I need to give you a bit of advice. I try to never involve myself in people's personal affairs, but I consider you a good friend. As a good friend, I'm telling you to let this girl go. I don't know what your relationship was . . ."

"There wasn't . . ."

"Whatever your relationship was, it's over. Your obligation, your responsibility, is to your wife and that adorable little girl in there. The woman in Coos made a choice. She chose to stay, then to fight."

"I just feel . . . like it's my fault, is all," Gordon lamented.

"Listen, that woman is an adult. You told me that she chose to stay. It's a done deal. Your arrangement with her was to get her to a safe place and guess what? Coos was until the colonel went off the reservation. Hell, man, you could've brought her here and all hell could've broken loose here."

"I hear you. You're right."

"I know I'm right. You need to let it go," Gunny counseled.

"You're right, but a call . . ."

"Would you just shut the fuck up about it? You calling back there won't save her—that's if she's still alive. The colonel won't listen to you, I'm telling you. Now, can you do me a favor?"

"Ah, sure, what?"

"Can we see if the chief has found us a house? It's not that I don't love staying here, but I'm sure you want your privacy back."

"Yeah, let's make a run into town," Gordon said with a smile.

Both men turned and headed for the slider when Gunny stopped Gordon and said, "Oh, and give me my phone back. I don't want you to do anything stupid."

Coos Bay, Oregon, Pacific States of America

Barone opened his eyes slowly, awakened from the sun's bright rays bursting through his office. Squinting, he rolled away from the sunlight and brought the pillow around to cover his head.

He lay there and thought about getting up, but the pounding in his head was telling him to stay put. Just as he was drifting back to sleep, a loud knock awoke him. He pressed the pillow harder against his head, hoping that he wouldn't hear it again. But again the loud knock on the door came, this time followed by Simpson's voice.

"Sir, are you in there?"

"Go away," Barone whispered to himself.

"Sir, it's your wife. It's an emergency."

Frustrated, he lifted the pillow from his head and called out, "Come in, for God's sake."

Simpson tried the handle but the door was locked.

"Sir, it's locked."

Barone threw the pillow in anger and rolled off the sofa. He grunted from the pain of moving and from the deep throbbing in his head. "God damn, I hurt," he said before he lumbered over to the door, unlocked it, and swung it open.

Simpson stared at Barone sadly. He had known him for a long time, and seeing him this way was disappointing and disheartening. Simpson was well aware of the troubles that Barone carried on his shoulders and why he had taken to the bottle. What distressed him more now was the information he had about his wife, which would only add to Barone's anguish.

Barone walked slowly back to the sofa and fell onto it.

"Sir, I'm sorry to bother you, but I knew you'd want to know . . ."

"What is it? Spit it out!" Barone lashed out.

"Sir, your wife is gone."

"What do you mean, gone?"

"When her day shift security detail showed up, they discovered that she, your daughter, and the night shift detail were gone. There's no evidence of foul play."

"Contact all the checkpoints and inform them!"

"Done, sir, we're on top of this. We will track her down," Simpson assured.

"That's it, nothing else? My wife is gone and no other info on it?" Barone yelled.

"No, sir, we're investigating it . . ."

"Get out, get the fuck out!" Barone screamed.

Simpson's eyes widened, and without hesitation, he turned and left the office, closing the door as he went.

Barone slouched farther into the sofa. Mixed feelings overcame him. He had resigned himself to the fact that their marriage was over; she had said it to him in so many words during numerous arguments following the massacre. He reflected on how often he missed out on family moments like the one depicted on the photo on his desk, where his wife and daughter stood smiling broadly during a trip while he was on deployment. Tears welled up, but he fought them back as he replaced his sadness with anger.

"I need a drink," he murmured to himself as he stood. He teetered back and forth but soon found his footing. He strode the short distance across the room to his desk and sat down. One drawer after another he looked into for something to drink, but each drawer provided nothing but disappointment until the last one. There, a half bottle of whiskey rolled forward from the force of opening the drawer. He picked it up, opened it, and drank straight from the bottle.

After his second gulp, his eyes caught a glimpse of a list that Simpson had left on his desk yesterday. He pulled the paper out to reveal a list of two dozen names. At the top was Major Ashley's name followed by names of Marines and civilians alike. He scanned the names, seeing if any were recognizable. His reviewed the list and stopped on a familiar name.

He took a long drink from the bottle and set it down. He leaned back in his chair and asked himself, "Brittany McCallister. How do I know you?"

McCall, Idaho

Gordon and Gunny were chatting about a hunting trip that Gordon was planning. The phone call and subsequent request from Gunny had forced Gordon to reschedule the hunt he planned for today.

"When was the last time you went hunting?" Gordon asked.

"Two legged or four legged?" Gunny joked.

"Four, of course. I've done enough two legged to satisfy a life-time," Gordon quipped.

"That truck up there is flashing their lights," Gunny remarked about the old Chevy Blazer coming toward them.

Gordon recognized the vehicle as Rainey's, so he slowed down and pulled his Humvee along the side of the highway.

Rainey pulled up alongside Gordon with his window down. "Gordon, your brother needs you urgently. It's his wife. She's in a bad way; he needs you. She's in the emergency room!"

Gordon didn't ask any questions, he just stomped on the accelerator and sped off toward the hospital.

• • •

Gordon ran into the hospital calling out for his brother. "Sebastian?"

"Gordon, down here!" Sebastian replied as he exited from a room.

"What's going on? Is everything all right?" Gordon asked as he approached his brother. He could see the fear and concern written on his brother's face.

"It's not all right; they don't know what's going on. She's gotten worse; she's in incredible pain," Sebastian rambled.

"Can I see her?"

"No. No, not a good time, they gave her something to sleep. It's the first time she's rested in days," Sebastian said.

"Brother, I'm so sorry. What can I do?" Gordon asked.

"They can't do anything for her here; I need to get her somewhere. I know you have a relationship with some people in the government. Can we get her to the air base outside of Boise or somewhere else?"

Gordon tensed up when Sebastian asked him the question. What help he could have provided he had destroyed not an hour ago. He steeled himself for what he was about to say, knowing that saying the words meant his life was going to get a little more complicated.

"We will find her help, I promise you. I'll do whatever I can, you know that," Gordon reassured.

"Thanks, brother," Sebastian said, then stood.

"I'll get to work," Gordon said.

Sebastian leaned in and gave him a hug. "Love you, brother." Sebastian then left the room and made his way back to Annaliese.

Gordon followed him out and exited the hospital; he squinted from the bright midday sun and looked for Gunny and the Humvee.

The rumbling of the diesel engine caught his attention as he turned to his left and saw the Humvee pulling up.

Gordon jumped in the passenger seat, turned to Gunny, and said, "Can I have that phone back?"

Cheyenne, Wyoming

Dylan burst into Conner's office in what was becoming very common trait for the young chief of staff.

"Don't you knock?" Conner blasted him.

"Sir, we've been trying to patch the call in here, but we can't," Dylan rattled off.

"What call?"

"Gordon Van Zandt! He's on hold now in the conference room."

"Great news. Get in touch with the others and have them come ASAP. I think we're going to be a go for this operation," Conner said with a wide grin as he made his way to the conference room.

Conner switched on the light. Most of the lighting in the capital building had been fixed, and with generators used as the primary power source, it was almost as if nothing had happened. Some elements of the past weren't working, like the elevators and old computer networking systems, but they were replacing those systems daily. The phone systems had been a struggle, but they too were back up for the most part. Some glitches still existed, but the progress that had been made showed that life was slowly getting back to normal.

Conner unmuted the conference speaker and said, "President Conner here."

"Mr. President, this is Gordon Van Zandt."

Conner could hear the conciliatory tone in Gordon's voice. He didn't know what prompted the call back, but he was confident Gordon was up to doing it.

"Gordon, this is a surprise! From our last conversation I thought I'd never talk to you again," Conner said, keeping his tone measured as he continued. "So, have you changed your mind?"

"Yes, I'm in."

"Great, here are the details . . ."

"One second, sir. Before I agree, I first need to discuss some terms."

Conner smiled at Gordon's lack of respect. He never would have thought of interrupting the President of the United States, even as speaker of the house. Normally he wouldn't have tolerated it, but in this one case, he would give Gordon a pass.

"First, I need something done immediately. I have a medical emergency here in McCall. I need this person to be transported to wherever she can get the treatment she needs. I can't stress enough that this needs to be done immediately."

"What's wrong with her?"

"I don't know, but she needs help ASAP."

The door to the conference room opened, and Baxter and Schmidt stepped in. Conner waved for them to sit down.

"Okay, we'll get a chopper ready to go as soon as we can. I don't know where we'll send her, but we'll get her the care she needs,"

Conner said as he gave Baxter a look that signaled for him to begin working on it.

Baxter grabbed another phone receiver and dialed out.

"Good. I also need a pallet of MREs, diesel fuel, 5.56, .308, 9-millimeter and .45 ammo, batteries . . ."

"Hold on, hold on. After we're done here, I'll have you give your list to my chief of staff. Let's get down to the details of the operation," Conner said, taking control of the conversation.

"Okay."

"I'll send two choppers there, one to pick up your friend, the other for you. We'll take you to just outside of Coos Bay; there you'll take a motorcycle into town. Here's what we need once you're there: I need to know in detail what's happening there. Don't leave out any details. I need to know everything. Understood?"

"Yes, sir, I'll give you everything you need," Gordon replied.

"And it has to be in person. I need you to physically meet with the colonel to gauge his mental state. I need to know if there is a revolt and if the colonel appears to be losing. If you can get me troop numbers, positions, equipment, et cetera, that would be ideal."

"I can't guarantee that," Gordon stated.

"Just do it."

"Yes, sir."

"Pack your bags. We'll be there by the end of today," Conner said while looking at Baxter for confirmation.

"We have two birds on the tarmac ready to go. We just need to know his grocery list and coordinates."

"Can you hold on for a moment?" Conner asked.

"Sure."

Conner muted the speaker. "Write down his list of equipment."

Conner unmuted the phone and listened as Gordon listed one by one each item he also wanted in exchange for his assistance. Once the list was confirmed, Gordon instructed them to send the choppers to the McCall Memorial Hospital.

"Great. Any idea where you'll take her?" Gordon asked.

Conner looked at Baxter for the answer. "The best place to take her will be here in Cheyenne."

"Sounds good. I've gotta sign off and make preparations . . ."

"Wait, do we have your number?" Conner asked quickly.

"Yes, the man I spoke with first, his name was Dylan, he has it. Thank you for helping."

"Glad it's going to work out," Conner said, then hit the disconnect button.

"Sir, if I might ask, is all of this worth it?" Baxter asked, rereading the extensive list of Gordon's requests.

"Believe me, this is well worth the investment. Major, I want you to command the mission. Get one of your best ops men ready. They're taking a trip."

"Yes, sir. I know just the man for the job. He's a good soldier and friend."

"You're sending someone with him?" Baxter asked, confused. "Don't you think that new development might upset Mr. Van Zandt?"

"He will go along. We hold the cards, he doesn't," Conner stressed.

The men discussed some details and Conner dismissed them. As they were leaving, he held Schmidt back.

"Major, I'd like a word with you."

Schmidt turned around.

"Close the door."

He did just that and went back to the table.

"Have you met with Wilbur yet?"

"Yes, sir. I did right after our meeting this morning."

"So, out of all the groups she identified which is the one that needs to be tackled first?"

"These Lakotahs are a problem that we need to stop now, mainly because they're right next door to us."

"Plans yet?"

"Yes, I think we'll let them come to us. If they hold their rally, we'll scoop them up then."

Conner nodded his approval.

"Who's next?"

"The Cascadians. The group in Washington is very radicalized and the Idaho group isn't far behind. Some of the details from Secretary Wilbur show they support armed resistance and rebellion. I wasn't prepared to give you my full brief but since you're asking, sir, I would suggest we have the local authorities arrest them and transport them here for interrogation and detention."

"Aggressive. I like it. I knew I picked the right man for the job."

"I haven't heard anyone mention it, but the epicenter of the eastern Cascadians are in the same town as this Van Zandt. It's either an uncanny coincidence or God is telling us something."

Conner adjusted in his seat and sat up. "I didn't connect it."

"Yes, sir. McCall is ground zero for the eastern Cascadians."

"You have my approval to do what you need to do. Just keep me up to date."

"Yes, sir."

"I like you, Major. I gave you the responsibility of commanding our response to these separatists for a multitude of reasons and one is I think I can trust you. I can trust you, correct?"

The expression on Schmidt's face grew intense. "Absolutely, sir."

"I thought I could. That means what you and I discuss will be kept between us. Not even General Baxter or the vice president are to be made aware of the missions I might send you and your men on."

"Yes, sir."

"Good, now let's discuss some additional details I want to see happen for this Coos Bay mission. And remember, these new details are between you, me, and the man you send."

McCall, Idaho

Gordon hung up the phone for the second time in as many hours. He had to move quickly to get everything in order for Annaliese's pickup and his own departure. Dread enveloped him as he thought about how he was going to explain his leaving to Samantha. He hoped that Annaliese's need for critical care would be enough to convince her to be gentle with him.

He turned to Gunny, who had been quiet the entire time he was on the phone, and said, "My friend, I keep asking you for favors and I have another."

"Sure."

"Can I keep the phone for a few days?"

"Not a problem, but can I ask why, at least?"

"Looks like I'm making a trip and it will come in handy."

"Another trip?"

"I know, seems like I can't stop moving, but it needs to be done."

Gunny leaned in and said, "Van Zandt, you gave us a home here by vouching for us. Whatever I can do for you I'll do. Letting you use the phone is nothing. It's yours."

"Thanks, buddy," Gordon said, then exited the Humvee and made his way to Annaliese's room, only to find her awake and seething in pain.

He watched his brother try to comfort her. He knew the helpless feeling his brother must have been experiencing—he had been there before himself with Hunter. He cursed the world they were living in now. Not often did he think about why it all happened, but now he did. Watching a loved one in pain caused him to ruminate on the type of person who could have inflicted such inhumanity. What could have motivated someone to commit the mass murder of so many people and set the human race on a course of apocalypse? Only six months before, this type of scene wouldn't have been playing out. Annaliese would be sitting in a fully functioning hospital with access to the care she now needed so desperately.

"Sebastian," Gordon said, barely above a whisper. He felt odd disturbing them during this moment.

Lost in his wife's pain, he didn't hear Gordon.

"Sebastian," he said louder.

Sebastian turned, tears in his eyes. He grasped Annaliese's hand tightly, as if his firm embrace would take away some of her pain. "Hey, it's not a good time."

"I have help coming. I called in a favor, you could say. They're sending a chopper here to pick her up."

Sebastian wiped his eyes. What Gordon had said gave him hope instantly. "When?"

"In a few hours. They're taking her to Cheyenne, Wyoming."

"How did you make this happen so fast? That's incredible."

"Let's just say that I was already speaking with them, but it's coming at a cost."

"What do you mean, a *cost*?"

"I have to go to Coos Bay."

"What? No, no, Samantha won't allow it, I can't allow it."

"It's done; the chopper taking me will arrive just after yours. Listen, I'll be back here in time to see you guys off. I'll have Samantha watch over Luke and . . ."

"What do you have to do in Coos Bay? What does Colonel Barone want? I don't understand."

"It's not Barone; I'm going there at the request of the president. He wants me to get some intel on what's going on there. It's a simple in-and-out operation. I'll be back before you will be, I'm sure of it," Gordon said, trying to reassure Sebastian that his deal was a sound one.

"There's no such thing as a simple operation. You know better than anyone," Sebastian countered.

"Why are you arguing with me? Annaliese needs the care; I did what I had to do. How about a thank-you?"

"I'm sorry. I'm grateful, thank you. I just don't want it at a cost to you or Sam. You guys have suffered so much already."

"Little brother, the deal is done. Now I need to go have this conversation with Samantha. That's not going to be fun," Gordon said, a frown etched on his face.

• • •

"You're nervous, aren't you?" Gunny asked.

"What?" Gordon answered his question with a question. His mind was elsewhere.

"We've been sitting out in front of your house for five minutes and you haven't budged," Gunny jabbed.

"I'm trying to figure out how to best phrase it."

"There isn't a best way. Just tell her what's going on. You can't sugarcoat this. Get in there and get this done."

"Can you get Jones and McCamey to take off for a bit while I talk to her?" Gordon asked.

"Sure thing."

Gordon stopped short of the front door. He knew time was running out but he couldn't help but reflect that soon he'd be gone again. He worried about Samantha, but he was even more worried about how his absence would affect Haley. His little girl had been through so much and this wouldn't help. Trying to reason with six-year-olds was impossible. He just hoped that one day she'd understand.

Finally ready, he opened the front door and walked in. He looked around but didn't see Samantha. The clang of a pot told him she was in the kitchen.

Gunny came in right behind him and immediately found the other two Marines. Without wasting time, they gathered themselves and left.

Gordon sauntered to the bar in the kitchen and watched as Samantha prepared some food. Whatever Samantha did, she did with a level of precision and intensity. She often would joke that it was how things should always be done, but he'd counter that she was just a perfectionist.

"I'm so glad you're home. How's Annaliese?" Samantha said while moving about the kitchen.

"Sam, we need to talk," he said somberly.

His tone said it all. She instantly stopped what she was doing. "What is it?"

"Annaliese is not doing well. They can't help her here. She's being transported to Cheyenne, Wyoming."

"Cheyenne? Why? What's wrong with her?"

"We don't know what's wrong with her, but they can't do anything here for her. I called in a favor with the vice president and they've agreed to pick her up and take her to Cheyenne for treatment."

"Thank God. When are they taking her?"

Gordon looked at his watch. "By the end of the day."

"Oh my God, how's Sebastian doing?"

"He's a mess, but everything will be better."

Samantha came out from the kitchen and put her arms around him in a tight embrace. "I guess your little excursion paid off in some way."

"Well, not exactly."

She stepped back from him and looked into his eyes. "I know that tone, I know that look. What else is going on?"

"This arrangement came at a price, and that price is me going back to Coos Bay for a short trip," Gordon said.

Samantha's face fell. "No, no way. You promised. You're not leaving us again."

"I have to. If I don't do this, they won't help her. It has to be done. Please understand," Gordon pleaded.

"No, no, no, there *has* to be someone else who can do this. You can't leave us again. I can't, Haley can't, go through this again. We barely made it last time you were gone," Samantha berated.

"This isn't the desert, this isn't San Diego. It's safe here."

"It's safe now, but there's no guarantee it will always be. This world is crazy out there, you know that. One day we can be playing happy family, the next we're fighting for our lives. I can't have you gone ever again. You promised, Gordon!"

"Sam, I have to go, it won't be for long. I'll return as fast as I can."

"No!" Samantha yelled.

With equal intensity, he yelled back, "If I don't go, she will die!"

The statement hit her like a ton of bricks. The last thing she wanted was for Gordon to leave again, but the thought of Annaliese dying was not something she wanted to deal with either.

"Sam, it's an easy trip. Let me explain. They're going to fly me in—no driving this time. All they need me to do is get some information on what is happening there."

"But you just told me the place is crazy. Those were your words, just yesterday!" She sat, dazed, on a bar stool.

"You're right, but I'll be fine. The colonel knows me. I'll go into town, say hi, take a look around, and leave. I'll be home in three days, tops," Gordon said, clearly exaggerating the ease of the mission. He knew that nothing was simple, specifically in this world and under the circumstances as they were in Coos Bay.

"Damn it, why does something always have to come up? Can't someone else go instead of you?"

"I wish there was, but it has to be me. I'll be fine and Annaliese will get the urgent medical care she needs."

"There's not another doctor? What about in Cascade?"

"Sam, the best doctors in a hundred miles are in McCall and they said she needs specialty care. They want to perform exploratory surgery to help diagnose the problem. That's crazy. In Cheyenne, they have modern equipment and the only way to get her there is by me doing this favor for the president."

With each second that passed, the truth of what needed to be done sank in for Samantha.

Gordon looked past her into the kitchen. He could see she was preparing food for her McCall Women's Auxiliary meeting that she held once per week. Not long after arriving in McCall she had founded it in hopes of spreading knowledge and skill sets that some women had lost during the modern age, like gardening, holistic remedies, canning, preparing meat, animal husbandry, and other old-worldly skills that were now needed. He hated that he had to ruin her outing, but the news couldn't wait.

Samantha hadn't said a word for what seemed like an eternity to Gordon. He sat down in the stool next to her and gently took her hand.

"Sweetheart, I'm sorry, but I have to go. This is the only way we can help Annaliese."

"I know, you're right, you have to go. Annaliese and Sebastian need you and it's who you are. To not let you go would not allow you to be you," she softly said as she raised her head and looked into his eyes.

"I'll be fine."

"Don't make those promises; I know how things are. This is the new world we live in and you have to go. There's no other way."

Gordon leaned over and embraced her.

Haley walked into the room and with excitement in her voice she yelled out, "Cuddles!" She ran over with open arms. Gordon and Samantha took her into their arms.

In the softest and sweetest tone she said something that defined everything and made it all so simple. "I love my family."

. . .

The remaining part of Gordon's day was spent preparing for his journey. He knew he had to pack light so he took only the essentials: Gunny's phone, food, water, and fire-starting materials were a critical part of his pack, as was extra ammunition.

While Gordon was preparing, Samantha was doing her part for the family. She and Haley traveled to Sebastian's house to get Sebastian and Annaliese some personal items and to get Luke, as he'd be staying with them while everyone was away.

Samantha drove the truck into short driveway of the small house that Sebastian, Annaliese, and Luke called home. The little fifteen-hundred-square-foot home had the feel and look of what you'd expect if you went to the mountains. The siding was a natural wood and the deck that spanned the full front was made of log. Large trees encircled the home and to the left what had been a lawn was now a garden.

Haley was excited to see Luke. Since the day they met, they had gotten along. Samantha was initially apprehensive about Luke after she heard his story, specifically how he'd snapped and killed Brandon. She discussed her feelings with Gordon, who dismissed her skepticism. She did see that Luke was growing more outgoing with each day spent with the family. He was acting like an older brother to Haley, and she couldn't deny that connection.

The day's events had weighed on her and what energy she had earlier was now gone. She hadn't put the truck in park for a second before Haley jumped out and tore toward the front door. She gave in to her fatigue for a moment as she slid down and rested her head on top of the old vinyl bench seat. Closing her eyes, she inhaled deeply. The rich smell of pine needles propelled her to their first time in McCall over eight years ago. She fell in love with Idaho the second she saw the grass-covered foothills outside of Boise give way to the tree-covered mountains. The alpine feel was something she had never experienced growing up. She had tried to explain its uniqueness to her friends but it often fell on disinterested ears. Upon their fourth visit a year later they finally committed and bought the place they were living in now.

A loud happy squeal from Haley jogged Samantha from her daydream. She couldn't waste any more time. She exited the truck and walked down the worn paver walkway to the front door.

"Luke?"

"Back here," Luke said from his bedroom, his voice a bit raspy.

Samantha looked around the main room and smiled. She loved that Annaliese was like her, a caring homemaker. Everything in their house was in its place and neat and clean. She wondered how after being sick for week Annaliese's home stayed immaculate. All she could surmise was that she had properly trained the men of the house.

Luke came out of his bedroom, followed by Haley, who was wearing a gorilla mask.

"Hi, Aunt Samantha," Luke said. His referring to her as aunt happened relatively quickly following their meeting. Wanting to give Luke a sense of stability and to not let him feel isolated, Sebastian and Annaliese asked if they could adopt him and he joyfully agreed to it. There weren't any legal proceedings, but the simple act of wanting him and declaring that he was family meant more than any court could give Luke. He fit right into the role as a dutiful son, nephew, and cousin. "What's going on?" he then asked, clearly unaware of the situation.

"Are you feeling all right, Luke? I heard you coughing."

"Yeah, just a chest cold. I woke up with it."

Samantha looked him over. He appeared well enough, but it was something to monitor.

"I'm sorry to be the one to let you know this, Luke, but Annaliese is being sent to a hospital far away and Sebastian is going with her."

A grim look came over his face.

"While they're gone, you'll stay with me and Gordon."

"And me, yay!" Haley yelped as she jumped up in the air, still wearing the tattered gorilla mask.

"Is she going to be okay?" Luke asked, concern evident in his voice.

"Yes, she'll be fine, she just needs care that she can't get here," Samantha answered as she rubbed his arm.

"How long will they be gone?"

"I don't know, but I can't imagine it will be for a long time. Why don't you go and get some things together while I go and pack a bag for them?"

Samantha wandered into Sebastian and Annaliese's bedroom. There she found the opposite of tidiness. The bed was unmade, with towels and dirty dishes on the nightstand. Sebastian must be beyond devastated. Her heart felt a pang when she imagined the physical pain Annaliese was experiencing and the emotional pain Sebastian was suffering. Not wanting to stay long, she found a duffel bag in the closet and began to stuff it with clothes. As she packed, she came upon a loaded .45-caliber pistol. She instinctually set it aside. She imagined Sebastian could need it and placed it in the bag as well.

When she was getting items from a chest of drawers, she found a Free Cascadia T-shirt. She pulled it out and looked at it. She didn't find it odd that Sebastian had gravitated toward the group; he was more of a free spirit than Gordon. But she wondered why Gordon hadn't yet made the transition. It wasn't for Sebastian's lack of trying. She knew Gordon like the back of her hand, though, and figured that the more his brother got involved, the more his interest would be piqued.

"I gave that to Sebastian," Luke mentioned, now standing at the doorway.

"Oh my God, you startled me," Samantha said as she jumped.

"Sorry."

"They have a pretty flag. I love the tree," she said, holding the shirt up as she examined it more closely.

"They're good people. You should come to a meeting sometime."

"Since when did you become involved with them?"

"A few weeks ago. Sebastian thought I was old enough to participate. Why doesn't Uncle Gordon join?" Luke asked.

"I don't know, Luke, sometimes Gordon can be stubborn. How does Sebastian feel about Gordon's reluctance?"

"Oh, he thinks he'll come around. He's not too worried."

"Yeah, I would agree with Sebastian. Your uncle Gordon takes a little longer to warm up to things sometimes, but I think he likes the concept of self-rule. Actually, I don't think it, I know he does. I know he pretends to be against it sometimes but he has no real love for the establishment, never has."

"That's good to hear," Luke said.

"I think it's good too," Samantha said,

"Is Uncle Gordon leaving too?"

"Unfortunately, yes, he is."

"Sorry."

Samantha looked over at Luke and smiled, moved by his sympathy. Each encounter she had with him helped push any negative thoughts about his previous behavior further from her mind.

Haley tugged on Samantha's sleeve. "Mom, why does Daddy have to leave again?"

The question alone tore at her heartstrings. "He has to go help Aunt Annaliese."

She and Gordon had talked with Haley earlier but the mentioning of his departure rekindled her tender emotions.

"I don't understand," Haley stated.

"I know it's all confusing, honey, but Daddy will be home soon. When we get home I'll set up a tent in the great room and we can camp out together, make it special."

Samantha's overtures didn't do anything to help relieve Haley of her sadness. Tears welled in her daughter's eyes.

"That sounds like fun!" Luke chimed in, in an attempt to help. "If it's clear tonight why don't we look for falling stars?"

Luke's persistence finally brought a smile to her face.

"Sounds like we're going to have fun tonight," Samantha said. It was a temporary solution, but in this situation, it was all she could do.

• • •

The chopper taking Annaliese and Sebastian back to Cheyenne arrived close to the expected arrival time. Working like a pit crew, the medical staff exited the chopper and scooped up Annaliese.

For the second time today, Sebastian's face was awash in tears. Samantha embraced him tightly.

"You be safe and watch over my sister," Samantha said. Tears now filled her eyes too.

"It makes me so happy that you two love one another. She thinks the world of you."

"Well, I think the world of her. She's amazing," Samantha said and gave him another big hug.

The crew chief on the helicopter hollered, "We gotta go!"

Gordon ran up and gave him a hug. "I love you, brother. Be safe."

"I can't thank you enough."

"It's what family does." Gordon looked at his brother and remembered the time Sebastian had stopped by his house for dinner well over a year ago. He looked so different now. His sandy blond hair was shaggy and hung below his ears. A trimmed and groomed beard graced his face, giving him an older and more rugged look. Even his blue eyes looked older. If this new world had one thing that was universal it would be its ability to sap every ounce of youthful innocence and idealism right out of anyone. A combat tour didn't even have the same lethal effect on one's psyche as this world did. The wars he and his brother had been through may have scarred their humanity, but this world had the ability to utterly destroy it.

Luke and Haley both ran up and grabbed Sebastian. Seeing them together brought a smile to his face.

"Luke, listen to your aunt Samantha and take care of them both, especially this one," he said, tussling Haley's hair.

"I will," Luke said.

"I'm going to miss you, Uncle Sebastian," Haley said as she squeezed him.

"I'll bring you something special back," Sebastian said to Haley. He picked her up and held her tight. "I love you, little one."

She wrapped her arms around his neck and gave him a kiss on the cheek.

He put her down just as the crew chief again hollered, "If you're coming, it's gotta be now!"

Sebastian took a brief moment to look at each one before turning and running onto the helicopter.

All four watched the chopper lift off slowly, bank, and fly over the hospital and out of sight. Not an eye was dry; even Gordon had to wipe tears away. Soon the choppy echo of the helicopter was gone.

They all looked at one another and didn't say a word. The next fare-well was scheduled to come at any moment, and for Samantha and Haley, this one would be even more difficult.

The thumping sound of rotors again echoed off the buildings and surrounding trees. As the sound grew louder, Samantha stepped close to Gordon and gripped his hand. Haley too drew closer. Gordon looked at her, smiled, and picked her up.

"I love you, baby girl," he whispered to her.

"I love you most."

"I love you from here to the moon."

"I love you from here to the moon and back."

"I think you have me beat there," Gordon said as he squeezed her tighter.

A black HH-60 Pave Hawk appeared over top the hospital. It circled the parking lot and set down not fifty yards from Gordon. When the main rotor stopped, the flight engineer, dressed in a dark flight suit and helmet, exited.

The man wearing the flight suit approached them. "Are you Gordon Van Zandt?"

"That would be me."

"Where's your gear?"

Gordon gestured to the pack and M4 on the ground before him.

"You have less crap than the other guy," the flight engineer commented.

"What other guy?" Gordon asked as he looked over the flight engineer's shoulder.

"The other guy we're taking with us. He came in on the cargo plane from Cheyenne." The flight engineer shrugged.

Another man suddenly stepped out of the chopper and stretched. He was clad head to toe in a green digicam uniform.

Gordon didn't like when plans were changed without him being made aware of it. Putting Haley on the ground, he walked past the flight engineer and up to the man who yawned and bent over to stretch his back.

"God, my back hurts from riding in that thing," the man complained.

"Who are you?" Gordon asked in an irritated tone.

The man stood and looked at Gordon. He was average height, approximately five foot ten inches. His straight, groomed black hair showed age as it was sprinkled with gray along the sides. "Excuse me?" the man replied, eyebrows raised.

"My mission to Coos Bay doesn't call for another person. This is a delicate plan and anything can jeopardize it."

"Let's not get off on the wrong foot. My name is Staff Sergeant Finley. I was ordered to join this op not eight hours ago," Finley said, offering his hand to Gordon.

"The president never mentioned I was being accompanied by anyone. It will be hard enough for me to get in, much less another person," Gordon said, not taking his hand.

"I have my orders and I'm coming. If I don't, the mission is scrubbed. I'll get on the radio and call that bird with the woman back," Finley replied defiantly.

Gordon knew the importance of being tactful, so he bit his tongue and nodded in agreement to the new plan.

"Let me go get my gear," Gordon said, and walked back to Samantha and Haley.

Under his breath, Finley commented, "Looks like the major was right, he is an asshole."

Gordon first stepped up to Luke and smiled tightly. "Watch over the girls, okay?"

"Yes, sir."

Luke had grown on Gordon, much like he had on Samantha. His

initial skepticism was replaced by real affection. He could see why Sebastian had a fondness for this smart young man.

"Thanks, buddy. I'll see you soon."

Gordon stepped in front of Haley and looked down.

Her little eyes told him the pain she was feeling inside. She cried out, "Don't go, Daddy, please stay."

Gordon swept her up in his arms and hugged her tightly. Tears welled in his eyes. The pain he felt leaving them again tore at his chest. If there was another way to accomplish what he had to do, he would have done it, but there was no way around it. "Oh, baby, I'll come back quickly. I promise. I won't be gone long."

"Last time you were gone a long, long time. Bad things happened."

A few tears ran down his face, as he didn't know how to answer her. He hugged her tightly and repeated, "I'll be home quickly. I will."

Samantha began to rub her back as Haley cried loudly.

Gordon wiped the tears from his face. He looked at Haley clinging to Samantha and smiled. "Should we make a Haley sandwich?"

"Yeah, I think we should."

He stepped forward and placed his arms around them both.

Gordon looked into Samantha's eyes and said, "I love you so much."

"I love you too. Be safe."

"I will."

He knew his good-byes were taking a long time when he overheard the flight engineer and Finley make a comment.

Gordon pulled away and looked at the men.

"Staff Sergeant Finley, I assume you have comms?"

"Yes, I do."

"I need to get your contact information."

"I can't give you my info," Finley remarked.

"Don't be that way. No one is going to be drunk dialing you. We're all in this op together. Hand it over," Gordon demanded.

Finley paused then and said, "Hold on." He dug in his pocket and pulled out a phone. He scrolled through the phone until he came to the number. "Here," he said once he found it.

Gordon took the phone and plugged the number into the phone he had. With Finley now going, he didn't have a need for a phone to call the president—he could just use his. He knew it was a risk, but leaving Samantha with a phone gave him peace of mind

Finley took the phone back and said, "Hurry up. We have to go."

"One second more," Gordon said as he walked back to Samantha. "Take this," he said, handing the sat phone to her.

"Won't you need it?"

"We have comms. I want you to have something. His number is programmed inside. Don't call unless there's an emergency or you see someone has called the phone."

Samantha took it, nodding appreciatively.

Gordon winked at her, and because he never felt you could say it enough, said, "I love you." He turned around and swiftly walked to the chopper and boarded.

The rotors began to whine and move and within moments they were spinning fast. The chopper lifted off and Gordon looked into the distance, unsure of what the future held for him.

JUNE 27, 2015

. . .

"The essence of lying is in deception, not in words."

—John Ruskin

Five miles outside of Coos Bay, Oregon, Pacific State of America

The smoke from the smoldering fire wafted over Gordon, waking him up. The dawn's light was just showing in the eastern sky and the chirping of the birds was announcing the pending morning. Finley was still sleeping, nestled in his sleeping bag. Gordon stood up and looked around at their campsite and the surrounding groves of trees they had called home for the night.

The ride to Oregon didn't go as planned. Their first stop was Mountain Home Air Force base for refueling, and from there the ride took a couple hours. The fuel range on the choppers prevented them from getting as close as had been discussed, so they were set down ten miles east of Roseburg, Oregon. From the landing zone they both set out on M1030 motorcycles. The bikes were rugged and handled very well off road. It had literally been years since Gordon had ridden a motorcycle, but when he got back on, his muscle memory kicked in. He soon was his aggressive old self, the pre-Samantha, pre-kids warrior.

He and Finley agreed that they wouldn't attempt to cross over into Coos Bay until the morning, as coming up on a checkpoint at night could be unnerving to both those approaching and to the guards. Best to approach in the light of day to alleviate any issues. Their final approach into town would be from the south along Route 42.

Gordon rolled up his bag and stowed it on his bike. As he was digging through his pack for something to eat, a clanging sound alerted him that someone had broken their makeshift perimeter detection devices, or in layman's terms, the cans they had strung on a string. He pulled his pistol from his shoulder holster and held it out in front of him in the direction of the sound.

Finley jumped up, grabbed his rifle, and was immediately at the ready. "See anything?"

Gordon didn't answer; he slowly walked toward where the sounds came from, a large group of trees and thick shrubs that flanked their campsite. He strained to see anything, but nothing moved in the trees. Silence now blanketed the area.

"Psst, what do ya think? See anything?" Finley whispered.

"If I did, don't you think you'd know?"

A loud crunching of leaves followed the cans clanging again.

"Whoever is there, come out!" Gordon ordered, and took a step toward the edge of their campsite.

A much louder crash of crunched leaves and broken branches made Gordon hyper-focus on the spot, his finger on the trigger. He was tempted to just shoot into the shrubs but he quickly assessed that whoever or whatever it was was clearly scared enough not to attack. With his decision made, he boldly walked toward the area to flush out whoever was there. Suddenly a large golden retriever came bursting out of the shrub.

"Holy shit, you scared me!" Gordon cried out.

Finley swiveled, rifle in his shoulder. When he saw the old dog he began to laugh.

The dog came up to him, sniffing and rubbing against his leg. He bent over and began to pet him but stopped when he felt large ticks all over the dog's body.

"Come here, pooch!" Finley called.

"Don't, the dog is gross. He's covered in ticks. And, hey, we should pack up and go. You nearly slept the morning away. We have a long day ahead."

Finley nodded and made his way over to his gear. "So, I hear you were a Marine?" Finley asked. They had mostly avoided small talk on their trip, Gordon still agitated at Finley's unannounced presence.

"Yes, a long time ago."

"You ever get trigger time in theater?"

"Yeah, in Iraq back in 2004. You? What's your story?"

"Three tours under my belt. I've been in for over twelve years now."

"Oh, a lifer?"

"I love this shit!"

"You love *this* shit?"

"C'mon, how many jobs allow you to blow shit up and . . ." Finley stopped when he realized how odd it must have sounded. He thought for a moment and further commented, "Yeah, I know everything has gone to shit, but I'm an action guy. I was made for this."

Gordon thought about his last comment for a second, then said, "I guess you're right. That's one of the four reasons one goes into the military."

"What are the other three?"

"You never heard of the four types? There are the ones who join strictly to get the benefits like college, then there are the super patriotic ones, there are the action guys like you, and then there are the killers, those who like to kill. The military gives them that license to do that."

"Seems about right. I love the action, but I also love my country and if I can get a bad guy in my sights, I don't mind putting him down. Maybe I cross several categories."

"I was like you, action and patriotism. But I have no problem ending a savage's life if need be."

"I heard you're quite a badass, a true no-bullshit kinda guy. I was briefed on your past and your trip with the vice president. You definitely have a reputation and that's cool."

Gordon ignored his comment, grunting. "You ready?"

"Let's do this!" Finley shouted with excitement.

Both men fired up their motorcycles and sped off out of the woods and toward Coos Bay.

McCall, Idaho

After tossing and turning most of the night, Samantha decided to get up and start her day early. She made a carafe of coffee, grabbed a book, and took a seat on the back patio. The dawn's glow was replacing the darkness, ushering in a new day. She read a few pages of *For Whom the Bell Tolls*, by Ernest Hemingway, but soon realized she wasn't retaining anything. She exhaled heavily and put the book down on the table next to her. She used to love Hemingway, but reading some of his works wasn't escapism anymore. She didn't find it enjoyable to read about death and war when her life was just that. As she waited to see the sun's first rays, her mind turned to Gordon. She was worried sick about him and wondered where he was in his trip. The temptation to call him on the satellite phone kept nagging at her, but she knew the delicate nature of what he was doing and didn't want to jeopardize anything.

The sun's rays felt good against her cool skin. She relaxed into the chair and closed her eyes. However, her slumber didn't last long as a knock on the glass sliding door behind her disturbed the peace and quiet. She turned and saw Haley, rubbing her sleepy eyes. She waved; Haley returned the wave and motioned for her to come. She jumped up and opened the door.

"Good morning, honey. You should be sleeping," Samantha said in a sweet voice.

"I had a bad dream," she whimpered.

"Come here, I'll take you back to bed," she said, picking her up.

"No, I want to cuddle with you," she said, burying her head into her neck.

"Are you sure?"

She nodded.

"Sure, I'd love that. Let me get a blanket from the sofa here," Samantha said as she grabbed a large animal-print throw from the sectional. They both sat and said nothing to each other for a few minutes. Haley broke the silence by asking, "What happened to Auntie Annaliese? Will she be okay?"

"Auntie Annaliese is sick so she went to go get better."

"Will she die?"

Samantha's heart skipped a beat. "No, honey. The doctors are going to make her all better." She rubbed her arm, and noticed that Haley felt a bit warm.

"You're a little warm, baby. How do you feel?"

"I'm fine, Mommy."

With everything that had happened to Annaliese, the thought of Haley getting sick made Samantha nervous. She tried to push aside the negative thoughts, but it was difficult.

"You sure?"

"Mommy?"

"Yes."

"Have you seen Diamond, my unicorn?"

Samantha chuckled to herself; the innocence of youth never failed to surprise her. "No, but let's go find her."

Cheyenne, Wyoming

Conner woke early and took advantage of the extra hour to work out. Excitement and the anticipation of news from Coos Bay were making him feel like a child waiting for Santa Claus. The operation to send Gordon had been hastily done, but if all went as planned he'd have the edge on Barone he'd been wanting since the day he heard about his mutiny.

The rigorous run on the treadmill made him sweat profusely. Each bead of sweat represented toxins and negativity leaving his body. The apocalypse had been good for him if you gauged it on weight loss alone. Since the lights went out he had lost over forty pounds, and when he looked in the mirror he saw the Brad Conner he knew in college. Never again did he want to go back to the overweight and lethargic man he had allowed himself to turn into. His captivity by the gang taught him that physical strength was critical in the new world. Even though he now had protection, he knew firsthand that no matter how much protection you have, you can't rely on it. That would pertain to Barone soon, he hoped.

He had renewed focus on reassembling the country, piece by piece, state by state. That included trying to get Texas, Alaska, and Hawaii to come back into the fold. The first thing to do, though, was eliminate the threats of Barone, the PAE, and the various separatist groups. Once that was accomplished, the reconstruction could progress unencumbered and he could work diplomatically on having those states return to the union.

The reconstruction effort would soon show much improvement once the steady stream of aid and equipment from Australia and other allies came. The projections were very promising—each month, more and more of the country would have their grids back and running. Conner was confident that everything could fall into place. He jumped off the treadmill with a type of energy he hadn't felt in years.

· · ·

Conner exited the locker room and looked at his watch. He had an hour until his first meeting. The thought of a cup of fresh coffee sounded great, plus he wanted to check on his friend, so he decided to make a run to Pat's.

Once in the armored Humvee, he called Dylan on the secure phone and informed him of his destination. Looking out the window, he marveled at how the city was changing so quickly. Each day it grew more and more as migrants moved in from all parts of the United States. They came looking for hope and so far, he was giving it to them.

At Pat's, many regular patrons sat inside. He exchanged handshakes and hellos before reaching the counter. Pat was busy behind it.

"Mr. President, good morning! The usual?" Pat asked.

"Yes, sir. The place looks great. You can hardly tell there was a brawl here."

"Yeah, it was mostly turned-up tables and spilled drinks. Nothing that couldn't be fixed."

"How are you?"

"Fine," Pat answered as he was pouring Conner a hot, steaming cup of coffee.

"You sure?"

"Yeah, I'm fine. No use crying over spilled coffee." Pat walked over with a paper cup filled to the top and handed it to him. "Here you go, sir."

Conner pulled out his wallet and removed a twenty-dollar bill.

"Glad to hear you're fine. Here," Conner said as he handed the money to him.

As Pat counted out his change, he clucked his tongue. "It's so funny using money again. I have to admit that it's been difficult to get people to use it."

"We have to start again somewhere, and what better place to start the use of a currency again than in the capital city? I realize it's not going to be easy for people to trust it, but we can't keep trading eggs and milk. Eventually we have to have an established and standardized currency to do trading and commerce with."

"Indeed. Your money is always good here," Pat said with a broad smile.

"Anything new going on here?"

"Ha. Things do happen here. Sometimes I think I've created a monster with this place."

"What does that mean?"

"Oh, it's nothing, but you know those guys, the Lakotahs. A few others came in this morning. I heard them mumbling about how their people were arrested the other night. After they left, I found some more flyers."

"Let me guess: pictures of me with a bull's-eye on them?"

"If it were I'd have it over there on the dartboard," Pat said as he reached down the counter and handed the papers to Conner.

Conner flipped through the sheets of paper. They were similar to those from the other night, but with some strikingly different language. What caught his eye were phrases like "tyrannical federal government," "free our prisoners of war," and "free the Lakotah people." The bottom called for a march for "freedom" coming in two days.

"Can I take these with me?" Conner asked.

"Sure, I don't need them; I was saving them for you anyway," Pat said, then made his way back behind the bar.

"I'll catch you later, thanks," Conner said, raising his cup. He stopped just before exiting and called out, "Can you contact me if these guys come back in?"

"Sure thing," Pat replied.

"Cheers," Conner said, and left. He walked out of the shop and jumped into the Humvee. "To the capitol," he instructed the driver.

As they sped off, he looked over the flyers again. He would have to stamp the Lakotahs out, but he wouldn't go looking for them. He'd let them come to him.

Warren Air Force Base, Cheyenne, Wyoming

Sebastian couldn't sleep. He had stayed awake all night as they ran test after test on Annaliese. Finally, the MRI showed the doctors what they needed to see. In her lower abdomen, a blood clot in an artery was cutting off blood flow to her lower intestine. Once they determined this, the doctors raced her off to have emergency surgery. The test result and surgery had happened so quickly that he hadn't had a real chance to talk with her.

One bad image after another kept coming into his mind. He pictured her on the operating room table covered in blood and the heart monitor flatlining. It took all he could to block those visions out of his mind. Never before was he so worried or had he felt such fear at the potential of losing someone. Having someone die close to him wasn't foreign; when he was younger his parents died and even though it upset him then, the fear of losing his wife felt even more tremendous. The only thing he imagined could be worse was losing a child. He could not even fathom how difficult it must have been for Gordon and Samantha to lose Hunter. Seeing their pain affected his own willingness to have children.

The yellowish glow of the fluorescent overhead lights and the roomful of empty chairs gave a feeling of dread. Sebastian was consumed with thoughts of his wife, his head in his hands. He didn't even notice that someone had walked up to him.

"Excuse me," the woman said.

Sebastian looked up, his vision a bit blurry from lack of sleep. After blinking a few times she came into focus. "Yes."

"Hi, Mr. Van Zandt, I'm Secretary of State Wilbur. I thought I'd stop by and say hello and check on you. I wanted to make sure that you and your wife were getting the best care possible."

He stood up promptly, rubbed his eyes, and said, "Ah, yes, everything has been good, very good."

"Is your wife doing well?"

"I have to assume so, she's still in surgery."

"I can assure you that we have the best available people taking care of her. She's in good hands."

"Thank you. Everything has been great. Sorry if I seem a bit out of it, but I haven't slept in over twenty-four hours and I'm nervous."

"I can understand."

"Any word on my brother, Gordon?"

"The last I heard, he landed in Oregon. They haven't made it to Coos Bay yet but are expected to arrive soon."

"They?"

"He is being accompanied by a Staff Sergeant Finley."

Gordon hadn't mentioned going with anyone else, but he really wasn't apprised of the mission so he let it go.

"I can't thank you all enough. Bringing her here to get care was very generous."

"You're welcome, Mr. Van Zandt."

"Please, call me Sebastian. Um, forgive me, but you look familiar. Have we met before?"

"Yes, we have, in Idaho. Your brother escorted me and Vice President Cruz out of Coos Bay a few months ago."

"That's it. I knew you looked familiar. I'm just so tired that I couldn't place the face."

"Here," she said, handing him a card.

Sebastian looked at the business card, which was a bit wrinkled and worn looking.

"Major?"

"It's an old card; my current contact information is on the back. If you need anything at all, please don't hesitate to reach out. We want to make sure you and your wife are taken care of."

Sebastian flipped the card over and looked at the handwritten phone number. "I will. Thank you again."

A man dressed in blue scrubs walked into the waiting room and approached Sebastian. "Mr. Van Zandt."

An intensity gripped Sebastian's face as he attempted to read the body language and tone in the surgeon's voice. "How is she?"

"She is doing very well. We were able to remove the clot with no complications. We will need to monitor her for a while to see why she had the clot to begin with."

Relief washed over him when he heard the words he had been praying for. "What do you think caused it?"

"Right now we don't know. Without knowing her history and based upon her age, we think she had acute intestinal ischemia."

"Acute intestinal ischemia?"

"There are several types but the way you described her symptoms—the sudden-onset pain, bloody stool, painful bowel movements, et cetera—led us to believe it was acute versus chronic, but we will be able to determine more after further tests so we can prevent a clot from ever forming again. I'll leave you with this: The worst is over. She will recover with no projected complications."

He let out a huge sigh. "Can I see her now?"

"She's in a surgical recovery room now but she's still under. We are slowly bringing her out of anesthesia and when she's fully awake, we'll wheel her back to a hospital room where you can see her. I expect that to take about an hour. A nurse will come find you and show you to her room after she's been transported there."

"Okay, thank you, doctor. Thank you so much."

"You're welcome," the doctor said, and walked away.

Wilbur had remained but had taken a few steps back during the conversation. "I know you must feel like a ton of bricks have been lifted."

Sebastian had forgotten Wilbur was even standing there, he was so dazed with the news. "Yes, something to celebrate for sure. Can you do something for me?"

"Absolutely."

"Have word sent to my brother."

"I will. If there isn't anything else I can do, I'll leave you to soak up this great news."

"Thank you very much."

Wilbur put her hand out and Sebastian shook it.

"Don't forget to contact me if you need anything."

"I won't forget. In fact you might regret giving me your number," Sebastian joked, the previous tension clearly gone.

Wilbur smiled, turned, and left. She had only visited out of a professional courtesy. She had been tempted to reveal her displeasure with Gordon to Sebastian but didn't think the timing was appropriate. After meeting Sebastian, she could see a family resemblance but that was where their similarities stopped for her. She found him easier to talk to and much more charming than his older brother.

With renewed hope for Annaliese, Sebastian began to pace the room. His excitement made it impossible for him to sit. He knew she wasn't completely out of the woods, as he was a realist, but he chose not to entertain any dark thoughts. With a heart filled with gratitude, he looked forward to seeing his beautiful wife.

Coos Bay, Oregon, Pacific States of America

Gordon's memory from his last time in Coos Bay proved to be correct. The first checkpoint they came upon was near the intersection of U.S. 101 and the Route 42, exactly where he said it would be. It was set up like many he had seen in Iraq, with barriers and Jersey walls channeling all traffic into one curved lane that led to the guard shack covered with sand bags. Two LAV-25 light-armored vehicles sat to either side of and behind the guard shack, their 25-millimeter Bushmaster cannons pointed down the controlled access. One armored Humvee mounted with a .50-caliber machine gun sat in a position in front of the shack.

They weaved left and right through the access until they reached two armed Marines at the guard shack.

Gordon pulled up first and took off his helmet. "Hi, my name is Gordon Van Zandt. I'm here to see Lieutenant Colonel Barone."

A Marine corporal looked at him, then looked at Finley behind him and asked, "What's your reason?"

"I transported the vice president a few months ago, and I'm here to talk to him about that."

"Who's with you?"

"That's my associate, Chuck."

"Do you have any ID?"

Gordon cocked his head and quipped, "Really? Who the hell carries an ID anymore?"

"I don't know who you are and without something proving you

are who you say you are, I'm not letting you in," the corporal said defensively.

"Do me a favor; jump on your radio and contact Colonel Barone and tell him that Sergeant Van Zandt is here. I'm a good friend of his and when he finds out you refused me access, he'll be up your ass," Gordon said, hoping to intimidate the Marine.

"Wait right here." The corporal took a few steps back, clicked his radio receiver, and called in for instructions.

Approximately ten minutes went by before an officer instructed the guard to turn away the two men.

"Sorry, no access. If you need to get something to someone, let me know, I can do it for you."

Gordon was nervous. He was afraid if he pressed it too much it could cause a scene and the entire mission would be jeopardized. He turned and looked at Finley, who returned his look with a wink.

"Can you please contact Colonel Barone directly with that radio?"

"No, sir, we can't. We have our own chain of command and he is refusing you access."

Gordon thought about what to do. He decided he'd try one more time and if that failed, he and Finley would have to sneak in. "Corporal, please contact your commanding officer, tell him I'm Sergeant Gordon Van Zandt, here to see Colonel Barone at his request. Also add that I was the Marine who escorted the vice president out of here."

"Sorry, sir, turn around," the corporal instructed.

"Please, Corporal, one more try, contact Master Sergeant Simpson too. He'll verify my identity," Gordon pleaded.

The corporal looked at him, and then looked at Finley. "Okay, one more time. Wait here."

Gordon took the moment to look around; there was no getting

past these LAVs and Humvee. If they attempted to force their way in, they'd lose.

The corporal approached Gordon and asked, "You're cleared to proceed to the second checkpoint about a mile or so down the road. Thank you for your patience. I'll radio ahead to inform them you're good to go."

"Thank you, Corporal," Gordon said. Putting his helmet back on, he turned to Finley and gave him a thumbs-up.

They drove on through the remaining parts of the checkpoint and soon were on open road again. The second checkpoint came into view after the last turn to the left. This one had even more vehicles and personnel. They pulled in and stopped just outside the door of the guard shack.

"I need you two to stay put. Someone is coming out to meet you," a Marine sergeant said.

Gordon had thought they were in, but his assumptions were premature. His plan was to tell them a bullshit story of information he had about the United States. Without any other options, that was the best he could do.

"Who's coming out?" Gordon asked.

"Just hold tight, sir," the Marine responded.

"How long do we have to wait?" Finley hollered from behind.

Gordon grew increasingly worried that things would not go how he had planned. So much was on the line. There was no way he'd be able to pull out and flee without causing the situation to go completely out of control or turning violent. He could tell that things were on edge since his last time there.

The Marine guard kept his eyes on Gordon and Finley, his hand on the pistol grip of his rifle. Minutes went by until the rumble of a Humvee could be heard

The Humvee stopped a few feet from the rear of the guard shack. The passenger side door opened up and an older Marine exited and walked up to the guard. They talked quietly and then the older one walked up to Gordon.

"Sergeant Van Zandt, I'm Staff Sergeant Phillips. I work for Master Sergeant Simpson. He sent me to come escort you in."

"Thank you, Staff Sergeant," Gordon said, the tension eased now.

"Who is your companion?" Phillips asked, pointing toward Finley.

"Finley—he's my partner and ex-army doggie," Gordon lied.

"I'm slumming it, hanging with the jarhead here," Finley chimed in.

Phillips grinned slightly and said, "He's a comedian too, I see."

"The real joke is he thinks that wearing a beret makes you look tough," Gordon joked.

Finley raised his middle finger at Gordon, and then blew him a kiss.

"All right, you two, follow us into downtown. Don't veer off, you might not like where you end up," Phillips ordered, jumping back into the Humvee.

Relief washed over Gordon. He had passed his first test, but what was coming was unknown. He put down his visor, started the bike, and followed Phillips.

As they passed each street on their way into Coos Bay, Gordon saw a once beautiful town turned into a battlefield. Passing a small community on his right, he saw what looked like two infantry platoons entering a series of homes. Civilians had gathered near them and were shouting. He could only assume they were in opposition to the raid.

The highway led them to just outside the main part of downtown and to a final checkpoint. This one was manned with tanks, light-armored vehicles, and endless strands of razor wire, barricades, and Jersey walls. Sandbagged bunkers flanked them as they proceeded through.

Inside town, the streets were covered in debris, trash, and abandoned cars. Signs of past fights were evident everywhere, as most of the buildings were riddled with bullet holes.

Gordon shuddered, thinking to himself, What have you done, Barone?

Phillips led them down to the USS *Makin Island*. Gordon never imagined he'd lay his eyes on the ship again, but here it was, towering over the dock.

Phillips walked up to him and said, "We'll find you and your friend a berthing spot shortly. We have plenty now."

Gordon took this opportunity to gather some needed information. "What happened here? It's not the same town I left three months ago."

"We've had a bit of trouble with the indigenous people, you could say."

Gordon found it strange to hear Phillips refer to the local people as "indigenous." It was very strange, as if he were treating them as though they were lesser than. But then again, he remembered, in the psychology of killing it's easier to kill and mistreat people when you don't equate them as equals or even humans.

Phillips escorted them onboard and into the bowels of the ship. As they made their way through the tight passageways and down ladder wells, he recalled Sebastian's last moments on the ship. Sebastian detailed how Gunny had escorted him through these very passageways to the flight deck. Gunny then was completely in league with Barone; Gordon chuckled when he thought of the irony that Gunny was now with them in Idaho. How quickly things could change and alliances shift.

Two decks down, Phillips brought them to a hatch. He opened it and inside appeared rows, stacked three high, of beds and small wall lockers.

Not having spent a single day onboard a naval vessel, Finley was excited somewhat by the experience. "Christ, you all sleep in these things?" he said with a laugh as he pointed out the small racks.

"Ah, yeah, sorry, these are the typical luxury accommodations the army gets," Gordon said as he tossed his gear on a rack.

"That's quality of life! We know how to live," Finely retorted.

"Quality of life? The military isn't about quality of life, it's about quantity of the enemy we kill," Gordon fired back.

"Quantity? I think we could say the army has more enemy KIAs than any other service!"

"I would also add it's about efficiency, and the Marines get a ton of shit done for the fraction of the cost the army does."

"I see you don't dispute my argument of total kills."

"The army is, like, ten times the size of the Marine Corps. I'd challenge that based upon percentages."

Finley raised his hand like a sock puppet and began to mock Gordon. "Percentages, percentages."

"Whatever," Gordon said, irritated with Finley's smugness.

"Oh my God, these beds suck!" Finley cried out as he lay on the rack.

"I thought you were a mountain-division guy. Aren't you boys supposed to be tough?"

"It's just stupid to make you guys live like this."

"Enough of the bullshit, let's take a walk around. I want to get eyes on things so we can get the hell out of here," Gordon said as his thoughts shifted to Samantha and Haley. "How about you call in and then we head into town?"

"Good idea," Finley said, sitting up. They made their way to the flight deck, where Finley made contact with command in Cheyenne. He was communicating their initial reports as Gordon scanned the deck. As he approached Finley, Finley turned away from him, as if trying to conceal the conversation.

"Hey, I'm on this mission too!"

Finley's back was now toward him.

"Hey, I need you to check on something!"

Finley only responded with his hand in the air, indicating for Gordon to be quiet.

"Hey!"

Finley swung around and asked, "What?"

Gordon shot him an angry look and said, "I need you to check on my brother and his wife!"

Finley rolled his eyes, and then asked into the phone, "Sir, Mr. Van Zandt is inquiring as to the condition of the woman."

Gordon could hear the voice but it was unintelligible.

Finley finished the call. "Thank you, sir, we'll check back in tonight."

"Well?"

Finley stared at Gordon, cold and irritated.

"How is she—are they okay?"

"First thing, let's establish something. Don't interrupt me again; second, while you think this is your mission, it's mine. You were our key to get in. I'm in charge of everything else. Do you understand?"

Gordon's first reaction was to tell him to go fuck off but he refrained. "Listen here, I might have been your *key* but I'm also cover for you. This is a joint mission, and I can rat you out any time."

"And if you do, your brother and sister-in-law will pay."

Gordon paused to bite his tongue. He was indeed in a tight spot and didn't have the leverage he often enjoyed.

"Do we understand one another?"

With a hard look, Gordon conceded. "Understood. Now, please tell me how my sister-in-law is doing."

"It wasn't good."

Gordon's face paled. "What?"

"She had something called intestinal ischemia."

"What's that?"

"Do I look like a doctor? I don't know, they said they had operated on her."

"And?"

"She's stable and your brother is with her. It looks like it will be okay."

Gordon breathed a sigh of relief. "Nothing else?"

"That's it. She'll be fine, and he's good. Now, let's go get some food. I'm starving," Finley said.

Elko, Nevada

Pablo threw the binoculars on the ground in disgust. His forces had taken a severe hit in the latest series of airstrikes from the United States Air Force. Numerous tanks, armored personnel carries, and trucks were ablaze. Smoke billowed from the metal carcasses now strewn along the high desert plains.

He grabbed his radio and screamed, "General Alejandro!"

Static cracked on his receiver, then Alejandro answered him. "Yes, Emperor." The sound of men yelling and screaming could be heard in the background.

"I need a status report!" Pablo barked.

"Sir, it's too early to know. We are still assessing the situation."

"General, when you're done, gather the commanders and meet me in the command post," Pablo ordered.

"Yes, Emperor," Alejandro replied.

Pablo wanted to be angry at someone but the only person he could be mad at was himself. He had ordered that most of the forces should be placed out of the city. General Alejandro had said keeping them inside the small city would conceal them in the open and prevent the U.S. forces from hitting them for fear of collateral damage. In his arrogance, Pablo had insisted they set up outside the city. There was no real justification for this decision, he just didn't want Alejandro to be challenging his authority so brazenly. Now his naïve decision had resulted in his forces being slaughtered.

A strong northern wind began to blow the black smoke horizontal across the eastern hills. The sound of rounds cooking off from the heat of the burning vehicles echoed and popped. An occasional scream from one of his men added to the concerto of horror before him.

His anger soon led to a deep feeling of defeat. His army could not keep taking these types of hits. The EMPs were supposed to have disabled much of the U.S. air capabilities, but either the United States had repaired some of their jets or they had been provided support. Maybe he needed help; his hubris had stopped him from seeking assistance outside of buying it. After today's events, he realized that he just might need an ally. The Americans were in disarray, but they were not going to give up without a fight. If his plans of a great Pan-American Empire were to actually come true, he would need to find someone to assist him in the fight. As he did so often, Pablo looked back on history to give him guidance. If Hitler felt the need to have allies like Mussolini, Stalin, and the Emperor of Japan, he too could use them.

Today had been horrible and he just couldn't think of anything else that could go wrong; but the radio came to life, dampening any hopes of that.

"Emperor, this is Major Silva." Major Silva was his new chief of staff; he oversaw all of Pablo's more personal matters. Hearing him meant something else was occurring outside of the military-operational scope.

Pablo picked up the receiver and hit the button. "Yes, Major."

"Sir, we've received an important message. Your attention to the matter is critical."

"What is it?" Pablo asked, frustrated by the string of incidents.

"Sir, this is personal. You may want to come back to receive the message."

Pablo closed his eyes and clicked the receiver. "Major, go to the secure channel and relay the message."

Pablo clicked the dial on his radio and waited for the major to come on. A brief moment elapsed before Major Silva's voice came over the airwaves.

"Emperor, are you there, over?"

"Go ahead."

"Sir, I regret to tell you, but we have received word that your father has had a major stroke. Your mother is requesting you come see him."

The transmission made Pablo sit straight up in his seat, his eyes wide with shock. Regardless of everything that had happened between him and his parents, he still loved them. They had never hurt him or wished ill of him; they had given him the best that life could offer.

"I'm heading to the command post now. Are you there?" Pablo spoke into the handset.

"No, sir, I'm at your residence."

"Good. Pack my things, and get your things together as well."

"Yes, sir."

Pablo turned to his driver and commanded, "Take me to the command post."

As the truck sped off, he thought about the situation. If his mother had requested his appearance it meant two things: one, his father was close to death, and two, they had forgiven him. He didn't know much about his father's condition but if he had one last chance to speak to him, he wasn't going to let that chance slip away.

McCall, Idaho

Samantha decided the best strategy for her and Haley during Gordon's absence was to carry on with their normal day-to-day plans. Every Saturday afternoon, she met with the other ladies of the McCall Women's Auxiliary. She found these meetings beneficial not only for the valuable information and skills they were taught, but also for the bonding. She was determined from day one to make McCall home and to fit into the community at large, and so she started the group. Word soon spread of how great it was and soon what turned into a handful of women meeting in their homes turned into dozens of women, and the meetings had shifted to a larger place. The owner of the Shore Lodge, a rustic, luxury hotel on Payette Lake, allowed them use of a large banquet room.

Samantha had just finished the meeting and was having casual conversation with Beth Holloway and a few other women when Haley walked up

"Mommy, I don't feel good," Haley said, coughing.

Upon seeing her flushed skin and watery eyes, Samantha jumped and attended to her immediately.

"Oh my God! Honey, you don't look good." She knelt down and placed the back of her hand on Haley's forehead. "You're burning up."

"My body aches," Haley said, grimacing as she tenderly hugged herself.

Beth squatted down too and said, "Does your throat hurt?"

Haley nodded and said, "It really hurts."

"What else hurts?" Beth asked.

"My whole body," she said, and began to cough hoarsely.

"I'm going to get her home. I'm sorry, I should've just stayed home when she first complained."

Beth turned and looked at the other women. "We should all call it a day. I'm not sure what Haley has, but flulike symptoms in the middle of summer is strange. I suggest we don't have the kids interact with each other until we know for sure what it is."

"I'm so sorry, Beth. She must have what Luke has," Samantha said as she gathered her things.

"What's wrong with Luke?"

"Dry cough, fever, diarrhea, body aches. It seems like the flu."

"Sickness is a part of life. The only thing we can do is get them better and hope no one else gets it."

Samantha nodded. "Thanks, Beth. We better head out. Please let the other ladies know that they should be on alert for these symptoms with their kids." With Haley in tow, Samantha rushed out of the Shore Lodge, her mind racing.

Warren Air Force Base, Cheyenne, Wyoming

A tugging pain in her lower abdomen jarred Annaliese from her deep sleep. Looking down she saw Sebastian, his head resting on the bed. She smiled at her husband, deep in sleep. She looked around the room, cognizant enough for the first time to take in her surroundings. It was your standard hospital room, with an old TV hung in the corner, two small chairs set against the opposite wall, and a small sink and cabinet next to them. They were very fortunate to have their own private room, especially considering how the need for care had skyrocketed with the volumes of refugees pouring into Cheyenne. In some ways, she felt bad because she was receiving special treatment, but wasn't about to refuse it. She knew everything she had received came with a hefty price tag, and she was grateful.

The tugging pain came again, this time like an electrical shock.

It made her wince and shift in the bed. The heart monitor on the wall recorded this as it beeped quicker with each flash of pain. Her movements woke Sebastian.

Seeing her awake, he widened his eyes. "You all right? Everything okay?"

"Yeah, just a bit of pain."

"Let me get someone," he said, jumping up.

"Wait, one second. Stay with me for a bit," she said, gripping his hand.

"Are you sure?"

"Yeah, it's only a little pain. I'll be fine. I want to talk with you."

Sebastian sat back down and looked at her with his concerning eyes.

"This might sound crazy, but what day is it?"

"It's Saturday, June twenty-seventh."

"Ha. Sorry, but I feel like I've been out of it for a while."

"Yeah, well, you have."

"Did we talk earlier or was that a dream?"

"I was wondering if you'd remember that. You seemed a bit groggy."

"Oh, no, did I say something stupid?"

Sebastian's eyes shone with sympathy as he tightened his grip on her hand and answered, "No, you were just mumbling some things. Nothing you should be concerned about. Don't worry; you didn't divulge any dark secrets."

"It seems like a dream."

"I'm glad it's just a dream and has passed now. It could have been a nightmare. You're going to be fine now, they removed the blood clot without complication, and now all you need to do is lie here, rest, and heal."

"Nothing is ever that easy," she said cynically.

"That's it, really! The prognosis is good. You just need rest."

She squirmed again as another jolt of pain hit her gut.

"Let me go get the nurse, I think you need another shot of pain meds," he said, jogging out of the room. He came back quickly, followed by a nurse who administered more pain medications via her IV.

"This might make her drowsy, which is good. The more rest, the better," the nurse said with a smile. "Is there anything else?"

Sebastian felt hunger pangs and needed to eat something. "Where can I get some food?"

"We have a cafeteria three floors down. I can have something brought up for you."

"If you don't mind, that would be great," Sebastian said. "I'd like to stay here with my beautiful wife."

"Honey, you can go, I'll be fine here by myself."

"No, I want to stay."

The nurse looked at the two as they debated, then winked. "I'll have something brought up," she said as she left.

"They're busy, why didn't you just go downstairs?"

"I'm not leaving you."

"You're silly, you'll have to clear your head and stretch your legs sometime."

"I will, just not now. You only got out of surgery this morning."

Annaliese closed her eyes as the pain meds began to course through her body.

"The pain meds look like they're already working," he remarked.

Not opening her eyes she answered softly, "Yeah, feels good." She reopened her eyes and said, "Any word from your brother?"

"No, but I should find out soon."

"I don't know how to thank him."

"I do. Bake him some of those lemon cookies."

"You think he liked them? They're so much better made with real lemons."

"Are you kidding me? He loved them. The lemon extract was a perfect substitute."

"I think he was just being nice."

"No, he really loved them; he couldn't stop talking about them."

"I was so embarrassed, I can't believe you made me serve them."

"Why? They tasted great. I can only imagine how they would taste with real lemons but considering what you managed to do with limited supplies, I applaud you. If you want to repay him, bake him a few dozen of those when we get back."

Annaliese's eyes grew heavy. "Okay, I'll do that. Um, yes, I'll make him cookies when I . . ." Her eyelids fluttered open and closed.

"Sweetheart, just get some sleep."

"Okay. I'm sorry, I'm just so tired."

She pressed her eyes closed but openly them quickly and said, "I love you, Sebastian."

"I love you too."

He watched as she breathed slowly, falling into a deep slumber. He took his hand and brushed some of her blond hair from her forehead and tucked it behind her ears. Standing, he planted a soft kiss upon her cheek.

The hum of the monitors was the only sound in the room, leaving Sebastian with his thoughts. He was worried about Gordon. If something happened to him, he didn't know how he'd face Samantha, much less Haley. He reached into his pocket and pulled out the card from Wilbur. Of anyone, she should know about the situation in Coos Bay. He picked up the phone on the table next to him. Surprisingly, there was a dial tone. He punched in the number and waited. It rang for a few moments until a voice he recognized answered.

"Hello?"

"Hi, this is Sebastian Van Zandt. Sorry to bother you, but you said to call if I needed anything.

McCall, Idaho

Nelson opened the door to The Bistro, a local hangout. The smell of smoke, baked goods, and coffee washed over him. Like Gordon, he had been invited to come and meet Charles, a representative from the Western Cascadian movement. For the most part, he stayed out of the local politics, but any excuse to get out of the house was enough for him, particularly after the struggle of the past few months. He had suffered greatly from the gun battle in Eagle, and for a time, it looked like he wouldn't make it. He felt blessed to be alive and promised to live his life with greater joy and gratitude. The death of his father hit him hard, but it was his mother who shouldered the brunt of the pain. Months had passed and she was still in deep mourning over the loss of her Frank. Many of her days were spent wandering their house in her nightgown. Nelson tried desperately to help with her depression but each attempt was countered with the same "Leave me alone" or "Let me be." Nelson didn't like conflict and after his attempts to soothe her failed, he decided to indeed just let her be. He went out of his way to make her life easy and effortless, but he stopped mentioning his father and her depression.

With his mother incapable of helping him while he was healing, Seneca jumped in and was there daily to clean his wounds, feed, and care for him. When anyone asked about his recovery, he always gave her credit. Ironically those weeks bedridden were some of the best he had ever had in his life. Each day was filled with countless hours of deep conversations, laughing, and tender touches. He sometimes joked that he had gotten better earlier but was just pretending so she'd be at his bedside daily. The selflessness she showed him endeared her again in his heart. It had taken him a long time to get over their breakup years before, but he never mentioned it and neither did she. He preferred to live in the present, rather than dwelling on the past.

Once he was able to get around again, he took the first chance he had to ask her out on a date. He thought it funny that even in a world turned upside down that romance was still alive and well. In fact, the intensity of the new world made romantic endeavors even more powerful because people never wanted to miss out on a chance to experience love. Not only did tonight provide him the ability to get out, it gave him a chance to see Seneca. It wasn't an ideal date, but then again, the luxuries of the past world weren't available. The Bistro was a hub, and the very least he could do was buy her a drink and enjoy her company.

Nelson surveyed the room. The volume was high with conversation, debate, and laughter. He had his judgments about the crowd but there seemed to be a fair representation of the town's people. Young and old, male and female all sat together discussing the political topic that brought them together: secession from the United States.

"Nelson, over here!" Michael hollered from across the room.

Nelson made his way to the table and sat down with Michael and another man.

"Want some shine?" Michael offered, handing him a tall glass of clear liquid.

"Sure."

"I'd offer you whiskey but I'm sure you know the joint ran out of everything months ago. The owner of the café now distills this. It's not too bad. Made with homegrown Idaho potatoes," Michael said.

Nelson took the half-filled tallboy glass and smelled it. The strong alcohol smell shocked his senses. The shine was absent of any specific taste, but it had a signature burn, and from what he had heard, a signature hangover if one indulged too heavily.

"Hmm, not bad, but I still like my Maker's." Michael raised his glass and they clinked glasses.

"This is Charles Chenoweth. He's from our movement in Olympia," Michael said, gesturing to a tall, bearded man to his right. He wore an old baseball hat that had the Doug flag emblazoned on it, the symbol of this movement.

"Nice meeting you, Charles. I'm Nelson," he said, putting out his hand.

Charles took Nelson's hand and shook it. "Nice meeting you too. Glad you could come out. Michael here has talked highly of you. He says you'd be a good asset to our movement."

"Not sure what Michael said to make you believe that, but I'm here to listen. I'm not joining anything just yet."

"And I appreciate that! I wanted you to meet Preston, a colleague of mine from Olympia, but he's not feeling well."

"So there are two groups in the movement, I've heard?" Nelson asked.

Michael jumped in and said, "We are equally focused on having independence for ourselves. We just differ slightly on how to accomplish that."

Charles grinned and responded, "I would agree with Michael on that."

Michael had invited Charles to come and visit to show a united front for the party. McCall had become the epicenter of the Cascadian Movement in the east. The factions had two distinct ideological, core-belief differences, but one common goal and that was independence for Cascadia. There were some differences on what physical boundaries constituted Cascadia. The western Cascadia included all of Washington State and parts of Oregon, Idaho, and British Columbia. The eastern faction agreed with those boundaries but wanted all of Oregon and all of Idaho. There were also strong divisions on how to approach the United States and Canadian governments with independence. Michael and many in the east wanted a peaceful and democratic separation but would be willing to negotiate a loose affiliation or confederation with the United States and Canada if need be. The west wanted nothing but a full separation and was willing to fight for it.

Michael was instrumental in establishing the foothold for Cascadia in the east. He was looking at elected office, but his dreams of power were not local but national. He felt it important to finally meet those leaders in the west and begin to formalize a relationship that could ultimately end with them merging under a common goal. He knew they needed the west to win their independence.

Wherever Michael went, he invited townspeople to come to their meetings. He felt that the more who listened, the more they'd convert to their cause. Before the lights went out, he rarely ever talked about the idea of seceding—for him it was a pipe dream. But as soon as everything changed, he saw the opportunity and grasped it. As each day passed without federal or state response, converting followers became easier and easier. At first people were resistant to change, but their patience was wearing thin as days became weeks and then months. No longer did he have to hard-close people on the idea of independence when all they had to do was look around and see that they were abandoned and left to survive on their own.

Michael knew Nelson and the others would be a great asset to their movement and hoped that if he could recruit Nelson, it would make it easier for Gordon to come along if both Nelson and Sebastian were applying pressure.

"Has Michael shared with you what Cascadia means?" Charles asked.

Nelson looked around the room for Seneca, who was supposed to be arriving any minute. He turned his attention back to Charles. "Yeah, he's mentioned it before."

"So, let me ask you, what can be wrong with it?"

"Listen, I know what I'm getting with President Conner and the government back in Cheyenne. With you, I don't know what I'll get in the end. I've seen too much to trust that the fix for the ills that exist is as easy as flipping a switch. Changing the name of our country and flying a pretty flag doesn't make things better."

"What you're getting with President Conner and his regime is more of the same. The government neglected us before all of this happened and now they're engaging in what can only be described as criminal neglect and abandonment. We have been surviving on our own for a long time now. Why not just make it official and be independent?"

Nelson was half listening to Charles as he kept looking toward the door.

"Am I boring you?" Charles snapped.

"I'm waiting for someone, sorry. I'm listening."

"Good, you invited someone else to come?" Michael asked.

"Yes, my girlfriend, Seneca," Nelson said, thinking that he liked saying the word *girlfriend* when referring to Seneca.

"Sorry to snap. I don't like to waste my breath. It's fine if you're not interested, just let me know."

"I'm curious, I am, really."

"Fair enough. Now, if you'll excuse me I'm going to start the meeting," Charles said, then stood and walked to the center of the room.

"Really glad you came out, Nelson, it means a lot. Sorry that Gordon couldn't make it. Where did you say he was again?" Michael asked.

"Not sure."

Michael wasn't one to press when he realized Nelson was not going to give up anything on his old friend. "No worries."

Seneca had snuck in unnoticed by Nelson. She sidled up beside him and planted a big, wet kiss on his cheek. Startled, Nelson jumped up. "Hey, so glad you came out."

Seneca hugged him and promptly sat down, seeing that the room was being silenced for the upcoming meeting.

"Michael, you've met Seneca, right?"

"Yes. Hi, Seneca."

"Hi. Um, what's this?" she asked, pointing at Nelson's glass.

"Kerosene."

"He's starting. Listen," Michael blurted out.

"Everyone, quiet!" Charles said loudly.

All eyes turned to Charles as the volume in the room went to zero. Nelson looked around. He estimated there were over seventy people in the main room; every chair and space to stand was taken, and there were more people out on the patio.

"Thank you all for coming tonight. Michael said the group looks bigger than last month's. For those new to our group, Cascadia welcomes you. It will take all of us here to enact the change we are looking for. Many of the new people here have come because you feel betrayed by the government, and you should. Like I have been saying since the day I helped found this movement, we can't trust those in the seats of power. Their only interests were themselves and their corporate sponsors. While the rest of us have fought each and every day to survive, those that allowed this to happen are doing just fine. Somewhere they are sitting in the comfort and safety of their bunkers. Their past transgressions brought this apocalypse and now they don't have to suffer from it. They knew it was coming; this is why they prepared for it to collapse. What they didn't factor into this collapse is that we are a strong people. We have now adapted to living without them, so with that knowledge the question begs to be answered, why do we need them at all? Why should we wait for them to crawl out of their bunkers to claim what is left? Here is my answer: We shouldn't. This is our moment to mobilize. We must organize, march forces on our state capitals, and not only declare our independence but seize it." Charles paused to take a breath.

The Bistro roared with applause.

"When Michael invited me to come to McCall, I jumped at the chance to meet our brothers and sisters who, like us in the west, are determined to live in a truly free country. I also came here to make sure we all can have a common approach to this. But before I go into detail let me first thank Michael for my warm welcome and the invitation. Michael, please stand, and everyone give this man a round of applause," Charles said, pointing at Michael.

The crowd again burst into applause accompanied by hoots and hollers.

"Our goal in the west is to march on Olympia on August fifteenth. There we will declare our independence from tyranny and send a message that we're creating our own independent state where human rights, the environment, social justice, and a fair trade economy will flourish. Cascadia will be a beacon to the world announcing that the days of a greed-based capitalistic economy are over. We will not destroy our environment, we will not pervert nature, but live within our means and within our ecosystem with the understanding that we're not dominant over it but take an equal part in it," Charles boomed.

The response was more tepid this time. Nelson took note of the less enthusiastic response; he himself felt uncomfortable with some of Charles's words. To him, it sounded like veiled socialism. If Nelson had a vision of independence, it didn't sound like this. He believed that government was a necessary evil and wanted it to come together for defense, to build roads and to staff police, and he even could get behind making sure the environment was protected; but when Charles attacked capitalism, he cringed.

Charles spoke for another fifteen minutes. He dove into how the new government would be structured under a parliamentary system and discussed a range of topics in depth, from defense to energy to a judicial system.

Nelson was impressed with how thorough and detailed he was; this showed him that the idea wasn't completely harebrained. But during Charles's speech, several items raised red flags for him.

Charles finished by saying, "I'm here to answer any questions so feel free to ask."

Only a few clapped their approval with Charles's speech. What started as a raucous chorus now suffered a blow of dispiritedness. Picking up on this, Michael jumped up.

"Charles, thank you so much for speaking tonight. Come on, people, let's give a hardier round of applause for our friend from the west," Michael said as he began clapping.

Luckily, Michael's following was loyal and did as he requested, but the excitement from earlier in the evening was definitely toned down.

Charles began to walk back to his chair but Nelson couldn't contain himself. He had to ask some questions. By now he had drank enough shine to make him a bit feisty.

"Charles, excuse me, Charles!"

Charles stopped in his tracks and responded, "Yes, Nelson, you have a question?"

"Yeah," Nelson answered. He looked around and decided to stand so he could be heard. "I have a question that I think others might have too."

"Sure, what's your question?"

"What type of economic system do you have in mind for Cascadia?"

A few others in the room nodded in agreement at question.

"Cascadia will have a fair trade economic system. We do not believe in free trade if it affects our people negatively. We also believe in fair market places. That is to say that anyone can grow, sell, or produce what they want; we want the government to oversee that marketplace to remove greed and manipulation."

"What does that mean?"

"Greed will not be a part of the fair market system. The people will determine the prices that will be fair and equitable, ensuring that all can afford and have access to them."

A few laughs erupted from the group.

"You want to regulate trade by going as far to price-fix products?"

"Yes, we will encourage trading or bartering, but the currency we create will not be based upon a gold standard or any type of commodity that one individual can own, control, or manipulate. Cascadia will control the value of the currency it uses."

"Charles, you're losing me here."

"I'm sorry you don't understand."

"Oh, I understand, it's just that you're losing my interest in this movement. You sound like a communist, and I can tell you I'm never going to support anything or any government that thinks that way."

"I can assure you, we're not communist. You can own or open any business you want. You can sell, make whatever you choose as long as it's priced with fairness in mind. We will take this fairness doctrine to include what you as a business owner will pay for the labor. We believe that a worker in your business didn't only work but has contributed to a business's success. The business will be required to pay an equitable portion of the profit on top of the fair wage."

Nelson began to laugh openly, and others in the crowd were now mumbling loudly.

Michael saw the tension building and quickly interjected, "Charles has an important meeting to get to. Charles, thank you for coming out."

Charles looked at Michael but was passionate about his beliefs and continued to talk. "I see nothing funny. We will provide a country that values justice, peace, and living within the sustainability of our ecosystem."

The crowd grew louder and Michael knew he had to calm it down. The differences that separated the two movements were front and center.

"Everyone, please be quiet. I want to thank Charles for coming all the way out here. He and those in the west have some different beliefs than we do, but we each need one another to execute a successful separation from the United States. You've heard me say it before. We are already independent of them; we have been for a long time now. We don't need some group of people who are foreign to how things work up in the northwest to tell us how to live anymore. The differences we have with our friends in the west pale in comparison to our differences with those in Cheyenne and Boise. We will work together to hash out these and come together."

Someone in the crowd yelled out, "Why? We don't need those in Olympia. Let's form our own country."

Others nodded in agreement.

"We need Olympia," Michael responded.

Crosstalk and yelling began to erupt from the crowd now.

"Everyone, please be respectful."

"What are you trying to do here, Michael?" a voice shouted.

"Everyone, please, no one is trying to do anything. Charles's group and ours have some different beliefs on some items, but we all have the same objective!"

It was getting difficult to hear as the shouting and loud conversations overtook the room.

Nelson turned to Seneca and shrugged. "Sorry. Not much of a date."

"Are you kidding me? This is fun! I'm just ready for the first punch to be thrown."

"Everybody, shut the hell up!" a voice bellowed over the others.

Chief Rainey, a latecomer to the movement, was standing on top of a chair near the front door.

"If this meeting is going to turn into a melee, I'll bring you all in on disturbing the peace."

The room went silent as all eyes were focused on the chief, his stocky build straining the small wooden bistro chair.

"Mr. Chenoweth risked his life to come here and visit us. He came here in good faith thinking that we're all in this together. You're not being good hosts if this is how you treat him. I heard what the man said and like many of you, I'm not in agreement with some of his ideas, but we need to be tolerant of others' beliefs. If any of us dream of the day of being a free country where our leaders understand us and are truly accountable, than we need to find a way to work together."

"But Chief—"

"I'm not finished talking, but when I am you can have the floor in a respectable manner. Let me conclude by saying this: I'm all for spirited debate, but it needs to be organized, otherwise we have a mob and many of us here know from firsthand experience what that can lead to. We have a wonderful community and we live in a beautiful place. I want to see it stay that way. This is why we need to have this work."

Rainey's face was a bit flushed from his speech. He hadn't felt such a passion since his wife was alive. He truly loved McCall and wanted to see the town flourish. Like many, he had been resistant to the idea of Cascadia, but after the weeks went by and no one from the federal government or state came to help, he understood their perspective. He increasingly felt that government or countries that grew too big couldn't effectively take care of their citizenry or understand their unique needs.

With the crowd subdued, Michael spoke. "Chief Rainey, thank you. I know many of you have questions and I want to answer them but I think we should postpone this meeting—"

A few groans and shouts interrupted him.

"We will adjourn for a few days. Once everyone has cooled off and is willing to talk in a respectful manner, we can continue these discussions."

Michael ignored the jeers and walked back to his table.

"Charles, I'm sorry about all of this, but as you can see we have a lively group."

"I'm fine, but we have a lot to discuss if we're going to move forward in a unified manner."

"How about we go back to my place for a couple of drinks?" Michael asked Charles.

"Sure. What did you all think of my little talk?" Charles asked, half joking.

"Do you really want my answer?" Nelson said.

"Maybe I don't."

"I dislike politics to the point of nausea. Please take no offense but I see Cascadia as becoming nothing more than a dictatorship closer to home than the one you say is farther away."

"I don't take offense. The world is full of people who take no interest in how their lives will be governed," Charles said.

"I don't think you can characterize us that way," Seneca said.

"Then what is it?" Charles asked.

"Maybe we just don't agree with you," Seneca replied.

"Charles, let's head back to my house," Michael prodded.

"You know, we're going too," Nelson said, turning to Seneca.

As Nelson drove home he reviewed the events of the evening. The more Charles's words marinated in his mind, the more he disliked the policies. If his strain of Cascadia came to power, it would make for a system that he'd strongly oppose. Maybe he would have to stop being so ambivalent about politics and get more involved. Charles was right when he said that some people don't take interest in how their lives are governed. When he looked deep inside, he was lazy that way. He'd complain but was never active in making changes to things that were imposed on him by politicians. Hell, he never voted and that was a simple action. But now, he could have a tangible effect on the trajectory of his future. Maybe he needed to get involved; maybe he needed to do something.

Cheyenne, Wyoming

Ever since Conner designated Schmidt to lead the division that would deal with the separatist movements, Baxter hadn't had a chance to sit down with him as secretary of defense to discuss it. He was curious as to what Schmidt had planned and didn't like being left in the dark. Knowing it was hard to peg him down at work, he drove out to his encampment on the outskirts of the city.

If he was being honest with himself, the truth was that Schmidt made him feel uneasy. Even though he was his senior and older he always felt intimidated by him, perhaps due to his ruthless reputation. As he stood outside his tent, he puffed up his chest and commanded himself to take control of the situation. He tapped on a wood sign that hung next to the front flap of the major's tent.

"Major Schmidt, it's General Baxter. You in there?"

"Yes, come on in."

Baxter walked into the tattered and old GP tent. A strong musty odor was the first thing he took in. He glanced around to see Schmidt sitting at his desk writing in his journal by the light of a candle.

"Major, sorry to disturb you unannounced."

"Quite all right, give me a minute," Schmidt replied, not lifting his head from what he was doing.

Feeling like an intruder, Baxter stood near the entrance.

Schmidt could feel this uneasiness so he blurted out, "Come on in, General, sit down."

Baxter entered the tent and took a seat on the far side of the tent. While he waited, he took in everything that was there. A large table covered in maps and papers sat in the center of the tent. Curious, he stood back up and walked over to it.

Schmidt looked over and cleared his throat.

Baxter took the hint but decided that he had every right to see what was on his table.

Schmidt closed his journal, stood, and asked, "General, what can I do for you?"

"You like a drink?" Baxter said, holding up a bottle of Jack Daniel's.

"No, thank you, sir."

"Not a fan of whiskey?" Baxter asked with a frown.

"I don't feel like drinking, sir," Schmidt answered, his posture stiff, as if he were at attention.

Baxter looked at the bottle and said, "This wasn't easy to find, I'll tell you. Maybe another day?" He put the bottle back in his bag.

"Sir, how can I help you?" Schmidt asked with a stoic face.

"This isn't really an official visit, more of a personal one. I just wanted to talk," Baxter said. The man's demeanor made him feel nervous. Behind his dark brown eyes was an intensity, a darkness.

Schmidt walked over to the table and began to roll up the maps and collect the papers.

"What is all of this?"

"Nothing, just maps and plans."

"For what?"

"I thought this wasn't an official visit, but a personal one."

"Major, you haven't reported to me or given me any indication of what you're planning as it pertains to these separatist groups."

"Right now it's not necessary. I'll brief you on anything that is pertinent to you."

Baxter took a bit of offense from his last comment so he shot back, "It's all pertinent, Major. I'm the secretary of defense."

"Actually, sir, according to the president, I have full control of this and don't answer to anyone but him. If I have anything that includes you or will affect you, I will bring you in."

"I can't believe the president would give you such blanket authorization."

"Sir, I don't want to get into a pissing match with you, but those are his orders. Many of the missions we'll conduct will be covert and secrecy is critical to their success."

"You'll need assets sometimes and that will have to go through me."

"General, I have my own people and if I need anything I've been instructed to go directly to President Conner."

Baxter was floored by this revelation.

"Is there anything else?" Schmidt asked.

Angry and confused, Baxter replied, "Nothing. I'll let you get back to whatever you were doing." He grabbed his bag and exited the tent. Once outside, he took a deep breath. He wasn't a man who liked to buck the system, but this he felt the need to challenge. For Conner to leave him and other senior staff out of critical decision making was foolish and counterproductive. Once inside his vehicle, he picked up the phone and dialed a number.

"This is General Baxter. We need to talk."

JUNE 28, 2015

· · ·

"All men can see these tactics whereby I conquer, but what none can see is the strategy out of which victory is evolved."

—Sun Tzu

Coos Bay, Oregon, Pacific States of America

Barone forced himself to watch as his men waterboarded Major Ashley. Before the lights went out, his opinion on the use of enhanced interrogation techniques was similar to many in the military—ambivalent. He saw the value from a theoretical standpoint, but never had witnessed it before. Now he could see why this was one of the top techniques. After only a few attempts, Ashley was divulging all he knew on the resistance. His information was being verified immediately, as timing was everything in this sensitive situation. Barone watched as Ashley was removed from the chair and escorted away to his cell. He shook his head at him. There couldn't be a greater disappointment than to have one of his most trusted officers turn against him.

Previously, the torturing of prisoners had usually been limited to male captives, but Barone was in support of implementing these techniques on women now. He needed to stop the resistance and if it required waterboarding a few women, so be it. The woman who would be the first unfortunate victim of this torture would be Brittany McCallister. During normal interrogations she refused to speak up; even the most vicious threats didn't cause her to budge. Barone was confident that this method would move her to speak.

Brittany was ushered into the large, dark room a few minutes after Ashley was taken out. Two Marines escorted her to the wet, wooden high-back chair and sat her in it. Her fear was evident as she began to tremble in anticipation of what was coming. Each man strapped her arms down and stepped back.

Another man, wearing a balaclava, walked in and approached her.

The sight of him sent chills through her body; her body began to shake uncontrollably.

"Brittany, do you know what's about to happen?" the man asked as he towered over her.

She looked into his dark brown eyes and answered, "Yes."

"We can avoid all of this. Do you understand? None of this needs to happen if you just tell us where the rest of the rebels are."

The temptation to tell them became enticing as the fear of what was about to happen shot through her body.

"Nothing? You have nothing to say?" the man said.

She closed her eyes and began to pray. Tears streamed down her face.

"Do it!" the man barked to the two guards. They stepped up and grabbed her arms.

"You have one more chance. Are you going to talk to us?" the man said, looking down on her.

Brittany kept her eyes closed; she couldn't bear to look at her torturer.

Barone was still in the room, hiding in the shadows, watching it all. As she walked into the room, he had the same inkling that he knew her from somewhere, but he couldn't peg it. He wondered if he'd seen her before around town, and her name and face somehow stuck. Maybe he had met her through his wife, but that didn't seem right. It seemed to him that he'd seen her . . . on the *Makin Island*. That clue sharpened his memory and he saw her vividly standing in the room with . . . Gordon Van Zandt.

The man took a thick towel and placed it firmly against her face and picked up a jug of water.

"Stop!" Barone yelled. He emerged from the shadows and walked briskly up to the man. "Stop!"

The man froze and sat the plastic water jug down and removed the towel.

Brittany breathed in deeply, as she had been holding her breath the minute the man placed the towel on her face. She opened her eyes to see Barone above her.

Barone looked into her eyes and asked, "You're friends with Gordon Van Zandt, aren't you?"

For the first time she answered a question about Van Zandt. "Yes."

"Did you know he just arrived in town yesterday?"

She looked at the Marines holding her chair down, then back at Barone.

Seeing this, Barone ordered, "Sit her up straight, then leave."

The Marines and the man in the mask obliged and left promptly.

When the large metal door slammed shut, Barone asked, "Did you know he was here?"

"No," she said, shaking her head.

"Do you know why he's here?"

"No, I don't know anything about it, I swear."

"Why won't you just answer our questions?"

"Because I can't. You'll use what I know to hurt the people I've grown to love," Brittany said sternly.

"What if I told you I was going to hurt Gordon? Would you tell me then?"

Brittany didn't answer, her mind racing. Why was Gordon here?

Had he heard that she was in trouble? Had he come to get her and Tyler? Was he really there? Was the colonel bluffing? All of these questions passed through her mind in a flash.

"Don't you have a child? I seem to remember a young boy with you," Barone said, his memory becoming clearer now that he had a greater recall of that moment in the sick bay of the *Makin Island* after Gordon had been wounded at Rahab's compound.

Brittany remained quiet. She knew Tyler was safe; she'd had him transported to a small farm on the outskirts of North Bend.

"I will find your boy, believe me."

"No, you won't, I can guarantee that," she said defiantly.

"Fine. I have Gordon, and you leave me no other choice but to torture him," Barone stated, walking off into the shadows.

The clang of the large metal door echoed off the concrete walls and floor as Barone opened it.

"Don't hurt him! I'll tell you anything you want, just don't hurt him!" she called out.

She heard Barone stop, close the door, and walk back toward her. He emerged into the light and stood in front of her.

"You'll tell us everything you know about the resistance in exchange for us not harming Gordon?"

She dropped her head in defeat and said, "Yes, I'll tell you everything."

"Good, but if you set us up or lie to us in anyway, I'll kill Gordon. Do you understand me?"

She lifted her head and looked at Barone, his hands on his hips. He stood like a giant above her. "I understand, but I do have another term."

"You know you're not in a position to dictate terms."

"I want to see him; I want to see him before I tell you anything, okay?"

Barone thought about her request for a moment. "We can arrange that," he said curtly, then walked away. "Clean her up and have her sent to a clean interrogation room," he ordered the man in the mask.

"Yes, sir," the man answered.

"And pick up Gordon Van Zandt and have him brought here as soon as you can. We're going to have a nice little chat."

Cheyenne, Wyoming

After being faced with their literature, Conner was anxious to discuss the strategy to break up the Lakotahs. He walked into the executive wing of the capitol and straight into his office. He had spent most of the night thinking over strategy, and the more he thought about the plan to eliminate the separatist groups, the more he knew he needed to bounce ideas off of someone besides Schmidt. That one person he knew he could trust would be Cruz. He grabbed the phone and dialed out to Cheyenne Mountain.

"This is President Conner; I need to speak with Vice President Cruz."

"Good morning, Mr. President, please hold."

The phone went silent for a moment, than a loud click sounded.

"Mr. President?" a different man asked on the other end.

"Yes."

"The vice president is on another line with your team up in Cheyenne."

"What?"

"Yes, sir, we patched him through this morning."

Conner didn't respond, he just hung up the phone. He had just spoken to Cruz yesterday, and he had never mentioned a call to anyone here. Curious as to what was going on, he stood and exited his office. He walked up to the conference room next door and grabbed the handle. Dylan was standing there looking sheepish.

"Good morning," Conner said.

"Oh, um, good morning, Mr. President."

"What's going on here?" Conner queried. Looking past Dylan into the room, he saw Baxter and Wilbur. On the phone he could hear Cruz speaking.

"Mr. Vice President, the president is here," Wilbur said, an edge apparent in her voice.

Cruz stopped talking.

Baxter stood and said, "Mr. President, good morning. Nice to see you."

"I guess no one is going to answer my question," Conner said. The guilty looks on all of their faces told him something suspicious was going on. He pushed himself passed Dylan. An uneasy feeling coursed through his body as the memories of General Griswald came front and center. "I know the business of government doesn't require me to be involved in everything but this doesn't feel right."

"It's nothing like you think it might be. I called them together because we are concerned about the separatist policy," Baxter said.

Conner kept a careful eye on everyone as he made it to his chair. He stood behind it and placed his hands on the leather and firmly grasped it.

"Brad, no need to be concerned, we're just worried that the policy needs to be open and more transparent," Cruz said.

"Dylan, close the door and sit down," Conner said.

Dylan closed it quickly, and meekly made his way back to his chair.

"Mr. President, we want to deal with these separatists—" Baxter said.

Conner shut him down. "General, be quiet," he barked.

"Brad, please don't be upset. We have the country's best interests at heart here," Cruz said, his voice reverberating from the center speaker.

"Andrew, give me a moment to let this sit. You know we have a history of intrigue and betrayal," Conner said. He thought about how to approach the situation. It really wasn't the meeting itself that disturbed him; it was the obvious nervous energy that he felt when the door opened.

The tension was high in the room as Conner sat silently stewing. Wilbur stared down at the blank pad of paper in front of her. Baxter had his hands clasped in front of him on the table, while Dylan sat nervously tapping his fingers on his leg.

"General Baxter, you said you called this meeting," Conner said, breaking the awkward silence.

"Yes, sir."

"Why?"

"Last night I drove out to talk with Major Schmidt, as I wanted to know more about his plans for the separatists. I hadn't heard anything and I was curious as to what he had in mind."

"Let me guess. He wouldn't share anything with you?"

"Correct. He said he was under your orders to not release any information. Is that true?"

"Yes, it is, and here's the reason why. The way we're going to deal with these groups will not be conventional. I will be asking him and his people to do things that will require the utmost secrecy, and if things go badly, I did it to protect my staff, give you cover, give you . . . plausible deniability."

"Brad, why would we need that?" Cruz asked.

"Mr. President, we weren't trying to hide anything, hence why we held the meeting here, in the executive wing," Baxter added.

A knock on the door drew their attention away from Conner.

Dylan jumped up and opened the door. To everyone's surprise, Major Schmidt entered the room.

Conner looked at the clock on the wall. His scheduled meeting wasn't for another hour. "Major, come in, please."

"Sir, I have something urgent to discuss with you," Schmidt said, his voice conveying concern.

"Go ahead."

Schmidt looked around at the table and then looked back at Conner.

Conner knew what the look meant. Still committed to the mission he had given Schmidt, he stood and said, "If you'll excuse me, I'll be right back."

"Brad, what is going on that we can't be privy to the information?" Cruz asked.

Ignoring him, Conner rose and began to walk toward Schmidt.

"General Baxter, what's going on?" Cruz asked.

"Sir, Major Schmidt just came into the room," Baxter answered.

Conner walked over to Schmidt, then leaned in and asked quietly, "Can this wait?"

"Yes and no."

"Which is it? Now's not a good time for this."

"I have been holding back something that I need to tell you. It's not time sensitive, but it's important."

"Wait for me in my office. I'll be there shortly."

Schmidt excused himself and closed the door.

Conner turned and looked at the three and said, "I understand everyone's concerns, but I need you to trust me. I need you to know that what I'm doing is in the best interest of the country. The more that you know, the more it jeopardizes what needs to be done."

"Sir, let me be the first to say that we do trust you. This was a matter of leveraging different ideas to ensure the missions you're about to conduct will be successful. There is no reason to isolate us from the planning," Baxter said.

"Mr. President, I agree with General Baxter. We do trust you, we just want to be able to help," Wilbur added.

Conner looked at Wilbur with a scowl. She was one of the reasons he didn't want to include anyone on the operations against the separatists—he didn't want it to become a debate. He deliberately chose to ignore her comment and asked, "Andrew, do you have anything to add?"

"Remember when you flew all the way to Miami months ago to ask me to become your vice president? You said you chose me because you knew you could trust me, and you can. I have always been there for you. I will never betray you. We may disagree about how things should be done, but once you make the decision, I will always back you faithfully. I think everyone here feels the same as me. Whatever you and Major Schmidt are planning, we can be a help to the overall success of these missions."

As he listened to his friend and vice president, he slowly walked back to his chair and sat down. He placed his chin in his hand and let everything that had been said sink in.

"Dylan, do you have anything to say?"

"Nothing, sir, I agree with what everyone else has said."

Conner took a long moment before he answered.

"You are right, all of you. I should be including you in these plans, and will be going forward, but I can't stress enough that it goes no further than us. What we're about to embark on is different than anything we have done before. We will deal with these groups in a way that will be unconventional and harsh. We don't have time to debate the actions we'll be taking; we cannot complicate it with disagreements about strategy. We will pursue these traitors and squash their plans for insurrection."

He paused and took a moment to stare at each one.

"In a sign of trust for you, I'll bring Major Schmidt into the room to discuss our plans. Dylan, please go get the major. He's in my office."

Dylan jumped up and left. Moments later he and Schmidt came back in.

"Major, please take a seat," Conner said.

Schmidt took a seat at the opposite head of the table. He was dressed in his faded green camouflage uniform; his 10th Mountain Division patches still adorned the shoulder of his uniform.

"Major, there has been a change. From now on you can discuss our plans with these three. No one else though will be allowed to know what we are doing. Okay?"

Schmidt nodded and said, "Yes, sir."

"Major, please detail what our plans are to date with dealing with the groups."

Schmidt offered few specifics about what he was doing but told the group that he had teams working on infiltrating the separatist groups that Wilbur had discussed earlier. When he concluded Conner asked, "Major, you came early to inform me of something important. I don't think you presented that information. Could you please share whatever concern you had?"

A flicker of unease was evident in Schmidt's eyes.

Sensing his reluctance, Conner pressed. "Major, it's okay, please share with us whatever you wanted to share with me earlier."

"Sir, it had to do with the Lakotahs. I think they're planning something that could pose a threat to you. I'm requesting we send in two kill teams to take them out."

Conner got the immediate sense that this wasn't truly the issue. For whatever reason, Schmidt was holding back, not wanting to present it in front of the others.

"Major, let's not do that. Increase my security, keep an eye on them, but let's wait for the rats to come into the open. We will proceed to track them for their rally soon."

"Yes, sir."

"So, is everyone happy now?" Conner asked.

All nodded.

"If that's it, let's get back to work."

Everyone stood and exited. Conner made a point to pull Schmidt aside. He shut the door to the conference room.

"Major, you can't bullshit a bullshitter. What did you really want to tell me?"

Schmidt paused briefly. "I have a bomb."

"A bomb! That's your big secret, a fucking bomb?"

"A nuclear bomb."

Conner's face lit up with shock.

"What do you mean *you* have a nuclear bomb?"

"We encountered a small group broken down on the side of the road a few months ago. They saw us coming and opened fire on us; we returned fire and destroyed them. When we searched their vehicle, lo and behold, there was a nuclear weapon."

"Why are you just now telling me this?"

"To be honest, sir, I didn't know what I was going to encounter when we first came to Cheyenne. There is a lot of distrust within my ranks of the government because of the perceived abandonment of the east."

"You have a nuclear weapon in your possession and didn't think to tell me or anyone about it?" Conner asked, anger in his voice.

"I'm sorry, sir, but that was the decision we made."

Conner walked away from Schmidt, angry and disappointed.

"Sir, I apologize—"

"That's it? You're sorry?"

Schmidt just stood watching Conner pace the room.

"Is there anything else I need to know about you, Major?"

"That's it, nothing else, except you need to have radiation detectors in place around the city. What if those people were coming here to use that weapon? No one would've known. It was by chance that we came upon them."

Schmidt's remarks hit home.

"You said they weren't American. Explain."

"After searching them we found equipment and documentation suggesting they were—"

"Let me guess. Venezuelan."

"Yes, sir."

"This confirms everything. They were the ones behind it all. They caused all of this," Conner said, holding out his arms.

"What would you like me to do with the weapon?" Schmidt asked.

Conner spun around and said, "Let's return it to its rightful owners."

Coos Bay, Oregon, Pacific States of America

Gordon looked at his reflection in the mirror. He bent over and splashed some hot water on his face. Water dripped down from this thickening beard. His pulled at the hair on his head, which was now the longest it had been since he was a child. He ran his fingers through the prickly hairs on his face and stopped when his hand touched the scar. Instantly his mind flashed to Hunter, then to Rahab plunging the dagger into his young son's chest. He blinked hard to erase the thought, but it was impossible to forget. Rahab was correct—the scar would forever remind him of Hunter and of the choices he was making in his life. He pressed his eyes closed hard and focused on Haley and Samantha; he focused on their smiling faces till he blotted out the grisly image of Hunter's dead body. He longed to hear their voices. The attempt yesterday had failed; the call had connected but there was no answer. He wanted to assume that the reason he didn't reach them was innocent and simple. Maybe she had the phone off or maybe she was taking care of something important and didn't hear it. He wanted to avoid thoughts of the worst-case scenario.

As he toweled himself dry, the door to the bathroom swung open.

Finley stood there, his clothes on and rifle slung. "Hey, your presence is being requested."

"Who's asking for me?" Gordon asked as he walked past him and into the berthing area.

"Some jarhead stopped by and said you're to report to the quarterdeck."

Gordon dressed quickly. He stepped past Finley and said, "I'll see you in bit."

"Fuck that, I'm coming with you."

"They didn't ask for you."

"I'm coming nonetheless."

Both men raced through the maze of passageways and ladder wells till they reached the quarterdeck, a space set aside next to the gangway that overlooked the dock.

Gordon approached a staff sergeant and said, "Hi, I'm Sergeant Van Zandt. I was told to come here."

"Van Zandt, you're to report to the police station. The Marine down there will take you."

"Roger that," he responded and began to walk down the gangway to the dock.

"Where are you going?" the staff sergeant asked Finley.

"I'm going with him, I'm—"

"You're not going anywhere."

"But I'm—"

"You were not requested. In fact, I was given specific instructions for you to stay."

"This is bullshit. I'm with Van Zandt there, I need to go!" Finley yelled as his temper flared.

"Sir, I'm only going to ask once. Go back to your berthing and wait for Sergeant Van Zandt to return."

Gordon turned and hollered, "Don't get your panties in a knot, I'll be back soon and hopefully we can leave after that."

He stepped off the gangway and approached the Humvee. Inside was a young lance corporal.

"Hi, I'm—"

"I know who you are. Let's go, I've been sitting here for over an hour," the lance corporal shot back, clearly irritated.

An amused look stretched across Gordon's face. He opened the door and climbed in. "Who am I meeting at the police station?" Gordon asked.

"A prisoner."

"Who would that be?"

"A woman is all I know. A resistance fighter we captured a few days ago."

Gordon stomach dropped. There was only one person it could be. "Is her name Brittany?"

"Yeah, I think that's right. Brittany McCallister."

Tijuana, Mexico

The rhythmic sound from the heart monitor comforted Pablo. Even though his father wasn't moving and his breathing was labored, the beeping reminded him that his father was still alive.

His mother sat on the opposite side of him, sobbing. Between her wails, she'd recite the rosary, ever the religious woman.

This was not the homecoming Pablo had imagined or wanted. For so long he dreamt of his father finally realizing how incredibly powerful his son was. He had always envisioned himself walking into his father's old office, victorious from battle. His father would tell him how proud he was of him. They'd embrace and his father would want Pablo to tell him in detail how he alone destroyed the greatest superpower the world had ever seen. Instead, he was stuck here, watching his father's labored breaths, knowing his once-powerful army was ever closer to destruction.

"Pablo," his mother softly said, breaking her silence.

"Yes, mother," he answered in a subdued tone.

"Thank you for coming," she said as she reached over and grabbed his hand.

"Mother, I'm so sorry for how everything—"

"Shh, not now, this is not the time nor the place. I'm just so glad you're here to say good-bye," she said, tears streaming down her face.

"I'm not going to be saying good-bye. He's not going to die," Pablo said. His tone was not convincing, and he knew it.

"Pablo, Pablo, your father is going to heaven. I know this is hard for you because of everything that has happened in the past. But you love him, otherwise you wouldn't be here," she said, squeezing his hand tighter.

Seeing his father lying there and his mother in deep emotional stress brought him close to tears, but he fought the urge.

"Pablo," a barely audible voice said.

He looked at his father and saw that his eyes were open slightly.

"Father, Father!" Pablo said jubilantly.

"Pablo, my boy," his father said, his voice just above a whisper.

Pablo leaned in to better hear him.

"Father, I'm here. Do you have something to tell me?"

And just as quickly as he had opened his eyes, they closed.

"Father, Father, wake up," Pablo said, his voice cracked with emotion.

Pablo kept talking to him with the hope that his father would wake again. This went on for two hours before his mother came over and put her arms around him.

"Do you want something? I'm going to step out for a moment," she asked him.

"Let's take him to the cabana on the beach. It was his favorite place. You know how much he loves the ocean air." While moving him was dangerous, they both knew it wouldn't change the outcome of the situation.

"Thank you," he said tenderly as he touched her hand. Gone was the monster that lived inside of him. His only focus in these moments was to comfort his mother and to enjoy his father's last moments on this Earth.

A tap on the door caused them to both look up. Major Silva stuck his head in, clearly embarrassed to interrupt the sensitive moment. He didn't say a word, but held up the phone for Pablo to see. At first Pablo was irritated by the disturbance, but he couldn't ignore his responsibilities. He was the emperor of an army on the verge of conquering the United States. He had to focus, knowing victory—or defeat—might lie ahead.

"Excuse me, Mother," he said softly, kissing her head.

He grabbed the phone. "Yes," he said briskly.

"Emperor, this is General Alejandro. I'm sorry to disturb you, but this matter could not wait."

Pablo walked down the hall till he came to a large study, the same one where he had concluded the purchase for his army from the

Venezuelan Minister of Defense and where his mother had declared that she would never turn her back against his father. His mother's declaration of loyalty to his father was a major turning point for him. He then knew he couldn't count on her, him, or most of his father's people in the cartel. He would have to do this alone and with his new army. It had broken him, as he had dreamt of his father next to him riding into battle, but that never came to pass. Soon after that meeting with his mother, he had seized power from his father and welcomed the army he now led.

"What is it?"

"Sorry to bother you, sir, but you instructed me to call you with updates."

"Yes, yes I did," Pablo responded.

"It is taking us longer to get the Villistas established and our forces were again hit by the U.S. Air Force."

"What is the damage?"

"Two tanks, three trucks, and twenty-three men were killed."

Pablo was frustrated. He hated not being with his men, but fate wasn't kind enough to sit back and wait. Accepting the realities of his situation, he said, "Just keep doing what you're doing. I'll be back soon."

"Sir, can I speak frankly?"

"Yes."

"We need you, sir. The men need their emperor. The sooner you can be back, the better."

Hearing this filled Pablo with pride. Finally he was receiving the respect and love he had always wanted from his parents.

"Tell the men I'll see them soon."

"Yes, sir."

"Is that it?"

"Yes, Emperor."

"Very well, good-bye," Pablo said, and hung up the phone. He reflected on what Alejandro had told him. Knowing that his men loved him made him feel responsible in a way that he had never felt before. He had to march on Cheyenne and kill every last one by looking them in the eye. However, the daily battering of his forces were taking a toll, and he know knew he would have to find an ally if he was to continue his conquest past the United States. His mind drifted once again to the question of what countries he could possibly align with. Given Conner's nuclear bombardment campaign months ago, Pablo's choices were few and far between, as many feared Conner and the United States, despite its weakened state. He would find a solution. Filled with pride and confidence, he exited the room headed to the one place that gave him the solace and space to find that answer: the beach.

McCall, Idaho

"Hi, honey," Samantha said to Haley.

She bent over and touched her forehead, feeling the heat radiate off of Haley's small body. The fever wasn't high enough to give her concern, but the dry cough did. She assumed she had picked up this sickness from Luke. He had only gotten worse since the day before, and it concerned Samantha. When she and Haley returned home from the Women's Auxiliary meeting, they found him in bed shivering from a high fever. His cough had worsened as well; it sounded like rattling in a cage. Samantha immediately put them both on a steady regimen of ibuprofen, but it didn't appear to be bringing down either of their fevers.

Using a cool washcloth, she wiped down Haley's hot skin. With each pass of the cloth, her mind went back years to Haley's first illnesses as a baby. Being that Haley was their second child, she and

Gordon weren't as worried when she got sick as they had when Hunter experienced his first illnesses. The first child always breaks a parent in and trains him. No matter how many books you read or how much advice you're given, many parents become nervous when their kids, especially their first, get sick for the first time. In the back of your mind, you know it's coming, and when it does it can sometimes feel like an out-of-body experience. She and Gordon would joke about how there were varying degrees of parental reaction to illness. There were the parents who, at the slightest sniffle, rushed their kids to the doctor only to be told what everyone already knew: The child has a cold, go home, get rest, and drink plenty of fluids. Then there was the group who never took their kids to see a doctor; it didn't matter if the kid was almost dead, blood coming out of their eyes, they believed that they had some type of home remedy that would fix them. Samantha and Gordon fell in the middle; only after trying everything at their disposal would they go and seek professional medical attention.

Her trip down memory lane was interrupted when a knock at the door echoed down the hall. Before she answered it, she wiped her hands down with antibacterial gel. She knew her chances of getting whatever the kids had wasn't high if she hadn't gotten it yet, but she couldn't take any chances.

She opened the door to see Seneca and Nelson, both wearing face masks.

She took a step back. "You're scaring me with those masks."

Nelson stepped in first. "I brought some masks over for you. I wasn't sure if you had any."

"How's Haley?" Seneca asked.

"She's as good as she can be with a fever, chills, and a bad cough. Luke is worse—he has bad diarrhea and his breathing is very labored."

"You're not alone in this, unfortunately. We've heard about quite a few other cases around town. People aren't panicked but they are definitely nervous," Seneca said.

"The man that Charles Chenoweth came with is now in the hospital," Nelson added, looking at Seneca.

"Charles Chenoweth?" Samantha asked.

"He's a representative from Cascadia. He came with a colleague who has apparently been hit hard. From what I heard, he has pneumonia now."

"How many others are sick?" Samantha asked.

"Not sure of the exact numbers, but it sounds like dozens," Nelson responded. "It's being monitored by the staff at the hospital. I'm just a bit worried about the respiratory nature of this thing. Would you mind if I go see Haley?"

"Sure, she's down in my bedroom."

Nelson nodded and took out a pair of latex gloves.

"First the mask, now the gloves? You're freaking me out," Samantha said.

"Not my intention, Sam. It's just a precaution. I can't afford to get sick—and neither can you. Here's an extra pair; use them, please."

Loud coughing came from the secondary bedroom where Luke was.

Samantha excused herself and went to him. There she found him lying on his side, his eyes closed. She approached the bed but stopped a few feet away to put on the mask and gloves.

"You awake, Luke?"

"I feel horrible. My whole body hurts," Luke mumbled.

"Can I get you anything?"

He mumbled something that sounded like no. His hair was wet from sweating. She reached over and brushed the hair out of his face and took the washcloth at his bedside and wiped his face. He shivered as she swiped the cloth across his cheek.

Nelson soon appeared behind her and said, "How is he?"

Knowing that Luke was slightly awake, she didn't want to answer. She placed the washcloth back and stepped into the hallway.

"He's worse than Haley, but that's probably because he's had this longer. I think Haley got it from him, and he got it from someone else. We need to track down the source."

"I'd help but . . ."

"No need to explain, your hands are full with taking care of your mom. Plus you're just getting back on your feet."

"I'm much better, thanks to Seneca, and my mom will be fine. I promised Gordon a long time ago that in his absence I'll look after you and Haley. I've done that and I will continue to do so."

"Thanks, you've been a good and dear friend," she said, touching his arm.

"It's what friends do, right? Plus, I might as well put all that EMT training to use. I know a few things," he said, winking.

"What would I do without you?" Samantha asked. She was truly grateful; Nelson was a rock.

"We'll go to the hospital and see if anyone else has been admitted with similar symptoms. Then we'll go see Chief Rainey. If anyone knows anything, it's that guy."

They chatted a bit longer, then she left.

When the door closed, Nelson looked at Seneca and said, "Toss the gloves and mask, and don't touch your face until you've washed your hands."

"Trust me, I will. The last thing I want is to get the shits," Seneca joked.

"I'm serious. I didn't want to alarm Samantha, but something's not right about this sudden onset of the *flu*."

"Now you're scaring me too." She paused. "Is there something you're not telling me?"

Nelson grimaced. "It might be the flu. I hope it's something as simple as that. But we have to prepare ourselves for the possibility that it could be something much, much worse."

Coos Bay, Oregon, Pacific States of America

Gordon sat in the small twelve-by-twelve-foot cinder block room. It was obvious this was some sort of interrogation room by its design and scarcity of furniture. The only thing on the wall was a mirror, which he knew was a two-way mirror. A skylight, the only source of light, cast a soft and yellowish glow. He marveled at how the Marine Corps, with all of its focus on precision and efficiency, still hadn't gotten past the annoying "hurry up and wait" problem. He shifted in the chair. The stainless steel seat provided no comfort, and after almost an hour waiting had become unbearable.

A Marine lance corporal stood guard inside the room. Gordon had attempted to make conversation but found out right away that wasn't going to happen.

The door to the room opened suddenly, and there stood Brittany. Gordon's heart seemingly skipped a beat at the sight of her. She looked exhausted. Her hair was greasy and pulled back into a messy ponytail. He saw several bruises on her exposed arms and neck.

Right behind her was a man who looked like an executioner; his tight black balaclava hid his face and his uniform was different from the others. He wore tan cargo pants and a black tight-fitted T-shirt. His large, muscular arms didn't show any tattoos or scars to identify him by. Forcibly he escorted her into the room and pushed her into the chair opposite him. With a deep, long glare, he studied Gordon.

"You like to hurt women?" Gordon snapped at the man.

The man didn't utter a word. He just took a place behind Brittany's chair and kept staring at Gordon.

"Are you all right?" he asked.

"I'm fine. You know me, not one to bitch and complain," she answered with a slight grin.

Her toughness, both mental and physical, was very attractive to Gordon; he couldn't deny it. More than once this valuable trait of hers had helped them while they had traveled together.

"How's Tyler?"

"He's fine, safe, nowhere near these goons."

"Good, I was worried about him."

She lifted her arms and shook the restraints and said, "I like jewelry but these aren't the bracelets I was hoping were in my future."

Gordon forced a smile. It was just like her to try to keep good humor in this awful situation. "I'm not going to ask what happened. It's obvious everything went to hell around here. I'm sorry. I shouldn't have left you."

"What are you apologizing for? I'm the fool. None of this would've happened if I just had agreed to go with you."

"What's going to happen to her?" Gordon asked the man in the mask.

He looked at Gordon squarely. "She'll be interrogated further, then she'll be tried."

Gordon knew the conclusion to those proceedings would be death. He had to get her out—he couldn't have another person's life on his hands. The only leverage he had was information. He made a snap decision: he would use that to set her free. "Tell Colonel Barone I need to see him immediately. I need to tell him something, something important."

"Don't bargain with these monsters. You can't trust them," Brittany pleaded.

"I have to try, and I will," Gordon said.

"I'll inform the colonel," the man in the mask said.

"But nothing can happen to her until I speak with the colonel. Colonel Barone and I go way back. I suggest you heed what I say."

"Please don't do anything, Gordon, this is my own doing. I already sold my soul just to make sure you were safe."

"What does that mean?"

"The colonel said he was going to torture you, so I promised to tell him what I knew in exchange for seeing you. There's no need for you to whore yourself out too."

"I promised you a long time ago that I'd take care of you. That is my word, my oath. You helped me several times and now it's my turn. That's what friends do."

Her eyes watered as he spoke. She reached across the table and took his hand. "I told you," she said softly.

"No touching!" the masked man ordered.

"Told me what?" Gordon asked.

"That you were a good man."

The masked man jerked Brittany to her feet.

"Easy, take it easy!" Gordon yelled as he stood up.

The guard took a couple steps toward Gordon. "Go ahead, do something," he taunted.

A devilish grin appeared through the hole over the man's mouth. "C'mon," he said as he forced her out the door. Just as the door was closing he hollered out, "Keep Van Zandt here till I get word back from the colonel."

Gordon didn't know where this would lead, and he didn't know what he would tell Barone. Conner stressed that he was to try to speak with Barone personally to get a sense of his mental state. He knew nothing would happen to Brittany until then. At least he had bought himself a small window of time to figure out exactly what he was going to say.

McCall, Idaho

When Nelson walked into the police station, his only hope was that he'd leave more informed. He had his suspicions about what was ailing Haley and Luke but he didn't want to jump to any conclusions and cause a panic.

"Can I help you?" a young police officer said behind the front desk.

"I need to see Chief Rainey."

"I'm sorry, but he's very busy today. He's in a meeting with the city council."

Nelson looked at his watch. "How long will it be? I can wait."

"We estimate it will be some time. I can take your name down so when he returns he can try to find you."

"Sure," Nelson said, then gave the police officer his name. He then exited and saw Rainey walking to his 1970 Chevy Blazer.

"Chief Rainey, wait!" Nelson hollered.

Rainey stopped and hollered back, "Hey, Nelson, what you got? I don't have much time."

Nelson jogged over to him. "Chief, I have some concerns about an illness around town."

"We all have concerns."

"So you're aware?"

"Of course we are. I just had a meeting with the city council and I'm headed to the hospital to see the mayor."

"The mayor's sick?"

"Yeah, he came down with it a few days ago. He can barely breathe. It's bad."

"What are they saying at the hospital?"

"Nothing right now. At first they were thinking it was some type of flu," Rainey said as he climbed into his vehicle. He was definitely in a hurry.

"I have some thoughts too, but I'm sure the professionals know better than me."

"Climb in, tell me on the way."

Nelson didn't need a moment to think about it. "Give me a second."

"Hurry up," Rainey answered as he put his vehicle in gear and began to back up.

Nelson ran over to his truck, where Seneca was patiently waiting for him. "Hey, I'm going with Rainey to the hospital. Follow me over."

"Okay."

Nelson ran back and climbed in the Blazer.

"What are your thoughts?" Rainey asked as he punched the accelerator.

"I was visiting the Van Zandts, and Haley and Luke have the same illness. At first it appears to be flu, but I'm thinking it's something different, I just feel it."

"Nelson, you're a smart guy and your gut instinct is right."

"So it's not the flu of some type?"

"It's not the flu for sure."

"Have they tested it?"

"Yes, they have," Rainey said as he made a hard left than a quick right. He pulled into the hospital parking lot, stopping the vehicle right next to the front doors.

"So what is it?"

Rainey got out and said, "Come with me."

Nelson followed right alongside.

Rainey stopped him just before they entered the hospital and said, "I don't know you as well as I know Gordon, but he trusts you, so I'll give you the same courtesy I'd give him. He's really talked you up. Says you're a solid man, a good man. I'm glad to see you're up and about now, considering you were a bit banged up when you first arrived."

"I don't think I ever told you, but thanks for everything you've done for all of us."

"My pleasure. Good people are always welcome here."

They both began to walk again.

"I hear you were a firefighter and an EMT back in San Diego," Rainey said.

"Yes, sir, I was."

"Then what you'll see won't make you too squeamish."

Nelson's heart was beating fast as they walked into the main hospital entrance. Inside, everyone on staff and those in the waiting room were wearing masks.

Rainey waved to the nurse at the front desk and proceeded down the main hallway. The sounds of coughing, hacking, and crying could be heard from the rooms that lined the hallway. Nelson couldn't help but feel a sense of doom. Rainey stopped just outside a hospital room and took out two masks. Turning, he offered one to Nelson. "I suggest you wear this."

There, Nelson saw the mayor lying on his side. Nelson knew he was asleep but he could have easily have been mistaken for dead.

"We brought him in several days ago. He was fine last week, then developed just a slight cough, then the fever, and bam, here he is. We've kept his sickness private for fear of people getting panicked. But this is spreading, no doubt about it."

"How many people has it affected?"

"At last count, over four dozen."

"Any idea how he got it?"

"It's all a guessing game. We had a visit from the governor's office early last week. He drove up here to talk with us; apparently the Cascadian business has them worried down in Boise. Anyway, he comes up, he was coughing and hacking. The poor bastard looked like shit from the moment he arrived. He's now down the hall. They say he might not make it, something about renal failure."

"Have you contacted Boise?"

"Of course we have; they're the ones who did the test."

"Chief, I think this is some kind of major respiratory illness. Please tell me the test they took say it's not."

Rainey just looked at him and didn't answer.

"What are we dealing with?"

"It's nothing they've seen before, but it does resemble something."

"What's that?"

"MERS."

Coos Bay, Oregon, Pacific States of America

Barone donned his tactical vest and loaded his magazine pouches. It felt good to be getting dressed for battle. He hadn't informed anyone of his plans to accompany his men on the final raids of the evening, so he imagined his presence would motivate them. He couldn't resist going; the information that Brittany had provided them was more valuable than Major Ashley's. This last set of raids would wipe out the remaining rebels.

A loud knock at the door was followed by Simpson calling out, "Sir, I need to speak to you!"

Barone walked out from behind his desk and opened the door. "I'm going on the raids tonight," Barone said, with a proud look on his face.

"Sir, I really have to protest. We can't risk losing you."

"Julius Caesar didn't sit on the sidelines. He rode into battle with his men and so will I."

"Can I recommend that you draft a chain of succession in case you die?"

"Top, since when did you become such a worrywart?" he asked, patting him on the shoulder.

Knowing he'd never win the debate, Simpson pivoted the conversation to another urgent topic: Gordon Van Zandt.

"Sir, you're supposed to meet with Van Zandt. Don't you remember?"

"That can wait till tomorrow. Tonight I'm going to have fun," Barone said as he gathered more gear.

"Sir, he has information about President Conner. He says it's very important."

Barone looked at his watch then said, "Two hours till we go green, not going to happen. I'll meet him first thing in the morning."

"I'll set the meeting for zero nine hundred," Simpson said, a tinge of defeat in his voice.

"Sounds good. On your way out, tell my guards to go get some chow. I want their bellies full for tonight's raid."

"Roger that, sir," Simpson said and exited.

Barone was tempted to take a drink, but resisted the impulse. He wanted his mind and senses clear for this battle. On his way out of his office, he stopped and examined his reflection in the mirror. "Looking good, Devil Dog! We're going to kill some fucking rebels tonight!"

Cheyenne, Wyoming

With Schmidt as his new weapon, Conner felt confident that success was around the corner. All the obstacles and distractions that prevented them from getting on top of reconstruction would soon be resolved. Equipped with the knowledge that Pablo Juarez planned to use a nuclear bomb against them in Cheyenne made the decision to use one himself much easier. The internal debate that had been raging was over.

Ever the realist, he knew that unpredictable events would still occur, and today was no exception. Conner's mid-morning briefing was interrupted with the news that a pandemic of what appeared to be a MERS-type coronavirus had hit Idaho. The virus had broken out in Mountain Home Air Force base, which was operating as the temporary state capital for Idaho. To date, they had no deaths but hundreds had become sick. Wilbur reported to Conner that it had spread up to McCall, where a smaller outbreak was under way. Conner was disturbed by the news, but he also saw it as an opportunity to remove another threat: the eastern Cascadians.

"Excuse me, Dylan."

"Yes, Mr. President?"

"I need you to do something. It's important."

"What can I do for you, sir?"

"Please find Major Schmidt. I've tried to contact him, but he's been unresponsive."

"I'll get right on that, sir."

Conner walked to the window and looked out on the city below. The town was alive with activity. With his approval, he had allowed more and more people to come into the green zone. It was a slow process but the quicker he could integrate the refugees, the more vibrant the city would become. The growth was explosive but necessary. He began to call Cheyenne the Shining City—a beacon of hope to the many who had no home. It would be a symbol of a new America, a new republic. The one thing he needed to do was stop those hell-bent on dividing and destroying it. He knew that if he pulled it off, he could be that leader in history books who had a truly transformative effect.

He spotted a young woman pushing a stroller, her dark hair pulled back with a blue bow. Every few feet he could see the baby's hands grab at the toys that dangled from the mobile over him. How innocent and sweet, he thought. If he could accomplish his goals, that child would never know the horrors that he and so many had seen. Seeing the baby made him think of his son and the child he would never meet, the little baby that had never been given a chance to live. It pained him even more to think of Julia, his wife and trusted partner for so many years. If she had only held on for a few more days, she'd be alive.

Schmidt finding the loose nuclear weapon brought the entire conspiracy into stark view. He now had the name of the man who caused him and his family—as well as the rest of the nation—unfathomable pain. Conner's urge to capture the brutal dictator was unlike anything he had ever felt. Violence coursed through his veins. He fantasized about standing before the man who was directly responsible for murdering his family and taking his life personally. But the sensible side of Conner knew that such an operation could jeopardize the plan of destroying the entire PAE army. Conner would be victorious and see Pablo and his army vanquished, but he would have to let his selfish desires go. The plan was in motion and soon it would be realized. The old saying came to mind: "Live by the sword, die by the sword." This is exactly what would happen to Pablo Juarez, the self-appointed emperor of his mercenary army. Conner would ensure he died by his sword.

A grin crossed his face as he continued to watch the mother and baby. She stopped the stroller and was cradling the baby in her arms. Right there in front of him was his purpose, he thought to himself. He must win for that little baby, for all of the youth out there. For the future. He had to be victorious over all that threatened them.

A tap at his door pulled him away. He spun around and hollered out, "Come in!"

The door opened to reveal Schmidt in his customary faded uniform.

"Take a seat, Major. I have an idea, a good one. You'll be jealous that you didn't think of it yourself." Schmidt nodded and sat across from him.

"Let's get to business. Major, we might have an opening in Idaho that wasn't there before. There's some type of pandemic that has broken out in Mountain Home and has spread as far north as McCall." Conner briefed him on the pandemic and his idea for using it as a way to roll a military unit into McCall to deal with the Cascadians.

"I'll have a plan by tomorrow or the next day," Schmidt said, standing up.

"Good man. How's the other op going?"

"It's in motion now, sir. The package will be delivered in a few days."

"Excellent, excellent. That's it, Major. Have a good night. In fact go get a drink on me at Pat's. Put it on my tab."

Schmidt nodded and exited.

Conner walked back to the window and looked out. The woman and baby were now gone, but what was not gone was his passion for making sure they would have a life and a country.

Warren Air Force Base, Cheyenne, Wyoming

"Oh my God, all this time together and you never told me," Sebastian cried out with laughter.

"I didn't want to. I don't know, it doesn't bother me too much. I just roll you over and you stop once you're on your side," Annaliese said, a smile gracing her tender face. Her recovery had progressed much faster than the doctors had projected. Soon she and Sebastian would be able to go home.

"No one ever told me I snored! I figured I did now and then, but you make it out like I'm registering on the Richter scale."

"Um, yeah, it can be bad, especially after you've had a few drinks. But I don't mind, really. You're easy to push over."

"What, now you're calling me a pushover?" he teased her.

"You know what I meant," she said, pinching his arm.

"Ouch! God, you're always hurting me—now you're beating me up emotionally too!"

"Stop! Me, hurt you? I can't, you're a big strong man. I wouldn't have married you otherwise."

Sebastian was lying next to her on the bed and went in for a kiss. As he pulled away, he realized he couldn't imagine a life without her. She truly was his soul mate. If anything positive could have come from the horrible events, it was his finding her.

"I love you so much. You're so beautiful," he said as he placed his lips gently upon hers.

She returned his kiss with a bit more passion.

"I love you too, Sebastian Van Zandt. I know this is corny but you're my prince charming. I dare any woman dispute that when they were growing up they didn't want a handsome prince to come and sweep them off their feet. You were that man; although you didn't come in on a white stallion."

"Actually it was a stallion, a sea stallion."

"Huh?"

"The helicopter, the one I crashed in, it was a sea stallion."

"Well, I guess I stand corrected, my prince did come in on a stallion, but I kinda swept you up with your broken leg."

"I'm not a stickler to following all the societal rules anyway. I liked that you swept me up," he said, then laughed. "Thank God you did sweep me up."

"You have to thank my father for that."

"He was a good man. I didn't know him long but I could feel the goodness in him. He was a special person."

Annaliese grew quiet as she thought of her father. After a long pause, she said, "He was a great man. . . . I miss him."

Sebastian leaned in and kissed her again. This time she didn't return his kiss. The expression on her face told him that her mind and heart were now with her father.

"Do you think my mother's okay?" she asked.

"I'm sure she's fine. One of your uncle's positive traits is that he's prepared. She's not in need of anything, that's for sure."

"You're right. I'm sure she's keeping busy with my brother and sister."

"Knowing your little brother, he's probably already taken over control of the place. He's a character, that one."

"Do you suppose I'll ever see them again?"

"Yes, I do. I do think you'll see them again one day," he said as he caressed her face.

A moment passed. They embraced, then she broke the silence with a question. "How is Gordon?"

"I spoke to Secretary Wilbur yesterday and she told me everything appears to be going well. They don't have a timeline on when they'll leave, but he's fine. I worry about my brother, but then I remember that he's my brother, and he's as tough as nails. I swear nothing will kill him. Even if he did die, God would take one look at his crusty ass and send him back."

"Don't say such things."

"I'm not saying anything Gordon wouldn't agree with."

"Gordon's a good guy. I really like him and Samantha. . . . Actually I love them both, they're family."

"Yeah, Gordo's a good guy. He's always been there to help me, no matter what. He always looked out for the little guy or the underdog. He's never been afraid of a fight. When we were younger, if he saw a smaller kid being bullied by older kids, he'd step right in and defend

the smaller one even if it meant throwing punches," Sebastian recalled, a slight grin creasing his face. "I never told you this story, but
there was this one kid, I think his name was Samuel, or maybe it
was . . . either way doesn't matter. Well, the kid was in special ed in
Gordon's freshman class. These boys, seniors, were picking on him.
Gordon saw this and immediately stepped in. Of course the three
seniors thought they could bully Gordon too because he was a freshman, and, well, they bargained wrong. One thing my old man always told us growing up was don't start a fight unless you have to. If
there is no way out and a fight goes down, be the first to strike.
Gordon was a good listener for sure. He struck first, hitting the first
boy straight in the nose. From what I heard, Gordon just started
whaling on them, one punch after another until the three seniors
were down. Then like nothing had happened and as cool as ice, he
picked up Samuel's stuff and escorted him to the bus. Needless to
say, those boys never messed with Samuel again."

"Your brother strikes me as a defender, a sheepdog type."

"He definitely is the sheepdog keeping the wolves at bay."

Annaliese reached and turned his face toward hers. She touched
his eyebrows, cheeks, and then leaned in for a kiss. After the kiss she
scratched his beard and asked, "How long do I have to be tortured
with this?"

He scrunched his face and asked, "What, you don't like the look?"

"Ahh, I do, but if given a choice I think I want baby-butt smooth
face over prickly, hairy face."

"What will you give in exchange for one baby-butt smooth face?"
Sebastian joked.

"Umm, how about a big wet kiss?" She giggled.

They kissed and laughed.

"You must be needing to go out and stretch your legs. I know you
have to be curious as to what's happening here," she said.

"I'm fine, don't worry about me."

Sebastian was curious; he did have a desire to see Cheyenne.

"Honey, please go ahead, go out, take a look around," she pressed.

He looked at her and answered, "Okay, since it's so important to you."

"It is important to me. I'm fine here, go out and see the sights."

"Fine, fine, I'll go out tomorrow, okay?"

"Good. Now let's get back to you shaving that face," she teased.

JUNE 29, 2015

• • •

"Everyone has a plan till they get punched in the mouth."

—Mike Tyson

Coos Bay, Oregon, Pacific States of America

It was early but Gordon was awake and pacing the berthing space, nervous about his upcoming meeting. After Barone sent word last night that he wasn't meeting with Gordon until this morning, his men took them back to the ship. He and Finley were under house arrest. They weren't allowed to go anywhere except the mess hall, and even that had to be under the watchful eye of two guards.

Finley groaned as he stretched. "My body aches. Christ, these beds fucking suck."

"Stop the whining. That's all you do. Suck it up, would you?"

"Fuck off, Van Zandt. God, you're such a stress case. By the way, who is this woman?"

"She's a friend."

"Bullshit, no one is willing to go as far as you have for a friend. You must have been sticking your dick in her," Finely chided.

"Go fuck yourself!" Gordon snapped.

"Fuck you!"

Gordon's temper flared and he stormed over to Finley. He put his face in his and said, "Say something else, go ahead, motherfucker, say something stupid. I'll fucking ruin you."

Finley stepped back; a surprised look gripped his face.

Gordon's anger had reached a point that he was truly willing to beat Finley to a pulp. He was tired of people accusing him of having relations with Brittany; he was tired of the comments and innuendos. Fortunately for Finley a knock on the berthing hatch saved him from getting pummeled.

Gordon walked away from him toward the hatch, his fists clenched. He opened it up to see two Marines.

"Colonel Barone can see you now," a Marine lance corporal said.

"Let me get my gear," Gordon said.

Finley quickly put on his trousers and grabbed a few things while Gordon was gathering a couple of items. They both met at the hatch at the same time.

"I don't think he asked for you," Gordon said snidely.

"Incorrect, the colonel wants to meet him too," the Marine said.

Finley shot Gordon a look.

"You won't need those," the Marine said, pointing at the men's pistols that were nestled in their shoulder holsters.

Gordon and Finley looked at each other and reluctantly removed their holsters.

"Let's go. The colonel is waiting."

McCall, Idaho

Samantha defied Nelson's recommendation of embracing the children. She couldn't stop herself from holding Haley. She went along with his instructions as far as wearing her mask and gloves, but

Haley's cries and pleas were too much for her to say no to hugging her child. She rocked her little limp body and sang her lullabies—anything to ease the pain, even just a little.

Nelson had paid a visit late last night with the news he had learned from Rainey. Because there wasn't a cure, the kids would have to suffer through the symptoms until it passed. He had been honest with her about the probable prognosis from other coronaviruses like MERS. When she heard that thirty percent of those who contracted MERS died from complications, it frightened her to action. She immediately called the number Gordon had given her. However, no one answered. Again, she was left alone to fight for Haley's life, and like before, she was determined to prevail.

"Hush little baby, don't say a word, Momma's gonna buy you a mockingbird," she softly sang as she rocked Haley. Haley's movements were slow, as fatigue was a large part of her symptoms too. Just the effort of lifting her arm took everything she had.

The temptation to take Haley and Luke to the hospital crossed Haley's mind, but without a real treatment she didn't see a reason to do so. She could do just as much good by monitoring and providing comfort at her house than at a hospital surrounded by other sick people.

Like usual, Nelson arrived on time. If he was ever accused of anything, being prompt was something that all could agree on.

She laid Haley gently back into the pillows and brought the blankets and sheets up to her chin. Brushing her sweaty head, she said, "I'll be right back, sweetheart." The only sound that Haley emitted was a series of loud coughs.

Samantha stepped into the hallway to see Nelson dressed head to toe in blue hospital scrubs, booties, latex gloves, and a mask.

"Look at you," she joked.

"I can't take any chances."

"I know, you're smart. I, on the other hand, can't help but hold them."

"Sam, you can't do that, you can't risk getting sick," he admonished her.

"It's the only thing I can do. You said there's no cure so all I can do is ease their symptoms, and one of those is emotional stress. They need me and I need to be there for them."

He sighed. "I can't argue with you on that. So, how are they?"

"Haley has gotten worse; she now has diarrhea and her cough is bad. I can actually hear the mucus in her lungs. Luke seems to have stabilized, though. I don't know if it's something to celebrate yet but I'm thankful he's not worse. His temperature hasn't gone above 103."

"That's good news."

"Let's go into the great room. It's so dark in the hallway and with you looking the way you do I feel like I'm in a horror movie."

They both made their way into the room. The sun's morning light cascaded through the massive east-facing windows. It was the views out those windows that sold the property for her years before. Standing in the orange light was Seneca; she had become inseparable from Nelson ever since the outbreak.

"Hi. I didn't know you were here," Samantha said.

Like Nelson, she too was adorned with protective gear and clothing. "Hi, Sam."

"I'd give you a hug but something tells me you wouldn't appreciate it," Samantha joked.

"Ha, no thanks," Seneca cracked.

Samantha walked passed them both and into the kitchen; she took off her gloves and removed the mask she had been wearing. She poured water from a pitcher over her hands and applied soap and began scrubbing her hands and forearms.

"I haven't totally abandoned your advice," she said, lightly mocking.

"You wouldn't be laughing if you got this," Nelson said with a serious tone.

"Anything new since I saw you last?" Samantha asked, now toweling her hands and arms dry.

"I stopped by and saw Chief Rainey on my way over this morning. The government rep from Boise died late last night." Nelson's schedule had turned into a routine of seeing Rainey in the morning, followed by Samantha, and then in the evening he repeated the process, if possible. He felt it important to bring Samantha the most up-to-date information as possible before making his visits.

"Oh my God."

She sat back on a tufted ottoman. The lack of sleep showed on her face. Her eyes were bloodshot with dark bags under them.

"I want to ask you about any possible natural remedies or holistic medicines we should try."

"Sam, we're not going to cure this with oregano or any other essential oils. This is serious. If it was so easy to cure MERS, SARS, or any other type of coronavirus it would have been done by now," Nelson said in a condescending tone.

"How do you know that?"

"Samantha, I never figured you for one of *those* types," Seneca quipped, trying to lighten the mood.

"What type is that? The one doing whatever she can do to keep those two kids alive in there?"

"Are we going to have this conversation? The best thing we can do now is hope that Boise can come up with something or you can reach Gordon and he can get direct help from Cheyenne," Nelson chimed in.

"I can't sit here and put the fate of Haley and Luke in someone else's hands. I need to try something, anything, that can at least alleviate the symptoms so it doesn't progress to pneumonia or any of the other complications. I have to try."

"While you're trying with those natural remedies, please keep trying Gordon. I think you have a better shot there."

"I'm not giving up on hoping he can help with Cheyenne, but in the meantime I'm going to talk with some of the ladies at the auxiliary, put our heads together."

"You do that."

She ignored his sarcasm. "Can you both do me a favor?"

"Anything."

"I need you to watch the kids later when I do meet with them."

Nelson didn't hesitate. "Of course, not a problem."

Loud coughing erupted from Luke's bedroom followed by a bellow. "Aunt Samantha, help!"

Samantha and Nelson ran down the hall and into his room. She approached the bed but Nelson held her arm. She turned and shot him a look.

"Put this on. Humor me, please. You're no good to anyone if you get sick," he pleaded.

Knowing he was right, she quickly put on her masks and latex gloves.

Luke coughed several times. His entire body shook when he did. Both she and Nelson could hear the large volume of mucus in his lungs.

There wasn't much Samantha could do other than provide comfort. She rubbed his back and whispered something unintelligible.

Taking a deep breath, he looked at her, tears in his eyes. He held up the hand he had been coughing in.

Samantha's eyes grew wide.

"Nelson, he's coughing up blood!"

Cheyenne, Wyoming

Dylan rarely showed anger, much less contempt, but after Conner told him the plan to restore the legislative and judicial branches of the government would be put off indefinitely he had to tell Conner exactly how he felt.

"Sir, you promised. You not only promised everyone on your staff but you promised the people that you'd bring back the two other branches."

"There's no time for it."

"Yes, there is. You don't have to be involved in the process. In fact, sir, you don't need to involve yourself in every detail about everything. Delegate and let your staff do these things," Dylan said, his voice elevated.

"Dylan, I don't have time for debate on every issue. Now is not the time to have a legislature sit around and possibly block or slow down what I'm trying to do. What I'm doing is too important."

"Sir, all I hear is *I* and *me*. This isn't about you, this is about providing a sense of stability to the people."

"I am providing them stability, and that stability will increase if we stick to my plan."

The door to his office flew open. An excited Baxter walked in.

Conner and Dylan looked up, startled by Baxter's unannounced entrance.

"What the hell?" Conner shouted out.

"Sorry, sir, no time for pleasantries," Baxter said.

"Dylan, please leave," Conner said.

Dylan walked out quickly.

"What's wrong with you? You barreling in here surely gives people pause that something's going on. Next time, be more tactful."

"I tried to call, but these damn phones keep failing. Our friends from the Republic of Lakotah are holding a large rally, and I mean large."

Conner looked at his watch then said with a slight smile, "Perfect, right on time."

"They managed to organize inside the green zone and are heading here, toward the capitol."

Conner opened his desk drawer, pulling out a small pistol. He tucked it in the waistband in the small of his back.

Baxter looked confused. "What's that for? I've never seen you carry. You're not thinking of going down there, are you?"

Conner ignored his question and picked up the phone. The phones were dead. He placed the receiver down and picked up a handheld radio.

"Major Schmidt, this is President Conner."

After a few moments of silence the radio crackled to life.

"This is Schmidt, go ahead, sir."

"Our guests have arrived."

"Roger that, sir."

Conner pocketed the radio and began to make his way to the door.

"Sir, you can't go down there. This group might be looking for a fight."

"General, if it's a fight they want, we'll give it to them."

"Please, sir, it's too risky."

"General, you can't lead a country sitting behind a goddamn desk!"

Tijuana, Mexico

The move to the beach house was successful, while unadvisable by the physicians. Pablo's father had now fallen into a coma, and the conversation about him shifted from his quality of life if he awoke to how best to let him go. So many family memories had been created at this house over the years. One of the first things Pablo did after arriving late in the night was to walk along the beach. Along his walk he thought about his life and how in an odd way he had been blessed. It was his own prodding that forced his father to in-

clude him in the "family business." So often his father told him he
wanted to see Pablo live an ordinary life. He had created wealth, not
ordinary wealth but true generational wealth. Pablo could have done
whatever he chose to do. He could have followed his father's wishes
and gone on to do something legitimate and safe, but his own desire
for approval went beyond a father's recognition for simple accom-
plishments. Built upon a deep-seated insecurity, and to show his
father that he could be a "greater" man, he went in the direction that
led him to the battlefields of America.

As he walked the beach, he wondered for just a moment what it
would feel like to walk away from it all. To live an easier life. To live
by the ocean, spend his days relaxing rather than planning for battle. He picked up a handful of sand and let it fall through his fingers.
But he reminded himself that the easy path was not the best one. He
was on a path that he couldn't turn back from now. He didn't have
the luxury to doubt himself—not now. He wiped his hands off and
went back to make the final arrangements for his father and his
army.

· · ·

Walking into his casita, he discovered that the cool ocean air had
blown through like a whirlwind, tossing papers and flipping pages
on books he had opened. He closed the doors, arranged the papers
on his desk, and noticed the red blinking light on his phone. He
called the last number that had called him, and the familiar voice of
General Alejandro answered.

"Emperor, hello."

"You called?"

"Yes, sir. Bad news. We lost contact with our team headed to
Cheyenne."

Pablo clenched his jaw. "Is this confirmed?"

"No, sir, but it's been a long time since we've heard from them."

"What does that mean, a long time?"

"We lost contact with them weeks ago."

"Weeks ago! Why am I just hearing about this now? I was told the weapon was in place in Cheyenne!"

"I just found out myself. Captain Garcia, the officer in charge, didn't want to say anything for fear of being reprimanded. He sent several teams out looking for them. This happened without anyone's approval and they've returned with no new information."

Pablo bit his lip. "I need you to turn those teams around and send them back out. Am I making myself clear? We must find them."

"Yes, sir."

"As far as our other forces, have you brought them inside Elko?"

"Yes, sir, and that appears to be stopping the U.S. Air Force from striking. They're afraid of collateral damage and civilian deaths."

"How are our forces to the south?"

"Good, sir. The United States hasn't struck them. In fact, it appears they're not aware that we split off units."

"That won't last. General, we need to move on Salt Lake City now. We can't wait for the Villistas to get up and running. Elko is not a strategic location. How many days do you estimate it will take us to get to the outskirts of Salt Lake?"

"Three days, sir."

"Three days?"

"That's the estimate for the entire army, including our forces to the south. That takes into account mobilizing the army to move."

"Understood. I'll meet the army outside the city. Do not move on the city till I arrive."

"Yes, sir."

"Good-bye, General."

"Good-bye, Emperor."

Pablo hung up the phone. Even though it didn't have the bravado of his original plan, the move on Salt Lake was important—strategically, his army could find safety there. He would use the city to shield his army from the American airstrikes. This would provide him time to get the support he needed.

The loss of the Cheyenne team with the nuclear weapon was troubling to him, but if the Americans had it, he doubted they would use it if they hadn't already. They already had thousands of others weapons at their disposal and his instinct was that they were shy on the nuclear front after their massive bombardment abroad. He just didn't want it in the hands of someone who would use it, specifically against him. With marching orders in place, he now faced the more difficult task: saying good-bye to his father.

McCall, Idaho

Nelson didn't like bringing Luke to the hospital, because the care and attention he'd get would be limited, but once he started coughing up blood, he knew the illness had taken a turn beyond what his own care could provide. He didn't fault the competence of the hospital staff and doctors, because he knew the outbreak had overwhelmed them. Determined not to allow Luke to go without attention, he pledged to stay with him and oversee his care personally when the staff wasn't available. He had begged Samantha to stay at home with Haley but she wanted to accompany Luke. She knew how lonely and scared he might be and while Luke knew Nelson, he wasn't family. Seneca offered to stay with Haley, and Samantha knew she was in good hands with her.

A familiar voice echoed from a room a few doors down. Nelson walked out into the hallway and saw Charles Chenoweth talking urgently to a nurse, pointing to a gravely ill middle-aged man.

Nelson presumed this was Preston, Charles's colleague from Olympia.

"Charles, it's Nelson."

Charles stopped and turned to face him. "Do I know you?"

"Yes, I met you at the bistro."

Charles remained quiet for a moment, then like a light turning on, he replied, "Oh, yeah. I remember you."

Charles put his hand out to shake but Nelson didn't take it.

"Sorry," Nelson responded.

"You're smart. I should be more careful too."

"Your friend in there, how's he doing?"

"Not good. I feel so bad for him; he has a wife and kid back in Olympia."

"Hi, I'm Samantha Van Zandt," Samantha said, interjecting herself into the conversation.

"Oh, hi, I'm Charles Chenoweth with the Cascadian Independence Movement."

"Nice to meet you, Charles. I heard you were in town."

"Van Zandt, how do I know that name?" Charles asked.

"Maybe my husband, Gordon Van Zandt—he's good friends . . ."

"With Michael Rutledge, yes, yes, I remember now. Sorry he couldn't make it the other night."

"I don't mean to pry, but you seem to be in a hurry. Are you leaving?" Nelson asked.

"Yes, I need to go back to Olympia."

"I can understand your urgency. Who wants to stay around here with everyone getting sick?"

"I'm not leaving because of that. I'm leaving because I know someone who might be able to help."

"Help, like medically help?"

"I hope so."

"There's no known cure or vaccine for MERS or the other coronaviruses, so I don't know what you can do," Nelson commented with skepticism.

"I don't know either, but we should try and I intend on doing that," Charles said. "That man in there is a friend, a dear friend, and I can't just give up. I won't just let him die without trying everything in my power."

"I agree with you a thousand percent," Samantha said.

"So what or who is in Olympia?" Nelson asked.

"My sister, and she might have a vaccine for MERS."

"How can she have a cure?" Nelson asked.

"My sister, Elle, works—or I should say used to work—for a lab. One of the projects she had been working on for years now was finding a vaccine for MERS. I remember her telling me this last Thanksgiving." He went on to explain how his sister was considered by many to be a prodigy. She had graduated high school at the age of fifteen and secured her doctorate in pathobiology from Johns Hopkins University by twenty-five. She was quickly recruited by Kimpter Laboratory in Seattle, where her focus was on finding a vaccine for coronaviruses, specifically SARS and MERS. It was this background that gave Charles the hope that if anyone would have a cure, it was his intensely bright little sister.

"If that is true we need to make sure you get there and back safely," Samantha said, excitement building in her voice.

"Got something in mind, Sam?" Nelson asked.

"Charles, you're not leaving here by yourself. It's far too dangerous out there."

"I agree that it's dangerous, but I don't really have a choice, do I?"

Samantha's eyes twinkled mischievously. "How do you feel about traveling with a team of heavily armed Marines?"

Cheyenne, Wyoming

Conner was shocked by the size of the rally. By his estimate, there appeared to be close to five hundred people on the capitol grounds. Many protestors held signs and chanted at the soldiers who stood watch at the checkpoint. They were demanding access to go petition the government.

"What do you think, General?" Conner asked.

"I can't allow you to go out there, it's too dangerous," Baxter answered.

"General, how many times have I said this isn't the old government? Neither you nor my protection detail has the authority to stop me, but you must support me."

The roar of the crowd made it difficult for Baxter and Conner to hear their conversation. Soon it was drowned out by an even louder commotion: the squeal of tank tracks and the rumble of engines.

"Major, thank you," Conner said, looking up to Schmidt.

"Of course, Mr. President," Schmidt said, getting out of the turret and jumping off the tank.

This tank was exactly what he needed. He would drive up to the west gate where the protestors were and then emerge from the tank. The effect would be perfect.

Conner climbed up and took Schmidt's spot in the turret. "Let's go, drive forward," he barked.

Baxter looked at the tank with Conner riding high and shook his head at the bravado that Conner was displaying.

When the crowd saw the massive tank, fear and disbelief spread through their ranks. Many stopped chanting and yelling as they started to step away from the gate.

The tanks lumbered toward them, through the heavily guarded and barricaded checkpoint, then stopped with a jerk. Conner's protective detail came running alongside the tank and stood ready.

Inside, Conner took a breath, closed his eyes in preparation for the tense exchange he was about to have with the group. When he was ready, he climbed out of the turret and stood upon the top of the tank.

Gasps and chatter erupted from the crowd as many recognized Conner.

Standing like a giant, he bellowed, "I'm Brad Conner, President of the United States! Who's the leader of this mob?"

Heads turned and the chatter grew louder after Conner's question. An uncomfortable moment passed before a man raised his arm. "Here, I represent the Republic of Lakotah!"

"What is your name?"

"My name is Mark Ironside; I'm a facilitator for the government of the Republic of Lakotah!" shouted the elderly man of Native American decent.

"Mr. Ironside, there is no government of the Republic of Lakotah, because no such country exists!"

"President Conner, we don't need you to validate our existence."

"No such country exists and this mob needs to disband immediately!"

"We are here today to formally present our declaration of independence. Today we declare ourselves a free people once again. The United States invaded our lands many years ago, and through force, we had treaties thrust upon us. Your government violated those treaties, which make your claims over our lands null and void. We are here today to tell you to leave our lands and to fully recognize us as a free and independent state!"

Conner smiled, his confidence buoyed by the platform he was speaking from. "Mr. Ironside, the country you speak of does not exist; we will not recognize your secession. I am now asking you again to disband this mob immediately."

Almost on cue, the rumble of tanks was heard behind the crowd.

Conner looked up and saw a dozen M60 tanks heading down the road toward them, flanked by hundreds of armed men. The show of force was incredible. He looked down at Major Schmidt and winked.

Schmidt's tanks and men spread out behind the crowd, effectively boxing them in.

Ironside whipped around and watched in fear as the tanks lined up behind his people. The anxiety in the crowd intensified as they began to stir, and the pitch of conversation escalated.

"Mr. Ironside, you have one chance to go in peace. We do not wish for this to become something that cannot be reversed."

Baxter couldn't believe the direction this was going. Conner told him he was only coming down here to talk, but clearly he had other ideas about how to handle this. By the look of the crowd there was a mix of what looked like fighters and non-fighters. He wasn't concerned that they'd lose a physical fight; he was concerned they might lose the political one if there was bloodshed.

"President Conner, we are not going to leave! We will not until you free those you have imprisoned and formally recognize us!" Ironside yelled. A few dozen in the crowd cheered.

"I don't know where all of you come from, but I am asking you to disband and go home. Do not be a part of this, you can't win. If you don't leave, I can't promise your safety!" Conner yelled.

"We will fight if need be!" Ironside yelled.

Conner again ignored him and hollered, "Please open up to allow those who seek peace with us to freely go home!" he yelled out to Schmidt's men.

Baxter stepped closer to the tank and said, "Mr. President, what are you doing?"

Conner looked down and replied, "Taking our country back."

"Sir, what are you prepared to do to those who don't leave?" Baxter asked, clearly concerned.

Conner didn't answer Baxter; he didn't have time for a debate on the matter.

Ironside turned to his people and yelled, "Do not leave! We can do this. We can't let them run over us like they did when they first invaded our lands!" His words were falling on deaf ears as droves of people in his group began to leave.

Conner watched the group's size melt away to no more than a hundred. He looked out on those hardliners who remained and knew that he had to go forward on his threat and take direct action.

"This is the last warning. You have thirty seconds to disperse or else!"

"Why won't you talk with us? Why are you resorting to violence so quickly?" Ironside yelled at Conner. He turned to those who remained and commanded them to lock arms.

"Your movement is violent in and of itself. Your desire to break away from the United States is a direct threat to its security and therefore must be dealt with harshly. Movements like yours weaken our nation and we will not negotiate with the likes of you. Like we did in Montana, we are taking a stand against all separatists!" Conner bellowed.

Unmoved, the group sat down and began to chant, "Lakotah, Lakotah, Lakotah!" over and over.

Conner was fully committed now to doing what he had to do. A burning desire now raged within him to crush those opposed to the United States. For too long he had used the strong opposition to his nuclear strikes to temper his responses to those he perceived as a threat, but seeing these people before him, daring to challenge him, that temperament disappeared. Unfortunately for the Lakotah, they had picked the wrong time to make a stand. Today was Conner's reemergence as a decisive and firm leader.

With a nod to Schmidt, soldiers marched on the Lakotah protestors. Those who had stood with Ironside rose with makeshift weapons and began to fight.

Conner watched with a glimmer in his eye as the soldiers and Lakotah clashed violently.

"Sir, we should go!" Baxter hollered.

"I won't retreat to the comfort of my office. This is where I belong."

The fighting was brutal but it took only a few minutes for Schmidt's men to subdue the Lakotah.

Schmidt walked into the fray with a collapsible baton extended and began to hit some of the protestors. Whoever got in the way of his reaching the leader, he struck. When he reached the old man, now cowering on the ground, he bent down, grabbed him by his bloodied T-shirt, and pulled him to his feet. Schmidt dragged him to the tank where Conner stood overseeing the fight.

Conner looked down on Ironside and smiled. He jumped off the tank. "I gave you a warning and you didn't heed it. You had your chance. I'm a fair and equitable man. I gave you a choice," Conner said, and snatched Ironside by the collar and turned him to face the aftermath. "You see what you caused? It didn't have to be this way."

Blood dripped from Ironside's chin and nose. "We will not surrender, we will fight for our freedom," he spat at Conner.

Schmidt struck Ironside on the head with the butt of the baton.

Conner wiped off his face and smiled. "You are no different than the other opportunists who seek to destroy our great country while we're in a weakened state. I will not allow it."

"We will never surrender, never!" Ironside declared, his voice garbled as blood filled his mouth.

Conner leaned in and stared into his dark brown eyes. "You've already lost. Right now, we are sending teams to clean homes out, and we are not stopping there. We will arrest anyone who proclaims allegiance to your group. We will try them and if they are found guilty we will execute them for treason."

Ironside's eyes ballooned.

"I got your attention, didn't I? Just remember that this is of your doing, not mine. Major, take him away from me," Conner ordered.

Schmidt forcibly took him to a truck and loaded him onboard with others from his group, many of whom couldn't walk. Their limp bodies were being carried and tossed in the truck.

Baxter walked up behind Conner. "So, this is the new strategy?" he asked angrily.

Conner pivoted and answered him. "Not by choice but by necessity."

Schmidt ran up and said, "What are your orders, sir?"

Conner patted him on the shoulder. "Great job today, Major. Great job!"

"Yes, sir. Your orders?"

"Just clean up. I trust you have it under control," Conner responded.

Baxter looked on as both men talked. Now more than ever, he was feeling isolated from how things were being conducted. He wasn't sure how to process his emotions but he felt jealous of Schmidt. Conner had without a doubt taken a liking to the young officer and was now confiding in him. Baxter never thought of himself as an envious man but for a multitude of reasons this emotion was overtaking him and he didn't like it.

Schmidt saluted, turned, and walked off.

"General, you look . . . shocked."

"Actually I am, sir. I don't think this operation with Major Schmidt was a coincidence. This was coordinated."

Conner took a step toward him and placed his hand on his shoulder. "Today we took a stand against the enemies of the United States.

You may not agree with some of my tactics or even the strategy, but what happened here today was necessary."

"I thought you were going to include us in these decisions," Baxter said, reminding Conner of his earlier pledge.

"General Baxter, you're just going to have to trust me."

"Yes, sir. Sir, if you'll excuse me, I want to go help Major Schmidt process our new prisoners."

"Good man, go do that. I think I'm going to go back and—" Conner said, then stopped himself short when he saw Pat in the distance.

Pat was staring in his direction, and when they locked eyes on each other, his face expressed disappointment. Conner thought about speaking to him, but he hesitated. He wasn't in the mood to hear objections, even from a friend. He wanted to keep the high he was riding for as long as possible. He raised his arm and gave a slight wave, then turned and headed back to the capitol flanked by his security detail.

Coos Bay, Oregon, Pacific States of America

Gordon and Finley sat pensively as the armored Humvee wound its way through the lifeless streets of Coos Bay. Samantha and Haley had been on Gordon's mind more and more. He hoped that soon he'd be on his way back to McCall. Each day that passed added to the pain he felt being separated from them.

"Is the phone turned on?" Gordon asked.

"Yeah, don't worry, Prince Charming, it's on. If we have coverage and she calls, it'll ring," Finley sneered.

Gordon ignored Finley's comment and stared out the window as they passed one empty house after another. After clearing the last checkpoint, the activity on the streets went from barely detectable to nothing. His assumption was that they were in a secure area, meaning that Barone must be close by.

"What are you going to do if it rings while you're talking with the good ol' colonel and it's your wife?" Finley asked.

"You're going to give me the phone is what's going to happen," Gordon said.

"Ha. You know something? I'm going to be a nice guy today. Here, take it," Finley said as he offered the phone to Gordon with a broad smile stretched across his face.

"Serious?"

"Yeah, take it. Don't ever say I never gave you anything."

Gordon took the phone. He immediately looked to confirm it was turned on. He unbuttoned the top pocket of his long-sleeved shirt and slipped the phone in.

• • •

The Humvee pulled up to a small white house with black shutters at the end of a cul-de-sac. Two armed Marine guards approached and escorted Gordon and Finley to the front door. There they were told to leave all weapons and then were frisked to ensure they didn't carry any guns. The guard frisking Gordon felt the phone and took it out.

"Sorry, no weapons, phones, or recording devices."

Just as the Marine reached for the phone, it rang.

The wrenching feeling in Gordon's gut was gone and replaced with excitement.

"Samantha?" Gordon asked into the phone.

"Gordon, oh my God. I . . . believe . . ." Samantha said, her voice breaking up.

"Sam, you there?"

". . . ordon, it's Hal . . ."

"What's wrong, Sam, you're breaking up!" Gordon spoke loudly into the phone; he could hear the urgency in Samantha's broken voice.

The phone suddenly went dead; he looked at it and pressed the button to redial.

"Sergeant Van Zandt, you need to go, the colonel is waiting."

"Hold on, I need to try and reach her," Gordon answered. Frustration built in him as the call wouldn't connect.

"That beep means no signal, boss," Finley said.

"Damn it!" Gordon exclaimed.

"Sir, the colonel is waiting," the Marine said firmly with his hand out.

"But I need . . . this call is important," Gordon pleaded.

Finley stepped in and said, "Really, Van Zandt? I'll go in first."

Gordon pushed the concern out of his mind, knowing that getting the meeting over with Barone was critical to completing the mission. He could not allow Finley to go in first; he needed to explain to Barone who Finley was. "No, I'll go. Here," he said, handing the phone to Finley. "If she calls, find out what's going on, please."

Gordon turned to the guard and held up a bottle of scotch. "Is this fine to bring in?"

The guard grabbed the bottle and examined it, then handed it back. "Sure." He hollered to his colleague. "He's clear."

Another Marine came out and escorted Gordon inside. He looked around and was surprised to see the small living room was empty except for two lawn chairs. The only light emanated from underneath a door at the end of a long hallway. The guard stopped him just before he entered the hallway. He was surprised that with all the troubles, Barone didn't have more men guarding him.

"Go ahead, it's the door at the end of the hall," the guard instructed.

Gordon nodded and walked the remaining distance down the

creaking wooden hall until he reached the door. He paused a moment before he knocked. He wasn't sure what he'd be encountering on the other side but he needed this meeting to be successful. With his nerves calm, he tapped on the door.

"Yes, come in!"

Gordon recognized the raspy voice; he grabbed the cold brass handle and opened the door. There in a queen-sized bed, Colonel Barone was sitting up, with half a dozen pillows stuffed behind him. He was wearing only a green T-shirt with matching green shorts. His leg was wrapped with a thick bandage. Papers, binders, and books were spread across the bed. The nightstand was overburdened with half-empty glasses, medicine bottles, tissues, bandages, and a Beretta M9 pistol.

Barone looked up from a pad of paper he was drawing on and said, "Come in. Sit down over there." He squinted and then added, "Van Zandt, what the fuck!"

"Hi, Colonel, good to see you," Gordon said, still standing.

"Close the fucking door and take a seat," Barone barked.

Gordon did as he said and sat down in a small chair against the wall. He surveyed the room, which resembled any ordinary bedroom. Chest of drawers and a dresser against the walls, small runner carpets at the foot of the bed. The most important thing he studied was Barone's leg.

"Did you trip?" Gordon joked.

"Motherfuckers were lucky last night. I took a round, but it will take more than this to stop me. You should've seen me. I kept fighting like a good Marine," Barone said proudly.

"Is it bad?"

Barone rubbed the bandage and answered, "Nah, stings a little but the meds help with that."

"This might help too," Gordon said, holding up the bottle of scotch.

Barone was clearly in need of bifocals, as he held the bottle at arm's length and read the label. "This is a very nice bottle of scotch. You're a good man and this is another example of that." Barone opened the bottle. He grabbed the half-full glass on the nightstand, took the last gulp, and filled it with his new gift.

"Sir, you know why I'm here. Meaning why I'm in Coos Bay."

"Out fucking standing, that is top notch!" Barone yelped after taking a long drink, ignoring Gordon's comment.

Gordon watched him in amazement. It appeared that the man just didn't give a shit about anything.

"I was sent here by President Conner. He wants to know what's happening with you. I wouldn't have done it if my brother and his wife hadn't needed medical care that could only be provided in Cheyenne," Gordon said. His voice cracked a bit; he couldn't help his nerves.

Barone finished the glass of scotch and returned it to the nightstand. In one quick motion, he picked up a pistol and pointed it at Gordon.

Gordon jerked in his chair as he stared down the muzzle of the handgun.

"What are you doing here, Van Zandt? Are you here to betray me too?" Barone bellowed.

Gordon held his hands high and said, "Colonel, if you shoot me, you'll never know why I'm here and what's going on."

Barone didn't flinch.

"Please put the gun down," Gordon pleaded.

"Ha, ha, ha, I'm fucking with you, Van Zandt," he said, laughing, then tossed the pistol onto the bed.

Gordon exhaled heavily and relaxed into the chair.

"You don't have to tell me what's going on, I already know," Barone said.

Gordon raised his eyebrows, surprised by Barone's admission that he was fully aware of Gordon's mission.

"What do you know?" Gordon queried, curious as to what Barone might divulge.

"That split tail. You're here for that woman."

Gordon was shocked by the remark and thought about Barone's assumption for his visit to Coos Bay. Not knowing how to answer or remark, he kept quiet.

"She is a good-looking woman, I will say that," Barone joked.

Seizing on his assumptions, Gordon asked, "Can you release her to me?"

"Van Zandt, I like you, always have. I still remember the day you came into my hooch after the shooting in the mosque. I looked into your eyes and saw a strong man, a determined man. You were deliberate then and you're deliberate now. I respect that about you. There needs to be more men like you."

"Thank you."

"How's your family holding up?"

Gordon was taken aback by such a personal question and the fact that Barone ignored his request about Brittany. But Gordon wasn't going to press too hard. Barone made him feel uneasy and he didn't want to set him off.

"Good, I think."

"You think? What the hell kind of answer is that?"

"You know how it is, sir, being out of touch with them. You have to assume they're fine."

Barone chewed on that and said, "I guess you're right. Mine left me. My wife and daughter just packed up and left me."

"I'm sorry to hear that."

"What's all of this about, huh? I mean, why do us men do the things we do?"

Gordon didn't answer, as it seemed like Barone was mostly posing the question to himself.

Barone reached over and grabbed the bottle of scotch and his glass and filled it again. He glanced over at Gordon and asked, "You want a taste?"

"No, sir, I'm trying to keep my wits about me."

"Good for me, now I have more to myself," he chuckled.

"Sir, can—"

"Everything I did, the mutiny, everything, was to make sure I could rescue my wife and daughter from harm's way and what do they do? They leave me just when I need them the most. That's fucking gratitude for you," Barone barked. He took another large gulp and said, "It's a tough world out there, especially when you can't even trust your own family. It's a real motherfucker. So now I sit here, bullet in my leg, war waging in the streets, and I have to ask myself, what's it all for? I'm just fighting to fight now because I don't know what else to do. You know that I was offered a way out? Yep! Old Timms came to me and said they would be willing to stop if I would leave. Here's the kicker: I honestly considered it."

Gordon was mesmerized. Here was the mighty Colonel Barone, the Butcher of Coos Bay, opening himself up to him. Without a doubt, this confirmed to Gordon that Barone just didn't give a shit anymore.

"I honestly tried to imagine myself up in the woods somewhere, retired, big fat belly and long hair. Can you see me like that?" he asked Gordon.

"Actually, sir, I can't."

"Ha, right answer. I can't see myself like that either. I am a fucking warrior, a Marine!" He finished the glass and poured more scotch.

"Sir, I'm here with another man—"

"I remember you telling me about your son being murdered. That's some shitty luck. You know we have that in common," Barone said, interrupting Gordon.

Gordon nodded. "I'm just trying to do the best for my daughter now."

"Van Zandt, we can only do what we can do. Just remember, the most important thing for you to do is keep them safe. That's your responsibility, period. There's no one out there who will do it for you. I tried myself to be a good parent, but being a career Marine made that hard. I gave my life, my soul, to the Corps and the country. Many say I'm a traitor, but I'm happy with the decision I made. How many who proclaim patriotic purity would have allowed their wife and daughter to be left to the mobs and criminals? If they did, I would say they were traitors in their own right. The most difficult thing for me to deal with is that after all I gave, after all I sacrificed, they abandoned me." Barone poured more scotch into the glass and shot it back.

"I'm sorry, sir."

"I don't need your pity, Van Zandt, that's life. Sometimes we get fed a shit sandwich."

"That's true."

"Sorry for barking at ya. Anyway, I can't surrender, I won't let them win. I'm close to victory, very close."

Gordon nodded slowly, understanding Barone's need to be victorious. While he was appalled at what Barone had done, he understood the basic need to win, as it was also ingrained in him.

"Thanks, Van Zandt, but just so you know, you don't have to kiss my ass for your lady friend. You've been a straight shooter and I always return the favor. You can take her with you, but she can't come back here. If I see her again, I'll serve the justice that you've saved her from, *capisce*?"

"Understood, sir."

"What do ya think?" Barone asked, holding up the pad of paper he had been drawing on.

Gordon looked at it and saw a rectangle with some inscriptions and a symbol that looked similar to the Marine Corps's eagle, globe, and anchor.

"What is it?"

"Every country needs a flag. This will be the one that flies over Salem as soon as I'm done cleaning up this mess here," Barone said with pride in his voice.

Gordon looked closer and asked, "What does that say?"

"*Sublimis ab unda*. It's Latin for 'raised from the waves,'" Barone answered.

"I like it."

"I'm envisioning a blue background to represent water, a mountain in the middle with an eagle, globe, and anchor, and the Latin phrase at the bottom."

"I look forward to seeing it when it's done," Gordon said, his patience starting to wane.

"You know something, Van Zandt?"

"What's that, sir?"

"I fucked up, I really did. I shouldn't have killed all those people. I knew better but I let my temper get in the way. I'd like to blame all of this on the old bitch of a mayor, but I can't. I ordered it, I gave my men the order to kill them all. If I could go back in time, I wouldn't have done it. I had something good here but I fucked it all up. Listen to me whining like a bitch. What's the saying about the ship has sailed? Well it has and I fucking sank it," Barone confessed, still staring at his etchings on the pad.

A loud ring of a phone came from the other side of the bedroom door. The door opened abruptly, surprising them, but who was standing there shocked them more.

Covered head to toe in blood was Finley. In his left hand he held the ringing phone, in his right, a Marines pistol.

"I think this is for you," Finley said, tossing the phone at Gordon. "And Colonel Barone, this is for you, compliments of President Conner." He leveled the pistol at Barone and squeezed off three shots.

Barone reached for his pistol but it was too late. The first shot was all that was needed. It hit him in the forehead. The back of his head exploded and his body fell limp. The other two shots struck him in the chest. Blood quickly began to soak through his shirt and onto the white sheets.

Everything happened so fast that Gordon didn't catch the phone. It fell to the floor with a thud but kept ringing. Stupidly, he looked down at it, still ringing, and thought about grabbing it, but what had just happened to Barone brought everything into clarity.

Finley pivoted to Gordon, pistol in hand, and said, "Sorry, buddy, but you gotta go too. Orders are orders."

Gordon reacted quickly and hit the pistol out of Finley's grasp with his left hand. The pistol smacked the floor and skidded under the bed. He then punched Finley with his right. Finley reeled from the blow to his face and stumbled backward. Gordon sensed he had the upper hand and charged Finley, tackling him. Both men hit the floor hard. A fierce grappling match began with Gordon on top of Finley. Gordon took advantage of his position and began to pummel him with one punch after another.

Finley tried to block but Gordon's intense attack was too much. Dazed from the barrage of punches, Finley managed to do the one thing he knew would stop Gordon's assault. He reached down to his side and pulled out the four-inch sheathed knife that he had just used to kill the two Marine guards. He gripped it tightly and thrust it into Gordon's left side.

Gordon lurched backward and cried out in pain from the knife blow to his side. After an instant, he rolled off Finley and crawled toward the pistol on the floor just a few feet away.

Seeing a chance to finish Gordon off, Finley got up and jumped on Gordon's back, forcing him to the ground. He hoisted the knife above his head, ready to strike, when the deafening crack from a pistol thundered in the room.

Gordon looked up and saw Simpson standing in the doorway, a pistol in his hand.

Finley bent over backward after the bullet ripped through his chest. With his last breath he tried to sit up, but Simpson prevented it by hitting him again with a 9-millimeter round. Finley fell onto his back and gasped before dying.

Gordon kept his eyes glued on Simpson in anticipation that he'd turn the gun on him, but it didn't happen. Simpson holstered the pistol, stepped over Gordon, and went to Barone's side. He looked over his old friend's body, covered in thick blood.

"Rest in peace, Devil Dog," Simpson said softly.

Gordon sat up but the stinging pain in his left side caused him to pause. He put his fingers through the hole in his shirt and felt the bleeding stab wound. "Fuck, that hurts."

"You all right, Van Zandt?" Simpson asked.

"Finley came in and started shooting; he shot the Colonel and then turned to shoot me but I stopped him. The next thing I know is I'm stabbed and then I hear a loud boom, I look up and there you are, saving my ass."

"Are you all right, can you walk?" Simpson asked.

"Yeah, just a small knife wound."

"Let's get you cleaned up and we'll talk later," Simpson said as he walked up to Gordon and put out his hand to help him up.

Gordon grimaced in pain as he stood. He looked at Simpson

strangely; he couldn't guess why he hadn't shot him. Lord knows he would have. "Top, why didn't you shoot me too?"

"Because I know you didn't have anything to do with this."

"How would you know that?"

Simpson pointed to a corner of the room.

Gordon followed his finger to a small bookcase but didn't see anything out of place.

"Inside that little cherub angel is a camera. We've been monitoring you and your friend since the first day you arrived. We intercepted his calls and heard everything; this is why I know you weren't part of this plan. Now go get yourself cleaned up and meet me later."

"But I . . ."

"Van Zandt, you need some medical care. Go, we'll talk later."

"Roger that."

Simpson patted him on the shoulder and left the room.

Gordon looked down at Finley's dead body lying in the center of a large pool of blood. Then he looked again at Barone. The pad of paper with the flag he had shown him not minutes ago sat next to him, his blood smearing the ink, making the Latin unreadable. He stepped over to the nightstand and grabbed the bottle of scotch. He poured some on his side then tipped it back and took a long drink. Anything to numb the pain.

At the sound of a ringing phone, he swiveled and looked around in a frenzy. He knew it was Samantha and he had to answer it. The pain in his side became secondary to finding the ringing phone. He got on his knees and looked under the bed. He saw it there, the screen illuminating the darkness. He reached in as far as he could and grabbed it; his heart jumped, knowing he'd be talking to her any moment. He clicked the button and brought the phone to his ear, but the phone slipped out of his hands and fell on the floor. "Shit!" he cried out. He picked it up again and put it to his ear, but before he could speak a voice, not Samantha's, spoke.

"Finley, are you there? Is it done? Have you removed Colonel Barone and Van Zandt?"

Gordon's eyes widened when he heard the questions.

"Hello? Finley, are you there?" the unknown voice asked again.

"He's here but he can't speak to you," Gordon answered.

"Who is this? Put Staff Sergeant Finley on the phone."

Gordon looked at Finley's body and said, "This is Gordon Van Zandt and Finley can't come to the phone right now on account of I killed him."

Cheyenne, Wyoming

Sebastian found transportation downtown via a shuttle that ran every hour from the base. He took in the city as the shuttle drove along, and was surprised by what he saw. Cheyenne was bustling with people in and out of the green zone. Cars were being driven and people were coming and going; and some of the windows were even illuminated with the bright glow of electricity. He knew the town's progress was the result of the federal government focusing most of its resources on one location, but it was nice to see something that resembled the past.

He got off the shuttle in front of Pat's Coffee Shop and looked through the large glass windows. The place was alive; people spilled out its doors and sat at small bistro tables on the sidewalk.

"Here ya go," a man said to him, holding the door open.

"Thanks," Sebastian replied. He walked in and the first thing that hit him was how loud it was. Laughter, chatter, clanging dishes and glasses, doors opening, and music, sweet music coming from the corner. A young girl sang a song he'd never heard before to the strumming sounds of an acoustic guitar. The inside of Pat's felt as if it existed in an entirely different time. The only clues that gave away their present circumstance were the TVs that remained dark. Compared to how they were living in McCall, these people were living in luxury. He wished Annaliese was well enough to travel with him and see this.

He got in a long line of people ordering drinks, and was pleased that it moved quickly. A man came up. On his chest he was wearing a name tag that said Pat. Sebastian laughed to himself when he saw the name tag. Who wears a name tag at a bar? he thought.

"What can I get ya?" Pat asked.

"I need a stiff drink, what do you have?"

"Several things. Do you like sweet, spicy, or just regular?"

Sebastian raised his eyebrows at the selection and answered, "Regular, I guess."

Pat turned but Sebastian stopped him.

"What's the spicy?"

"It's my homemade vodka infused with jalapeños."

"Ahh, no thanks, I'm a gringo. I'll go with the regular."

Pat turned back, grabbed a mason jar, and half filled it with a clear liquid out of a plastic jug. He quickly spun back and handed it to Sebastian. "That'll be three bucks."

Sebastian looked at him oddly because he hadn't been charged money for anything in a very long time. "I don't have any money . . ."

"Have anything to trade? I can set you up with an account and you can pay me back with—"

Sebastian interrupted him and said, "Secretary Wilbur told me I could put it on her tab."

"She did, huh?"

"Yeah, I'm in Cheyenne for a short time and she told me it was on her. A favor of sorts."

"I don't know you, but I'll just have to trust you this time."

"I'm not lying, believe me. My wife and I are over at the base. I guess you could say we're guests of the president," Sebastian added, hoping that referencing the president would make him seem more important.

"Guests of the president? Well, well. You must be a bigwig," Pat joked. He handed over the drink. "Enjoy."

Sebastian found a small table near the back in the corner and took a seat. He relaxed into the wooden chair and tipped the glass back. The bite of the "regular" vodka was present at the start and carried through all the way down. The second sip wasn't as harsh and the third even easier. By the time he reached the bottom of the jar the vodka was having just the right effect on him.

"Need another?" Pat asked, hovering over Sebastian. The line had cleared down and he was making his rounds, checking in on the customers.

Sebastian smiled. "Yeah, that would be great, thank you."

Pat soon returned with another glass. "I'm not boasting but I'm friends with President Conner so I was kinda playing with you when you mentioned you were here as a guest of his. I don't know who you are, but just watch what you say. And if I were you, I wouldn't wear that shirt around here."

Sebastian looked down at the Republic of Cascadia shirt. It ended up in the bag that Samantha had packed, and he had thrown it on this morning without thinking.

"Why what's wrong with it?"

"The president and many others around here don't take kindly to separatists or secessionists."

The door swung open and a group of soldiers walked in. Pat looked down at him. "Time for you to go. Sorry, but I have to ask you to leave."

Sebastian looked at Pat in shock at his request.

"It's for your own good. You can come back tomorrow or another time, but now is not a good time for you stay here," Pat said with urgency.

"This is about the stupid shirt?" Sebastian exclaimed, standing up. No sooner was he out of his chair than Major Schmidt marched over to him.

"Take that fucking shirt off," Schmidt ordered.

Sebastian looked at Schmidt and then at the four soldiers behind him.

"Are you deaf? Take the shirt off!" Schmidt barked.

"Last time I checked this was a free country," Sebastian shot back.

"Major, please, I've asked the man to leave; he was just on his way out. I don't need another altercation in here," Pat pleaded.

Schmidt ignored Pat and pressed on. "I'm going to ask you one more time."

"Then what, you're going to jump me? You can't fight your own fights, you need to come with your goons and threaten people?" Sebastian said.

The others with Schmidt fanned out in anticipation for a fight.

Sebastian never looked for fights in his life, but he never ran from them either. By the looks of it, if he struck Schmidt, he'd only get another hit or two before the other men took him down. He couldn't see a chance to win. He then thought of Annaliese and his need to let his bravado go so he could make it back to her.

"I normally wouldn't do what thugs demand but since you don't plan on fighting fair, I'll give in to your demands," Sebastian said as he pulled off the shirt and held it in his clenched left fist.

Schmidt looked at Sebastian, now standing shirtless, and said, "Time for you to leave. Get the hell out of here and don't ever come back! If I see you in this place or anywhere in the green zone, I'll kick your ass!"

"Major, please, can't you see he's doing what you asked? Just leave him alone. He'll leave," Pat pleaded, then turned to Sebastian and asked, "You're leaving, right?"

The Van Zandt temper was now boiling in him. He wasn't seeking a fight but Schmidt kept antagonizing him. "You know something, I can't leave town as I'm here at the request of the president, so you, my friend, can go fuck yourself!"

Schmidt nudged closer to Sebastian.

"As far as this shirt goes, here, it's yours now," Sebastian said as he tossed it in Schmidt's face.

Schmidt's temper was now on the precipice of erupting too. The engagement earlier had gotten him riled up; now seeing Sebastian wearing a Republic of Cascadia shirt added fuel to his internal fire.

Sebastian stared hard at Schmidt. "You better try to kick my ass now, because I'm not leaving town. I'm here to stay and I plan on coming back here tomorrow and getting a drink. If you want to fight, come by yourself, stop hiding behind your men for protection. Only a pussy talks about fighting a lone stranger when he has four of his buddies backing him up."

Schmidt's top was about to blow, the typical cool and stoic demeanor gone. He inched closer to Sebastian, who held his space, but was stopped when Pat put out his arm.

"Major, that's enough. This man here is a guest of President Conner's," Pat begged.

"Fine, I'll stand down from kicking this guy's ass, but make sure he gets out of my face now," Schmidt sneered.

A grin appeared on Sebastian's face as he could see Schmidt backing down.

"Get out of here now and don't come back tomorrow, you hear me? I don't need this," Pat exclaimed.

Sebastian stepped out from behind the small table and headed for the door, keeping his eye squarely on Schmidt and his men.

A few feet from the door he heard some laughter; he turned to see Schmidt's men slicing up the T-shirt.

Sebastian turned back, took a step, but was stopped when Schmidt hollered, "What's your name, Cascadian?"

"Van Zandt, Sebastian Van Zandt! You better remember it," he said, then exited the coffee shop into the warm night air.

JUNE 30, 2015

• • •

"When it is obvious that the goals cannot be reached, don't adjust the goals, adjust the action steps."

—Confucius

Cheyenne, Wyoming

It was rare for Conner to meet anyone at his residence, but this meeting was unique. Besides his personal protection team, no one would know about this secret liaison. It had to be that way if the missions he and Schmidt were working on were going to have a chance to succeed.

The violent breakup of the Republic of Lakotah supporters had given him a boost in confidence. His actions yesterday were a clear departure from the old Washington, D.C., Conner. He put himself at greater risk, but that risk translated into greater results. Word of his stance on top of that tank had spread through the tent cities, bars, and homes of every person in Cheyenne. Conner was now taking on an almost mythical status and he loved it.

With the Lakotahs' threat diminished, he felt like one concern was cleared off his plate. He still needed to go to Porcupine, South Dakota, and complete the task of ridding the United States of that separatist threat, but that could wait. He had contacted the governor of South Dakota and advised him on their troubles there. The governor said he'd do what he could do on his end but support from Cheyenne was appreciated.

With this newfound confidence and sense of completion, Conner decided during the night that he'd finalize plans on dealing death blows to two other enemies of the United States, the Pan-American Empire and the Cascadian Independence Movement.

However, with every step forward, there were obstacles that hindered the progress. He had received news from Schmidt early last evening that Finley might have failed in his attempt to assassinate Barone. This development concerned him, and with the mission an apparent failure he had to find another way to dispose of Barone if he survived.

A tap on his home-office door alerted him that his visitor had arrived. He walked briskly to the door and opened it.

"Major Schmidt, so glad you could come by, thank you. Please come in," Conner said, motioning to a couple of tufted leather chairs in front of a fireplace.

"Yes, sir, my pleasure," Schmidt said, standing near a chair.

"Please, Major, sit. I appreciate your penchant for protocol but it's not necessary," Conner instructed him.

Schmidt sat down and held his hat in his hands.

Conner walked over and asked, "Do you need anything, coffee or tea?"

"No, sir, I'm fine."

"Well, let's get down to brass tacks," Conner said. He leaned forward. "What is your plan for the Cascadians in Idaho?"

Schmidt laid out his plan for Idaho. It called for sending five thousand troops and most of his tanks. They would take two weeks to get to Mountain Home and another few days to get to McCall. Upon arrival in Mountain Home, they would drop off supplies to help with the outbreak. This would be the cover. When they hit Mc-Call, they would quarantine the town, and then the plan of creating a false flag incident, like an attack on Schmidt's forces, would justify systematically neutralizing all of those involved with the Cascadian Movement. The sheer numbers were to ensure they could overwhelm them. He would begin his march toward McCall on July 5.

After discussing Idaho he shifted to the PAE. Schmidt told Conner the plan was still in motion and within a few days it would all be over.

Schmidt moved to discussing Coos Bay. They discussed the plot against Barone, and clearly, Gordon's allegiance was brought into question. That led Schmidt to discuss his encounter with Sebastian the night before. Schmidt requested that both Sebastian and Annaliese be arrested. This idea drew criticism from Conner.

"I won't arrest him or his wife. I don't want him contacting them back in McCall and warning them," Conner said.

"But, sir, what happens when he talks to his brother?"

Conner considered. Gordon was a wild card, particularly considering neither of them knew the exact circumstances of Finley's death. But he didn't want to risk it. "Just monitor them, nothing more, and make sure they're not doing something that would jeopardize us."

"Sir, we don't know if the other Van Zandt is here to cause trouble. We can't be sure."

"Why do you have a hard-on for this other Van Zandt?"

Schmidt's face was flush with anger, and Conner could tell that there was something deeper than his disrespect toward the United States.

"It's personal, isn't it?" Conner asked.

Schmidt turned away from Conner and finally confided, "Yes, sir. Sergeant Finley was a friend, a good friend. We served together but along our trip here he stood out and was a big part of my team. You asked me to send one of my best to take care of this and I did, but now he's gone, murdered at the hands of Gordon Van Zandt."

"I understand you're upset, but death is commonplace. You have to move on from this."

"Don't get me wrong, sir, I know this world holds no guarantees. I have no misgivings about this, but when I know the person who committed such an act and that person's loyalties aren't to this country, it makes me want to exact revenge."

"And revenge you'll get, Major, later than sooner."

Schmidt disagreed with the decision, but ever the loyal soldier, he replied, "Yes, sir."

"After we clean out the Cascadians and PAE, we can move on the Arizona group."

"Yes, sir."

Both men continued to discuss options and processes for how the operations would be conducted. After an hour they were done.

As Schmidt was leaving, Conner called out, "Major, thank you for your loyalty."

He turned and answered him with pride. "It's my pleasure and my duty. I love my country, I love everything it stands for. I'm an American soldier; it's my honor to serve."

Conner nodded his response but out of nowhere he felt he needed to give the major something to fill the void he was lacking with the loss of his colleague. "Major, I've changed my mind. You do what you feel you need to do with the Van Zandts here. I just don't want to hear about it. Keep it discreet."

Schmidt smiled and then quickly left.

McCall, Idaho

Hearing Gordon's voice yesterday gave Samantha hope and a little peace of mind. She explained what was happening and told him to hurry home. Haley's symptoms seemed to have stabilized, but her cough was still violent and her fever stuck at 103. However, Samantha was hopeful that Charles would return with a vaccine. He had left yesterday night, accompanied by Gunny and two other Marines. Whatever the man's politics were, she couldn't fault him for trying to find a solution.

Nelson had brought Luke home once it was determined that the blood from his coughing had come from broken blood vessels in his throat and not his lungs. Samantha agreed with the decision to bring him home, as the hospital was now overloaded with sick people.

The day before, while Seneca watched over Haley, Samantha had gone and met with Phyllis Smallbach, a local and Idaho native. She had been one of the first to join her auxiliary and for Samantha she was a godsend. Most of her sixty-eight years had been spent living a life as a modern-day homesteader. The skills and knowledge she offered the auxiliary group were priceless. Phyllis had been preparing her whole life for this type of event, and when it happened she was ready. She never panicked, she just acted. The moment Phyllis heard about the outbreak she went to work to find a natural remedy or relief for the illness. When Samantha had shown up, she had something to give her that she believed would help Haley and Luke.

Samantha was surprised by how simple it was. First, she gave her pine-needle tea to help provide vitamin A and vitamin C. She told her that pine needles have four times the amount of vitamin C than a lemon. She swore that the medicinal qualities of the tea would also help with cardiovascular health, which for their ailments was important. The other remedy she gave Samantha was licorice. At first Samantha didn't know if she was joking, but she went with it. Phyllis first explained that the licorice got its characteristic sweetness from glycyrrhizin, and that it had proven anti-inflammatory qualities. She proceeded to tell her that for centuries many cultures had used it to soothe coughs and reduce inflammation, soothe and heal ulcers and stomach inflammation, control blood sugar, and balance hormones. Phyllis was exuding excitement as she continued to detail the other healing properties and that, most importantly, it had a potent antiviral agent and could be used to treat flu, herpes, and even hepatitis.

Samantha's head was swimming with all of the information. She had always been moderate in her views on medicine and health, not one to discount either modern conventional or natural homeopathic cures. But in this case, she had to act. When she came home, she proceeded to give Haley and Luke the remedies. She was realistic and knew they wouldn't see immediate relief, even though she prayed for a miracle as news came that more and more people were dying.

Like before, on the road and in Eagle, Nelson had been a huge help to her, and now with Seneca at his side, Samantha had a powerful team helping her with the kids. This morning he showed up with some bags of intravenous fluids for the kids. He stressed that they had to stay hydrated.

"I'll hook them up when they wake up," he said, placing the IV bags on the counter. There he saw the pine-needle tea.

"You think this will do anything? I mean, c'mon," Nelson joked as he swirled a spoon through a pot of pine-needle tea that was on the kitchen counter.

"What?"

"This hippie stuff you have here. What's next—are you going to burn dried sage throughout?"

"I don't need your little cracks right now," Samantha shot back.

He stepped into the laundry room and said, "Sorry, that was a dick thing to say."

"It's all right; I just need you to support me. I don't think that stuff will cure them but if it can help relieve some of their symptoms, I'll do it."

"You're right, I'm sorry."

"Stop apologizing, you wouldn't be you unless you were being a smart ass."

"Great, that's all anyone thinks of me. I can see the epitaph on my gravestone now. 'Here lies Nelson Warner, A Real Smartass.'"

"Anyway, moving on to something else. Anything new to report?"

"Glad you asked. I stopped and saw Rainey earlier this morning. He's saying that he received communiqué from Boise. Apparently Cheyenne is sending troops here to help with the outbreak."

Samantha exhaled deeply and said, "Thank God! This is great news!"

Nelson stopped himself from saying something that would have moderated her enthusiasm. He wasn't completely confident that the federal forces coming were there to provide a cure but more to contain the outbreak and quarantine them. He presumed that if they had a cure they would have sent one, not a force. Knowing that mind-set was important, especially a positive and hopeful one, he didn't bring up his suspicions of the true intent of the federal forces.

"I think the kids have a real chance," he said.

"They really do. It just seems like everything is finally coming together. Gordon is coming home, Charles's sister might have a cure, and the government is actually coming to help. These are all positive steps."

Nelson refrained from additional comments. "So, what did Gordon have to say?"

"I talked to him for a good ten minutes. He said everything was fine and his mission was complete. He said he'll be coming home soon. It was so good to hear his voice. I just wish we had some word from Sebastian and Annaliese. One of my tasks today will be making a call back to Cheyenne to inquire about them."

"Sam, can I say something personal?"

She stopped what she was doing and looked at Nelson. "Personal? As long as you promise you're not going to make some sort of passive-aggressive joke."

"It's not a joke. From the bottom of my heart I wanted to tell you that you're an amazing person, a truly strong woman. I've seen you grow and adapt like no one else I know. I've known you for so long and you are not the person I knew before. The kids and Gordon are lucky to have you and I'm fortunate to have you as a friend."

"Aww, that's so sweet. Thank you. I know I wasn't as prepared as I could have been, but what I've found is that everything is about attitude. I know I had a time there where I wasn't at my best, but I changed my outlook and everything else followed. And you've been invaluable to my family. Thank you."

"I love you guys, you're like family."

"Knock, knock!" a voice called out from the other room.

"Back here," Samantha replied.

Seneca walked in. "Hi, Nels. Sam, how are you this morning?"

"Much better than I was the other day. *Hopeful* would be a better word," Samantha answered.

"Hopeful? You *are* optimistic," Seneca blurted out.

Samantha looked at her strangely. "Is there something you're not telling me?"

Nelson cocked his head and shot Seneca a look that could kill. He turned back to Samantha and opened up. "I shared a thought with Seneca this morning after I met with Rainey."

"Oh? And you didn't think to share it with me?"

Nelson gritted his teeth. "This is not a fact, it's just my opinion, so please don't take it as truth."

"Go ahead."

"I don't think the federal forces coming our way are coming to help. I think they're coming to quarantine us."

"You can't know that."

"Sam, there is no cure for MERS or any other type of coronavirus. I think it makes sense for them to come and contain this outbreak. Whatever this is spreads faster than MERS and is lethal to three out of ten people."

"But Charles's sister might have a cure, she's been working on this for years, he seemed to think . . ." Samantha stopped herself as she could see the look on Nelson's face. "You don't think he's coming back, do you?"

Nelson just looked at her, quiet, but his eyes told her the answer.

"You don't. I can see it written all over your face."

"Seneca, thanks a lot," Nelson snapped.

"I didn't do anything," she shot back.

They began to bicker.

"Both of you, stop, please, just go," Samantha begged, her hopeful demeanor now dashed.

"Sam, I don't know if what I think is true, I just—"

Samantha held up her hand signaling for him to stop.

Nelson closed his mouth and didn't utter a word.

Faint crying sounded from the hallway beyond the kitchen.

Samantha looked at them both and said, "Excuse me, I have to go take care of the kids. I'll see you both later."

She brushed by them both and headed toward Haley's room.

Nelson turned to Seneca. "Did you not hear me this morning when I asked you to keep my opinions to yourself? This doesn't help. I realize that we all need to deal with possibilities, but let me deal with those, not Samantha. She needs to stay upbeat and hopeful because she needs to believe that the kids will get better," he chided.

"But—"

Nelson cut her off, "There's no *buts*. From now stop being the town crier. It's hard enough for her without Gordon here. She can't be focused on those issues; that's for us to worry about. Let her worry about it when we know it's a reality, not a theory."

Seneca nodded her agreement and acknowledgment.

"Let's go before we fuck anything else up."

Coos Bay, Oregon

"If I live long enough, I think my entire body will be covered in scars by the time I'm fifty," Gordon commented as he rubbed his hand across the thick gauze bandage taped to his side.

"You're lucky the blade didn't hit anything," the corpsman replied.

"I can tell you this—it hurt like a motherfucker."

"I bet it did. Okay, you're all done. Here is another dose of pain meds," the corpsman, said handing him a small white envelope.

Gordon took it and said, "Let me guess: Motrin. Don't you have anything else?"

"Motrin is standard issue, and we reserve our hardier pain management drugs for other real wounds."

"I guess you're right, it's just a flesh wound," Gordon quipped as he put his shirt on.

Gordon finished gathering his stuff and left the clinic, heading toward city hall. The only thing on his mind now was getting home. Of course with everything that had happened, he wasn't sure how he'd be getting there. He had the motorcycle but not enough fuel. He needed to convince Simpson to give him another Hummer. Hell, he'd take a lift on a chopper if that was offered.

The grounds of city hall were not like they were the last time he was there. It reminded him of scenes from Iraq during the height of the war in 2004, litter and debris everywhere. With each footfall he heard the sound of crunching glass against pavement. The face of the building was covered in large black pockmarks and bullet holes; not a window was left untouched. Large boards with cutout gun ports covered the gaping holes where the windows once sat. Like birds in their nests, teams of Marines sat behind sandbagged positions manning machine guns. It no longer looked like an administrative building; it looked like a war-torn fortress.

Once he was inside, the place hummed like it did when he was there before. Marines, civilians, and sailors went about their tasks of operating the besieged city. He strode easily but focused down the hall till he came to Simpson's office. Standing outside the large oak door were two Marine guards who immediately stopped him upon his approach.

"What can we help you with?" a Marine asked.

"I need to see Master Sergeant Simpson."

"Do you have an appointment?"

"Yeah, I do."

The large door flew open and there in front of him stood a captain and gunnery sergeant, neither he recognized, both in a hurry. Gordon got a quick glance inside and saw Simpson packing.

"Master Sergeant, it's Gordon Van Zandt."

Simpson looked up quickly and barked, "Get your ass in here."

Gordon squeezed by the men exiting and the guards and stepped into the office. With the windows boarded up, the only light in the room came from several portable lanterns.

"Want a drink?" Simpson asked.

"No, thank you. Um, I'm glad you wanted to see me. I have something to ask."

"Go ahead."

"I need some transport back to Idaho. I was hoping you could help in that department."

"I don't see why not. After all you helped us."

Gordon didn't know what that comment meant, but he continued, "A Hummer would be great, with enough fuel to make the distance."

"Done."

A knock on the door made Gordon jump. A slight panic ran through his body as he imagined a scene like yesterday happening again.

"Come on in!" Simpson hollered.

The door swung open and there stood Timms. A smile stretched across his face as he strode in and walked up to Simpson. "Master Sergeant, glad to see you."

"Good to see you too, Mr. Timms," Simpson responded. The men shook each other's hand.

"So, is this the man here?" Timms asked Simpson.

"Yes, it is, Mr. Timms, this is Gordon Van Zandt."

Gordon adjusted in his chair, unaware of what was happening.

"Mr. Van Zandt, nice to meet you, I'm—"

"Van Zandt, this is the new mayor of Coos Bay. He's taking over and putting this whole mess behind us."

Timms stepped over to Gordon, stuck out his hand, and said, "From the good people of Coos Bay, thank you."

Gordon looked at him then shot a look at Simpson. "What's going on?"

"I know this is going to come as strange but you and your friend did us all a favor."

"Favor?"

"Yes, you brought down the Butcher of Coos Bay, allowing us to restore order. You see, Mr. Timms and I were working behind the scenes to overthrow the colonel. The issue we were having was one of logistics. I mean, we could do it, but could we do it without causing further upheaval? We thought not, but we were willing to remove him. Then you and your friend showed up. You gave us the opportunity to have him killed without us actually pulling the trigger. We can say he was killed by men from the United States. This story works the best. Those hardcore followers will feel defeated and leave or we will mop them up."

"Don't be so sure of yourself," Gordon challenged.

"We are sure of ourselves; we have been planning this for some time and have identified a solid number of those in Barone's high command who were only following him out of fear. We know this to be the same within the enlisted ranks. People weren't following him out of respect."

"So you used me and Finley?"

"Don't look at it that way," Timms said as he sat down next to Gordon.

"You seem somehow disappointed or upset," Simpson said.

"No, I'm not, I just was worried all along and you knew, you knew Finley was here to kill him and you let it happen."

"Yes, I knew something was odd when you showed up with another person. That's why we bugged your berthing space and monitored your movements."

Gordon was in shock by this revelation and didn't know what to say. In many ways, it didn't matter. Barone, a man who factored heavily into his life in the Corps and out, was dead, and he was free to go home.

"What happens now? I see you packing," Gordon queried.

"Time for me and many of my men to leave and go find a new home."

"Why?"

"Let's just say that they can't stay here. Too many raw emotions. It will be hard to have them stay and get things back in order."

"Where will you go?" Gordon asked. A thought came to mind of asking them to come to McCall, but he didn't know if he could trust them. These Marines had once sided with a man who was a mass murderer and had committed heinous crimes against civilians. However, he knew how valuable in this upside-down world a small army of warriors could be.

"Not sure, but we'll soon march out of here. Probably head somewhere north, maybe the panhandle of Idaho."

"I wish we could find a way to have them stay, but this was the deal we struck with the resistance leaders and civilian leaders, and they thought it best they all go," Timms added.

"I can understand," Gordon said.

"What're your plans, Mr. Van Zandt?" Timms asked.

"Heading home as soon as I can get a vehicle to take me."

"Let me work on that for you," Simpson chimed in.

"Thank you."

"Give me an hour. I'll have a vehicle for you then."

"Now, for the matter of Brittany McCallister. Where can I find her?"

"The jail where you met her the other day, you'll find her there," Simpson answered, then looked at his watch. "In fact she might have already been released."

"If you have nothing else, I'm going to go down and see to her," Gordon said as he stood.

"Very well, see you back here in an hour."

"Nice meeting you," Timms said as he and Gordon shook hands.

Gordon couldn't leave quickly enough. The entire conspiracy was so odd to him. He never saw it coming, but how could he? He wondered if Barone had any inkling, or whether he was so consumed

with hate and anger that he never saw the betrayal playing out be- /
hind the scenes.

Once outside he pulled the phone out. He had tried all night to
contact Samantha but no connection could be made. This time, the
screen showed a strong signal. He closed his eyes, said a short prayer,
and hit the green dial button. After a series of clicks the phone began
to ring. Hearing this made his heart skip a beat.

"Please answer, please answer," he said to himself as he made his
way through the mostly deserted streets.

"Hello."

When he heard her voice he almost cried, he was so worried and
had missed them dearly. "Sam, oh my God, it's so good to hear your
voice."

"Gordon, are you there, hello?" she said.

"Sam, can you hear me?" he asked as he looked at the screen
again. He saw he had the signal strength, but her responses indicated
otherwise.

"Gordon, hello?"

"I'm here, Sam, can you hear me?"

"I can't hear you, Gordon, but I know it's you. If you're there
please hurry home. Haley is sick. There's some type of pandemic,
some sickness has swept through. She's not doing well, she needs
you, please come home."

"Sam, can you hear me, Sam!" He now spoke loudly into the
phone.

"Gordon, I hear you, but it's very faint."

He had now stopped his march toward the jail and focused on
the phone. "Sam, what's wrong with Haley?"

"She's very sick; so is Luke. We are doing the best we can do, but
you need to come home."

The thought of losing his little girl sent fear down his spine.

"Sam, I'm coming home soon. I'm leaving in about an hour. It will take me a day or so and I'll be there!"

"Where are they dropping you off?"

"I'm driving back."

"Why? Why are you driving?"

"Long story, everything is fine on my end. I'll be home soon."

"There's something else too," Samantha said.

Gordon could hear more concern in her voice. "What is it?"

"The government in Cheyenne is sending help, but Nelson and others don't think they're coming to help, so to speak."

"What do they think?"

"That they're coming to quarantine us."

"Honey, everything will be fine, I'll be home soon. I love you," Gordon said, his answer different from the concerned thoughts spinning around in his head.

"I love you too. Please hurry back."

"I will. Tell Haley I love her," he finished, and hung up. Then the reality of everything he had to accomplish before he could leave hit him like a ton of bricks. He pocketed the phone and took off running as fast as he could, considering his wounds, heading for the jail.

Warren Air Force Base, Cheyenne, Wyoming

A light tap on the door halted the debate Annaliese and Sebastian had been having about her ability to get up and move. She insisted she was fine, while he wouldn't allow it. He believed she needed more time to rest.

"Come in," Sebastian called out.

The door opened and Wilbur stepped in.

"Secretary Wilbur, what a surprise to see you here," Sebastian said.

"I've been meaning to stop by to check on you. How are you doing, Annaliese?"

"I'm good, thank you."

"I'm sorry, I don't think we've actually met. I'm Secretary of State Wilbur, but please just call me Bethanny," Wilbur said, holding her hand up in an awkward wave.

"Hi," Annaliese said, looking at this relatively young and attractive woman. Few people would have thought Wilbur attractive, but Annaliese could see it. Wilbur hid her beauty behind stiff clothes, pulled-back hair, and relatively no makeup.

"You're the person I wanted to talk to. The timing of your visit is uncanny," Sebastian said.

"Oh, is it?" Wilbur responded.

A nervous undertone to her voice told Sebastian that something was wrong.

"Mr. Van Zandt, can I speak to you in private?"

"No, whatever he knows, I know; we make decisions together," Annaliese said defiantly.

Wilbur looked at her then back to Sebastian, who nodded his approval.

"The mission in Coos Bay has gone horribly wrong."

Fear traveled down Sebastian's spine upon hearing that.

"We sent one of our men with your brother, and apparently your brother killed him."

"What? I'm sure Gordon had good reason if he did. Believe me, he wouldn't have otherwise," Sebastian said, quick to his brother's defense.

"What has happened there has consequences here. I'm concerned for your safety. I would suggest you don't go out again like you did the other night, and if you do, stay away from Pat's. You don't need any more altercations with Major Schmidt."

"What altercation?" Annaliese asked.

"It's nothing, I'll explain later," Sebastian replied.

"I have credible word that Major Schmidt wants you both arrested. I'm concerned for you both. I've asked for greater security here. I spoke to your doctors and once you're able, I've arranged safe passage to anywhere you want to go."

Annaliese was scared by the things Wilbur was telling them. She reached over and took Sebastian's arm.

"Who is this Major Schmidt?" Annaliese asked.

Wilbur just looked at Annaliese. She wanted to spew out everything she disliked and distrusted about him, but she knew that wasn't the smart thing to do.

"Mr. Van Zandt, just please stay put. No more trips until the one that takes you both away."

"Okay, but what about my brother? Any more news, anything?"

"No, but I can tell you that the administration is not happy. That's why it's important for you both to just lay low until I can get you out."

"Why are you doing this?" Annaliese asked.

Wilbur took a deep breath. "We made you both a promise to take care of you. I don't know what happened in Coos Bay but you're not a party to it. You came here seeking help and I will honor our country's pledge to do that. If I can do anything in my position I will make sure that we keep the mantle of hope and freedom over one of fear and tyranny."

Sebastian and Annaliese could see the passion in Wilbur's face.

"I'll leave you two. Thank you for listening, and please, I cannot stress this enough—stay close to the phone. If I call and say it's time to go, don't hesitate," Wilbur said. She then turned and exited.

Sebastian rushed to follow her into the hallway. "Madam Secretary."

"Yes."

"You're not telling us everything. What is it?"

"I'm worried about you two."

"Why? Because of Gordon? Or Schmidt?"

Looking straight and hard into Sebastian's eyes, she said, "Government has the capacity to do wonderful things and can be an instrument for good, but it can also be an instrument for evil if left in the wrong hands."

Coos Bay, Oregon

As Gordon drew closer to the jail it became apparent that word of Barone's death must have leaked, as he saw groups of Marines and others loading vehicles. The streets were still vacant but soon he knew the word would spread to the people; they'd be out too. Some would merely come out to survey the area, but others would be seeking retribution.

He reached for the handle on the front door of the police station when it burst open. Several Marines brushed past him, loaded down with boxes and arms. Their focus was on getting what they could and not on him.

Aside from the men he encountered on the way out, the place was empty. He meandered down the debris-covered hallway toward the holding cells. At the end of the long hallway stood a massive metal door with a small window. He peered through the thick glass and saw people in cells but couldn't make out any of them. The only way to find out if Brittany was in there was to get inside.

Next to the door was a sliding window and control station for the cells. Before he entered the cell block he picked up a set of larger-than-average-sized keys; he hoped these would be useful. A strong smell of fecal matter and urine overcame him as he entered; placing his arm over his nose and mouth only slightly alleviated the grotesque odor.

"Brittany! Brittany, where are you?" he yelled out.

People began to stir and respond after they heard his calls.

Each cell he looked into housed numerous people, their arms dangling between the bars in a desperate attempt to grab him. Pleas for help and release followed him as he quickly strode down the passageway.

"Brittany!" he called out again.

"Down here, last cell on the right!" she responded frantically, waving her arms.

He jogged the remaining few feet to her and grabbed her hand. "Glad I found you. Are you okay?"

"I'll be better once I get out of here," she replied.

He fumbled with the keys, trying several until he found the one that turned the tumblers hard to the right. With a loud clank, the lock unhinged and he swung the door open.

She jumped into his arms and hugged him tightly and said, "Thank you, thank you. I'm so happy to see you. Where are the guards?"

Gordon grimaced from the tight embrace as her affection brought back the reminder of his earlier fight. "Let's get you out of here," he said, letting go of her and grabbing her hand.

"Where are the guards?"

"Gone, they abandoned their posts . . . listen, too much to explain, let's get you to a safe place," Gordon said urgently.

"No, we're not leaving until we let everyone out of here," she said, holding firm and not moving.

"We don't have a lot of time; things are probably going to get bad soon."

"These are my friends and neighbors. I'm not leaving without them."

Gordon saw the stubborn Brittany he'd met months ago on the road. There was the same woman who had saved him and kept him sane for those harrowing weeks after Hunter's murder. He acquiesced and began to open one door after another. People began pouring out of each open cell and took off toward the exit.

"You're free, go, go," she said loudly.

Gordon opened the last one and a man he remembered seeing before stepped out and walked up to Brittany. She embraced him and kissed him tenderly on the lips.

"You okay? How bad did they hurt you?" she said as she petted his handsome and chiseled face.

"I'm fine. I was so worried; thank God you're safe," the man said.

Gordon looked at them both, shocked to see Brittany acting in this intimate way.

They again embraced tightly and kissed.

"Let's go, sweethearts, we have to go!" Gordon barked.

She looked at Gordon and said, "This is Gordon, the man who saved me and Ty months ago."

The man walked forward and extended his hand. "Nice to meet you. I'm Major Ashley. Brittany speaks highly of you. Thanks for getting us out."

"Well, Major, it's time to go. Colonel Barone is dead and when the word gets out, this place could erupt into total chaos. There's a new mayor and he told me everything will be okay, but I don't trust human nature."

"Please tell me our new mayor's name is Timms," Ashley commented.

"Yeah, it is."

"The plan worked," Ashley said, smiling.

"We don't have time to waste. We need to go before shit hits the fan!" Gordon stressed, taking Brittany by the arm.

"I'm capable of taking care of myself," Brittany snapped.

Gordon cocked his head toward her and said, "This isn't a conversation or debate, let's go." He led them out of the cell block through the police station and back onto the street. The level of activity had increased just in the short time he had been inside.

"C'mon," he said, and began to head back toward city hall.

"Gordon, stop!" Brittany exclaimed.

"What? Let's go."

"I'm . . . we're not going with you," she said, looking at Gordon then turning to face Ashley.

"Really?" Gordon asked, shocked.

"Yes, you go, we'll be fine," she said softly, and walked up to him. She placed her palm on his face and said even more softly, "Thank you for everything; you saved my life more than once. You gave me another shot at life and love." She looked at Ashley when she mentioned love. "I'll never forget you. I don't know why you came back but you did, and you did what you said you would. You took care of me, but you don't have to do that anymore."

"I . . . uh, are you sure? You can come back to Idaho with me. You, Tyler, and the major."

"No, I can't. My place is here."

Gordon stared at her, then looked beyond her to Ashley. "One second," he said as he ran back inside the police station. A minute later he emerged and handed her a note. "This is my address in Idaho. If you change your mind you can find me there. You're welcome at my home anytime, all of you."

She took the note and carefully put it in her pocket.

"Come here," he said as he reached for her and hugged her. "Be safe out there. Tell Tyler I miss him," he said. He was happy for her but also felt an urge to press his case for her to come with him. He didn't know Ashley and didn't want to leave her in a situation that could turn bad again. However, he understood that she was trying to build something with Major Ashley and she was sincere in her objection to leave with him. He had to let her go.

"I'll tell him. He'll be upset that he missed seeing you, as he misses you so much."

Gordon's heart sank for a moment, knowing he would never see her again. "Good-bye, Brittany McCallister," Gordon said.

"Good-bye, Gordon Van Zandt."

Gordon turned away and jogged off. He stopped suddenly and spun around. He saw that she was still watching him. "Stay frosty. It's brutal out there . . . but you know that already."

• • •

Gordon's short trip back across town was uneventful, but the sounds of gunfire and the occasional scream in the distance told him the word was out and the retribution and paybacks were clearly under way. It brought back memories of Iraq and how some Iraqi civilians mishandled justice post–Saddam Hussein. He understood the violent expression of anger and resentment that had stewed for years among those who had suffered under the Baathist regime, so when he witnessed it he found it hard to involve himself or his Marines. What he feared most was that Coos Bay would continue its spiral into violence even after Barone's death. This is why he wanted out of there, and quickly.

City hall was more frantic than when he had left it not an hour before. He found Simpson still holed up in his office packing and preparing for his own departure.

"Top, any timing on my Hummer?"

Looking up a bit flustered, Simpson said, "It's not there. Hold on one minute," he said as he brushed by Gordon and barked at a guard, "Get ahold of Gunny and tell him to get that Hummer out front ASAP!"

"Yes, sir," the Marine guard said and marched off.

"Top, I have another request."

"What you got?"

"Is it possible to get an armored Hummer, a TOW variant with a missile system?"

Simpson gawked at Gordon, mouth agape. "Can I ask what tanks you plan on blowing up?"

"No plans, just prepping for whatever might come my way."

"Can I just get you a fucking tank too?"

"Actually, can I get that with a half dozen missiles and a half dozen Javelins too?"

"Are you fucking serious, Van Zandt?"

"Yes, I am."

"Listen here, you helped us but what you did would have been done if you weren't here. It just helped give us a better cover story to hopefully keep some of the chaos at bay, but I don't think what you did is worth all of that."

"I realize it's a crazy request, but that could give our little town enough firepower to help resist anyone who had something like a tank."

"Who exactly is going to be attacking you with tanks?" Simpson joked.

"To be fair, how do you think the citizens of Coos Bay would answer that question now?"

Simpson thought for a moment and said, "Van Zandt, I really don't owe you anything, but I will help you this one last time."

"Thanks, Top. Oh, and can you toss in some C-4?"

"Go find Gunny Wallace and tell him what you want. You do realize with these extra asks that you won't be leaving as quickly as you want, right?"

"Understood."

Simpson walked over to Gordon and put out his hand. "I imagine this will be the last time we see each other."

"Maybe so. I don't make grand assumptions anymore, but if you find yourself near McCall just keep going."

"That's rude."

"Just joking. I wish you the best, Top. I know plotting against Colonel Barone wasn't easy for you and took courage. I'm just sorry it all had to happen, meaning what the colonel did. I know from talking to him he regretted it, but it was too late."

"Colonel Barone was a conflicted man. I went to war with that man, but he had become someone else. After what happened I couldn't go along with it any longer, but I felt it best to stay close and plot his demise from inside. You know, sometimes I think he knew all along."

"Really?"

"Yes, I do, but we'll never know and it really doesn't matter anymore. He's dead and his chapter in this whole fucking apocalypse is now over. You be safe out there, Van Zandt."

"Good-bye, Master Sergeant."

"Good-bye, Sergeant Van Zandt."

JULY 1, 2015

. . .

"Death is not the greatest loss in life. The greatest loss is what dies inside us while we live."

—Norman Cousins

Tijuana, Mexico

Tears ran down Pablo's face in a steady stream. He hadn't cried like this in many years, but he couldn't control himself as he watched his father's body being laid to rest in the family crypt. Having ordered the doctors to pull life support the day before was hard, but necessary. He was sad that his father hadn't gotten the chance to see him forge a new empire that people around the world would hear about for millennia.

Seeing his mother wail, so heavy with emotion that she was unable to walk, made it tougher for him. He wished he could stay in Mexico for a bit longer to comfort her, but if he was to finish what he started he needed to leave immediately. Last he spoke with General Alejandro, his army was a day and a half outside of Salt Lake City. He ordered them to halt and wait for his arrival later in the day.

Dressed in his uniform after the funeral, he walked into the banquet room to seek out his mother, but she wasn't anywhere to be found. He went from room to room, ignoring others in his family until he found her in her father's office. There she sat weeping in his leather chair.

"Mother, there you are," he said softly, walking toward her.

"He would spend so much time in here. He was such a business-man, your father," she said, looking at the desk.

He walked up to her side and knelt down. "Mother, come to the wake."

She looked at him with her swollen red eyes and touched his face. "You look so much like him when he was a young man. So hand-some, strong, and confident. You're just like him."

"Father was a good man. I don't know if I have that in me. I'm different that way. I'll never have the moral strength that he had."

"My boy, you are like him. You have a dream, a vision, and you go get it. You don't know the word *no*."

"That's true," he said as he kissed her hand.

"He never told you, but after you left he sat me down and told me how proud he was of you," she confided.

Hearing this took him by surprise.

"He was angry with you because he didn't approve of your tac-tics, especially forcing him out, but he knew the day would come when someone challenged him. He was happy it was you."

"Father was proud of me?"

"Absolutely, Pablo, he loved you. He respected your intelligence and courage. When he came back from seeing your army land in San Diego, he told me that you had done something that he could never do. You had topped him; you were now the rightful patron of the family. However, because of how you had overthrown him he was still angry and needed more time," she said, and began to cry again.

"I cannot express enough how much these words mean to me. Having his approval, love, and respect is all I've ever wanted. To know that he was proud of me validates everything, it justifies the entire endeavor. I can leave today with my head held high and my heart full."

"My beautiful boy, I wish you could stay, but I know you must leave. Stand up and let me look at you."

Pablo did just what she asked and stood.

"You're so handsome, my emperor," she said, then kissed his hand. "Go, fulfill your destiny."

"Thank you, Mother. Your words have moved me to action. I will go and finish this. I will immortalize the Juarez name forever," he said, then turned and strutted off.

Still aglow from his meeting with his mother, he walked up to Silva and said, handing him a piece of paper, "Take this down. After we take Salt Lake City, send out this proclamation."

Silva looked it over and nodded in agreement.

"Let it be known that after we plant our flag in Salt Lake City, it will be forever known as Juarez."

Warren Air Force Base, Cheyenne, Wyoming

Sebastian slammed the phone down and exclaimed, "We have to go, now!"

Annaliese sat up in bed, fear gripping her body from the panic in Sebastian's eyes.

"What's going on?" Annaliese asked.

"It was Secretary Wilbur. We have to leave. Men are coming to arrest us!"

"Who's coming to arrest us?"

"No time to talk, c'mon!"

Sebastian helped Annaliese out of bed and into a wheelchair. The only thing he took was the pistol on the nightstand next to the phone, tucking the .45-caliber Sig Sauer P220 into his waistband. He wheeled her to the door but stopped short of exiting right away; he opened it slowly and peeked out. The hallway was uncharacteristically quiet; this gave him a chill as he felt the impending doom of what was coming for them.

"We have to get to a loading dock, wherever that is, so please, no more questions. I need to concentrate," Sebastian barked as he wheeled her at a running pace down the hallway toward the elevators and stairs.

He parked her wheelchair at the stairs and went to pick her up but she stopped him. "Are you crazy? We're three stories up."

"I can't risk getting stuck in an elevator; stairs are the safest."

The elevator chimed just as he picked her up into his arms. When he stepped to the stairwell door, the elevator door opened to reveal several uniformed men. One of them was Major Schmidt.

Schmidt saw Sebastian and smiled a devilish grin.

Sebastian kicked open the door and walked into the dimly lit stairwell. He knew he couldn't move fast with Annaliese in his arms, so he'd have to fight them. He cleared the first level of steps and sat her down.

"What . . . what are you doing?" Annaliese asked in fear.

"Trying to make sure we can get out of here," he replied as he pulled out the pistol and took up a covered position behind the railing at the bottom.

The upper door burst open and the men he'd seen earlier came charging into the stairwell.

Sebastian committed himself and shot the first two men. One tumbled down the stairs and came to rest next to him. Sebastian picked up the man's M16 rifle and a pistol that was holstered on the man's hip. He tucked the pistol into his waistband and slung the rifle. "C'mon, that bought us a few minutes," he said as he went to pick Annaliese up.

"I can walk."

"No, let me carry you."

"I can walk; just don't ask me to sprint," she said as she snatched the Beretta M9 pistol he had just taken off the man. She held it up and said, "Let's do this."

He smiled and gave her a big kiss on the lips. "That's my girl."

Sumter, Oregon

Gordon looked at his watch, then bent over in an attempt to stretch his back. Sleeping on the hard ground aggravated old wounds and was another reminder of the hard life he lived. All through life he did everything he wanted at an extreme, but at the cost of his body. He was only in his mid-thirties but his body had the experiences of someone twice that old. He longed to be back in Samantha's arms and in his own bed. Simpson had honored his word and given him an armored TOW variant Humvee with six TOW missiles, six Javelin antitank missiles, a crate of C-4, detonators, and fuses. He also threw in other goodies for him as well: a crate of M18 antipersonnel mines, a crate of hand grenades, an M240 machine gun with five thousands rounds. He couldn't wage war for long but he could definitely be a pain in someone's ass if they came knocking in McCall. After driving through the late evening, early morning fatigue weighed on him, so he found a quiet brush-covered ditch and camped for the night. With his Hummer topped off and two additional five-gallon cans of diesel he'd be able to make it back, but it would be tight. However, fuel wasn't his biggest concern. The threat from road bandits and modern-day highwaymen were the obstacles he worried about. He was alone and still almost three hundred miles from home, and the roads ahead were not the well maintained. Each mile he traveled would get him closer to home but each bend in the road could spell disaster.

After plotting his route using an old Rand McNally map, he packed his gear and headed back on his way. The first town he'd pass through would be the tiny little town of Sumter. Each town he had journeyed through since the lights went out was a different experience. Some were heavily guarded and others wide open. He had no idea what to expect when he approached the edge of town, but he was cautious. No signs of real life were initially present, but as he made the right turn into the main part of town he saw more activity. He slowed down further as he approached a little establishment called the Elkhorn Saloon. Gordon came to a full stop when a woman with blood running down her face and chest jumped in front of him.

"Please help!" she cried out, waving her arms.

Gordon couldn't get involved; he had to make it home. He turned the steering wheel and began to accelerate around her when she jumped on the hood. "Please, they have my daughter and they'll kill her."

"Get off!" Gordon yelled at her from the safety of the reinforced armored Humvee.

"My daughter, please!"

Out of the corner of his eye he saw the front door explode open and a young teenage girl come sprinting out toward them. Behind her were two men and they appeared intent on stopping her. The young girl, no older than thirteen, only made it the length of the cars parked out front before one man tackled her to the ground. The girl hit the ground hard with the man on her back.

The frantic woman jumped off the hood and dashed toward her daughter. When she reached them, she began to kick one man when the other man who had been in pursuit punched her in the face.

Gordon had seen enough. He pulled to the side of the road and stepped out, his rifle at the ready. He just couldn't allow this to happen. Getting involved could put things in jeopardy for him, but he couldn't rest knowing he'd allowed these men to brutalize these women.

"Get off the girl!" he ordered from across the narrow road.

"Fuck off!" the man who had punched the woman barked. He proceeded to grab the woman by the hair and began to drag her back toward the saloon.

Gordon calmly slid the two-point sling over his head and walked across the road.

The young girl was wrestling under the weight of the man who had tackled her. She cried and begged, but he was now trying to pull her pants down.

The two men seemed to be oblivious to Gordon's steady approach. Either they didn't care or were so blinded by their desire to hurt these women that they didn't take notice when he walked up to them. Remaining quiet, he let the rifle hang and pulled out his pistol. He stepped up to the man who was hurting the teenage girl and said, "Hey!"

The man looked up, his eyes red with rage and pure hatred. His leathery tanned skin was covered in an uneven and dirty beard that stretched from his face to his neck. The last thing the man saw was Gordon's pistol in his face.

Gordon didn't seek this fight, but he also wasn't about to get his hands dirty or risk going hand-to-hand. He was going to start and end this altercation quickly and efficiently. He looked into the man's eyes and just squeezed the trigger.

The back of the man's head exploded. The force of the bullet ripping through his skull flung him back and off the girl.

She wiggled away from him and Gordon in fear.

The man who had been dragging the woman looked up in shock and fear after hearing the loud shot. He dropped the woman but Gordon dropped the hammer on him right after. A well-placed

.45-caliber round hit him in the chest, forcing him to fall backward against the front door of the saloon. His body twitched but he wasn't long for death as he breathed a few times then expired.

The woman sprang up and ran toward her daughter, then embraced her tightly.

Gordon holstered the pistol and turned to them. "You okay?"

"Please help him, inside, please!" the woman begged.

"Who's inside?"

"He's a friend, they'll kill him."

Gordon looked at them both and decided that he'd extend his aid by helping out the man inside.

"How many are inside?"

"Six . . . no, sorry, four, you killed two of them," the woman said, clearly flustered from the ordeal.

Gordon turned back and approached the front door. He stopped shy of opening it when he noticed a few windows. He stepped over and peeked inside the dark room. All he could see were shadows but he did hear men yelling. He walked back to the entrance, moved the dead body, and with one fluid motion flung open the door and stepped across the threshold with his pistol at the ready.

Warren Air Force Base, Cheyenne, Wyoming

The ground floor of the hospital was busy, and no one seemed to notice them as they walked in an odd, hurried but slow-paced walk. Annaliese was trying to move fast but the pain in her incision radiated from her lower abdomen throughout. She had reduced her pain medication a couple of days ago and now she wished she hadn't.

Frustrated by their slow speed, Sebastian saw a wheelchair, grabbed it, and put her in it. He then began to run down the hall. Nowhere did he see a sign or posting that directed him to the loading docks.

He abruptly stopped at a nursing station and asked, "Where's the loading dock?"

The woman working at the desk looked at him strangely. "Is everything okay, sir?"

"Where's the loading dock?" he repeated.

Her eyes were wide with surprise as she noticed that he was armed. "Ahh, down the hall, take a right, go through the door on the left. The stairs will take you down one level to the loading dock."

"Thanks!" Sebastian said and took off running.

He made the right and sprinted down the last hallway, dodging and weaving around people, carts, wheelchairs, and beds. He slid to a stop at the end of that hallway and helped Annaliese up. He opened the door and they both began to descend when the door above him burst open. He craned his head but couldn't see who it was from his vantage point. "Let's hurry."

"I'm moving as fast as I can."

They reached the door at the bottom and opened it. Sebastian blinked a few times, adjusting his eyes to the bright light of day, and saw a parked Humvee. A man in plainclothes stepped out and waved to them.

"That must be our ride," Sebastian said.

They scurried along the loading dock but they couldn't move fast enough. Several uniformed soldiers appeared from the door they had just burst through.

Sebastian looked over his shoulder and knew he had to engage them. "Help her!" he cried out to the man next to the Humvee.

A door at the opposite end of the dock exploded open and more soldiers poured out, rifles at the ready.

Sebastian knew the situation was quickly deteriorating, and to have a chance he'd either have to surrender or kill them all. The option for surrender was dashed because he knew that only meant possible torture and death anyway. So with the clarity that today might be his last day, he decided he'd go down in a fight. He let go of Annaliese's arm, spun around with the pistol in hand, and began to shoot. His shots hit the men charging toward him. Schmidt, who had just emerged from the doorway, ducked back inside.

Annaliese, taking her cues from Sebastian, held the Beretta out in front of her and started to shoot the half dozen soldiers who had appeared at the opposite end of the dock.

The man from the Humvee reached Annaliese and pleaded, "Ma'am, we need to get out of here."

Annaliese nodded but kept shooting until the pistol's slide locked to the rear. She jumped in the truck and yelled for Sebastian to do the same.

Sebastian fired a few more rounds until his Sig P220 also ran out of bullets. Not having another magazine, he dropped the pistol and swung the rifle into his shoulder. With no more men coming from the door he had come from, he turned to engage the soldiers Annaliese had been shooting at. He couldn't see them, as they had taken cover behind Dumpsters.

She called out again. "Sebastian, hurry up!"

The distance to the Humvee seemed much farther than the eighty feet he had to clear. He lowered the rifle and began to sprint toward her, his eyes locked on hers. The expression on her face dramatically changed as she screamed out, "Behind you!" Before he could react, he felt a searing pain in his left leg as a single bullet ripped through his thigh. His leg gave out as he fell to the ground hard. He looked up and saw the Humvee was only a few yards away. He struggled but stood and began to run again when another bullet clipped his right calf. He again fell to the ground. He cringed in pain but began to rise again as more and more men poured into the loading dock.

Annaliese screamed and started to get out of the Humvee.

"No! No! Take her away, get her out of here! Go!" Sebastian commanded the driver.

"Sebastian, get up!"

"Go!" he yelled.

The man put the Humvee in gear and slammed on the accelerator.

"Stop, no, stop! Sebastian!" she screamed out.

Sebastian climbed back to his feet and brought the rifle up to his shoulder to engage the men when a boot to his lower back forced him to the ground again.

Sebastian rolled over, still holding the rifle, but Schmidt slammed his arm down and pinned it.

"Get it over with!" Sebastian barked.

"You're no good to me dead, Van Zandt. I need you for something else."

Sumter, Oregon

Gordon stepped into the dimly lit and musty barroom ready to fight but he found only a single man standing in the middle of the room. His sweat-soaked T-shirt was torn and bloody and he was panting heavily. Gordon scanned the room quickly but saw only turned-up tables, chairs, and smashed bottles and glass along the floor.

He turned the pistol on the man and asked, "I assume you're the guy I was sent in here to save?"

"Save? I had this under control."

Gordon laughed at the man's cockiness. He looked closer at the floor and saw pools of blood, and most bizarre of all, an ear. He looked back to the man, eyebrows raised.

"It's not mine," the man said with a smile.

The man was impressive in stature. He stood just shy of six feet but to Gordon the air he gave off made him look taller. His wide shoulders supported his large chest and two muscular arms. His thick black hair was slicked back and he sported a manicured goatee.

"Are you going to shoot me? If not, please put that away," the man said, his piercing brown eyes still focused on Gordon in a skeptical stare.

"What happened?" Gordon asked as he holstered the pistol.

"Let's say it was a misunderstanding," the man said as he turned away from Gordon and walked to the bar. He picked up a full shot glass and tossed it back; he looked behind the bar and pulled out a bottle of Jack Daniel's, unscrewed the top, and began to drink directly from it.

"Looks like I'm not needed. I'll bid you farewell then," Gordon said as he turned and made for the door.

"Have a drink with me," the man blurted out.

"Normally I'd say yes, but I gotta get home."

"Where's home?"

Not wanting to answer him, Gordon just said, "Have a good day."

Outside, the woman and her daughter were gone. Gordon looked for them but they were nowhere to be seen. He strode across the street to his Humvee but stopped short when he considered the cars parked out front. He turned back around and looked at them. The temptation was there to see if he could take one, but he knew the men who had fled could be back and in greater numbers. Pushing the idea out of his mind he stowed his rifle and jumped in the Humvee.

"Hey, where ya heading?" the man said, now standing in the parking lot, the bottle of Jack in his grip.

"Listen, I don't know you. I'm not going to tell you anything. This was just a chance encounter; I helped out when I saw the woman," Gordon said.

"I'm headed to McCall, Idaho, after a few more stops around

these parts. You headed in that direction? I wouldn't mind the company on the road."

The mention of McCall piqued Gordon's interest. He laughed to himself when he thought about how strange it was that he'd encountered this man in the middle of nowhere and he was headed to the exact same place. Gordon lost his faith long ago in the war-torn streets of Fallujah but sometimes things like this made him reconsider that maybe somewhere there was a divine spirit looking over him. Either way, the coincidence was too much for Gordon to look past. He looked at the man and said, "What's your name?"

The man took a swig from the bottle and strutted across the street. He stuck out his hand and said, "Nicholas Knight. Nice to meet you."

"Nice to meet you too, Nicholas, but I like to travel alone."

"Your loss," Nicholas smirked.

"Maybe so. Safe travels—maybe we'll meet again," Gordon answered as he fired up the Humvee.

Over the rumble of the engine, Nicholas asked, "What's your name? I didn't get it."

"I'm Gordon Van Zandt. Now, don't get yourself into any more trouble," Gordon said loudly.

Nicholas nodded.

Gordon gave a wave similar to a salute and punched the accelerator.

Nicholas watched him drive off, took another long swig of whiskey, and said to himself, "Trouble—hell, that's my middle name."

JULY 2, 2015

. . .

"Power tends to corrupt and absolute power corrupts absolutely. Great men are almost always bad men."

—Lord Acton

Twenty-five miles west of Salt Lake City, Utah

Ever the believer in divine signs, Pablo couldn't stop thinking about what his mother had shared with him. Pablo declared that he'd see the mission through and ensure the Pan-American Empire would succeed not only for his glory but for his father's.

The voice of the chopper pilot sounded in his headset.

"Emperor, General Alejandro is on the command frequency. He is requesting to speak to you."

Talking into the microphone, Pablo said, "Of course."

The pilot turned the knob on the radio and gave Pablo a thumbs-up.

"General Alejandro, how are you?" Pablo asked with a joy in his voice that was never present before.

"Emperor, I wanted to check on your ETA. We are in place awaiting your arrival."

The pilot then pointed out to a spot in the far distance.

Pablo leaned forward and looked until he saw tiny dots that stretched east to west for miles. "I think we see you, General."

The pilot held up his hand and flashed his open hand twice.

"General, we will be landing in ten minutes."

"We still can't see you, but your loyal soldiers look forward to the triumphant reunion with their emperor."

"I too look forward to seeing my men. Great things are coming for us, General, great things."

"Sir, I thought I should tell you that we have received an envoy from the United States."

"What are they doing here?"

"I just received the call from our forces along the northern flank. They pulled up in a truck, white flag displayed."

"I don't understand. Why would they come all the way here?"

"The American says he has come on the behalf of President Conner."

"Where are they now?"

"We cleared them through; they're being escorted to me now."

"You cleared them through?" Pablo thundered. "This doesn't make sense. Did anyone look in the truck?"

A long pause preceded Alejandro's response. "There wasn't anything in the back, sir. The truck bed was empty."

Pablo thought about this unusual maneuver by Conner. Could his victory be at hand? Could Conner see the writing on the wall, and was he now willing to plead for peace?

"Sir, I see your helicopter now. I look fo—"

The radio went silent just as a bright flash painfully blinded Pablo. He jerked away from the haloing glow and cried out, "Argh!"

The pilot flinched and turned his head away, causing the helicopter to drop suddenly.

Pablo turned back and blinked his eyes repeated until his vision adjusted. What he saw now was awesome. A large mushroom cloud towered over the desert; the dots that had represented his army were lost in the immense and fast-moving debris cloud on the surface.

"Turn now, get out of here!" Pablo yelled.

The pilot followed his instructions but just as they turned, a violent shock wave hit the helicopter broadside. The force of the shock wave destabilized the chopper. Alarms sang out inside the cockpit as the pilot struggled to regain control. The helicopter soon began to spin rapidly.

Pablo looked out the window to get his bearings but the intense spinning made it impossible. A feeling of vertigo overcame him as the helicopter spun hard and fast toward the ground.

"Ahhhhh!" he cried out as he closed his eyes and prayed. This could not be how it all ended for him. How could this be, he thought, how? How could this be? He opened his eyes for the last time to see the brown and tan earthly tones of the ground before darkness enveloped him.

Cheyenne, Wyoming

Conner didn't know when he'd get the word but each time the phone rang or someone knocked he expected it to be Dylan or Baxter there to tell him the exciting news.

He neglected the pile of paperwork on his desk and instead spent the greater part of the day staring out his office window to the now bustling city streets of Cheyenne. He was proud of what he'd accomplished so far and now he had confidence that he could do the same for the rest of the country. For the first time in a long time, he felt true hope. His initial reluctance to deal with his domestic enemies had disappeared. He now questioned his previous mind-set that operated from a place of dialogue or open warfare. He had never thought of using deception and covert actions to tackle his problems, but in the span of a week, he had done away with Colonel Barone, the Republic of Lakotah, and soon the Pan-American Empire. He expected to get some pushback from some in his staff, but once his allies gave him their approval to do what he needed to do on his soil, his conscience would be clear. He knew Baxter would be upset by the secretive manner of the operation, but he always toed the line.

The day before, he had been informed that their mission to Coos Bay had been successful. Timms, the new mayor of Coos Bay, had contacted Cheyenne to inform them of what had transpired and gave Conner the information that he and Schmidt had been curious about—whether Finley been successful. Apparently he had been, much to Conner's relief.

The phone's loud ring made him jump. He hoped it brought news of another foe slain. He swung his chair around and looked at the second button glow and flash. An internal line. He reached out, picked up the receiver, and said, "President Conner."

"Sir, this is General Baxter."

Yes, this was the call. A smile stretched across his face as he knew what was coming next.

"There's been a nuclear detonation in the Utah desert. We don't have any other reports, but it appears to have been set off approximately in the last location we had for the PAE army."

"Hmm, that sounds like a good thing," he said, in a weak attempt at trying to sound surprised.

Baxter paused, then said, "Sir, what's going on?"

"General, please come see me and I'll tell you everything. Today is a day to rejoice."

"Yes, sir, I'll be there shortly."

Conner rested back in his chair and placed his arms behind his head and began to hum a tune.

The phone then rang again. He assumed it was Cruz calling to discuss the news of the nuclear blast, but it wasn't. It was Schmidt.

"Mr. President?"

"Yes, Major."

"Sir, you told me to call you if my men saw anything suspicious with General Baxter and Secretary Wilbur."

Conner sat up in his chair with anticipation. "Yes."

"Last night, one of my men saw them gather at General Baxter's quarters."

"Who is *them*?"

"Secretary Wilbur and your chief of staff, Dylan. We didn't see the general, but it's assumed he was there."

"How long were they together?" Conner asked, his fist clenched.

"About two hours. Then they left and all were followed back to their residences."

"Thank you, Major."

"Yes, sir."

"Is that it?"

"Nothing more, sir."

"Oh, and good job on delivering the bomb. You've given our country a chance to rebuild."

"My pleasure, sir."

"I'll see you tomorrow, then?"

"Of course, sir."

Conner hung up the phone. He didn't have to think too hard to know what Baxter, Wilbur, and Dylan were meeting about; he knew they were still upset about his secret operations. He imagined them commiserating and plotting a way to become more involved in the government. He didn't want to act rashly, but with this new information, he'd keep them at a distance and monitor their movements.

McCall, Idaho

Knowing that Gordon would be home tomorrow gave Samantha joy and hope. Everything for her and the kids had been improving. The natural concoctions that Phyllis had made had given Haley and Luke some much-needed relief from their painful symptoms. The illness had not progressed, and for Haley her fever had reduced to a manageable level. Luke's was still high but it hadn't gone above 102 since she had been administering the pine-needle tea and licorice leaf. Upon seeing the positive results, she had sent the ever-skeptical Nelson into town to tell the doctors that these remedies were proving to be helpful. They weren't out of the woods yet, and the virus was still proving to be deadly, so she figured spreading this information would be well-received. Each time she saw Nelson he brought stories of others dying and increased numbers contracting it. The town and surrounding area had come to a standstill from what was now clearly a pandemic. She hadn't received any other news about aid from the federal government and Boise had also been nonresponsive. The rumors were that it had hit them hard there too.

The kids were asleep. During the moments they were resting she spent her time preparing fresh medicines and food that they could keep down. Soup had been great way to hydrate them and give them nutrition that could keep their strength up. She walked into the garage to get some canned chicken for her chicken noodle soup when she heard the phone ring.

Excited to hear Gordon's voice again she instantly stopped what she was doing and ran back inside.

With a hop in her step and glee in her voice she picked up the phone. "Hi, sweetie."

"Mrs. Van Zandt?" a man's voice asked.

She didn't recognize the voice on the other end. Hearing some-one else other than Gordon startled her. "This is she."

The man cleared his voice and said, "You've called the offices of President Conner several times inquiring about Sebastian and Annaliese Van Zandt."

"Yes, yes, I have. How are they?"

"Ma'am, have you been in contact with your husband, Gordon Van Zandt?"

The man's question alarmed her but she answered anyway. "Yes."

"Can you tell me where he is?"

"Who is this?"

"Ma'am, you've called wanting information on his brother and sister-in-law but we need to know the whereabouts of your husband first."

"I don't understand; he went there for you. Why don't you talk to him yourself?"

"We've tried, but we can't reach him. Is he okay?"

"Yes, he's fine, he's coming home. He'll be back in McCall by this time tomorrow. Who is this?"

"Good, so he'll be back in McCall tomorrow. Please relay a mes-sage to him for us."

"Please answer my question."

"Tell him his brother has been arrested for treason and if he wants him to survive the verdict that will be imposed, he and the leaders of the Cascadian Movement will need to surrender to us."

Samantha's heart was in her throat. "Who is this?" she asked, barely above a whisper.

"My name is Major Schmidt. Tell him he can give me his answer when I arrive in McCall," Schmidt said, then hung up.

JULY 3, 2015

• • •

Cheyenne, Wyoming

Conner cleared the main executive conference room for this meeting with his top staff. A small army of lower level staff had been in the room working on new congressional districting. No one had arrived yet, so it gave Conner time to look at the maps and printouts that were draped across the table and pinned to the walls. He leaned in and stared at a map that showed congressional districts. Each state was broken into a grid pattern. It resembled nothing like the districts he was familiar with. His staff was getting rid of the gerrymandering that was so prevalent before. However, these districts were nothing more than suggestions, because the state legislatures still held the power to district. He appreciated his staff's passion, but they lacked political experience. After he was done with his announcements today, they'd be a bit more aware of how things worked, politically speaking.

One by one they all entered the room and took their seats. Conner stood, smiling and overtly happy, his hands on his hips as he hovered at the end of the long conference table. To him, this was a briefing and a celebration.

With everyone settled in their seats he called out to Dylan, "Bring in the refreshments."

Dylan walked in with several bottles of champagne. Conner grabbed one of the bottles and popped the cork.

Many in the room were shocked by this break in protocol. Seeing Conner so happy was one thing; seeing him open a bottle of champagne was something entirely different.

"Dylan, pour everyone a drink."

Dylan poured the glasses and handed them out. When everyone had a drink he turned to Conner.

Conner began his prepared speech. "Several things happened this week that were pivotal to our ability to rebuild. We destroyed a separatist movement; we removed a tyrant in Oregon, reunifying those states with us; and late yesterday, we destroyed the entire Pan-American Empire army."

Several people murmured and talked but soon fell quiet. Everyone was obviously aware of what had happened to the Lakotah, but the news of Barone and the PAE was a surprise.

"Many of you have been suspicious of my new tactics, so much that a few of you openly challenged me. I heard you, told you I'd include you in on some of the operations, but I couldn't include you on the specifics of the former two operations." Conner took a moment to collect his thoughts and continued. "You all knew about my mission in Coos Bay, but what you didn't know was my sole objective was to assassinate the colonel. I didn't want intelligence; I wanted to get rid of the man. I knew by doing so, his entire organization would collapse. We have been getting spotty reports and the one thing that stood out to me was that the resistance he was facing was fierce and the loyalty from his troops was not solid. If we could

remove him we would end his insurrection. So, along with Major
Schmidt, we did just that. We were able to get in a good man to do
the job, but we needed a patsy to help get him close and that was the
man Gordon Van Zandt. The mission was successful, but it came at
a price, and that was the loss of Staff Sergeant Finley. Mr. Van Zandt
proved his loyalties were with Colonel Barone and apparently after
Staff Sergeant Finley did his job, Mr. Van Zandt killed him. Our
country lost a good man and we will remember him, but he sacrificed
himself for a great cause and that was preserving our country." He
paused as a few in the room looked at each other uneasily. "So, let's
raise our glasses first to Sergeant Finley and to our successful mission in Coos Bay," Conner declared, raising his glass high.

All in the room raised their glasses and repeated with Conner,
"To Staff Sergeant Finley!"

"Now, let me get to the best news. Late yesterday, we destroyed
Emperor Pablo and his Pan-American forces outside of Salt Lake
City. We delivered the lethal blow by means of a nuclear weapon—"

Crosstalk erupted in the room at the mention of the nuclear
weapon.

"Be quiet, please, let me finish!" Conner yelled.

The room fell silent.

"The nuclear weapon that we used against the PAE was meant for
us. It was the last of their weapons; it was the weapon that was supposed to have destroyed us in Cheyenne Mountain but for whatever
reason never made it. We came into possession of this weapon not
long ago; Major Schmidt captured it when he was heading here and
we . . . I have no doubt that the weapon, if it had made it here, would
have been used against us. I ordered Major Schmidt to deliver the
weapon back to its rightful owners, the PAE. Yesterday that package
arrived under the guise of a peace envoy. Sadly the mission was a
suicide mission and we lost two men." Conner picked up a piece of

paper. "A Private First Class Browning and Specialist Walter gave their lives so that we could live another day. They too gave all for this country." Conner put down the paper and picked up his glass. "To Private First Class Browning and Specialist Walter."

Soon everyone was on their feet, clapping. Conner nodded and took in the praise. He let a few moments pass before instructing everyone to sit back down.

"Now we can move forward without the threat from these forces. However, our work is not done. There are more separatist factions to deal with and we are moving on them now. I won't go into operational details but soon, our country will be free of everyone who wishes to stop its advance toward reconstruction."

The words *won't go into operational details* struck a nerve with a few in the room, one of them being General Baxter.

"Sir, I'm not here to rain on any parades and I don't want to take away from these recent achievements. They were important and I applaud our forces for successfully carrying those out. But I feel the need to remind you of the promise you gave us."

"I'm aware of the promise, but as president, I have the privilege to change my mind. Ever since the episode with General Griswald months ago, I've been forced to become more watchful. Our country and this government are fragile," Conner said, pacing around the room.

Dylan jumped in and said, "Sir, you keep breaking promises. Days ago you put off Project Congress. We had been working on that for a long time; there are hundreds of people and candidates who had been working hard. Many people are upset, the people desire it—"

"Desire it? I don't think so; the people don't give two shits. The people care about having running water and electricity, they care about food, they care about having access to health care and they want to live in peace without the threat of violence. It's what you care about, Dylan—it's what you and others in here care about because you're from the political class. Go ask anyone out there on the street and have them prioritize having a congressman or having clean water, and I can guarantee their answer. I'm not getting rid of the idea all together, just for now. We have too much to work on."

Dylan began to shake his head but stopped short of saying anything else.

Wilbur then spoke up. "Mr. President, abolishing the plan to reestablish the Congress and then undergoing these covert black operations might not be the best PR for the country to our allies—"

Conner cut her off as he had Dylan. "Madam Secretary, I've spoken with our allies; they have promised to continue to support us." He puffed up. "I will continue to operate under the emergency powers granted me under the National Defense Authorization Act. Until I see that we are ready, I will continue the reconstruction while simultaneously pursuing the eradication of any threats on American soil." Conner walked to the door and opened it. A moment later Major Schmidt walked in with several armed soldiers.

The tension in the room was palpable as each soldier walked in and took up positions throughout the room. Conner closed the door once everyone was inside.

"Everyone knows Major Schmidt. He and his men have become an effective weapon for the United States. I want you all to thank him for everything he has sacrificed."

Several people applauded but many sat in fear.

"Mr. President, what is going on?" Baxter asked.

"General, after the bombs destroyed our bunkers we have known that the only way for it to have happened was with inside help. I believe even today we are faced with those within our ranks who would do us harm or undermine our goals of achieving a stable nation."

Several people began to stir in their chairs and look around uneasily.

"Recently we tried made an arrest of a suspected separatist. While Major Schmidt and his men were en route to execute the warrant, the accused was tipped off. What that tip resulted in was a gunfight that left four of our people dead and two wounded. We captured one of the persons but the other was able to flee and is still at large. We happen to believe that the tip came from someone sitting here. Someone in this very room helped a suspected separatist flee." Conner walked over and stood near Wilbur. He placed his hand on her chair and leaned in.

Wilbur began to sweat.

Baxter's eyes darted around the table. He hadn't been the one who made the call but he was aware it had happened. Fear now rushed through his body as he wondered if Conner was aware of his secret meeting with Dylan and Wilbur. This meeting hadn't involved much more than discussing options to help temper some of the more aggressive and totalitarian positions that Conner had made. No one was advocating removal. He had begged Wilbur not to make the call but she said that arresting the Van Zandts was illegal, as they hadn't done anything wrong. She argued that without evidence of any wrongdoing, an arrest couldn't be justified. She maintained that practices such as these, arresting political rivals or innocent people, could be the beginnings of a slippery slope toward a dictatorship.

Conner leaned farther until his head was past hers and he was staring just feet from Dylan, who sat across from her.

"Why, Dylan, why did you do it?" Conner asked.

"What? I didn't do anything," Dylan shouted out, surprised.

"Major Schmidt, arrest Dylan, get him out of here. I don't want to see him."

"Sir, Mr. President? This is a mistake, I didn't do anything! I didn't warn anybody. Mr. President, please, you've got the wrong person," Dylan pleaded as two soldiers stepped forward and grabbed him by his slender arms.

"I trusted you," Conner said, looking at Dylan with disgust.

"Mr. President, please!" Dylan begged as he was dragged out of the room and down the hall.

"Sir, what's going to happen to him?" Baxter asked.

Wilbur was in complete shock but she couldn't fall on her own sword. There was important work to be done, and she knew she had to be at the helm of it. Someone had to keep Conner in check. It wasn't right that Dylan was being arrested, but she assumed they could work out a way for him to be released. Her mind started swimming with ideas as she nervously glanced at Baxter.

"He will be detained for as long as need be. We will find the right time to try him, but now we are busy," Conner answered as he walked back to his spot at the head of the table. He leaned forward, picked up the glass that still had champagne, and raised it. "We've all been through so much. We've all suffered and lost loved ones. But day by day we are rebuilding, and we will be whole as a nation again, soon. Tomorrow is a fitting day to celebrate our recent victories. Tomorrow we will celebrate the Fourth of July, but with new vigor. We will have a national celebration the likes of which haven't been seen since the first Fourth of July was celebrated those many years ago. We are now free from the threat of an invader, we are free from the threat of a tyrant, and we are free from the threat of traitors who would tear our nation apart."

Everyone stood with their glasses in hand. Conner could see some trembling; the shock at what just happened was still running through their bodies. He knew he had struck fear in them and that was exactly what he wanted to do.

Raising the glass even higher, Conner said, "To the United States of America!"

New Meadows, Idaho

If Gordon had been blindfolded he'd still know he was close to home by the rich smell of pine in the air. The drive from Sumter to New Meadows had been uneventful and Gordon was thankful for that. However, it was an eye-opening trip. He saw a landscape filled with people working the earth to plant gardens and crops or out working with what livestock they had. Everyone was living the life of their ancestors. They were outside, working with their hands to make ends meet; but now making ends meet had a new meaning. He laughed to himself when he passed an abandoned fast-food restaurant. How easy it was to feed the population before. People had taken the easy access for granted so much that it was commonplace to throw huge amounts of it away. He remembered the dinner parties where people were so picky over what they ate because they could be; he himself was guilty of those behaviors too. Food had become an industry, and he understood how that happened. However, along the way of industrializing food so that the masses could be fed, the people forgot where food came from. But now, food was no longer taken for granted—it became the fuel to sustain existence again. As he made the turns past the new farms and freshly tilled fields, he wondered if food would ever become what it had been in the Before, or if people realized the gluttony of the past was not a good thing at all.

Samantha had called him the moment she had gotten off the phone with Schmidt. So many things had been going through his mind after learning that Sebastian was in custody back in Cheyenne. He could only presume that it all had to do with what happened in Coos Bay. If the pandemic hadn't rushed him home, the news that federal forces were coming to McCall to arrest him added to his motivation to get there. He was happy that he had asked for the armament he now possessed. He now had some tools that they could use to protect themselves from whatever was coming their way.

The drive gave him the opportunity to reflect on the past few months. So many things had happened to him and his family since the lights went out back in December. One thing that became abundantly clear to him was that his actions were always reactive rather than proactive. He didn't want to do that anymore. Samantha and others throughout his life had accused him of being "hardheaded and stubborn," and now without a doubt he knew they were right. It took the murder of Hunter to show him that he couldn't just go off half-cocked in this new world. If he wanted to survive he needed to carefully plan his actions.

After what had just happened to him in Coos Bay and to Sebastian in Cheyenne, he needed to be active with regard not only to protecting his family but in creating a place for them to flourish in. The way he could do that was to be a part of a new political system, like Cascadia, where he could dictate the rules and laws that he and his family lived under. What happened in Coos Bay gave him a glimpse of what a corrupt and desperate system looked like—both Barone's and Conner's. Conner had ordered his execution, after all. He understood the desire and necessity for Conner to rid himself of Barone, but what had he done? Now his brother was captive and he was a fugitive. If Conner was ruthless enough to attempt to assassinate him, what else was he capable of? He had to marshal the people of McCall to protect them from what was coming, and instead of convincing them, he needed to be in charge of the entire thing. If he wanted to keep his family safe, he would have to create and then lead this new system. He couldn't trust anyone else to do this. He had to be the one.

With each passing mile he plotted just how he'd make his way to the top of the political food chain in McCall. He had the skill set, the knowledge, the connections, and some firepower. Those things would give him a seat at the table. Once there, he'd find a way to be the one at the head of it.

• • •

The northern checkpoint to McCall sat in the middle of Highway 55, adjacent to the entrance of Brundage Mountain Ski Resort. Stretching from one side of the road to the other were three rows of abandoned cars. Barbed wire, broken glass, and metals spikes were strewn in front of that a narrow chute made from old railroad ties that directed a single car or vehicle into the main guard. Rainey had designed what he thought was a very effective checkpoint.

Gordon went into the chute and was cleared quickly. He saw Rainey and motioned him over.

"Chief, how are you?"

"We've seen better times. What do you have there?" Rainey asked, motioning to the TOW missile system mounted on the hood of the Humvee.

"It's a blender," Gordon joked.

Rainey laughed. "Where have you been?"

"Oh, here and there."

"I won't ask further. I do advise you take a mask and gloves before you make your way into town, though."

"How's it going?" Gordon asked, eager to get Rainey's thoughts on the pandemic.

"It's not good, but we have hope that Charles Chenowith will pull a Hail Mary and find a cure."

"Listen, Chief, I want to help out."

"Sure thing, we have some shifts open . . ."

"Not that—I want to help more than that. I don't want to be a body that you use to help fill a schedule here or there. I want to help in the decision making."

"We leave those sorts of things to our elected leaders."

"Chief, I have some critical information that you and the town leadership need to be made aware of. I know you're busy now, but can we and the mayor and city council meet later?"

"Well, the mayor is sick, but I can pull the others together. Say, around one this afternoon?"

"I'll be there," Gordon answered. With that, he fired up the Hummer and drove off toward his reunion with Samantha and Haley.

• • •

The empty streets of town were the first change he noticed. Mother Nature had a way of reminding everyone who was really in charge of things.

When he arrived at his house, there was a sadness that hung over it, like an invisible dark cloud. He jumped out of the Hummer and quickly jogged to the front door. He found it locked and knocked to announce his arrival.

A moment later, he heard the loud clack of the dead bolt being unlocked. The door opened, and there stood a weary but smiling Samantha.

"You're finally home, thank God," she said as she embraced him. They held each other and kissed.

Her body felt good to his touch. He had missed her so much. He pulled her away when he felt the warm tears soak through the fabric of his shirt. "You're crying."

"I just missed you so much. This whole thing with the kids has me really scared," she said softly, wiping tears from her face and eyes.

"We'll get through this. Just remember, Haley is a Van Zandt.

We're stubborn. We won't let a little ol' virus take us out," Gordon said, attempting a little humor.

Samantha smiled. "She's awake right now. She refused to take a nap ever since I told her you'd be coming home this morning."

Gordon again kissed Samantha then made his way into the house. He marched down the hall toward Haley's bedroom when Samantha stopped him.

"Here, you'll need this," she said, handing him latex gloves and a mask.

Gordon hesitated at first but realized the importance of not getting sick. He donned the protective items then entered Haley's room.

"Dada," Haley said.

"Hi, baby, how ya doing?" Gordon asked as he quickly stepped across the room to her bedside and sat down.

Haley instinctually rolled over and embraced Gordon, who didn't hesitate to reciprocate.

"I missed you, Dada. I'm happy you're home," Haley said, her head now resting in Gordon's lap.

A wave of emotions washed across him as he looked down at her gaunt face. Her eyes were sunken and her skin was ashen. Her little body looked thin and weak. Tears began to well up in his eyes as he saw just how sick she was.

Within minutes she was fast asleep in his arms. She had waited patiently to see him, and with that fulfilled, she gave into the fatigue. Gordon watched her labored breathing and leaned back against the headboard. He too decided to let sleep take him and soon he was sleeping.

• • •

Gordon shot up, sweat beading on his forehead. He looked beside him and saw Haley lying sweetly, her chest rising and falling. Instinctively he looked on his wrist for his watch but he had taken it off early that morning. Knowing he had set a meeting with Rainey and the city council he sprang to his feet. When he entered the hallway, he heard a noise coming from the kitchen. He made his way toward it and was surprised when he encountered Nelson.

"Looky who's awake. How ya doing?" Nelson asked, stopping what he was doing behind the counter in the kitchen.

"Hey, buddy. What time is it?"

"Oh, about twelve-thirty."

"Good, I was worried I overslept."

"You were sleeping like a baby in there."

Gordon removed the mask and gloves and placed them on the counter.

With a pair of tongs, Nelson grabbed them and immediately tossed them in the trash can. He then took a spray bottle filled with bleach, sprayed the spot the gloves had been placed, and wiped it all up with paper towels.

Gordon watched him curiously.

"Gotta keep up on this shit, man. The last thing you want is to get sick," Nelson commented, tossing away the paper towel.

"Sorry, wasn't thinking."

"How was the trip?"

"A clusterfuck."

"What happened?"

"Too much to tell right now. Where's Sam?"

"Oh, she went to go see her friend Phyllis."

"Who?"

"The lady cooking up home remedies for the kids."

"So you're holding the fort down?" Gordon asked.

"Just helping out, that's all."

"Once again, Nelson is here when I'm not. Thanks, man, you're a good friend."

"That's what friends do. But do me a favor—can you please stop running off?"

"That I can't promise. I'm sure you heard about Sebastian and Annaliese?"

"Yeah, sorry to hear. What are you going to do?"

"I don't know, but when I do, I'll keep you in the loop. I'd stay and chat but I have a meeting with the chief and city council at one," Gordon said.

"God, man, don't you ever stop and rest?"

Gordon looked at him squarely. "If you stop moving in this world, you die."

• • •

Timeliness was very important to Gordon so when he looked at the clock and saw it read 1:12, he became a bit agitated. When people were late to affairs, regardless of how trivial some might have thought they were, like a dinner or cocktail party, he took it personally. He wanted to assume that something so big had happened that they were detained; and the way things happened now, that very well could be the issue. However, he still hated waiting.

He stood from the old office chair in the city hall conference room and began to pace the room. When he folded his arms he was reminded of the knife wound he had sustained in Coos Bay. Beneath his cotton T-shirt, he could feel the bandage. He ran his fingers up and down the thick adhesive, his mind now revisiting that fight with Finley.

The door opened, jarring his thoughts, and there stood Rainey, his buttoned short-sleeve collared shirt soaked with sweat stuck to his body.

"Sorry, Gordon, we were all at the hospital."

Gordon nodded.

"I really hate having you wait but we had to go."

"Shit happens."

"Yes, sir, it does, and more shit just happened."

Gordon cocked his head.

"The mayor is dead."

Gordon sat down with the knowledge. "I know this outbreak is bad, but how do you feel about our chances of surviving this?" he asked.

Rainey pulled a chair out and sat down across from Gordon. "You want me to be honest with you? It's very bad. The state government in Mountain Home is paralyzed from it, and all we've heard from Cheyenne is that they are sending aid, but we don't know when that will arrive and just what it will look like. In the absence of a vaccine or cure, we will have to just sit and let this go through the population."

"Unless Charles and Gunny Smith are successful."

"Come on, Gordon, what are the odds that Charles's sister has a vaccine?"

Taking a deep breath, Gordon nodded. "You're right, it's a long shot and seems pretty unbelievable."

"Right now, we've done all we can do to isolate the sick and provide comfort. We've put into action some strict quarantine protocols. I just don't see Charles or the Feds coming with a cure. Without a vaccine or cure, we'll have to just let this take its course."

"Have the doctors been giving everyone the natural remedies that Phyllis has been concocting for Haley and Luke?"

"Yes, they have been, but it only helps some of the symptoms. People are still dying."

Gordon looked at the clock and then back to Rainey. "Is the council coming?"

"No, they're meeting now to select an interim mayor till we can hold an election."

Gordon didn't like hearing that he wouldn't be able to present his concern to the entire council.

"So, what did you want to tell us that was critical?" Rainey asked.

"I don't know how to put this without it sounding paranoid, but the federal forces coming are not coming to help us. They're coming to arrest me and those affiliated with Cascadia."

"Where did you get this information?"

"My wife received a phone call from a Major Schmidt back in Cheyenne. They've arrested my brother and said they are coming here. They demanded that I and the Cascadian leadership turn ourselves in or they'll try my brother for treason."

"Treason?" Rainey asked, shocked.

"Chief, in all honesty it could be said that what you, my brother, and the other Cascadians were doing was possibly seditious, even treasonous."

"You're siding with them?"

"No, no, don't get me wrong, I just can see how President Conner might view this is all. Just because I can understand their motives doesn't mean I condone them. Christ, man, they have my brother. You think I'm on their side?"

Rainey, normally a calm man, looked nervous. He ran his fingers through his hair. "As if we needed something else to worry about."

"Chief, you have a lot on your plate. This is where I can help. I have experience, I've led men in battle before—"

"Battle? You think we're going to war?"

"I didn't say war, but I'm not about to surrender to them, which means things could get ugly."

"I need to inform the council of this immediately," Rainey said as he stood.

"I want to come too."

Rainey looked at him and said, "Of course you're coming. I want you there when I nominate you."

"Nominate me for what?"

"I don't know what the title will be, but anyone who leaves town in military choppers and returns with missile systems and other military gadgets is someone I need doing more than perimeter checks."

Gordon smiled. He wasn't one who liked to receive praise but in his mind, Rainey was right. He had a skill set and resources that the town could use, and if they were going to defend themselves from another force, they needed him. Now he wouldn't be just a player out of many; he was carving out that leadership role he set his mind to having.

JULY 4, 2015

• • •

"We hold these truths to be self-evident, that all men are created equal . . ."

—Thomas Jefferson

Cheyenne, Wyoming

General Baxter took the glass of whiskey and tossed it back. His index finger nervously tapped the side of the glass as he contemplated having another drink. He typically hated waiting but given the present circumstances, the waiting he had to endure was torment. He knew setting up another secret meeting with Wilbur was risky, but he needed to confer with her so they both knew how to proceed following the arrest of Dylan.

His front door opened and closed quickly with a loud thud. He had a sudden vision flash before him of him getting ambushed and arrested. That nervous anticipation dissipated as Secretary Wilbur appeared in the doorway.

"General, good morning," Wilbur said.

"Madam Secretary, please take a seat."

She strode across the small den of his residence and sat across from him.

"I don't think—"

"Don't talk, just listen," he said, interrupting her. "I asked you to come over here to tell you I'm out. I have no interest in working against President Conner or Major Schmidt. They haven't done anything to me and I believe a strong case can be made that they are doing what is best for the county."

"I had a feeling that's what you were going to say. So what happens from here then—you turn me in?"

"Nothing happens. We continue to do our jobs and forget we ever conspired or mentioned working against the president."

"What about Dylan? Aren't you afraid he'll squeal?"

Baxter poured another glass of whiskey and tossed it back. "No, I'm not worried about him. I took care of that."

"What does that mean?"

He then looked at his watch and said, "This meeting is over. When you leave, you forget everything that has ever been said or mentioned before, like it never happened. If you wish to continue down this reckless road, you'll do it alone, understand?"

"Understood," she answered and stood up.

"Good, now please see yourself out."

As she walked to the open doorway she turned and blasted him. "I never cast you as a coward, General."

"I'm not a coward, I'm a survivor. Now please leave."

She pursed her lips and pivoted back around. When she reached the front door a feeling of doom began to come over her. What did he mean by saying, "I took care of that," in reference to Dylan? She stopped and looked over her shoulder. With a quick and nervous nod, she turned the door handle and swiftly walked onto the sidewalk. With the door separating her from Baxter she inhaled deeply, collected herself, and marched toward her vehicle. Quietly to herself she said, "What did you get yourself into, Bethanny?"

McCall, Idaho

Gordon opened his eyes to find Samantha looking at him. He smiled. "Good morning."

"Good morning."

He was surprised he was waking so early after such a long day before and what seemed like an endless night caring for Haley and Luke.

"I was going to wake you, but you were sleeping so soundly," Samantha said as she reached out and rubbed his arm. They both had so much to deal with. Samantha was heartsick about Sebastian and Annaliese. It was another problem in a series of problems that kept piling up.

"Gosh, what a tough night."

"We've got it easy. The poor kids."

"You're right, I should be thinking of them."

"I remember you telling me you had a meeting with Michael this morning—when is that?"

"Oh God, I forgot all about that. I told him I'd meet him at his house at eight."

"So, tell me, what happened yesterday?" she asked while pushing him in earnest.

"Tell you what?"

"Stop it, you said something big happened at the city council meeting, but with the kids and then you passing out from exhaustion last night, you never mentioned it."

"Oh, well . . . you're looking at the new McCall defense chief," Gordon said, a grin from ear to ear.

Samantha raised her eyebrows. "What exactly does that mean?"

"You suggested I take on a bigger role in town. I know it's not the open spot on the council but it's a start."

"What's your job, what are your responsibilities?"

"I'm in charge of organizing, training, and equipping the McCall militia."

"Militia?"

"Yes, McCall will have its very own army, for lack of a better word. I'm in charge of them."

"This is in response to that Schmidt person?"

"Yes, and of course to other threats that our town might face."

Samantha rolled onto her back and sighed.

"What's wrong?"

"Everything. If it's not one thing it's another. Just when I think we're catching a break, we get slammed with something else. It's just so . . . crazy. How are we going to stop them when they come for you and the others? We don't have an army, we just have a bunch of regular town folk, no training, no big guns. How are we going to stop them if they come here with tanks and tons of soldiers?"

Gordon began to caress her arm and whispered, "Don't worry about that, that's my job. You just let me figure it all out. I have a thing or two up my sleeve that just might work."

She looked into his eyes and trusted what she saw. Gordon had proven to be resilient and if anyone could snatch victory from the jaws of defeat it was him. "What time is it?"

Gordon looked at the old wind-up alarm clock and answered, "Seven on the nose."

"Good, you have some time then," Samantha purred as she crawled over and got on top of Gordon.

They kissed passionately and soon the concerns and worries were gone as they lost themselves in each other.

• • •

Eight o'clock came quickly and Gordon was on his way to meet Michael. He had much to discuss with him. Having secured a place within the local government, he now needed to secure a place within the dominant political party of the area.

Loyalties in McCall were already strained between those loyal to the United States and those now swearing allegiance to the Cascadians. The momentum the Cascadians had been experiencing had stopped when word came that the federal government was coming to provide support. Michael and some of the local Cascadian leadership swiftly promoted the idea that the government wasn't coming to help but to quarantine them so that they'd all die off.

Gordon respected Michael's endless energy and drive to better his family. He never sat idly waiting for someone else to take care of them. If he didn't know how to do something he'd find someone who did and pick their brains till he had the knowledge. Gordon knew this was an important trait and was the reason Michael had been successful before the lights went out and was successful now.

Filled with promise, Gordon got out of his truck and walked up on Michael's house. Michael was outside, focused on laying a straight chalk line on a board he was about to cut.

"Look at you, always working on something," Gordon joked.

"Welcome back, stranger."

"Good to be back."

"One second," Michael said as he snapped the chalk line. The thin string left a dusty red line on the board.

"Thanks for meeting me."

Michael stopped working and motioned Gordon to come sit down on a small deck off the front of his house.

"Thirsty?" Michael asked.

Gordon loved how everyone in McCall was always polite, even given the threats that they all faced. He smiled. "I'm fine."

"How are Haley and Luke?"

"Good as they can be. I wish we had some word from Charles or

Smitty. It would just be nice to know what their status was," Gordon lamented.

"I know, this pandemic is a problem. Don't take this wrong but I fear it will be used to stop our process."

"I don't take it wrong, I actually agree with you. That's why I'm here."

Michael looked at him with raised eyebrows. "There *are* miracles, I guess."

"I would have come sooner, but there just weren't enough hours in the day," Gordon said.

"That tone—what's that tone I'm hearing?"

"I heard about your skepticism in regard to the federal forces coming here and you're right. They aren't coming to help us out—"

"I knew it!" Michael blurted out.

"They're coming to stomp us out. They're coming for me, you, and everyone who holds a leadership role in Cascadia."

Michael's face turned white upon hearing the words fall from Gordon's mouth.

"They are coming here to McCall to arrest us all for treason," Gordon continued. "You okay?" he asked. He could see fear in Michael's face.

"I'm all right. I guess I knew this day could come and now it's here. I don't know why I didn't think that they'd just roll over and let us have our own country," Michael said, the tone in his voice now subdued by the reality of it all.

"Actions have consequences. Always have, always will."

"If they arrest us, what will happen?"

"Oh, one of two things. Either they lock us away somewhere and throw away the key, Gitmo style, or they'll execute us. I really don't know; either way, your family, the life you know, it's over, Michael. The dream you had of Cascadia is gone, unless . . ."

"Unless we don't let them stop us, we fight back," Michael said, his voice raised.

Gordon nodded and said, "That's right, Michael, we have to fight."

"Let me guess—you have a plan?" Michael asked as he leaned in closer to Gordon.

"It's a delicate situation for us locally; there are many that believe the government is coming to help. We must show them that their intentions are not good. Just how we do that is something I can't answer right now."

"Any idea of when they'll get here?"

"Nope, but I've already got a plan on how to stop them when they come our way. But before I detail that to you, I need something from you."

Michael looked surprised. "What do you need from me?"

"Before that, let me fully explain everything so you have context." Gordon then detailed everything to Michael; he could no longer keep things from those he knew he could trust. He needed to build a coalition, and for him there was only one side he could go with and that was with the Cascadians. He detailed his travels to Oregon months ago, Annaliese's sickness, and the deal he struck with Conner. He explained in exhaustive detail what just happened in Coos Bay and how he had barely survived. He told him Sebastian's situation and how that weighed on his mind. He then finished with the details of his new position within the McCall city government. For Gordon it felt like a confession, and when he was finished, he had a deep feeling of relief.

"Gordon, this is crazy, all of it," Michael said.

"I know."

"I'm sorry about Sebastian."

"I just don't know how I'm going to get him back, but I can tell you that I'm not surrendering to them."

"I'll do whatever I can to help," Michael offered.

"Do you mean that?"

"Of course I do. I just don't know what I can do. But if you want me to help spring him, I'm in."

Gordon looked at him squarely and said, "I want to help you build a new country."

Michael almost fell out of his chair. His eyes were wide with shock. "Really?"

"I want to be a part in this new government you're trying to form."

"Of course, of course," Michael responded, palpably excited about Gordon's conversion. "What did you have in mind?"

"A leadership role. I'm tired of listening to what people tell me to do. I want to make the rules."

"I can't guarantee a leadership role, but you can start in the ranks—"

Gordon cut him off and said assertively, "If Cascadia wants to be free, then it will need the ability to fight. It will need an army."

"We have a leadership structure already; I don't really have the power to put you in one of those positions."

"Did you miss the part of my story where I mentioned I'm in charge of creating a militia to defend McCall? Between you and me, that will be the bedrock, the foundation of an army. What I need you to do is give me a position of power and influence. You do that and I'll give Cascadia an army."

Fifty-three miles west of Cheyenne, Wyoming

Perched in the turret of the lead tank, Schmidt turned and looked upon the small army he had following him. The column of tanks, trucks, and vehicles stretched for miles behind him. He felt blessed to be in the position he was in now. He was given the honorable position of cleansing the United States of the enemies who sought to divide it and split it apart. This was the greatest purpose a fighting man could be given. His mission would have a real and lasting impact on the future of his country and he took it seriously. He would do anything to make sure his country's flag flew proudly again, everywhere.

Conner had met him in the early morning hours to send him off with his five-thousand-man-strong army. Of any day to do it, the Fourth of July gave it greater meaning. The trust that Conner gave him was something he didn't take for granted. Conner's actions yesterday against his chief of staff sent shock waves through the administration. Schmidt respected that decision and knew it would go far to silence opposition to the tough decisions the president had to make.

Schmidt was disappointed that his men hadn't been able to find Annaliese Van Zandt, but having Sebastian in his custody would give him leverage if he needed it. He didn't know how involved Gordon was in the Cascadian Movement, or if he was involved at all. For Schmidt, the arrest of Sebastian was a way he could get in front of Gordon and then exact revenge for Finley. He would satisfy his own personal revenge while giving the United States another victory.

He reached into a pocket of his tactical vest and pulled out a laminated map. They were only fifty-three miles outside of Cheyenne, with another eight hundred miles to go. By his calculations they'd be arriving on the outskirts of McCall in six days. Their route took them along old interstate highways, state highways, and county roads; his plan was to avoid any large cities and make no contact with civilians unless it fell within his rule of engagement. Initially, his plan was to make a stop at Mountain Home but he changed that so as to not contaminate his men with the virus. Instead, they would slip around the base and head north toward McCall.

In retrospect he felt foolish for calling Gordon's wife and telling her they were coming. This lost for them any element of surprise they would've had. He was usually a disciplined man, but he allowed his personal emotions to interfere with his judgment.

"Sir, is it nice to be back in the saddle?" asked Corporal Cast, his tank driver.

Schmidt folded the map and placed it back in his pocket. "Yes it does, Corporal, yes it does."

"You expect we'll get much action?"

"Oh, I don't think we'll have much of a fight. These folks are more bark than bite. That's not to say we shouldn't be on our toes, but I imagine we'll mop them up in a day or two."

"I just hope we get a chance to finally use this," Corporal Cast said, referring to the 120-millimeter rounds for the tank's main guns.

"Don't fret, Corporal; we just might have a chance to use it. Our mission to destroy these groups has just begun. Be patient. Our time will come and this old tank will get an opportunity to show us what she has. Now, no more questions. Focus on driving."

"Roger that, sir."

Reaching into a side pocket he pulled out an old photo. It was a photo of him, smiling, his arms embracing a young woman who held a baby. He stared at it as his mind raced back to that time. No one really knew Schmidt, much less took the time to try. He was hardnosed and efficient, allowed only a few people to get close. Staff Sergeant Finley had been one of those men. Now he was gone, like the people in the photo. Deep feelings began to rise in him but he stopped them. He quickly put the photo away and focused back on the mission and task ahead.

With the rising sun at his back, he pressed forward toward the wide-open plains of western Wyoming and eastern Idaho. Soon he'd be in the central mountains of Idaho, where he'd strike another blow for the United States and seek the retribution his soul needed.

JULY 7, 2015

• • •

"One of the penalties of refusing to participate in politics is that you end up being governed by your inferiors."

—Plato

McCall, Idaho

As Samantha sat on the back deck, she looked out at the dark clouds in the east. She loved summer thunderstorms, especially in the evenings. Back in San Diego, she and Gordon would cuddle up on the long sectional couch with the kids and watch the dazzling display the lightning would showcase on the black sky. She smiled when she thought of those long-ago days, the *ooh*s and *ahh*s that followed each flash, the kids laughing and squealing when the thunder would roll. It was hard for her to get excited about the storm coming their way now. Haley was still sick with no sign that her symptoms were subsiding. The natural remedies seemingly lost their potency, which caused great concern. For Nelson, the greatest concern was that Haley had stopped urinating, which could be a symptom of something far worse, renal failure. Renal or kidney failure had been a major cause of death from NARS, and the only way to stop her kidneys from failing was to stop the illness. Though that seemed impossible, Luke's condition had vastly improved to the point that his fever had broken and he could now walk around on his own. His recovery gave them hope.

Every day brought news of more death from what had now been given an official name, NARS (North American Respiratory Syndrome). The pandemic had spread to towns all along Highway 55 south of McCall to Boise. With no word from Gunny or Charles, chance of a cure seemed weak at best. Even if Charles showed up with a vaccine of some type there wasn't the assurance that it would even work.

Gordon's days had now been consumed with preparing for Schmidt's arrival. The members of the Cascadian leadership took offense to Gordon's abrupt entry into their ranks, but after many conversations, he was given the newly created title of defense minister. This title didn't mean much but it gave Gordon a position at the head table with the Cascadian political machine. With his role as McCall defense chief, he covered all the bases.

Gordon unlocked the front door and walked in; his body was feeling the fatigue of sleepless nights. His eyes focused on Samantha sitting on the back deck. The house was silent, almost too quiet. A flutter in his chest hit him as he rushed down the hallway to Haley's door. His fears of seeing a lifeless Haley were alleviated when he saw her little body lying there, each breath labored. Emotion filled him when he imagined losing her. If he had any fear left in him, it was that. Losing Hunter had been unbearable, but if he lost Haley he had no idea how he or Samantha would cope.

Haley shifted in her bed and began to cough. He was about to enter her room to provide comfort when a hand touched his.

"No, don't," Luke said.

Gordon looked at Luke's frail frame. The skin on his face was drawn back; his cheekbones protruded sharply and his cheeks were hollowed. Even though his appearance looked bad, this was an improvement for him. Luke had survived the virus, and for them, he was a walking and talking sign of hope.

"You should be resting," Gordon said after closing Haley's door.

"I was but my back hurts from all the lying down and I'm starving."

Gordon smiled. "Come on, let's get some food in your belly."

Both walked into the kitchen, where Luke began to open a can of fruit salad. Gordon saw Samantha was still sitting outside.

"Hey, if you don't need my help, I'm going to check on Sam."

"Sure," Luke said, his mouth full.

Gordon opened the slider and stepped onto the deck. His first step produced a creaking sound, which startled Samantha.

"Hi," she said. A glimmer of happiness appeared on her face when she saw him.

He walked over to her side, bent down, and gave her a big kiss on her cheek.

"Sit down next to me," she said, patting a small spot on the oversized chair she sat in.

He did what she requested and immediately put his arms around her. He looked out over the mountains and saw the dark clouds. "A storm's coming. The rain will be needed for sure."

"I hope it's not too late for our little garden," she said, her eyes now focused on the tilled and dry dirt they had spent so much time working on two weeks before. So much had happened since they planted the garden that no one took the time to water it.

"Our garden will be fine."

"I need you to do something. I know you're busy, but . . ."

Gordon could see her getting emotional. "What? Anything."

"I'm beginning to think that our only hope in saving Haley is with this vaccine, but there's no word from Smitty or Charles, nothing, and I'm just worried that we're running out of time," she said. Tears began to stream down her face.

"Haley's strong; she'll make it. Look at Luke. He made it and Haley got sick a couple days behind him so I think that any day now, she'll be up and about."

"I'm not a fool, Gordon. I know she's not peeing anymore and her feet are swelling. I know what that means."

"She'll be fine."

Samantha cut him off and barked, "You don't know that for sure, you're guessing. I need you to do something!"

"What would you like me to do?"

"Go find Smitty and Charles. I told you that I needed you here, that I needed you to be with us, but if Haley is going to survive, we need to try every last method. We're losing precious time."

Gordon didn't know how to answer her. She was very emotional and in some ways, he knew she was right. He was leaving Haley's life in the hands of other men. He knew what Haley's new symptoms meant, but he didn't want to say anything, as if keeping quiet about it would make them disappear. He had concerns about Schmidt's forces and he hadn't yet made any plans on how to get Sebastian back, but if he were to try to plead a case for staying and preparing for that, it would fall on deaf ears with his wife. It wasn't that she didn't think those were issues, it was that she prioritized Haley's life above everything else.

Knowing the only answer to her emotional request was to give her what she wanted, he answered, "I'll leave immediately."

She reached out and took his face in her hands and said, "I don't know if you'll find them or if this will be a success, but we have to try. I hope you understand that I can't lose her, I can't."

He placed his hands over hers and said, "I understand, you don't have to explain yourself. I love you, Samantha; you're the most incredible woman and mother. I don't know what I did to deserve you."

She stared deep into his blue eyes and said, "Thank you, but stop being so mushy and get your ass out there. Your family needs you."

• • •

Gordon hadn't finished packing his Humvee for the trip to Olympia when a familiar sound echoed in the distance. He paused and listened to ensure his ears weren't playing tricks on him. As he stood leaning against the cold metal door, the sound of heavy chops of propellers ripped through the air.

"Looks like we have some visitors," Gordon said out loud. He jumped in, fired up the Humvee, and sped off down the driveway.

Cheyenne, Wyoming

Conner's hands shook as he read the paper he was just given. It was a transcript of operational details from Schmidt. If Conner could use one word to describe Schmidt it would be effective. He had executed a wide-ranging operation that Conner couldn't have imagined as a possibility and completed it without anyone knowing. While Schmidt had been planning his troop movement toward McCall, he had created and deployed much smaller operations to infiltrate and eliminate the other groups, very much like what they had done to Barone.

Before his departure, Schmidt had mentioned he had other irons in the fire. While they were tackling the Republic of Lakotah and PAE, Schmidt had been busy deploying two-man teams to other locations. A team was in place in Arizona, two teams were sent back to Georgia, and a team had made it to Olympia, Washington. These teams had two objectives: get close to the leadership and gather intelligence. The team in Washington reported back that they had easily made contact with the Western Cascadian leadership and were now settling in. Their hope was to provide critical information to Schmidt as he began his movement to Olympia after dealing with the Cascadians in McCall.

A slight tap on the door signaled that his new assistant was there. She was unlike Dylan in her approach and demeanor, and after the brazen betrayal from Dylan it was welcome.

"Come in!" he hollered.

She opened the door slowly and stuck her head in. "Mr. President, sorry to disturb you but I have some important information."

"It's okay, Heather, come on in," he answered, waving her in.

Heather stepped forward. Her body showed an uneasiness and tension that Conner wasn't familiar with. When she reached the front of his desk, she quickly wiped away a tear from her cheek.

Conner picked up on her tension right away, and when he saw the tear he immediately asked, "What is it?"

"Mr. President, it's Dylan," she said as she clasped her hands together in front of her. "He's dead. The guards found him in his cell," she said, her voice showing emotional strain.

"What? How?" Conner blurted out, shocked by the news.

"I just received the call. They found him lying on the floor. He slit his wrists."

• • •

Conner looked down at Dylan's cold, pale body. A wave of emotions ran through him as he thought back to the first time he met him those many years ago. They had been through so much together and after losing Julia, Conner had no one else closer to him besides Cruz.

"Why, why, Dylan? Why did you betray me? Why did you do it? It didn't have to be this way," Conner said, placing his hand on Dylan's cold stiff hand. He removed it and put it back in his pocket. How strange dead skin feels, he thought. You can tell that the person or soul isn't there anymore.

He took one more look at his old friend and colleague, said a quick prayer, and stepped away. He would miss Dylan, but he would never forgive him for what he did.

As the door to the mortuary closed behind him, he looked down the hallway before him. Half of the lights were on, and those that did illuminate were dim and flickering, making it almost impossible to see the door at the opposite end. He paused to take in the scene, thinking it an appropriate analogy. This hallway seemingly represented the path he was on: the areas that were lit became his vision and plan for the country and the dark or faint places were the surprises and obstacles that were out there but he couldn't see. He stood under one of the flickering lights and sighed. No longer would he be caught in the darkness. Not if he could help it.

McCall, Idaho

Rainey and several police officers had also heard the helicopter and followed it until it landed in the hospital parking lot. Not taking any chances, Rainey and his men converged on the helicopter with guns drawn.

The ramp on the helicopter lowered and a uniformed crew chief slowly stepped down, waving his hands.

"Get on the ground!" Rainey ordered.

The man did as he was ordered and dropped to the ground. Rainey and his men kept their positions, ready to engage whatever threat might appear from the helicopters.

A moment passed, then three other people appeared from the darkness inside the belly of the CH-53 Sea Stallion helicopter and walked slowly down the ramp.

"Stop right there and get down!" Rainey ordered.

"Chief, it's Gunny Smith. I'm with Charles Chenowith and his sister," Gunny barked, his arms held high.

Rainey leaned in and focused his eyes. He had only met Gunny twice but the man looked familiar.

"Chief, we have the vaccine! Please let us proceed," Gunny pleaded.

Just then Gordon came speeding into the parking lot, the Humvee's tires squealing as he abruptly stopped behind Rainey's parked truck.

Utter relief and joy filled Gordon as he laid eyes on Charles and Gunny. He assumed the woman was Charles's sister and the box she was carrying was the vaccine.

Not waiting a minute, Gordon hurried over to them. "You were always one for flashy entrances," he joked.

Gunny smiled and said with a wink, "You know me, always the show boat."

"I assume you're Charles?" Gordon asked.

"Yes, nice to meet you. I've heard a lot about you. This is my sister, Elle," Charles answered.

"Are you in charge?" Elle asked Gordon.

"I can help you with whatever you need."

"I need a place to set up, a lab with power so I can begin to synthesize large batches," she said, placing down her large case. She pulled out a mask and gloves and put them on.

"I'm McCall Police Chief Rainey. Who are you?" Rainey asked, walking up.

"Chief, this is Elle. We need to get her set up immediately," Gordon answered excitedly.

"Who?"

"The woman who has a cure!" Gordon said.

"Before we get everyone worked up, let me first say that what I have has never been tested on humans. I can't guarantee it will work, so please temper any expectations," Elle cautioned.

"Let's not waste any time, let's get her a place to set up!" Gordon barked.

"Right this way!" Rainey said.

As they rushed off, Gordon turned to Gunny. "Where did you get the bird?"

"It's one of Master Sergeant Simpson's choppers. I had an interesting encounter a day ago in central Washington."

"Interesting encounter?"

"Long story, but I ran into Top and a convoy of his men on their way north. I recognized the vehicles and took a chance to see if they'd help. Long story short, he said yes and here I am."

"Don't bullshit me. What did you have to give in return?" Gordon asked, curious.

Gunny looked down and away, not wanting to answer the question, but knew he couldn't get away with it. "I thought it was better to make a deal than not arrive or arrive too late."

"What did you do?"

"I offered them the vaccine after we mass-produce it."

"Oh, that's cool."

"So this bird will stay here until then."

Gordon looked at the chopper. His eyes widened when an idea came to mind.

"I know that look, Van Zandt. What's spinning in your fucked-up brain?"

"We just might be able to use this old chopper if the timing presents itself."

"That negotiation is on you. Leave me out of it," Gunny snarled, holding his hands up.

"Did Top say where they were headed?"

"He didn't, but when I saw him, I fully expected to see the colonel. Needless to say it was a risk on my part, but the roads between here and Seattle are not safe. We barely escaped an ambush from some bandits."

"I'm not going to second-guess you. You made it, so that's all that matters."

Both men discussed Barone's demise and how so much had changed. The bond they shared was deep and out of everyone there, Gunny was one of Gordon's oldest friends, besides Nelson. To have the privilege and blessing of people close to him he could trust was priceless and, in this world, a rarity. Gordon recognized how lucky he was, even given the bad things that had happened to him. For the most part, he and what remained of his family were fortunate. However, he needed to protect these blessings, and that didn't happen by chance but by deliberate actions.

JULY 10, 2015

• • •

"I came, I saw, I conquered."

—Julius Caesar

Horseshoe Bend, Idaho

"Burn it down! Burn down every building, home, barn, shack that displays this!" Schmidt ordered his men, clutching a Doug flag.

Without question, his men executed his orders. The first building to go up in flames was the small city hall. His platoon commanders were breaking away and going into the residential areas looking for any open display in support of Cascadia.

As the hot flames began to engulf the city hall building he jumped off his tank and approached a line of half a dozen people who had been taken prisoner. He walked by each one and looked at them; all but the last man had their heads bowed down in fear.

"It was an easy request but you chose not to follow it. Now you see what you've brought upon yourselves?" he chastised them.

The fearless man at the end of the line spat at him.

"Stand him up!" Schmidt ordered.

Two of his soldiers rushed over and picked up the man, whose arms were tied behind his back.

"You spit on me, but this isn't a shocker. You spat on the United

States when you embraced your silly idea of independence. Our country suffers an attack and before the ashes settle, you people rush to abandon it. You pack of traitors; you lack any sense of loyalty. While the president fights every day to get the country back on its feet, you selfishly work to destroy those efforts."

"Where were you when we were starving? Where were you when gangs came through here, threatening us?" the man scolded.

"Right there is a selfish comment. Just because we didn't come and wipe your ass right away, you blame your government and seek to destroy it."

"We don't seek to destroy anything; we just choose to live how we want."

"Again another selfish comment; it's about what *you* want, not what *you* can do for your country!"

Screams, cries, and occasional gunfire could be heard in the distance as his men made their way through the small town, going house to house.

Horseshoe Bend was the first town they encountered where they had seen open displays of Cascadian support and would also be the first to feel his wrath. The tiny city hall sat upon the main highway so as his convoy was passing, Schmidt saw the Doug flag flying out front. He immediately ordered his troops to halt as he investigated. That is where things turned very bad for the townspeople of Horseshoe Bend. The local mayor admitted to being the first elected Cascadian in the town, and his council was also proud Cascadians. Within mere moments, Schmidt acted, ordering the people to be arrested and the town sacked. Taking lessons from the past, he knew the only way to end these groups was to crush them and all those who supported them.

"You won't get away with this!" the man screamed.

"Get away with it? Do you know how stupid that sounds? Is someone going to arrest me? I'm not breaking the law, Cascadian,

I *am* the law!" His face was reddened, dark energy coursing through his veins. "In accordance with the powers vested in me by the President of the United States, I declare you enemies of the United States. Your punishment for treason is death; this sentence is to be carried out immediately!" Schmidt barked.

Cries, moans, and begging spewed from the six captives.

"Lieutenant, carry out the sentence!" Schmidt ordered a man standing behind him.

"Yes, sir!"

Schmidt turned away and walked back to his tank. He pulled a small pad of paper out of his pocket and began to take notes. As he wrote he blocked out the intense scene that was unfolding behind him as his men lined up the six town leaders against a small hillside.

"Ready, aim, fire!" the lieutenant ordered. A short burst of gunfire followed, ending the cries and whimpers.

On his pad of paper Schmidt wrote July 10, then stopped. "What's this little shit town called?"

"Horseshoe Bend!" one of his men called out.

"Thank you," he answered as he wrote the name next to the date and closed his pad. Turning around, he shouted, "Let's clean up this place. I want to be in McCall by tomorrow afternoon at the latest!"

McCall, Idaho

With the full support of every person and resource in McCall, Elle's vaccine was distributed widely within twenty-four hours of her arrival. The sickest were treated first but eventually every person in town was given a shot. All were praying it would work, as there were no guarantees on its effectiveness. Miraculously, some of the sickest were showing signs of improvement.

Haley was one of the first to receive the vaccine. With Nelson's help, she was given the shot, and by the late morning her fever was gone. However, she was not completely out of the woods, and Nelson worked immediately to address her kidney issues.

With Haley and the town on the mend, Gordon pivoted to tackle the other issues. He was a man who usually had a plan, but he couldn't come up with one for Sebastian's situation specifically. He knew how he could stop Schmidt, but not at the risk of his brother. Situated in a large conference room in the police station, or what Rainey now called "the command post," Gordon pinpointed locations for an ambush on a map in front of Rainey, Michael, Charles, and Gunny.

"Gunny, you'll be here at this location." Gordon pointed to a small road that broke off from the main highway and crossed over a small bridge south of the much larger Rainbow Bridge.

"Got it," Gunny answered.

"Set up ambush points here, here, and here," Gordon said, pointing to several locations on the road. Based upon the topographical map, the area he had pointed to was where the road narrowed and heavy forestation would provide cover for his men.

"We'll be up here at the Rainbow Bridge. I only have enough C-4 to blow this bridge, not the one to the south . . ." Gordon commented.

"Blow the bridge?" Rainey gasped.

"Only if we have to; it's a backup plan in case our ambushes fail," Gordon answered him.

"That would cut the one main route we have to Boise. We can't do that," Rainey asserted.

"We can still go there via New Meadows, but if we fail here they will cross over, and then there's not much in between them and us," Gordon stressed.

"He's right," Gunny said.

"Okay, I have trust in your plan, but it makes me feel uneasy."

"I don't want to do it either, but we can't allow them to cross over it. To the south, we'll have several points of ambush just in case they come up that way. The advantage we have is that the bridge to the south is very small and the road even narrower than the highway. They can get pinched there. If Schmidt is a smart man, he won't commit all of his forces there, because there are a lot of choke points."

Hollering reverberated through the door, disturbing the men.

Rainey looked up at the others and said, "What the hell is going on? I'll be right back." He walked away and opened the door, allowing the commotion's sound to envelop the room.

One of Rainey's police officers ran down the hall and stopped in front of him. "Chief, we just got a report from the southern checkpoint."

"What is it?"

"A man just showed up and reported that he survived an attack to the south."

"What kind of attack? Come on, man, spit it out."

"I didn't ask, sir."

"Where is he?"

"They're bringing him here directly."

"We need to activate the teams, we need to get people into the field now!" Gordon barked.

"I agree, we need to mobilize immediately, just in case this is Schmidt," Gunny agreed.

Rainey just looked at Gordon and said, "You're in charge of these types of operations; the ball is in your court."

Gordon nodded and turned to Gunny. "You missed my training but you obviously don't need it. Here is a list of the men in your rifle company," he finished as he handed Gunny a list of one hundred and twenty names.

Gunny snatched the list and looked it over. "These men have their own arms and vehicles?"

"Yes, addresses are next to their name, the asterisks indicate your platoon commanders, and the double asterisks are your squad leaders. I did the best I could with what limited time I had to locate these men and organize them. I've given you a Hummer with an M240 machine gun and you have all the Javelins. I'll keep the TOW up north of the bridge."

Gunny smiled and looked up. "Roger that, Van Zandt. Ambushes are easy, and if all fails we'll adapt and overcome, right?"

"Right," Gordon answered.

Michael was looking over Gunny's shoulder like a curious child. "What can I do?"

"You'll stay with me at the bridge."

Rainey then spoke up. "Me?"

"Chief, you need to stay in town, organize fortified road blocks at all the choke points north of Donnelly along the 55, West Mountain Road, and Farm to Market Road. You're in charge of the town defenses," Gordon said.

"I'm on it," Rainey responded.

"Gunny, go gather your men and rally in Donnelly. From there we'll go to the Rainbow Bridge, set the charges, and place the ambush sites."

"Roger that, I'll see you in Donnelly."

"Correct. Say, in ninety minutes? And we're on channel one— use the radio protocol I have listed on the second page."

"Roger that, I'm out." Gunny marched out of the room and disappeared.

Gordon turned to Michael and said, "Here is the list for the other company of men. Help me rally them. Let's meet at the Lake Fork Merc in an hour fifteen." Gordon tore off the bottom half of the list and handed it to Michael.

"And me?" Charles asked.

Gordon looked at Charles. He didn't know the man, didn't know his talents or skills, but didn't want to turn him away, given his new title as defense minister within the party. "It's best you stay with me and watch. You know how to handle a gun?"

"Yes," Charles quickly answered.

"Good, we'll get you set up. Michael, see to that," Gordon ordered. He clapped his hands. "Everyone has their jobs, so let's do it," he barked.

• • •

A car raced down the street and swung into the parking lot of the police station. A panicked man jumped out, running inside.

"We need help, please!" the man begged.

"Sir, please calm down!" a young police officer requested.

"They killed everyone, they just killed everyone!" the man screamed hysterically.

Rainey was still at the station working with some of his officers and making arrangements to fortify their checkpoints. Upon hearing the man he rushed out to talk to him.

"Who killed everyone?" Rainey asked.

The man swung around and said, "The military, the military!"

"Sir, calm down!" the police officer again asked.

"I won't calm down, do something! They killed everyone and are coming here!" the man bellowed, his skin flush with fear.

"The military? What do you mean 'the military'?" Rainey asked, stepping in front of the man. He held him steady by grabbing his shoulders and looking at him in the eyes. "What did you mean by 'military'?" Rainey asked again slowly. He needed to know without a doubt that this was Schmidt's forces.

"The United States military! They were Americans!"

The answer confirmed it for Rainey. His heart started pumping with the news. "Where did this happen?"

"Horseshoe Bend."

"When?"

"This morning."

Rainey turned to one of his officers and ordered, "Contact Van Zandt and Gunny Smith, tell them Schmidt hit Horseshoe Bend this morning."

Rainey then focused back on the man. "Tell me everything. Give me details so we can prepare."

"They were soldiers; they killed everyone who had anything to do with Cascadia. They killed them all, no question. If you were flying a flag or said you supported Cascadia, they killed you. I barely made it out," the man said. His breathing was rapid as he spat out his answers.

"Did you warn the sheriff in Cascade?" Rainey asked. Cascade was the country seat of Valley County, thirty miles south of McCall.

"I did, I did stop by, but no one was there. I knocked but they weren't there. I raced up here instead. I didn't know where else to go."

"Sir, thank you, you're safe here, so please sit down and rest. We'll find a place for you to go in a bit."

"What are you going to do to stop them?" the man blurted out.

"We're working on that now."

"How? How are you going to stop them? They have tanks, trucks, machine guns, and thousands of soldiers. How are you going to stop them?" the man yelled.

"Please calm down," Rainey pleaded.

"Leave, everyone needs to leave before they get here. You have to warn everyone!"

"Enough, sit down!" Rainey yelled.

The man looked at Rainey. His panic had turned into uncontrollable hysteria.

"I'm going to tell everyone!" the man bellowed.

"No, you're not. We don't need others panicking. Take him into custody. Don't let him go until it's over," Rainey ordered his officers, who jumped on the man instantly and subdued him.

"No, no, let me go, I don't want to die!" the man screamed from underneath a pile of police officers.

Rainey stepped around him and walked outside the station to see if his commotion had drawn unwanted attention. The streets were empty, which gave him a moment of relief. With no more time to waste, he walked back inside and barked, "Let's go, men, we have checkpoints to man. Let's do this!"

• • •

The plan was set, and all sided with Gordon that the Rainbow Bridge needed to be rigged with explosives as a backup. If it came down to it, getting rid of the bridge was a sacrifice, but one that would stop Schmidt's advance. If the plan went right, Schmidt's forces would be trapped on the narrow highway with nowhere to go. They'd be sitting ducks pinned between a rocky cliff and the Payette River. Once they were trapped, Gordon would bring the brunt of his small but lethal force against them. It seemed like a solid plan, but Gordon's experience told him two things: timing was everything, and to always, always expect something to go wrong.

Banks, Idaho

Schmidt couldn't believe the hour. He looked at his watch again and then asked his driver the time. "Is it really nineteen thirty?"

"Yes, sir."

"It stays light out late up here," he said from the turret of the tank. He ordered the column to a full stop when he spotted another Doug flag hanging from a local business. He was determined that everyone would know the United States was not tolerating separatists. Even if he had to stop at each individual house, he would stomp out every single individual that espoused secession. As Sherman went through Georgia during the American Civil War, he would plow through Idaho and then continue on to Washington till not one supporter of Cascadia stood. "All units, set up perimeter security and refuel. Third platoon, please meet me"—he squinted to read the name—"at Bear Valley Outfitters."

He stepped off the tank and stretched. He looked around and took a deep breath. "Ahh, this air is clean. This is really God's country up here, it's so beautiful."

A platoon of soldiers double-timed up to him and stopped.

"Sergeant, go find the owner of that flag," Schmidt said, pointing.

As his soldiers went for the building, his satellite phone rang. He took it out of his pocket and recognized the number. Gordon Van Zandt.

"Mr. Van Zandt, how can I help you?" Schmidt asked. He then held the phone away from him and got his driver's attention. "Psst, order our advance team to halt, refuel, and stay put till further orders."

"Sorry, what was that?" Schmidt said into the phone.

"I want to meet you. I have something to offer for my brother," Gordon said.

"There's nothing I'm interested in other than you, Mr. Van Zandt."

"Where are you so we can meet?"

"I'm a patient man. I'll see you in McCall tomorrow."

"Don't you want to know what I can offer before you turn me down?" Gordon pressed.

"No, I'm not interested. I'll see you tomorrow, Mr. Van Zandt. Good night," Schmidt said and went to press the button. He could hear Gordon still talking but he didn't care. Schmidt pocketed the phone and walked back along the long column. Crashing sounds erupted followed by a few gunshots in the building. A moment later his men exited, ripped the flag down, and began to burn it. Schmidt slowly strolled down to a canvas-covered Humvee. He tossed open the flap and peered into the darkness. A strong aroma of body odor and feces wafted out.

"We really need to clean you up," Schmidt said, holding his nose. "Just spoke to your brother; we'll be seeing him tomorrow. How are you doing, any complaints?"

Sebastian struggled with the restraints. He mouth was gagged so he could only grunt his response.

Schmidt could see the fire in his eyes and hear the resistance in his sounds. "You Van Zandts are a tough bunch. But sadly you picked the wrong side."

Sebastian wiggled closer to the back of the Humvee, his arms and legs bound and tied together in a hog tie. He grunted louder, expressing his disgust for Schmidt.

"Soon it will all be over and the balance of things will be restored," Schmidt told him, and closed the flap.

Rainbow Bridge, Idaho

Gordon looked at the phone, suppressing the urge to toss it in anger. He turned back to face the soldiers that had just been captured in their ambush on the north end of the bridge.

Schmidt's patrol had made it to the Rainbow Bridge all the way from Cheyenne without any contact or threat. This had given them a complacent mentality, so when the first roar of the 50-caliber machine gun Gordon had sounded, they were confused and thought it was the roar of the river crashing below. Gordon had the ambush ready for them, and as soon as they crossed over the span of the bridge, they were hit hard by the armor-piercing 50-caliber rounds. The light armor on the two Humvees was not enough to stop the onslaught. Within less than a minute, all were killed, expect for one.

"How many in the main force?" he asked a baby-faced private first class. The man was on his knees with his hands behind his head, fingers interlaced.

The man looked at Gordon then darted his eyes back and forth at Michael, Charles, and the other men around them, then down to his fallen comrades. Looking back at Gordon he began to whimper, "Please don't kill me."

"We won't kill you if you tell us everything we want to know," Gordon pressed.

"We have about five thousand men, um, over a dozen tanks . . ."

"Tanks?"

"Yes."

"Not a problem, we've got TOWs and Javelins."

"Please don't kill me, please!" the man continued to plead.

"I won't kill you if you tell me everything, I told you that. Now, how far back are they?"

"Um, about twenty miles."

Charles looked at Gordon, concern written all over his face. Gordon knew they were running out of time. He turned and hollered to Jones and the other Marines who had come with Gunny from Coos Bay. "Hurry up, guys, place those explosives quick! Double time!"

"They could be here any minute," Charles said, his voice trembling.

"There's a prisoner with them—do you know what vehicle he's being held in?" Gordon asked, ignoring Charles's comment.

"I, um, I can't be sure. I only heard about him but I don't know which vehicle he's in for sure," the man said, panicked that his answer was not enough.

Gordon took his pistol out and placed it against the man's temple. "Where is the prisoner?"

"I don't know, please, I really don't know. If I were to guess I'd say he's mid-convoy, but I've been with the forward patrol since we left Cheyenne, please believe me."

Gordon pressed the muzzle of the barrel farther into the man's temple and placed his finger on the trigger.

"I'm telling you the truth, I've told you everything. Please don't hurt me."

"Why are they doing this?" Charles asked the man.

"The president has had enough with insurrectionists and secessionists; he's not negotiating anymore. He's called on us to wage war against every group," the man said

"Do you know if they killed anyone in Olympia?" Charles asked.

The man hesitated as he thought.

Gordon pressed the muzzle harder.

"The major sent a team there. I know that, nothing more."

"What are your plans after McCall?" Gordon asked.

"We're to go to Olympia next."

Gordon now looked at Charles.

A loud whistle caught their attention. Jones gave a thumbs-up and called out, "The bridge is rigged."

"Is there no other way?" Michael asked, slight doubt about destroying the bridge evident in his question.

"No," Gordon answered, his pistol still pressed against the man's head.

"What about everyone south of the bridge? We're trapping them down there," Michael said.

"From the sounds of it, they're killing everyone," Charles added.

"When was the main force moving north?" Gordon asked.

"Last word we got informed us to stop and refuel."

"Are you sure blowing the bridge will work?" Michael again said.

Gordon was annoyed by Michael's constant interjections. "We have to stop this advance and if our ambush fails, this does it. I need to get my brother but I don't know how I can do that without risking the entire operation," Gordon said, removing the pistol from the man's head.

He looked up and said, "It's getting dark soon; I don't think they'll move till morning. Schmidt said something about tomorrow, but we need to be sure." Gordon walked over to Jones, who was getting behind the wheel of a Hummer to head back to Gunny's southern position. "Jonesy, hold up."

"What ya got, Van Zandt?"

Gordon liked Jones from the first time he'd met him, in Oregon months ago on his hunt for Rahab. He proved to be a smart, brave, and resourceful Marine.

"You and I are going for a ride south to recon."

"Okay, let me inform Gunny."

"What's going to happen if they get to the bridge before you can get him?" Michael asked just after walking up behind Gordon.

Gordon turned to him and said, "It pains me to say this but I'll blow the fucking bridge myself. We can't risk them crossing over. Even if I don't have Sebastian, we can't risk the lives of everyone in the town."

McCall, Idaho

Haley was sitting up in her bed. A fragile smile was stretched across her face when Luke walked in with the gorilla mask, making monkey noises and jumping around.

"Luke, you need to keep resting too. Please don't get her too worked up," Samantha said tensely.

He pulled the mask off, his shoulder-length hair clinging to his face. "Sorry, Auntie Samantha, I just thought she could use a laugh."

"No, Mommy, he's funny. Please, pretty please can he play with me?" Haley begged.

"You both can play a board game or cards, but no horsing around. And only after you finish your soup," Samantha ordered, pointing at the bowl on Haley's nightstand.

"Okay," Haley answered, a bit disappointed.

"I'll go get a game. What do you want to play?" Luke asked.

"Go fish!" Haley squealed.

Luke rushed out of the room and down the hall.

Samantha approached the bed and sat down, and placed her hand against Haley's head to see if she was warm.

"I feel fine, Mommy."

"Can't a mother check? You had us worried there, both you and Luke."

"I knew I was going to be all right, I saw it."

"You did, huh?"

"No, I did, I saw it in a dream."

"Was it a good dream?"

"Yes and no," Haley said. Sadness came over her.

"What's wrong, sweetie?"

"In my dream, I was there, you and Daddy, even Luke, but . . ." Haley grew quiet.

"But what?"

"Uncle Sebastian, he wasn't there. Something bad happened to him."

"Your Uncle Sebastian will be fine," Samantha said, assuring her.

"Why do you and Daddy lie to me?"

"Why would you say that?"

"I know there are bad people. I know bad people killed Hunter.

You tell me all the time that things will be fine, but I hear you and Daddy talking."

Her comment hit Samantha hard. It was the struggle of parents everywhere: You try to protect your children, but they are always listening.

"Do you believe Daddy and me when we tell you we'll do whatever we can to protect you?"

"Yes."

"Good. Now finish your soup before Luke comes back." Samantha kissed her on the head and stood up to leave.

"Mommy?"

"Yes?"

"I know you and Daddy will always protect me. But Daddy won't be able to protect Uncle Sebastian."

Banks, Idaho

The huge flames from what had been the Bear Valley Outfitters warmed Schmidt's face. As each flame danced and licked the remnants of the local landmark, Schmidt's message to the town was loud and clear.

The sun would soon be dipping below the mountains to the west. He thought about the call from Gordon and laughed to himself. He knew he held all the cards. Family ran deep in most people, and given that, he'd soon be able to exact the revenge he so dearly wanted against the man who had killed his friend.

His patience was growing thin. He didn't want to camp; he knew he could make it to the valley by twilight. Once in Round Valley, he and his forces would be in a better location to protect themselves.

"Corporal Cast, contact all units. Let's fire this up, we're headed north!"

"Roger that, sir."

"Have our forward elements move into the valley and scout a position to camp for the night."

"Sir, we haven't heard back from them."

This news alarmed Schmidt, who barked, "Where were they last contacted?"

"Here, sir, at this bridge," Cast answered, pointing at a spot on a map.

"When did you speak to them last?"

"Not twenty minutes ago, but I requested they'd check in every ten."

"Are you sure it's been that long?"

"Yes, sir, it was the same time you were on the sat phone."

Schmidt was never a believer in coincidence. In the pit of his stomach, he knew his foolish threats to scare and intimidate Gordon had only alerted him to his advance. The highway they were on was narrow and a perfect place to ambush someone. His army was vulnerable until they could reach the open valley. If he were Gordon, he'd lay in wait for them, but then again, attacking them would jeopardize his brother. Confusion about how to move came over him.

"Let me see the map," he ordered. Snatching it, he studied it until he found where they were. "Where was the last known location of our forward patrols?"

"Right there."

The Rainbow Bridge was a perfect location to conduct an ambush; it was narrow and both the entrance and exit of the bridge were followed by sharp turns. He looked at the topographical lines and saw that a cliff would be to their left and the river would be to their right.

The only way for him to call this ambush was to knowingly place

Sebastian in the front and let Gordon know he would be there; this would tell him if they were heading into something.

He examined the map closer and saw another route into the valley. He didn't like the idea of splitting up his forces but he should at least explore it.

"Corporal, radio the company commanders. I want Alpha and Bravo to break off here," he said, pointing at a small bridge in Smith's Ferry. "Tell them to take this route; we'll all meet up here in this valley. The rest of us are heading to the Rainbow Bridge."

"Yes, sir," Corporal Cast said as he picked up the handset and began to contact company commanders.

While his orders were being passed down, he would set up his rendezvous with Gordon. He pulled out the phone, pressed the green talk button, and waited for Gordon to answer.

Rainbow Bridge, Idaho

Gordon had just settled into his seat for the ride south to recon Schmidt's position when his phone rang. He pulled it out of his trouser pocket and quickly answered it.

"Yes."

"You're at the bridge, aren't you?"

Gordon motioned for Jones to stop before he answered Schmidt's question.

"I have your brother and I don't have any qualms about killing him," Schmidt continued.

"I'm not at the bridge."

"Bullshit! This conversation is over."

"Hold on, don't hang up," Gordon pleaded, his defiant tone changing quickly.

"You want to meet? Let's meet."

"How do I know you have my brother?"

No response. Gordon could hear the sound of gravel and unintelligible sounds, then Schmidt's voice saying something that he couldn't understand.

"Hello?" Gordon asked.

A moment passed, then a voice he remembered came across the phone.

"Gordon, don't do anything this fucker says. Don't do anything except kill this piece—"

"There's a valley just a few miles from the bridge. We will be there in an hour," Schmidt said, and hung up the phone.

"Major, hold on, Major? Damn!" Gordon bellowed.

"Let me guess, change of plans again?" Jones joked.

Sandy, Utah

The abrupt stop of the vehicle jolted Annaliese awake.

"I think we're here," said the man who had saved her in Cheyenne.

Eli Bennett had driven Annaliese all the way from Cheyenne to the outskirts of Sandy, Utah. When Wilbur asked if he'd help rescue two people, he had no idea it would take him this far. Getting out of Cheyenne proved difficult, but coordination with Wilbur made it possible. Eli had been a civilian contract worker at Warren Air Force base, providing avionics services before the lights went out. He had met Wilbur at Pat's Coffee Shop soon after she had arrived there. Many a night after leaving Pat's, they discussed politics, and soon she came to trust and confide in him. Even though both were single, neither had ever explored a romantic relationship; however, they both shared a passion for an open and free country. When she made the call telling him that she needed him, he didn't hesitate. Now he was parked outside a large metal gate in the middle of the desert with a woman he had met only ten days before.

Their exodus from Cheyenne had been relatively uneventful. After spending several days in a safe house, he ushered her from the city. When asked where she wanted to go, she didn't hesitate. She told him to go to Sandy. He didn't know what to expect but he was fully committed to her safety.

"How do we get in?" he asked.

Annaliese's recovery, while not the most ideal, had gone well, considering they were on the road. "I'll be right back," she said, exiting the Humvee. She approached a fence post ten feet from the gate. She carefully bent over, and upon standing back up, she held a key in her hand. Seeing how uncomfortable she looked, he got out and assisted her in opening the gate.

Once inside and with the gate locked back up, she told him where to go.

He drove for what seemed like five minutes when a bright light ahead blinded him. He slowed down and eventually stopped.

Annaliese opened the door and said, "It's me, Annaliese!"

The light flashed on her face quickly before being pointed toward the ground.

"Annaliese, you and your beau are not welcome here!"

"Uncle Samuel, he's not here! Please, we need you, I need you!"

Samuel walked out of the darkness and into the light of the headlamps. He strode up to her and stopped just a few feet away. "What happened? Who is this?" he asked, flashing his light into the cab of the Humvee.

"Please, we're tired. I'll explain everything later."

"Who is that? Where's Sebastian?"

"His name is Eli Bennett, he saved my life! And Sebastian, I don't know where he is, but I need your help. Please, help me!" she begged.

He looked at her again. This time the resentment in his eyes was gone. Regardless of what had happened he had the capacity for forgiveness, especially for his niece. He walked up to her and before he could put his arm around her, she embraced him tightly and began to sob.

"Uncle Samuel, I need you to help me save Sebastian," she sobbed.

He returned her embrace. He looked at her face as tears streamed down and softly said, "C'mon, let's get you inside and cleaned up. We'll talk about Sebastian and what we can do, but let's first get you and your friend inside."

With his arm around her, supporting her as they walked, he said, "Your mother will be so happy to see you. It's been too long."

Rainbow Bridge, Idaho

A harvest moon was rising, casting a yellowish glow over the rocks, pavement, and tall pines. With Gordon's sight limited, the sounds of the river were more pronounced. The mighty North Fork of the Payette crashed and moved underneath of him.

He stood on the north end of the bridge, waiting, a lone man ready to meet the man who held in his hands his brother and last member of his childhood family. Gordon couldn't and wouldn't allow Schmidt north of the Rainbow Bridge, and with the lack of time to react, he simply waited at the bridge for Schmidt to arrive.

The first sign of Schmidt's arrival was the squeaking and rumble of tank treads upon the pavement. He squinted hard and saw a black mass moving toward the south end of the bridge. As it moved closer, he was able to focus and see the outline of the body and barrel. Six other vehicles followed behind the tank, but it for sure was not the force the private first class or man from Horseshoe Bend had described.

The tank came into full view when it turned and faced him head on at the opposite end of the bridge. The turret opened and out popped a man. He couldn't make out who it was but he could only assume it was Major Schmidt.

The man began to walk toward him; Gordon too began to walk till he faced the man he believed was Schmidt.

"Gordon Van Zandt?" Schmidt asked.

"Major Schmidt?" Gordon replied.

"Yes, I'm Major Schmidt, U.S. Army."

"So, before I—"

Schmidt cut him off by saying, "You broke your word. This is not the valley we had agreed to meet in. If I can't trust you when it comes to a simple meeting, how can I trust we'll be able to conduct this transaction?"

"I can't let you pass this bridge. You and your army will never cross the bridge. You don't have jurisdiction here. This is Cascadia now."

"Ha, there is no such place, just a fantasy in the minds of fools."

"Remember a guy by the name of George Washington? I'm sure King George had the same sentiment you have," Gordon shot back sarcastically.

"This is a nice land you have, I'll say that. This area is quite beautiful. Too bad it's not really yours," Schmidt said.

"Where's my brother?"

"He's back in one of the vehicles, but if you want him you'll have to come with me, as will the other Cascadian traitors."

"I have something else that you'll be interested in. I know you heard of the NARS outbreak. Well, we found a cure, a vaccine. I will give you this vaccine in exchange for my brother and for you turning your people around and heading home."

"Mr. Van Zandt, the deal is off," Schmidt said, then turned and began to walk back to his tank.

"Stop!" Gordon yelled.

Schmidt turned, walked right up to Gordon's face so that he was inches away, and said, "I don't know why I offered a deal, because I'm going to march my army up to McCall and destroy it along with you and your family."

Hearing the threat against his family was all Gordon needed to push him over the edge. Unable to stop himself, Gordon head butted Schmidt. The impact from Gordon's forehead busted Schmidt's nose wide open. The shock from the blow forced him back a few steps, but Gordon was right on top of him, leveling punch after punch to his face.

Schmidt reeled farther back from Gordon's powerful punches until he fell onto his back. Gordon then pounced but Schmidt rolled out of the way. Gordon hit the concrete road hard, his knees and elbows taking the brunt of the jump.

Schmidt saw his advantage and kicked Gordon in the side, the blow knocking the wind out him.

The fight brought Schmidt's men pouring out of the vehicles and onto the bridge to assist their commander.

"Back away, he's mine," Schmidt ordered as he stood.

Gordon was still on the ground but moving to get up. Again, seeing an opportunity, Schmidt kicked him in the stomach, but when he pulled back for another kick, Gordon grabbed his leg and twisted it. Schmidt's knee popped and he fell onto the road.

Gordon had the clear advantage and he was going to take it. He pulled a pistol from the small of his back and placed it in Schmidt's face. "Give me my brother!

Schmidt's men raised their rifles but Schmidt yelled, "No, don't shoot! Get his brother!"

Schmidt's soldiers brought Sebastian out of the back of a Humvee but wouldn't walk him past the front of the tank. Gordon could see he was limping and that he looked frail. "Sebastian, it's Gordon. I'm getting you out of here!"

"Don't trust this motherfucker, brother! He's deceiving you!" Sebastian cried out.

Gordon rammed his pistol into Schmidt's face and ordered, "Have your men let him go!"

Suddenly, a loud explosion followed by heavy machine gun fire could be heard in the distance. Somewhere south and, by the sound of it, miles away, a gun battle had just broken out.

Gordon looked to the south just long enough for Schmidt to sense he was distracted. Schmidt hit the pistol out of Gordon's hand with one hand and punched him in the face with the other.

Gordon fell back and hit his head against the concrete railing of the bridge.

Schmidt scurried up and hobbled back toward the tank and his men.

"Gordon!" Sebastian yelled. "Run, get out of here!" With what little strength, he had he kicked one soldier in the side of the knee with his good leg and used his body to push by another, both men falling to the ground.

Sebastian began to make his way toward Gordon but Schmidt grabbed him and dragged him back.

"Give me my brother or I'll destroy you and your entire army. You have one chance or I'll kill you all!" Gordon screamed.

"You don't have anything to barter with, Van Zandt! You're a stupid, stupid man!" Schmidt responded as he took a pistol from one of his soldiers and placed it at Sebastian's head.

"Brother! Save yourself, fight another day. Please, go!" Sebastian cried out.

"Schmidt, you're making a mistake. You and your army will never make it!" Gordon shouted.

"Enough talk, I hold all the cards!" Schmidt yelled as he pulled the trigger.

The bullet passed through Sebastian's head. For a second he stood, staring out, before he dropped to the ground with a thud.

"No! No!" Gordon screamed in agony at seeing his brother fall. "Open fire, open fire!!"

With that command the hillside behind Gordon came alive with heavy machine gun fire. A heavy barrage of bullets rained down on Schmidt and his small convoy.

Responding to the attack, Schmidt's men began to fire back, but the onslaught was too much. Gordon's men were ripping them apart.

Knowing he needed to get off the bridge, Gordon ran back and took cover behind the corner railing on the north side of the bridge.

With a roar, Schmidt's tank fired, the round hitting the embankment behind Gordon.

In response to the tank fire, Gordon heard the familiar pop and whiz from a TOW missile system. The thunder of it launching soon ended with the metal-crushing sound of it impacting Schmidt's tank. The direct hit shoved the turret partially off the chassis, killing all inside.

It was difficult for Gordon to see what was happening, but he could tell that Schmidt's forces were overwhelmed and losing. Moments later he heard the cry of "Cease fire, cease fire!"

The haze from the gunfire drifted through the moon-lit sky, accompanied by the cries of the wounded on Schmidt's side.

Gordon stood and started for the south side of the bridge. His slight jog turned into a full sprint until he reached Sebastian's body. He fell to his knees and picked up his brother's body and laid it in his lap. "I'm so sorry, little brother. I'm so sorry, I couldn't save you." Gordon was so engrossed with Sebastian that he didn't take notice of his men who came across the bridge.

Michael walked up to him and said, "Gordon, I'm so sorry."

"I failed, once again, I failed," he moaned.

A man came up to Gordon and said, "No sign of Major Schmidt."

This got Gordon's attention quickly. He looked up and asked, "Are you sure? There's no way he could have survived that."

"No, sir, we can't find him. He's not with dead."

McCall, Idaho

Samantha shot up in bed when she heard Haley's screams. She grabbed the pistol on her nightstand and raced down the hall to her room. When she opened the door she found her sitting up but no longer crying. Instead, she seemed to be talking to herself.

"Haley, sweetheart, is everything all right?" Samantha asked, walking into the room, gun in one hand, flashlight in the other.

"I'm fine now, Mommy," Haley answered, evidence of tears still on her face.

Samantha put the gun and flashlight down and brightened the lantern on her nightstand before she sat on the bed. "Honey, you were screaming and crying."

"I'm okay now, Mommy."

"Bad dream?" Samantha asked as she embraced Haley.

"No."

"Well, everything will be okay, I'm here now," Samantha said, rocking her.

Samantha sang a lullaby, and as she laid Haley's head back down on the pillow she asked, "Who were you talking to?"

"What?"

"When I came in your room, you were sitting up. It looked like you were talking to someone."

Haley turned away from her.

"Haley, it's all right. What's wrong?"

She rolled back over and asked, "Promise me you won't get mad?"

"Oh, honey, I promise. What is it?"

"It's Uncle Sebastian."

"What do you mean?"

"I was talking to Uncle Sebastian. He came to me and told me that he was fine and to be a good girl."

Samantha didn't know how to deal with Haley's stories but decided to just play along. But deep down, she was a bit freaked out.

"I had a nightmare that he died and then he was sitting on my bed. He talked to me," Haley explained.

"Okay, we'll talk more in the morning. Time to go back to bed," Samantha said as she lowered the brightness of the lantern. When she stood up to leave, the phone began ringing in her bedroom; she jumped when she heard it. Chills spread through her body and the hairs on her neck stood. She knew who was calling and why.

JULY 11, 2015

· · ·

"Only the dead have seen the end of the war."

—George Santayana

Smith's Ferry, Idaho, Republic of Cascadia

The image of Sebastian being murdered was burned into Gordon's memory. The temptation to mourn Sebastian was strong, but he knew doing so now was not smart, nor would his brother approve. So to fight the urge, he kept himself busy after the battle. Along with the others, he surveyed the battlefield and took inventory of what spoils in equipment and hardware they had seized.

The battle to south of Rainbow Bridge, just east of Smith's Ferry, was the main engagement. Schmidt had sent his main force across the river and into the hills through small unimproved roads with the hopes they'd reach Round Valley. Once there they'd be able to envelop Gordon.

What Schmidt didn't know and the reason he also failed at the Rainbow Bridge was he assumed Gordon didn't have an organized and armed force of his own. Schmidt's hubris cost him the battle and his small army. The men Gunny's company didn't kill ran off and dispersed into the countryside. Fugitive number one was Major Schmidt himself. Gordon wanted him like nothing else.

With the battle won and the spoils counted, the men from Mc-Call all gathered around Gordon, Charles, Gunny, and Michael. They had been chatting near the wreckage of a smoldering tank. Gordon noticed the men gathering first, their eyes focused on the men they considered their leaders. He stared back and saw in them pride and fear, but not hope. Then an idea came rushing to him like a freight train at high speed. This was his moment. This was the time for him to rise and take a position of strength. Very few times in history do moments like this come along, and he wasn't about to let it slip past. Then thoughts of Sebastian came to him, followed by anger. Some would rejoice in their victory then settle back into a haze of complacency. He had seen it before and knew the natural instinct for many was to avoid conflict. But he knew he could prevent that mind-set from setting in. He not only wanted revenge for Sebastian, he needed it. If he was going to get it, he had to be the one calling the shots.

He looked over at a man he knew from McCall, a friend of Michael's and an ardent Cascadian. In his hands, he held a Doug flag that was duct-taped to a large stick. He walked over, took the flag, and jumped on the tank.

Standing tall on the charred tank, Gordon held the flag high and began to speak. "Some of you know me and some don't. My name is Gordon Van Zandt. I'm a simple man who wants to live in peace. I'm like you, all of you, no better. I want to live in a place where I know my family will be safe from the types of thugs who sought to harm us. Together we all stood and fought back against the tyranny that our government has resorted to, just to retain power. Together we all, citizens of Cascadia, defended our new land. Together we came and took a stand against tyranny and for liberty! Today we proclaimed to the powers in Cheyenne that we won't be silenced, our voice will be heard until it's so loud that all will hear the name

Cascadia. Today, we made history, for today we gave birth to our new country, the Republic of Cascadia. Years from now men will talk about this day and wish they could have been here among us as we declared our independence and formed a true republic!" Gordon thrust the flag high above his head and hollered, "Long live the Republic of Cascadia!"

Cheyenne, Wyoming, United States

Conner knew his luck would eventually run out. Too many great things had been happening; he just didn't think the end of that record would be so devastating.

Schmidt had survived the Battle of Rainbow Bridge and fled into the mountains. There he had found a safe place to call from his sat phone, in the hopes that Conner could rescue him. If it had been just any commander, Conner would have left him to his own devices, but Schmidt was no ordinary man. He was Conner's hammer, and a builder needs his hammer.

Conner picked up the phone and dialed out. "Get General Baxter in here, ASAP."

Fortunately for Conner, Baxter was just downstairs. Within minutes he was sitting before Conner.

"I need a SAR team to be deployed to Idaho immediately," Conner ordered.

"A SAR team to Idaho? Who the hell is in Idaho who needs rescuing so bad?" Baxter asked.

Almost embarrassed to tell him, Conner opened up about the mission there and what had happened. He detailed exactly what Schmidt had told him.

If Baxter were not a disciplined man, he would have laughed out loud upon hearing the story. He didn't like knowing that a major

U.S. military force had been beaten by a ragtag group in Idaho, but deep down he was happy that Schmidt was humbled. He also hoped that this event humbled the president too, to the point that he and the others would be included in the planning and implementation of all military exercises. Knowing that the timing wasn't right to gloat and demand a new way, he kept his opinion to himself.

"Did the major give coordinates?" Baxter asked.

"Yes, it's all here," Conner said, handing Baxter a piece of paper.

"I'll get right on this, sir," Baxter said as he stood up to leave.

"This goes nowhere."

"Yes, sir, I wouldn't want to embarrass the major."

"It's not about embarrassing the major, it's about not advertising that we can be beaten. This type of thing will only embolden others!" Conner scolded.

"Yes, sir."

"General, this was a serious loss for us. We have lost a sizeable force, approximately five thousand men, along with tanks and other equipment."

"Yes, sir," Baxter acknowledged.

Conner could sense the slight joy in Baxter. He knew Schmidt wasn't liked by the others but to rejoice in your allies' losses was disgusting to Conner.

"General, are we good?"

"Sir?"

"You know what I mean. Are we good, between you and me?"

What pleasure that had just been displayed on Baxter's face vanished.

"Yes, sir, we are good."

"Glad to hear it. Go get the major and leave me."

Baxter turned and exited.

Conner knew this wasn't over with the Cascadians. If they had enough of a force to stop Schmidt, they were more of a serious threat than they had anticipated. He swiveled in his chair till he was facing the large window; he leaned back, closed his eyes, and let it all sink in.

A knock on his door jolted him out of his thoughts. "Come in."

Heather walked in and placed a message on his desk from Cruz in Cheyenne Mountain. Before he read it, he had the sinking suspicion that more bad news was coming. So as to not add to what was a bad day, he pushed it aside, swung around, leaned back, and pondered his next step. He had achieved much in the past weeks, so a few missteps were bound to happen. Like the chess master plots his move with an eye for his opponent's countermove, he would now wait to see what the Cascadians did next. He had many other pieces in play on the table, but he wouldn't rest until he checkmated Gordon Van Zandt.

McCall, Idaho, Republic of Cascadia

The first thing Gordon saw when he parked the Humvee at his garage was the small brown hummingbird. He stared at the little bird, mesmerized by the blur of its wings. Moving in jarring and rapid motions the bird moved close to the shattered windshield before darting away. He quickly looked to see where it had flown but it was gone. He'd seen the bird before; it was one that he and Haley had watched weeks ago in the garden. It had found a home close by and was just going about its day unaware of the tragedy that had occurred hours ago. Its life was going on peacefully, unlike his, which had taken another radical turn. But maybe the little bird had its own troubles and he just wasn't aware. Maybe in its short existence it was fighting to cling to life like he was.

Once again, Gordon's life had been hammered at the hands of men with murder and power in their hearts. The battle last night was decisive; they had dealt a severe blow to Schmidt and Conner. However, this was only the first battle in the war—a war he never asked for, a war that he knew would be bloody and horrific. Gordon was a man familiar with history, and never in history had civil wars been conventional. Civil wars brought out the worst in people; it showcased bitter and personal rivalries that made it a type of warfare that knew little boundaries.

Even though Cascadia had won, Gordon had lost. He had already lost his son and with him went his soul, but now he had lost his only brother and with him went his heart. Gordon refused to lose anyone else close to him. He would do whatever was necessary and utilize whatever means were at his disposal to ensure his family was safe. The only way he knew to do that was to take the fight to them. He would not rest until everyone who had been involved in Sebastian's death had fallen. Even if it meant killing thousands, he would not stop until he and Cascadia were free.

His meditative state was broken when the sound of wood and metal drew his attention to the front door. He looked and saw Samantha, then Haley came from behind her and grasped her leg. Finally Luke appeared and stood next to Samantha. All were staring at him as he sat in the bullet-riddled and smashed-up Humvee.

So much had been lost since that fateful day over seven months ago. When their old lives came to an end in San Diego, he did everything he could to make it work, but it failed. As they drove down the long road he came face-to-face with the horrific consequences of making a wrong decision. The purpose of bringing Samantha and Haley to McCall was to find a sanctuary from what the world had become, but even there he had failed. He failed to see things or failed to anticipate the evil that lived in the hearts of others. Now he had crossed the line of departure and there was no going back. He was at war with the very country he had sworn to defend so many years ago.

He looked at his family, what remained of it, anxiously waiting for him to come to them. The new world was harsh, unforgiving, and cruel, but he would never surrender or give up. He knew that in order for him and his family to survive he would have to embrace the new world, let it envelop him like a warm blanket.

He opened the door and painfully stepped out. He looked down at his clothes; they were torn, bloodied, and stained. He'd remove them later, but what he could never remove was the torn person he'd become.

EPILOGUE
OCTOBER 19, 2066

. . .

McCall, Idaho, Republic of Cascadia

"Oh my God, that is one of the craziest—no, it's the craziest—story I've ever heard," Sebastian exclaimed.

"Don't be so rude," Hunter reprimanded him.

"I wasn't being rude."

"It is a crazy story, Hunter. I'd feel the same way if someone told me my life too," Gordon said.

"It's not a story, Granddad," Hunter said, trying to explain his outburst.

"Good to see you both have the hot Van Zandt blood," Gordon joked.

"Mom never let us forget," Hunter replied.

"Oh, your mother, she's a firebrand. Did she ever tell you what she did to the man who tried to assassinate me during the '22 election?"

Hunter and Sebastian looked at each other then back to Gordon.

"Ah, no, what happened?"

"That's for another time, but I'll let you know, and soon."

"Please tell us, c'mon," Sebastian begged.

"I want to know why you faked your own death," Hunter said.

"I will, I will, be patient."

"I really need to be writing all of this down. I'm hearing stuff that no one knows about," Sebastian said excitedly.

"I better do it, little brother; I seem to remember you flunked English."

"But I aced sign language," Sebastian remarked, holding up his middle finger.

"While you boys scrounge around for something to write on, I need to get up and stretch these old bones."

Gordon slowly walked around the house, but like so often, the back deck called him. There he had many memories of his friends, Hunter, Haley, and most importantly, Samantha, the love of his life. He walked out and sat in the same spot they'd sit. For a man who was so practical and pragmatic, he was equally sentimental. What the boys didn't know was the house hadn't changed a bit; it was exactly like it was when he bought it almost sixty years ago.

After the great civil war, they left McCall and moved to Olympia, the new capital of the republic. There they stayed for many years, but he never thought of it as home. When time came for him to "retire" from politics, he came back to McCall and the old cabin. Its walls held a collection of memories, many of them happy ones from before the war and even before the lights went out. Many objects throughout were a trigger to that happier time. When he looked at the carpet, he didn't see worn-out and stained fabric, he saw the place where Hunter crawled when he was a baby or where Haley would play with her dolls. When he looked at the dusty and faded drapes, he saw the kids' favorite hiding spots. Whenever he'd see the cracked mirror that hung above the vanity in the master bath, Samantha's youthful and beautiful reflection would be cast. This place held memories that could not be replaced. He longed for his life before;

so many times he would press his eyes closed tight, pray, and imagine that when he opened them, he'd be there, but as a young man again and free of all the physical and emotional scars. In his vision, he would hear laughter and turn to find Samantha playing with Hunter and Haley. They'd see him and smile and beckon for him to come and join in on the fun. No matter how real every dream and vision he had, he'd wake to the truth, to the now, a place where he was alone.

A loud banging on the door startled Hunter and Sebastian. They looked at each other then looked outside to see if it was Gordon, but he was still sitting.

"Didn't you lock the gate?" Hunter asked.

"Of course I did."

Hunter walked to the front door, turned the handle, and almost jumped when he saw who it was. "Mom!"

"Can you believe that he hasn't changed the lock on the gate?" she said, holding up a key.

"What are you doing here? How did you know?"

Haley walked right in and looked down the hall then into the kitchen; she looked at them and asked, "Where is he?"

Sebastian pointed to the back.

Haley put her hand on her chest as if catching her breath when she caught a glimpse of him.

"Why didn't you tell us? Why did you lie to us?" Hunter asked, a tinge of irritation in his voice.

She turned to him, and with a motherly tone of admonishment she answered him. "Sometimes parents lie to protect their children."

Sebastian looked on as he watched what had been a familiar battle his whole life, the two alpha personalities, his mother and brother.

"I just don't understand the whole cover-up! This is huge!" Hunter barked.

Haley walked up to him and placed her hand on his face; she

gently patted his cheek and said, "Sweetheart, we did it all for you and your brother. I know you're having a hard time with this but trust me when I tell you that your grandfather had no choice but to surrender to the political forces that spawned within the republic. Building a nation is different than governing one. I"—she looked outside, then faced Hunter again—"we will tell you everything. We will tell you and your brother how it all came to be. Just know that he did it for family. Everything that man has ever done has been for family."

Hunter saw the raw emotion in his mother, which softened his attitude. He trusted her and would wait for the answers to be revealed.

She hugged her two sons before rushing to the sliding door. She paused for a moment to calm her nerves then walked onto the sun-bleached deck.

Her shadow cast long across Gordon as he sat with his eyes closed. She looked down on the man who had done so much for her.

He breathed deeply through his nose and captured a scent of a woman. With his eyes still closed, he smiled and said, "It must have worked this time." Thinking it was Samantha, he put out his hand and asked, "Is that you, my love?"

Haley smiled as a tear quickly ran down her face. She took his shaking and wrinkled hand. "It's me, Daddy."

Gordon opened his eyes, smiled broadly, and said, "Haley, my little baby girl, you came home."

Don't miss the other books in the New World series by G. Michael Hopf

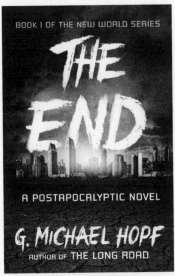

BOOK 1 OF THE NEW WORLD SERIES

THE END

A POSTAPOCALYPTIC NOVEL

G. MICHAEL HOPF
AUTHOR OF THE LONG ROAD

978-0-14-218149-2

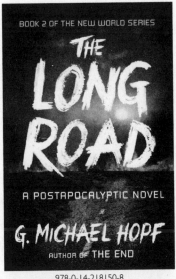

BOOK 2 OF THE NEW WORLD SERIES

THE LONG ROAD

A POSTAPOCALYPTIC NOVEL

G. MICHAEL HOPF
AUTHOR OF THE END

978-0-14-218150-8

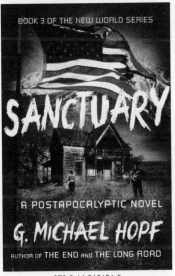

BOOK 3 OF THE NEW WORLD SERIES

SANCTUARY

A POSTAPOCALYPTIC NOVEL

G. MICHAEL HOPF
AUTHOR OF THE END AND THE LONG ROAD

978-0-14-218151-5

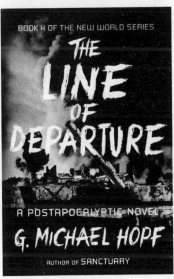

BOOK 4 OF THE NEW WORLD SERIES

THE LINE OF DEPARTURE

A POSTAPOCALYPTIC NOVEL

G. MICHAEL HOPF
AUTHOR OF SANCTUARY

978-0-14-218152-2

PLUME

www.gmichaelhopf.com